Three GIs Home From The War
And It's The Summer Of Love

The girl floated toward them carrying a single, freshly-cut flower. She went into a graceful hover in front of them.

"Peace," she said. "I'm Sunshine."

"You surely are," Tyrell managed.

Sunshine held the flower out to him.

"You guys are soldiers, aren't you?"

Oh shit. Jeff thought. *Now we're going to get the lecture on how we're monsters who go out and kill Viet Cong babies. Howinhell'd she spot us? The duffelbags? Couldn't be. We saw some longhaired guys carrying them. Oh. Yeah.* He ran his fingers across his nearly-crewcut head. *A dead giveaway. But what could he do, buy a damned wig?*

"Uh... yes," he managed. "Or, rather, not any more. We're civilians now, honest. Discharged just about an hour ago."

"That's groovy," Sunshine said. Her voice was tinkling bells and a forest brook. "Soldiers need love, too... Don't they?"

This, directly at Tyrell. She came very close to him, and touched his arm.

"Yes ma'am. I'm Tyrell." was the best Tyrell could manage.

"Far out," Sunshine said.

About The Authors

International bestselling authors and screenwriters Allan Cole and the late Chris Bunch were collaborators for nearly twenty years. Together, and separately, they published over forty novels and sold more than 150 TV and movie screenplays. Their most noteworthy collaboration produced the eight-book Sten series, hailed as "landmark science fiction" by Publishers Weekly, among others. Especially notable are their critically acclaimed novels about America's wars. Besides Freedom Bird, those books include, The Wars Of The Shannons, A Daughter Of Liberty, A Reckoning For Kings: A Novel Of Vietnam.

For details about the books, as well as Allan's life and work, see his homepage at http://www.acole.com. For information about Chris, see his Wikipedia entry at http://en.wikipedia.org/wiki/Chris_Bunch. Both authors are also featured in the International Movie Data Base (IMDB.com)And be sure to read about the authors' hilarious years as Hollywood screenwriters in Allan's popular blog, My Hollywood MisAdventures at http://allan-cole.blogspot.com/

Links to all formats of the books can be found at: http://tinyurl.com/4712141

FREEDOM BIRD

A Novel Of The Summer Of Love

by

Allan Cole And Chris Bunch

For Kathryn, Karen, Philip
And
Elizabeth Rice Bunch

ISBN-13: 978-0615518138
ISBN-10: 0615518133

A MODEST DISCLAIMER

All of the people, places, times and events depicted herein are
wholly and completely fictional, including Ronald Reagan,
LSD25, Haight Street, Ashbury Street, the entire Year of 1967,
the City of San Francisco and the State of California.
The Mind is a *Terrible* Thing to Waste...

WEDNESDAY: DAY ZERO

"Fly Trans-Love Airways...Gets you there on time..."

—Donovan

mutants revolve your head and nervous system, do acid, do the holy cities. spinspiril. do yurself and bod. create free forms, novas, do free.

freeall

freal

f real 1"

—Berkeley Barb

It is July, 1967
And we are at 28,000 Feet
Near Guam...

CHAPTER ONE

... AND THE 707'S cabin was quiet except for the high whine of the engines. Here and there seat lights pooled the darkness. Some men were trying to read. One just sat staring, his face empty.

There were nearly a hundred and eighty men on the *Braniff* flight. In a long line they would be hard to distinguish as individuals except by their race. All of them wore short-sleeve khaki uniforms, sleeves marked by rank. Mostly Army, some Air Force, a scattering of Marines.

They were all about the same age - very early 20's.

And they all had one thing in common:

They were going home.

A stewardess exited the rear galley carrying a tray with three ice-filled plastic glasses and five airline bottles of Scotch.

She stopped at the first lightpool five rows up. Three young men stopped their quiet conversation as she put the glasses and bottles on their tray.

"Welcome to yesterday," she announced.

One of the soldiers grinned. "I didn't know they made poets so pretty."

"Thanks. But, I wasn't trying to be poetic," she said. "We crossed the International Date Line about five minutes ago. It's Wednesday now."

The young black sitting next to the window thought for a moment. "Are we past Guam yet?"

"Oh yes. Hours ago."

"Whew," the third said in exaggerated relief. "Guess we stand a chance of makin' it." He was a solid, rangy blonde who, in overalls, could have been a 4-H Club Poster Boy.

"Why is Guam so important?"

The dark-haired soldier who thought the stewardess a poet twisted the cap off one bottle, poured and passed that, along with a second bottle, across the aisle to the other two.

"The last time we came through," he said, "somebody counted the engines and came up one short... so the Army - in its kindness - thought we'd better stop for refreshments. They picked Guam."

"I've only embarked there once," the stewardess said. "We didn't layover, but it also didn't look like it was one of the party spots of the Pacific."

"You got that shi... stuff right" the dark haired soldier laughed. "We never met any of the natives. But we saw some sailors... some Air Force. And some pretty lonely dependents."

"How long were you stuck there?"

"Long enough to find to meet a whole lot of mosquitoes and find out nobody would let us get into trouble. Then they bolted us back on the plane... and sent us to our – He raised his voice slightly – "DES-tiny."

The stewardess' professional smile vanished.

"That's not what I'd say about Vietnam," she murmured. "Excuse me. I've got to go help clean up the forward galley."

She walked away. The two soldiers on the aisle leaned out, looking at her shapely form. The black started to do the same, then caught himself.

"Nice legs," the dark haired soldier said.

"Bet they go all the way up to her ass," the blond added.

"Speaking of which, Nebraska, we gotta start watchin' our own ass. You too, Mister Goddamned Tyrell Harris."

"I ain't done nothin' else for fourteen months, the black said in a deliberate drawl. "What else is new?"

"What's new is that every fu... dammit, I'm doing it, too... is that we're all garbage mouths. I go back to LA, walk in the door, and say to my dad, 'Hey, asshole, how's it hangin'' and he'll have a coronary."

The black smiled. "You got a point, Jeff. I talk like that, and Momma'll have the preacher over with a case of Lifebuoy soap. I've got to remember, we're all going be civilians. Cleancut, upstanding American soldier boys who've done their duty to their country and all."

The dark haired man was still staring down the aisle after the stewardess.

"So she doesn't think Vietnam was all that airborne ranger, huh? I woulda just said It Sucks."

He lifted his glass. "Like I heard somebody in a movie say once... departed friends."

They drank. All three of them were more than a little drunk. The subject they'd all skirted for hours had been opened.

"You're sure about Atherton and Mills," Nebraska - real name Steve

8

Applegate - asked. He looked to be the youngest of the three, but was the highest ranker - the three stripes and a rocker of a Staff Sergeant were sewn to his sleeve. On his left breast he wore two rows of ribbons.

"Sure about Mills. About three months after I wrote to his unit, I got a letter back. It was from his brother. KIA for sure. He told me the letter from his CO said he died of..." and the dark haired man's voice mocked officialese "...wounds suffered in an enemy ambush. He died without pain."

"Yeah," the black guy named Tyrell Harris said. "Nobody ever kicked without a smile and a prayer on his lips. At least the way they tell it."

The dark haired soldier's hands unconsciously touched the single metal device on his left breast, a Combat Medic award. Specialist Four Jeff Katz.

"So what," he said. "If you got hit, would you want anybody to know what it was really like?"

"Fu... I mean, hell, no. Damn glad the Army went and lied about things when I zigged when I should'a zagged," the black said. As stated: he was Tyrell Harris. Of the three, he would have stood out the most. But not for his color. Like Katz, he was a Specialist Four. But he wore three rows of ribbons, including the Silver Star and Purple Heart. Above the decorations were paratrooper wings and the Combat Infantryman's Badge. The overseas cap on the seat beside him had the round red-white-blue "glider" patch of an airborne soldier. He was related, in a sometimes roundabout and sometimes scandalous ways to a family that had fought in every American war from before the Revolution onward.

"About Mills, I don't know," Jeff said, returning to the subject. "The letter I sent got bounced down to 193rd Evac, then returned to me."

"You didn't have his home address."

"Course not. Don't know if I would've written if I'd had it. Who wants to know for sure? Better thinking he got a glory wound, went home, got out and is chasing women up and down the entire state of New York."

"Yeah," Nebraska agreed. "Better like that."

They drank and refilled their glasses in the suddenly uncomfortable silence.

"You know," Tyrell said, ostentatiously changing the subject, "I've been thinking."

"I could'a guessed," Nebraska cracked. "Smelled the woodsmoke burning."

"Screw you," Tyrell said giving Nebraska the finger. His lingo dropped into GI slur. "First thing I do, when I get home and send this uniform off to the Salvation Army, I'm gonna go out and buy me an M-14."

"For Chrissakes why?"

"Shut up. Gonna get the whole damned thing chromed. Barrel, receiver, all of it. Get me a stock custom-made out of teakwood."

"Uh-huh," Jeff said skeptically.

"I'm gonna get me a little stand made out of marble. Then I'll put that rifle out in my momma's rose garden..."

"Yeeaahh?" Jeff said. He couldn't help but be caught up in Tyrell's mad dream.

"... And every morning... just when the sun comes out, I'm gonna come out and piss all over the son of a bitch!"

The three laughed and drank some more. Then Nebraska turned serious. He leaned across the aisle to Jeff.

"How well you know San Francisco?"

"Pretty good... I guess. I've been there half a dozen times with my folks. Couple of times by myself... before I became... unattached to college."

"What's the best hotel in town?"

Jeff considered. "The Mark... Mark Hopkins. My folks used to stay there. Or maybe the Fairmont."

"Thanks." Nebraska settled back.

"What's a shitkicker like you want to know about hotels? Especially expensive hotels?"

"Part of my plan. After we have that drink when they turn us loose... and you guys head for home, I'm gonna get me a suite in the most expensive hotel I can find... For three days..... I've been saving for this son of a gun a long time.

"Then I am going to throw me the biggest, best party I can. Callgirls... and I don't care if they're a hundred bucks a night so long as each one's prettier'n the last. The best booze. Hit the topdollar nightclubs. I am going to swing!"

"Why, Nebraska, you decadent bastard," Jeff said in vast admiration.

10

"I didn't know farmboys went crazy," Tyrell said.

"Not crazy at all," Nebraska said. "Look. I'm goin' back to Grainton. Back to daddy's farm. Probably gonna marry the girl I was going out with before I went in... She lives 'bout three miles away.

"That's gonna be my life. That's the way I want it." Nebraska said this firm, unbudging. Then: "... But something you city guys might not know. Farming ain't exactly the most lively way to spend your life... sometimes.

"So ten, twenty year from now, I'm sittin' on the combine seat... goin' up and down and back and forth and out of my tree... I'll get this secret little smile on my face.

"And people will wonder, and maybe even ask. But I won't tell them that I'm thinking back to those three days in Frisco."

"I will be a son of a bitch," Jeff said slowly. He toasted Nebraska with the dregs of his scotch. "Damned if that isn't the most sophisticated idea I've heard since the first sergeant decided I was a troublemaker."

"Thank you, son," Nebraska said. "Only thing... kind of a pity you guys couldn't do the same thing. Be a lot more fun. Hell, I'm gonna get the suite anyway. Hotel's on me. I'm gonna be Fat City... besides, my dad sent me a money order last month."

He turned to Tyrell. "How about it? Memphis'll manage to get along without you for 72 hours, wouldn't it?"

"Naw," the black said. "Women'll be whoopin' and cryin' in the streets. But let them wait... I'll give my momma a call from Oakland."

He stuck out his hand. "Staff Sergeant, you got yourself a Party Point man!"

"What about you, Jeff? Prob'ly need a medic sooner or later. Shit... Ooops. This is hard. Anyway, I forgot you have some kinda big family deal, don't you?"

Jeff hesitated. Then reached a decision. He twisted the caps off the two remaining bottles and poured drinks. "They'll be too busy schmoozing and talking about real estate to miss me. Yeah. Yeah, I'll hang out with you."

He lifted his glass. "San Francisco, here we come... right back where we never started from," he sang, then knocked the drink down.

The stewardess came back down the aisle, and stopped by them again.

"You three look like you just solved the world's problems," she

11

said.

"Better than that," Jeff said. "We've just made a pact... Set the plan. For three days we're... gonna rock... gonna roll. Gonna tear the town down."

"Look out San Francisco!"

"It's a good town for a party," the stewardess said. "I ought to know. I live there."

"Hey," Nebraska said. "Maybe we could give you a call. You could show us some hot spots. That is, if your boyfriend don't mind."

The stewardess caught the emphasis on boyfriend. She grinned and ruffled his hair. "Nice try, GI."

"Miss," Jeff said. "Don't listen to him. Here I am. I saw you when I walked on this plane, and there were little bluebirds singing, and flowers blooming, and I fell in love forever and ever."

He came awkwardly out of his chair, knelt and took her hand.

"I'm housebroken, no bad habits, over 21, and a good Jewish boy with a foolish career ahead of him as a doctor making tons of money. Couldn't you find it in your heart to let me worship you from afar?"

The stewardess laughed. "You were doing okay until you hit the doctor bit. *I don't care/Too much for money...* and she hummed the second two bars of the verse.

"Go back to the flowers and bluebirds. It'll get you farther. Especially in San Francisco... these days."

"My heart has been torn apart," Jeff muttered and sat back down. The stewardess moved past him, toward the rear of the plane. Her hand, seemingly by accident, brushed across his cheek.

Jeff put his hand to his cheek. "Damn," he said, almost in a whisper. Shook his head, and looked at Nebraska.

"So what've you got in mind? Once we get out of these monkeysuits and start looking like real people?"

"I read some magazine stuff about Frisco. Said North Beach is The Place. Topless bars and all kinds of loose women."

"Your information's got a long beard on it, son. It's *totally* nude, now."

Tyrell blinked. "You mean... nothing? Nothing at all?"

"That's what I heard."

"How do they get away with that?"

12

"San Francisco's different," Jeff said. "Not as uptight as other places. Plus I bet they're paying off the cops. They've got one dancer... Carol, uh, Doda, that's her name... got a 44 inch chest."

"Forty-four inches? Lord Above, that'd be a mouthful," Nebraska marveled.

Tyrell turned serious. "Uh... is there going to be a... problem? With me being...?"

"A black cat? Hell no. Only color San Francisco knows is green. You got dollars, they'll decide you're an African prince or maybe a jazzman, and hand you the keys to the city."

"Maybe," Tyrell said. "I'll believe it when I see it. Lot of crap back in Memphis about them being integrated. But there's streets you'd best not walk down and bars you damn well don't go near. Classy joints, too. If you're like me, you don't walk in the front door even if you're the star act."

"Everywhere isn't the south," Jeff said. "Loosen up. We see any white sheets... me and Nebraska will ratpack 'em. I've been known to walk drag, Tyrell, and you don't see any CO patch on my ass."

"Besides," Nebraska put in. "You're airborne. You got steel teeth. Rip 'em in half the long way, right?"

"Right," Tyrell said.

"Not to mention that this shit... there I go again... I mean, stuff... is getting way too serious... and we're low on scotch," Jeff said, and got up.

"Hey," Nebraska said.

"Yeah?"

"Give it another try."

"You don't think I'm walking back there just for my good looks do you? Ah feel good/Doo-ah-ooo-ah-ooo," Jeff chanted, and headed for the galley. But his heart was fluttering like the first time he was under fire as he made his way back.

He heard the two stewardesses talking, and stopped, just outside its entrance.

"Am I getting old," Jeff's lady of interest was saying, "... or was this flight the rowdiest ever?"

"Nobody told you?"

"Nobody ever tells me anything."

"This is a real special flight, Sam. Every one of these guys is getting out of the service."

"Okay. The company goofed. Somebody did tell me that."

"Bet they didn't tell you how it worked. When their tour was originally up in Vietnam, all of the guys on this plane would have had three, four, five months left to go in the Army.

"So the Army offered them a deal. Extend your tour for a month... and get a discharge. The boys on this plane are the ones who survived that month... Those thirty days in the jungle..."

"Jesus, mercy," Jeff's object of interest said. "Hey, there young man. Want to play dice with your life? You willing to gamble another month for a Get Out Of Jail Free card?

"You know," she went on, "I never used to be anti-Army. But seeing these guys board, and they're* all happy and really just a bunch of kids. Then we pick up the ones coming home at Tahn Son Nhut. Same guys... just thirteen months different.

"A lifetime different. No wonder they've been calling this flight the Freedom Bird.

"Now this kind of thing... it really..." she searched for a word to describe her disgust. She found Jeff's: "... it sucks, that's what." She said it with such force she surprised herself. She laughed to cover her embarrassment. "Of course, these days there's a <u>lot</u> of that going around."

Jeff heard a giggle. "Samantha, you have a very dirty mind."

Laughter... and Jeff stepped around the corner.

"Uh... could I have some more gruel? Please?"

The other stewardess moved past him, indicating the drink tray. Next to it was three nearly-full trash containers of empties.

"Take whatever you want," she said.

A red light flashed on a panel.

"Oh Lord," the stewardess said. "My master's voice. Are pilots born Nazis or do they learn that in flight school?"

The other woman, the one Jeff had heard called Samantha, shook her head. "What can you expect of somebody who can't talk without moving his hands?"

"Excuse me," the other stewardess said, and headed for the plane's cockpit.

Jeff fielded five more tiny bottles, and looked for an excuse to say more. Samantha gave him the opportunity. She looked at the bottles.

"You order five scotches every time. How come? Why not six?"

Allan Cole & Chris Bunch

Jeff suddenly felt a lot more sober.

"Well... see, fourteen months ago, back in Oakland, before they sent us over, me, that blond-headed guy Nebraska and old Tyrell Harris got together. There were two others with us. Dick Mills and a guy named Atherton.

"We got along fine. For starters, we all thought the Army, well... We used a rude word - *sucked*. I saw your big ears." He shrugged. We're just home and haven't been verbally potty trained yet.

"Anyway,.. All That. And we were all planning to get out of the Army when we came back... which separated us from the lifers going in.

"We got friendly. Then we got stuck on Guam, and got a little tighter... And we thought it'd be cool if we all got together at the end of our tour... and had a drink.

"Sort of like one of those promises you see made in the old World War II movies... Hell. We were kids.

"Anyway. There were five of us... then..." Jeff's voice was suddenly hoarse. He pushed on. "But... only three of us caught the Bird."

Jeff found his vision blurring. He turned away, blinking rapidly. Then he turned back.

The stewardess had a Kleenex out, and was dabbing at her own eyes.

"It gets real smoky back here," she explained. "The air conditioning... you know."

"So anyway," Jeff went on. "We're sort of drinking... for a couple of guys that didn't seem to make it. I guess... I guess maybe we're still kind of... childish."

"I don't think so."

The enginewhine was quite loud in the galley.

"Uh... you know," Jeff said, "I've never been able to figure out what you say... you know, like in a bar, when you see somebody you... you think you might like. So...

"I guess I might as well mess it up big, then. And go back and get real shit fac-. Uh... Sorry... drunk.

"But... I'm going be in San Francisco for three days. And... If I wanted to call somebody... and maybe have dinner with them. Or maybe just a drink or lunch... uh... what would happen if I asked?

Oh. I'm Jeff Katz, by the way. "

He put out his hand.... hesitant. Samantha grabbed it and give it a firm shake.

"Glad to meet you, Jeff Katz. Now, for your questions:

"First, you really are drunk. Second, if you did ask... and somebody took out a napkin... like this... and wrote down Samantha Vaughn, 834-2258... like this... and passed it to you, saying that she's got a week's downtime... Why, you'd probably lose it or forget where you put it when you got straight."

She handed the napkin to Jeff. He put the bottles down on the galley sideboard, and took out his wallet.

"If... If I asked, and somebody did something this wonderful..." he glanced at the scribbling on the napkin... "I'd have that name Samantha Vaughn, uh, 834-2258, tattooed on my mind.

"Plus stuck right here. In front of that driver's license that proves to God, man and any MP that I'm a real live California civilian and back in The World again... And I'd call. God would I call! At midnight. At three a.m. At dawn."

"To use the GI vernacular - you are pushing it again, Jeff. Just call. Once. And see what happens."

He picked up the bottles. "You know... fourteen months of nothing going right and everything going wrong and pretty damn' bloody... maybe things will go right.

"We are going to by God San Francisco."

Samantha smiled. "Maybe. Like the song said, 'I believe in" magic.'"

"Now... get back to your seat, soldier. I've got work to do."

Jeff Katz went back to his seat. Not drunk, not sober, but certainly not touching the 707's rubber matting as he went... And in thrall with a beautiful woman who actually used the word "Vernacular."

THURSDAY: DAY ONE

"...Oh Lord/ Pride of Man/Broken in the dust again.."
—Hamilton Camp/ Quicksilver Messenger Service

"Somethin's happening here/But you don't know what it is/
Do You, Mister Jones
—Bob Dylan

"...Jeans of blue/Harley Davidsons too/Old Angel, young
Angel/Feel all right/On a warm San Francisco night..."
—Eric Burdon/ The Animals

CHAPTER TWO

THE BIG OLIVE drab buses from March Air Force Base groaned through the gates of Oakland Army Terminal - past the MP shack - and made a creaky, brake squealing stop in front of the OARTS Admin Building.

The driver of the lead bus pulled the door handle, and shouted: "Okay. We're here. Everybody out."

In a worm-fight of duffelbags and struggle, the soon-to-be-civilians clustered there way off the bus.

Jeff paused by the driver. "I," he announced, "am not short. I am *next!*" And he kissed the driver on top of his baseball cap.

"Lucky fucker," the driver muttered.

"How long will it be before they' turn us loose?" Tyrell asked.

"Three days. Maybe. If they've got their heads out. Which they don't. So that means three days... if you're lucky."

The statement hit the young men like a howitzer as they saw their plans for a three day party about to explode. Nebraska was the first to recover. A determined, pure farm stubborn look came over his face.

"Nobody, but nobody stops this party," he announced. "Least of all the U.S. Damned Army!"

"What are we going to do?" Jeff asked.

"Hide and watch," was all Nebraska said. "You'll get the drift."

There were shouts: "Gentlemen. If you'll all form up... please have the six copies of your separation orders ready... Three ranks..."

The first sergeant looked tired and hung over. Almost everybody in the formation in front of him was also tired and hung over.

"Okay. I need a section leader. Who's senior?" Quick looks around at stripes. SP/4's... a lot of Sergeants or Specialist Five's... One of the looks fell on Nebraska. Just as he knew it would. He'd already checked the rank terrain. "Staff Sergeant. You. You look senior."

Nebraska was ready. He put his duffel bag down and doubled to the front of the formation. "Sarn't Applegate, Top."

"Fine. Take charge of these men and march them down there... past the barracks... we'll assign you bunks later... turn right and go down three rows to Bay D as in Delta."

"Uh... right. First Sergeant."

Nebraska turned, frantically sifting his mind for what command elements he remembered from Basic Training.

"Uh...Group...Ten-hut !"

There was a change in the formation of exhausted, wrinkly-fatigued soldiers. From shambles to motley.

"Left... sorry, Right... Face!"

The group of men turned. There was snickered order from the ranks: "Right shoulder... duffelbags!"

"You men in the ranks! This is not a joke," the first sergeant shouted. "You're still in the Army, goddammit!"

Someone shouted: "What're you gonna do... send us to Vietnam?"

Laughter... and the first sergeant seemed to shrink. Without saluting he spun and went up the steps into the admin building. Most likely in search of the hair of the dog that bit him.

"I got your bag, Nebraska," Tyrell shouted. "Oh yeah. You want your camera?"

"Hell yes."

Applegate caught the Petri as it sailed through the air. "Now," Jeff observed, "let's see if the Old Man's Driver remembers which foot to start off with."

"Knock off the shit," Nebraska said. "Okay," he commanded. "Grab your stuff."

Suddenly he found the whole thing damned funny. "Forward..." and his voice went falsetto, "... HOOP."

And the shambles shambled forward.

Outside Bay D, a master sergeant was giving out The Word to a rigidly-formatted, bright-green-new-fatigued group of soldiers. They all looked pretty much like Tyrell, Nebraska and Jeff had fourteen months before.

The master sergeant wore sharply creased khakis and rows of ribbons. None of the new soldiers could... nor would they bother to... read the ribbons and realize that none of the decorations were for anything other than Time Served Somewhere or Awards of (Dubious) Administrative Merit.

"You troops better get your heads out," he shouted. "Get your heads out! Because you are all going to Vietnam, goddamit! The Viet Cong do not play games! You straight up and fly right... or you will all be fucking dead, I promise you!

"We just got a shipment of combat soldiers. Real soldiers, just back from Nam. You look at them. Real close. "These guys lived... They were

Strack! They got their shit together! And they lived! Do like they do... and you'll live, too, and come back home."

Jeff heard what sounded like a marching cadence.

"Now you take a look at these soldiers... and learn to soldier just like they do!"

The "cadence" became audible.

"Hep, hoop three four, hep five two one... change step, hep! Hep two, hep three, cadence, cadence, cadence call."

A ragged shout:

"FUCK THE ARMY."

A shout from their still unseen leader:

"Column right... wanderin'"

And the formation hove into view.

The master sergeant had time to pick up some details:

The staff sergeant evidently in charge of the formation was walking backward, shooting photographs. He saw one man in the front - also walking backward - animatedly talking to a friend. Some idiot to one side was skipping like a goddamned schoolgirl.

The shambles came closer. The leader slung his camera, and prepared to bring his men to a halt.

"Hippity-hop! Platoon... stop !"

The master sergeant heard his Vietnam-bound trainees look at the old pros and start laughing. It was the sound of discipline crumbling.

"Holy shit," he muttered to himself. "We gotta get rid of these clowns. Yesterday!"

And, ignoring the soldiers he'd been haranguing, . he tucked his clipboard under one arm, and scurried away, looking for the first sergeant. Desperate action was required.

"Sergeant, you know you're entitled to a full physical when you're being released from active duty?"

"Yessir."

"That'll take... 48 hours."

"Oh."

"How do you feel?"

"Great, sir."

"You look great. You got two arms, two legs, a head and I guess the rest under those shorts. You got any problems you want to tell me about?

Allan Cole & Chris Bunch

Medical problems, I mean?"

"Nossir."

"Sign here... and here. You're A-l, like they used to say, properly attested to by a Captain in the United States Army, Medical Corps. Right?"

"Thank you, sir."

"Next!"

"Be a sonofabitch," the clerk said. "Harris, it says here you got the Silver Star, right?"

"Uh... yeah."

"But there wasn't any award ceremony that I can see. "

"We were mostly in the field. So we didn't do parades," Tyrell said.

"You want to stick around? We could get a ceremony up... maybe by tomorrow afternoon?"

"Fuck, no."

"Didn't think so. Sign here."

The finance clerk owled through the pay records. Twice. Frowning.

"Uh...some kind of problem?"

"Yeah," the clerk said. "Look. According to your records, you qualified for Pro Pay, right?"

"First in my class, first on the test."

"Fine. Which you draw when you were up at Lewis, and then they send you to Vietnam. You get that for... let's see, three months, and then no more. You got any idea what happened?"

"Sort of," Jeff said, tentative. "First sergeant didn't like me."

"Why not?"

"Well... he came in on sick call. Said he had a cold, and wanted some penicillin pills. Had the clap, of course. Didn't want to get in trouble with the Old Man."

"So?"

"So we give him a shot in the butt and somebody gave him his pills. The pills turned out to be Pyridium. Which made him pee bright red. He thought it was gonna fall off for a couple days.

"Top thought I did it. So he decided I was superfluous to the TO&E, and cut my pro pay." Jeff shrugged. "Shit happens."

The clerk laughed, then went through the pink payment vouchers again.

"Problem is, he didn't back his act up. Nobody ever cut orders like that."

"Which means?"

"Which means you're gonna get... oh, $350 more than you thought you were gonna, on separation pay. Unless you think that's unfair."

"I never argue," Jeff said, "with a dedicated professional."

"Great. Have a drink for me when you're out of this fucking Army."

"I will do that. Believe me, I will do just exactly that!"

"Next!"

"Group... ten-hut!"

Nebraska pivoted and saluted the first sergeant, standing on the Admin Building steps. The topkick returned the salute.

"Men... I want to thank you," he said. "This is the fastest out processing we've ever managed here at Oakland. Normal proceeding would have taken 72 to 84 hours. But thanks to your cooperation, all of you are finished in record time.

"You have all your necessary paperwork now. You are free to leave. There are pay phones inside the barracks if any of you wish to call a cab, or if you live here in the Bay Area. There will be two buses in half an hour, for San Francisco International Airport.

"But any of you who have already made other arrangements... you can still draw bedding from our supply sergeant.

"And we have steak on the menu tonight."

He sounded almost as if he were pleading.

"That's all. Group... Ten-hut! The mess hall will open in ten minutes. Dis-missed!"

The Oakland Army Depot Permanent Party had all the steak they could eat that night.

Only five men from Nebraska's shambles stuck around for chow.

The shabby yellow cab had barely stopped in front of the green Admin Building when it was Combat Assaulted by three men wearing newly-issued green Class A uniforms.

Jeff, Tyrell and Nebraska hurled their duffelbags into the cab's trunk, piled inside and shouted: "SAN FRANCISCO," to the driver.

The cab accelerated for the gate.

A Military Police first lieutenant, resplendent in greens, armband, spitshined boots and pistol belt, was giving watch instructions to the MP gate guard as the cab pulled through. His black plastic nametag read SANDERS.

Lieutenant Sanders glanced up. And saw three clenched fists sticking out the open window, one brown, two white. From each fist protruded a middle finger.

Before he could pick up his jaw, before he could shout an order, before he could remember his olive drab sedan with the red light on top, the cab was out the gate, out of his jurisdiction, out of the Army, out of his life.

For the moment...

"Not many cities as pretty as this one," the cabbie proclaimed proudly as the cab pulled through the toll gates onto the approach to the Bay Bridge.

San Francisco spread in front of them, the Bridge arcing high over the blue Bay waters that echoed the bright blue, cloud-spattered sky above.

The city's low hills and buildings were golden in the late afternoon sun, and the Golden Gate was a graceful draftsman's sketch to the right.

It seemed to wait, expecting and promising.

"People from around here call it The City. They don't need no other description.

"Yeah. Pretty. Shines like a woman in the night. And delivers what she promises and don't look like a harridan in the morning.

"Ain't but a few cities as beautiful. Paris, maybe, from some views. Copenhagen. Hanoi, possibly. Saigon. Before the Americans."

Tyrell looked at the driver's hair. It was gray, and it hung from his shoulders and was held in place with a flowery headband.

"You," he asked - a tinge of skepticism in his voice - "were in Vietnam?"

"That I was, mister. Back when the French had it. Second, no third time I shipped out. Carrying U.S. War Surplus guns to the Fightin' French. Didn't do 'em a hill of shit. But yeah. I been in Saigon - San Francisco's better, though. Always glad to come back. Always sorry to be leavin'. Where you three want to go? The Airport?"

"Mark Hopkins, please," Jeff said.

The driver half-turned, looking astonished. "You sure?"

"Yep."

"Damn. That's a new one. Most GI's coming out want to go to the airport. Bus station. Some, North Beach, looking for a party. Others, that

23

mebbe got more on the ball, the Haight. But the Mark... sure. Why not."

Nebraska frowned. "We were gonna go to North Beach, later. Is there something the matter with that?"

There was a silence. Then: "I don't rain on any man's parade. But... let's say North Beach used to be interesting. Back in what they called the Beat Generation days. Now... hell, I'm starting to sound like a frizzly old fart croakin' about Them Wuz Th' Days. Life... and a party... is what you make it and where you find it."

"What's about that other place... I think you called it The Haight?"

Another silence as the driver thought. He shook his head: "I'm not gonna tell you. Maybe I *can't* tell you. Don't have the words. Maybe nobody can. And I don't want to give any preconceptions. But... the Haight's... interesting. Changing some, from what it was.

"But everything changes. When I feel like that... it's time to move on. Go somewhere else. Maybe back to Torremolinos for awhile. Maybe I just get twitchy when I start feelin' rooted. Forget that shit. But if you got the time, check the Haight out. Like I said, it's interesting."

That was it. Evidently the cabbie had said all he intended.

The three recently ex-soldiers stared out the window, as San Francisco drew nearer.

"Now," Nebraska said. "If we can't find a party in a town as pretty as that, we're even dumber than we look."

"Speaking of which," Jeff said, "we do look pretty dumb. I mean... in this uniform?" He plucked at one of his sleeves and made a face as if he was smelling something evil.

"What's the matter with it?"

"First, we're civilians, right? I am not going to wear this fucking - goddamit I got to stop that cussin' - uniform one second longer than I absolutely have to And that second stopped when we drove out the gate and flipped off the cop lieutenant.

"Next, I'm getting sick and tired of going somewhere and somebody spots me for a GI and figures I'm nothing but a sucker.

"Third, there's a bunch of people who ain't real big on Vietnam. Remember? Even Stars & Stripes has run stories about them. Why cruise for trouble?

"Let's do it right. Dump anything that's got U.S. Army on it. Socks, low quarters, jockstrap... hell if I want anybody to look at me and think

Grunt."

Jeff leaned forward. "Mister, we changed our mind. You know any real good clothes stores in Frisco?"

"Don't be calling it that to the natives. Makes 'em hostile," the cabbie advised. "Clothing stores? How much money you want to spend?"

"We don't care. A good one. One that'll sell us clothes so *nobody* can think we look like GIs. You know. Wild clothes. Like, maybe, those suits the Beatles used to wear. Edwardian, I think they called them?"

The cabbie glanced in his rear view mirror at the three men, noting their carefully-cropped hair.

"You don't want anybody to look at you and think soldiers, huh? I got just the place. Wild it is..."

"Shitfire," Nebraska muttered. "Not *this* wild!"

He turned to the clerk and held up the garment. It was a mail shirt, constructed of small metal rings.

"People really wear something like this?" he wondered.

"It's very, very popular right now. At a party, you will be the center of attraction, I can *promise you*. My... friend just bought one last week."

The clerk looked quite average to Nebraska, if you ignored his gauze tee-shirt and paisley bellbottoms with hugely flaring bottoms. He had short hair and a moustache. But for some reason, his voice made Nebraska uncomfortable. It was... too smooth. As if he was taking acting lessons, Applegate thought.

Tyrell came out of a dressing room. He wore a natty, narrow-lapelled suit, tasty Italian half-boots, a lacy shirt and a tie that would shame a color wheel.

Nebraska whistled at all the glory.

"There it is," Tyrell mocked. He struck a pose and warbled: 'Reach out, an' I'll be there.' All I need is a three cats for the harmony and some doo-wop girls and I'm set!"

"Yeee-ah," Nebraska said. "Won't be any trouble pickin' *you* out of a crowd. What do you think of this?" He held out the mail shirt.

"That, my friend, is out there. Way out. Are you planning' to look up King Arthur while you're here?"

"It would *certainly* show off your chest to its maximum advantage," the clerk purred. "And remember, it's better to be blatant than latent."

Allan Cole & Chris Bunch

The store phone rang. "Excuse me." The clerk went behind the counter and picked up the phone. "White Swallow Boutique. This is Roger. Oh! So you finally decided to wake up, you lazy bitch! My. You do, do you? How much would it be? Mmmm. That is. expensive.

"But it's blonde, you say? Two... no, three grams would be perfect. Now, about tonight..." and the clerk's voice sank to a intimate tone.

Nebraska leaned over to Tyrell. "Is he, uh..."

"You asking me, brother? I'm not from the big city. But if he isn't, he'll surely do until one comes along."

"I heard Frisco's got a lot of... guys like him. And there were always these jokes goin' around. But..."

"Nebraska, does it bother you?"

Applegate started to answer, then thought about it. He grinned. "Naw. Not unless he wants to double-date with me."

"So don't buy that Knight of the Round Table thing. First time you try to get out of it you'll either cut your self on the can opener or rip your nose off."

Tyrell walked to a rack. "What about this little item?"

It was a two piece ensemble, denim jacket and bellbottom pants. Except that it looked like somebody at Levi Strauss had gone nuts with the Clorox bottle, all shades of brown and tan.

"Looks like one of the Jersey cows we got."

"Jersey *bull*, remember? Think about it. I'm not sure what that dude meant by blatant and latent, but like they say, it pays to advertise. You need this..."

Tyrell went into motion, selecting clothes as he went. "This... naw, you're too straight to wear it. This. These two shirts. Man, you honkies not only got no rhythm, but you don't know how to dress, neither."

"Hang on there, Tyrell. This shit's expensive! I'm gonna wear it for three days, then what? I put this on and go parading through Grainton, hell Omaha, and there'd be a lynch mob."

"Got you covered on that, too. Stash it for five years, and it'll be the height of fashion in Nebraska. Word travels slow when it's going by Pony Express."

"Funny. Real funny," Nebraska growled, knowing it was true. "Where the hell is Jeff?"

"Waiting for my cue," was the answer, and the store's other dressing room opened.

"What is this," Tyrell complained. "First the farmboy dresses up like Sir Galahad, and now you're trying for Errol Flynn."

"And what, exactly, is wrong with that," Jeff asked. "Consider the rep."

Jeff wore a silk peasant shirt, with belled sleeves, a deep vee neck, red velvet pants and floppy boots that came nearly to his knees.

"This, like that guy'd probably say, is definitely me." He pirouetted like a ballerina.

Tyrell just stared at him. Jeff looked at himself in the mirror. Yeeck! Maybe he <u>had</u> drifted a tad. Tyrell steered him to the rack. In a few moments he was outfitted from toe to neck.

Then Jeff saw the jacket. Denim like Nebraska's. And treated with the same mad Clorox bottle. But this was midnight blue with swirling patterns drifting into purples. The sleeves and pockets and arch of the back were studded with rivets. Now *this* was a jacket! He lifted it from the rack and tried it on. Fit like it was born to him.

"What do you think?" he asked Tyrell, putting on a James Dean swagger and leer.

"Rebel Without A clue," Tyrell said. But Jeff knew there was more envy than bite.

"Awright. Knock off the crap," Nebraska ordered. "I want a drink. Let's pay for this stuff and get out of here."

They piled clothing and went to the counter as the clerk ended his phone call. "My," he said, We have some big spenders today."

"Let me ask you something," Jeff said. He went back into the dressing room and came out with the brand new set of Class A greens. "Do you have a trash can where I can dump this?"

"I shouldn't say anything," the clerk said. "I should just let you be foolish. But I am soft hearted." He smiled at the three, and let the smile linger on Nebraska.

"I will *buy* that uniform. Twenty-five, no, thirty dollars."

"What the hell are you going do with it?" Tyrell wondered. "Against the law for a civilian to wear Army uniforms."

"It's not for me. My tastes are a bit loftier. But you have no idea how many of these hippies come in here, looking for something unique. Old band uniforms, military wear, anything that, in their words, will ' freak the straights.'"

"You've got a deal, brother," Jeff said. "Hey, guys. Not only can we dump the monkey suits, but pick up a buck. You in?"

Nebraska was shocked. "We can't do that. It's government property."

"Sorry for breaking my promise, and I'll buy the first round," Jeff said. "But fuck the government!"

"Come on, man," Tyrell said, coming down on Nebraska's side. "You have to put it on for the plane ride home or you don't get standby. And what about the Reserve meetings? Remember... you two draftees have Reserve meetings to think about."

"First, all I have to worry about is a PSA puddlejumper to LA, which is going to be twenty bucks or so. Second, I'll worry about the Reserves when I worry about the Reserves. This is San Francisco, son. And I am Freddy Feelgood for the next three days."

Jeff looked at the clerk. "Start ringing it up, my friend."

"Thanks," Tyrell said. "But you didn't have to cut in."

Jeff gave the shrug of a man whose pocket was fat with unexpected cash. "Consider it a gift from my old first sergeant. Plus, Nebraska said he's picking up the hotel tab. We'll gang up on you for dinner. Okay?"

"Damn. I've got some generous friends," Tyrell said. "It'll be hard adjusting to those tightassed peckernecks back home. Hey, Nebraska, mind if I practice my yowza bosses on you... since you're the closest thing to a redneck around?"

But Nebraska was not listening. "Would you look at that," he said softly. "Come here, come here, little one. I am the cat and you are a bowl of sweet cream."

Indeed, the "sweet cream" was walking down the street toward them.

Floating would have been a better description. The girl's bare feet were in contact with the pavement, but it seemed as she flowed toward them that she'd mastered levitation.

She was perhaps fifteen or sixteen. Her blonde hair fell long and straight like a waterfall to either side of a dreamily-smiling heart-shaped face.

"What's she wearing?" Jeff whispered. "Looks like my grandmother's tablecloth."

She wore a white lace dress with a neckline just above small, pert breasts. She was visibly not wearing a brassiere. Around her neck hung a coral necklace, with a tiny brass bell at the center.

"Is she wearing *anything* under that," Tyrell wondered.

"Skin colored panties?" Jeff ventured... hoping otherwise.

The girl floated toward them carrying a single, freshly-cut flower. She went into a graceful hover in front of them.

"Peace," she said. "I'm Sunshine."

"You surely are," Tyrell managed.

Sunshine held the flower out to him.

"You guys are soldiers, aren't you?"

Oh shit. Jeff thought. Now we're going to get the lecture on how we're monsters who go out and kill Viet Cong babies. Howinhell'd she spot us? The duffelbags? Couldn't be. We saw some longhaired guys carrying them. Oh. Yeah. He ran his fingers across his nearly-crewcut head. A dead give away. But what could he do, buy a damned wig?

"Uh... yes," he managed. "Or, rather, not any more. We're civilians now, honest. Discharged just about an hour ago."

"That's groovy," Sunshine said. Her voice was tinkling bells and a forest brook. "Soldiers need love, too... Don't they?"

This, directly at Tyrell. She came very close to him, and touched his arm.

"Yes ma'am. I'm Tyrell." was the best Tyrell could manage.

"Far out," Sunshine said.

"Ty...rell." She trilled the syllables. "That's psychedelic."

Tyrell, who'd been named after his paternal grandfather who reputedly was more than a bit of a bastard, had never considered his name psychedelic. Whatever the hell that meant.

Sunshine stroked the front of his outfit.

"That's an out of sight suit," Sunshine said. "It makes you look really sexy. Maybe we could get together, sometime. Trip out and maybe... you know."

She giggled. "You guys ever go to the Haight?"

"No," Jeff said. "Not yet, anyway."

"You ought to. It's a real turn on. Really what's happening."

She dug into the tiny purse hanging around one shoulder that no one had noticed. Took out a pencil and a rather battered business card. She used Tyrell's chest as a desk, and he wanted to kiss the top of her head and work south from there.

Then she gave him the card. "Tonight. At the FBI Girl. A party."

29

Jeff, maybe, was the closest of the three to coherent. "Sunshine... what is an FBI Girl? Not J. Edgar Hoover's daughter or something like that?"

Sunshine giggled again. "It's a place, silly. Near the Haight. It's got food... and bands... and really groovy people."

"Is it... a special party," Nebraska wondered. "Maybe you shouldn't be inviting just anybody, I mean." He felt momentarily protective. This could be his little sister. Then he glanced down her inviting neckline. The hell it could be.

"Yeah. Special. Every party is special. Tonight it's for Mulberry Street. The Dead are in town, maybe they'll come down. Or maybe the Airplane. It'll be groovy."

"Doesn't sound like we'd be welcome," Jeff said, wondering what an airplane, let alone The Airplane would do at a party. And Dead? Come to think about it, why a party for a street? This was very, very strange.

"Oh no. Parties shouldn't be just the same old people. You can't change like that. And we've all got to change our heads so we can change the world. Right?"

"Uh... right."

"Somebody said there'll be tripper's punch" she said. "That'd be far out. Tyrell, maybe you and me could trip together tonight."

Tyrell's mouth was very, very dry.

"... If I'm there," she said. "If not... some other time. I know we'll see each other again Tyrell. Here... down in Sur, maybe Morning Glory Ranch... that's our karma. Isn't it?"

"Uh... yeah. Sure. Karma all the way," he said.

"Groovy." Sunshine smiled once more, and made the peace sign. "I love you guys," and hover went into forward motion and she drifted on.

There was a long very complete silence.

"What was that all about?" Nebraska wondered.

"Beats me," Jeff said. "And what is this tripping she wants to do with you, Tyrell?"

"I'm new, myself, remember? But whatever it is, I'm her man. She's..." Tyrell caught himself. Glanced around at his friends waiting for The Stare.

But all he saw was smiles. Nebraska clapped him on the back, nearly knocking him off the curb into the street in front of an oncoming bus.

"That cabbie was right," he said. "This is a magic town. You get a stew's number, Jeff, and somebody falls in lust with you, Tyrell. And we haven't

30

been in town longer than an hour.

"Now, all I gotta do is connect, and we're there!"

Tyrell smiled, an apologetic smile that neither Nebraska or Jeff caught. Then he turned and stared off down the street, at the small figure of Sunshine gliding away.

One way or another, he was *going* to... to take a trip? No, just trip. And damn, damn, damn, he prayed. I'd pure love for it to be with her.

He carefully put the flower in his breast pocket.

CHAPTER THREE

THE CABBIE KEPT fish-eying them in the rear view mirror, checking out their flashy new duds, contrasting supershort hair and ostentatiously bigearing the conversation. He was alert, Jeff surmised, for any subversion. The cabbie was a frizzly old fart, pushing forty, maybe forty five. He had a San Francisco Sheriff's Reserve card sealed in plastic dangling under his cabbie ID.

From the moment they'd hailed him the cabbie had been cold water on their leaping hormones, still sizzling from the encounter with the golden-haired Sunshine.

He'd started by making them stack their duffel bags on the front passenger's seat - obvious ransom for the fare.

"Where you wanna go?" the cabbie asked as they piled in and he edged the car into the North Beach traffic.

"Mark Hopkins," Nebraska said.

The cabbie's eyes popped.

"Not so fast, Lone Ranger," Jeff admonished Nebraska. "First we have to score some luggage and phone for reservations."

"What the hell for?" Nebraska goggled. "I got me a perfectly good duffel bag. Why spend bucks for somethin' I'll never gonna need? Where I come from, only folks with luggage are travelin' preachers and vacuum cleaner salesmen."

Jeff sighed. "Duffel bags don't wash at the Mark. The door man won't even let us in the place to get thrown out. They like their guests to carry luggage. To them, duffel bags equal flakes."

"Fine by me, son," Nebraska said. "I am a flake! Least for the next three days. Shit, that's the whole point, ain't it?"

"Not until we get that goddamned room booked, you aren't," Jeff said.

Tyrell was getting edgy. Sunshine had blown him away. The heavy presence of the cabbie, however, was yanking him back to earth. Jesus, Tyrell thought, she's *white*.

WHITE!

Strange how that encounter had made him dangerously color blind. He'd better keep his head straight. Otherwise he might end up being forced to kill some honky son of a bitch. Tyrell was in no mood for confrontation. He had definite plans when he got home. Plans that called for gettin' along with Whitey.

"Uh... how do the folks at this fancy hotel of yours feel about this black is beautiful business?" he asked.

"You mean... if we got luggage? And reservations?" Jeff said.

"Yeah."

"We got money to pay the bill, right?"

"Sure we do."

"I say again my last, little brother. It'll be the green they're looking at. And that'll be beautiful as all hell." Jeff leaned forward to address the cabbie. "Say, aren't there some surplus stores down on Market? Over near the Greyhound Station?"

"Yeah," was all the cabbie said.

"Then, that's where we want to go." He turned back to his friends. "Here's the plan. We'll buy something real cheap. Just to get us into the hotel. We can rent a locker at the bus station to stash our duffel bags. Okay?"

Everybody said okay. The cabbie, however, wasn't pleased. He grumbled something about hippie hustlers as he pushed for Market Street. Jeff and his friends decided to ignore him. It wasn't easy. His mutterings continued - just low enough so they could pretend not to hear if they wanted, but loud enough so that his comments were impossible to miss.

"Damn town goin' to hell in a hand basket... Somethin' oughta be done... Sure didn't fight no Germans for no hippies... Dope and stealin'... Girls cussin'... Sex everywheres... No shame... Can't blame the commies... Uh, uh... No way... I blame the parents... Yep... parents..."

Jeff wished he'd shut up about parents. It was a subject he was desperately trying to avoid.

The cab driver's mutterings cut off - as if by mental command. He leaned over and snapped on the radio. Music blared. It was obviously something the cabbie liked, because he cranked it up real loud. Tyrell couldn't stifle his groan. Don Ho, the white on white Hawaiian. "Tiny Bubbles." The cabbie sang along at the top of his voice. A fanatic of the Mitch Miller Sing Along school.

...*Tiny bubbles...* Don Ho sang. *"...Tiny bubbles..."* echoed Ho's backup and the cabbie. ... *In the wine...* "... In the wine..." the cabbie offkeyed back.

Tyrell had been worried about what the customary tip was to a San Francisco cab driver. He had planned to make the ride his treat.

33

But had been trying to figure out how to ask Jeff what the tip ought to be. Now he wasn't worried any more. The tip would be smaller than those stupid bubbles.

Bad valves, bent pushrods and dead con rod bearings rattled like machinegun fire and overwhelmed the cabbie's voice. As they slowed for a light, a battered VW Beetle pulled up beside them. It was painted with bright swirls of dayglo - orange and pink and green. The little car was overflowing with girls. Shrieking and squealing and having a good time. Tantalizing little breasts danced as they bounced about. Flashes of naked flesh. One of the girls was passing an album to another girl in front. Jeff saw her fumble with something under the dash. A car record player he guessed. As she fumbled, the girls spotted Jeff and his buddies in the cab. Single males! Wow! "You're beautiful," someone shouted. "Come on over and groove," yelled another.

There was only one guy in the car. He was behind the wheel. Nebraska thought he'd never seen such an ugly fella. Skinny kid. Pimples. A wispy beard. He caught Nebraska's eye. Gave him a shit-eating grin.

The song blared from the Vee Dubb's banks of Sweet Sixteen speakers: *Good mornin' little schoolgirl/Can I come home with you/Tell your momma/Your poppa/I'm a little schoolboy too...*

The light changed and the hippie guy flashed a peace sign at Nebraska. The Vee Dubb belched away in cloud of black smoke. The sound of the music and the girls' laughter drifted back like a heady perfume.

I wanna be your chauffeur/Wanna ride your li'l machine...

"I think I just died and went to heaven," Nebraska said. "If I didn't, shoot me now, boys, 'cause I hear the good Lord a callin'."

"Filthy hippie bitches," the cabbie snarled. "Spreadin' crabs and VD to decent folks. Whyn't they stay home where they belong?"

"Just kids havin' some summer fun," Tyrell blurted. For some reason he felt he should stick up for the girls in the Bug.

He flashed on the vision of Sunshine, smelling so clean and sweet standing there with the outstretched flower in her hand. The last woman he'd been with smelled like a rice paddy. Not that Tyrell was a man with vast sexual experience. A couple of whores in Vietnam... and he felt like a guilty shit afterwards and never was that hot to repeat the experience. Despite the lies he had told his friends back home, he'd only gotten laid a few times. In his country world, girls mostly kept their pants on until marriage.

"Yeah, mister," Jeff broke in, feeling contrary himself. "What are you so hot about? Don't you have kids of your own?"

"Not a one, and me and my wife get down on our knees every night and thank the good Lord we don't," the cabbie shot back. "And I'll tell you why. 'Cause you kids got no appreciation. You been handed everything on a silver platter. Your folks spoil you. Buy you anything you want. Why, I've seen workin' men's sons drivin' brand new cars and they ain't even outta high school.

"And what thanks do their folks get... nothin', that's what. Kids spit in their eye and run away from home. It's happenin' all over the country. Thousands of kids runnin' off. Scarin' their folks to death. Gettin' pregnant. Takin' up narcotics. Whinin' for more money when they get hung out with the law.

"Yeah. That's the way it is. And to think I fought a war for you. Me and millions of other guys. Excuse my French, but, damn you kids make me mad. Every one of ya runnin' off first chance you get. And where do you run? Why, to San Francisco. The city of free food, free dope, and all the sex you can get."

"You oughta get a job with the Chamber of Commerce, mister," Nebraska said. "Slogan like that should really bring in the bucks."

"Think I'm kiddin', huh?" the cabbie said. "Okay. Call me a liar. But tell me this, first. How come you're here?"

"I dunno," Nebraska said. "We were in a hover pattern round Guam and we flipped a two bit piece. It came up San Francisco."

"Nobody said diddly about stuff bein' free," Tyrell said.

"You tellin' me none of you guys heard of the Summer Of Love?" the cabbie asked.

Jeff wanted to say, no, but hum a few bars and I'll give it a whirl. Instead, he raised a hand and swore they were newborn ignorant.

"What, are you from another planet?" the cabbie said.

"Something like that," Jeff answered. "It's too complicated to explain. Let's just say we've been out of town."

"Way... way... way the *hell* out of town," Tyrell snarled.

The cabbie decided to believe. Or he just wanted to hear himself motormouth.

"It's all those hippies over on the Haight," the cabbie said. "The Diggers fill 'em full of rock and roll and dope and brainwash them."

Nebraska wondered what a "Digger" was, but stayed silent.

"They publish these radical newspapers encouragin' kids to sin and riot. More they write, the more kids we get comin' in from God knows where. Draft dodgers. Deserters. Drug addicts from Canada and New York.

"That's what's been goin' on up to this year. Then things got real bad out."

"Oh, yeah. Like how?" Jeff asked.

"They declared this the Summer Of Love. Sent the word out all across the world. 'Come to San Francisco. Where everythin' is free. An' anythin' goes.' And they've been comin'. And comin'. Figure there's gonna a be at least a million of 'em by the end of summer. Think of that. One million drugged up kids. Livin' off the kindness of the good folks of San Francisco."

It sounded fine to Nebraska. And Jeff. Also Tyrell. Although they believed not one word of it.

"We got 'em camped out in the parks, the streets, even in folks doorways. Garbage every place you go. Foul talkin' kids. Smokin' marijuana. No respect for authority. Defacin' the flag. Even our nig..." he glanced at Tyrell in the mirror and shifted... "... our colored people are upset. Fillin' up their neighborhoods with white trash. And we got some good colored folks here, I tell you. They know trash when they see it."

A sudden silence descended on the cab as first Jeff and then Nebraska considered murder. Tyrell had already passed that point. The cabbie was quiet as well, maybe realizing he had gone too far.

"Right here is fine, buddy," Tyrell said. He just wanted out of the cab.

The dismal mood fled as soon as they bailed out.

They marveled, not quite sure what they were marveling at. But marveling just the same.

Nebraska was the first to get it.

"No uniforms," he said. "And... and people are *normal-sized!* Not short little shits in black pajamas.*"

"Welcome to the real world," Jeff realized. "Now, Where's a surplus store?"

Nebraska looked, then spotted one, further down Market. They loped off.

Tyrell lagged a bit behind, eyes and head turning, looking like a Hick In The City and not caring who noticed.

Allan Cole & Chris Bunch

From a cheap jewelry store's outside speaker, drumroll and:
...Put silver wings/On my son's chest...
And Jeff bellowed over Barry Sadler's mellerdrama the GI's version of
the song:
*"...Entrenching tool/And all the rest/One hundred men/Will test
today/And ninety-nine/Be legs to stay..."*
And then for Tyrell Harris it was complete serendipity as he looked in
the next storefront and saw the sign:

CHOICE, NOT CHANCE. GO ARMY.

Inside the recruiting station sat a very lonely Sergeant First Class in
Dress Greens.
Tyrell sympathized with his solitude by giving him the finger, and they
were bouncing on, toward that surplus store.

"Why in hell," Nebraska wondered, "would somebody want with *this*?"
The object in question happened to be an electric-blue 250 pound practice
bomb, standing near the store's entrance. Price: $2.00
"Damfino. Cut it in half and put sand in and you've got the world's
biggest ashtray for drunks, maybe," Tyrell said. "But how about *these*?"
These were some very battered, very surplus jungle boots. "These boots
were made for walkin,'" Tyrell sang...
"Come on, you guys," a suddenly business-like Jeff said. "Here's what
we wanted. Quit goofing on the war toys."

They left as the proud owners of three cheap, black briefcase type pieces
of luggage, with loose, white stitching holding the sides together. Cost, five
dollars each. They had stuffed the rest of their new clothes inside the cases,
checked a map they'd picked up in the store, and decided they were close
enough to the bus station to walk, even lugging the heavy duffelbags.
They were silent for a few blocks as they drank in the sights, sounds and
smells of American civilization. Even the hard end of Market Street was
pure exotica. The scent of burgers and fries and grilled onions wafting on sea
breezes. Tall people nourished on those burgers and fries going about their
business. Shop windows jammed with strange new things.
All around the sounds of their very own language swirled about and
smothered them in warm comfort. Their heads rubbered back and forth and
back again. Checking it out.

Especially the women.

American women.

Each and every one of them. How unusual. How... sensual. Even the sight of little old blue-haired ladies amazed them. Made them dumb with shyness.

They saw a girl, maybe nineteen, exit a shop and wave a hand for a cab. She was wearing an expensive, light knit mini skirt. Cut half a whisper below mystery.

They couldn't remember legs looking this good - even in a bikini. But it wasn't just the shortness of the dress or the loveliness of the legs that stunned them. As far as they could tell, the girl wore nothing under the dress. They stopped and waited in respectful silence until she had climbed into the cab and taken off.

"Did you see what I saw?" Jeff whispered.

"Jesus... nipples," Nebraska said.

"I swore I saw hair," Tyrell said.

"Me too," Jeff said.

"Aw, man, you did? I musta missed it," Nebraska mourned.

They spoke in hushed tones, as if they were in a church discussing sacred relics rather than private parts.

"Maybe the cab driver wasn't lying" Jeff said, hopeful to beat hell. "From his warped point of view, I mean. And speaking as the official Team Doctor, we need a prescription for someone like that. Correction. Three someones."

"Summer of Love, huh?" Nebraska said.

"You were right the first time, Nebraska, my friend," Tyrell said. "We musta got our asses shot off in 'Nam. And we died and went to heaven. Although, no way is it any kinda heaven my momma and the preacher man ever told me about."

"Naw," Jeff said sadly. "It won't work out. The only lucky thing that ever happened in my life was making it through fourteen months of Vietnam and getting out in one piece," Jeff said.

"I don't know, boy," Nebraska said. "Maybe you're on a streak."

"Yeah, maybe we're *all* on a streak," Tyrell said. "Come on. Let's get movin' while we're still hot."

Any remaining thoughts of cabbie lies faded when they reached the Greyhound Station at Seventh and Market. The ground did serious abrasive damage to their jaws as they dragged them about the station staring at what

Allan Cole & Chris Bunch

had to be a living poster for a B movie, with a title like: "Invasion of The Sex Mad Underclad Rock 'n' Roll Teenagers."

The buses were lined up in four incoming lanes. All manner of kids swarmed off. White and black and all the colors in between, hailing from every inch of America and points beyond. They carried duffel bags, knapsacks, potato sacks or bound-up cardboard and paper bags. They wore exotic costumes with every imaginable color lighting up the space around them. Many wore fancy, Indian style headbands. They were decked out in beads and bangles and Jesus locks. The sound of bells came from everywhere.

Jeff felt like he had dropped into some kind of ancient fair. You could smell incense and once in a while the faint odor of marijuana.

Tyrell spotted some kids openly smoking dope. Music blared out from countless portable radios.

As they wandered about in a daze, looking for the rental lockers, they saw scraps of paper posted in every conceivable place. "Marsha Collins. I'll be at Tracy's Doughnuts on the Haight until July 23. Love, Tina," read one. "Have you seen this boy? $500 Reward!!" There was a picture, a name and a phone number on the sign. It was a high school graduation picture of the boy. Short hair, clear eyes, neck like a jock's. Obvious upper middle class.

Jeff looked at the boys shuffling around him. Hair to their shoulders. Beards. Snapping their fingers to the music. Goosing their girl friends. Eyes dancing with the prospect of all the fun they were going to have. He looked back at the picture of the straight looking kid. Yeah, he was probably here. But if he was, he sure didn't look like *that*.

Nebraska nudged Jeff. "Come on. Make that phone call. Let's get goin' to this Mark Hopkins place. This child's feelin' weary and in need of strong drink."

Jeff brought himself back to reality and found it just as depressing as he'd predicted.

"Uh, guys... I think we're up Crap Creek without a paddle."

Two huhs.

"We're tryin' to look civilian, right? Look around? You think that a real zootcapri hotel like the Mark would want people like *these* guys stayin' there? Even if they were the Beatles, say?"

Nebraska's expression suddenly matched Jeff's.

"Hell. You're prob'ly right," he said. "First dream, down in flames."

He forced a smile. "No big damned deal," he said. "So we'll end up at

39

some kinda motor inn. We can still party!"

But his voice rang with hollow disappointment.

"I'm sorry..." and Jeff brightened. "The hell I am. I'm apologizing for wasting fifteen bucks on these junk suitcases. Hang tough. Doctor Katz is gonna implement Plan B."

And he headed for a phone. A few minutes later, he came back beaming happily, told them to forget putting the duffelbags into storage and let's get a cab. The Mark's expecting us. Half-believing in sudden miracles, Tyrell and Nebraska followed him.

A portable radio sang: *...Do you believe in magic/In a young girl's heart...*

The Mark Hopkins was twenty stories of 1920's elegance. It consisted of a tall, central tower, flanked by two wings - all decked out in buff-colored brick. Perched on top was its famous cocktail lounge - The Top Of The Mark -commanding one of the most startling views of a city noted for its vistas.

Tyrell and Nebraska craned their necks and nervously licked dry lips as a big black limo spilled out a couple dripping in jewels and arrogance. Tyrell gulped. Nebraska shifted from foot to foot.

"Let's go," Jeff said, and marched into the hotel like he owned it - trailing his vastly intimidated friends. "Just shut up and let me handle it," he hissed as they approached the front desk.

Nebraska and Tyrell gaped when the clerk's eyes turned from suspicion at Jeff's clothes to obsequious welcome as he announced his name.

"Yessir, Mister Katz, I sure do have your reservation. Your father called ahead and said to treat you and your Army buddies real well. We got your room ready for you and if there's anything you need... just ask. The Mark Hopkins is very proud to have you three here," the clerk oozed on."

He leaned closer to Jeff, lowered his voice. "Is it true all three of you got Silver Stars for bravery."

"Actually," Jeff corrected, "I just got the Bronze. My friends, here..." he waved an imperious hand at his marveling buddies... "were the ones who got the Silver." Then he indicated Tyrell. "In fact, he saved my life. Threw himself on a Viet Cong grenade. They recommended him for The Big One... you know, the one that Audie Murphy got. But no. A terrible miscarriage of justice."

The clerk gaped at the man in the neon clothes. "On a grenade? My

Allan Cole & Chris Bunch

God, did he get..."

Jeff shook his head. "He doesn't like to talk about it," he said. "The wounds were pretty... personal."

"Awful," the clerk said, shaking his head. "And so young."

Tyrell felt his nuts crawl up into his shorts. What was Jeff saying? That they got blown off?

The clerk moved on to the money part.

"Your father said you'd be paying cash. At the end of your stay."

"That's right," Jeff said. "My dad wanted to pay for everything. But I didn't think that was right. Now that we're no longer serving our country, we have to start getting used to civilian life and taking care of ourselves."

The clerk thought this was absolutely marvelous of Jeff and his incredibly brave friends. A few minutes later, the guys were clambering out of the elevator and walking down a hallway with carpeting as thick as elephant grass.

"What's this about your daddy callin'," Nebraska wanted to know.

"He didn't," Jeff said. "I just *said* I was my dad."

"Now, that's what I call a hustle," said an admiring Tyrell.

"Must be nice," Nebraska said, "to have a daddy who's a big time doctor."

Jeff went suddenly silent. His eyes narrowed. His lips thinned. The blood fled his face. "Yeah. It's simply wonderful," Jeff said after a long uncomfortable moment. "Just a thrill a minute to be such a lucky guy."

"I'm sorry," Nebraska said. "I was just foolin' around. I got no right to judge another man's troubles."

Jeff was instantly back to square one. He laughed and said Nebraska was probably right the first time. And to just forget it, he was feeling pretty sensitive. People from Whittier, by God, California, tended to get that way, he said. Seeing as how it was the birthplace of Richard "Tricky Dick" Nixon, he hoped this was understandable to the rest of America.

The bellboy was stashing their gear as they came into the room. He handled the duffelbags gingerly, as if they were covered in muck. But Jeff's hefty tip brightened his day and he bowed out of the room with a broad smile.

Nebraska and Tyrell were dazed at the opulence surrounding them, a yawning suite of rooms with antique furniture and fine art copies on the wall.

"Fuck. Can I afford this?" Nebraska asked.

41

"Watch the fucks," Tyrell said, automatically.

"Sorry about that. Still. My wallet took one look at this place and hauled for cover."

"No sweat," Jeff said. "I got it for the same price as a single room. Guess some high roller cancelled out at the last minute or something. And we, gentlemen, are the beneficiaries."

He threw himself onto a bed and nearly sank out of sight in its softness.

"Well, what do you think?" he asked.

Tyrell stomped on the floor. Hard. His foot made a soft, feathery sound.

"Some hooch," he said. "It's even got a real floor. Of course, it's the least you could do for a guy like me. Seeing as how I went and saved your worthless white hide, and all. And lost my balls to the war effort."

"I was making it up as I went along," Jeff said. "Worked didn't it?"

There was a loud bang from the other room and Tyrell dropped that *real* floor as if there were incoming rounds raining from the ceiling of the suite. He didn't feel too stupid, however. Because Jeff was somehow curled on the rug beside him.

Nebraska gave them an evil grin as he entered the room from the adjoining suite. He had a big fat bottle of champagne in one hand, sans cork. In the other were three glasses.

"I guess I should'a yelled 'incoming,' before I popped it," he said when he spotted his friends sheepishly getting up off the floor. "For a second there I thought I shot myself."

"Gimme some of that sinful brew," Tyrell said. "If my momma calls, tell her I'm just sipping my nerve medicine."

"Your daddy must really rate," Nebraska said to Jeff. "They had this stuff cooling in an ice bucket and there's a basket a fruit in there that'd feed two villages -and that's *before* we pacified their asses."

"Oh, he rates. He rates," Jeff mumbled as he swallowed his champagne in one go. Nebraska and Tyrell followed suit, then refilled the glasses.

Jeff raised his glass.

"Gentlemen," he said with grave formality. "We have a perilous mission before us. A year and a half ago we swore a solemn oath with two absent comrades in arms. We pledged that the five of us would hoist a brew together in this fair city.

"Well, here we are. But there are only three of us to redeem said promise. And the mission now has grown in even greater proportions. Three to do the job of five.

"Are we men enough for this task?"

"Lead me to that bar," Tyrell said. "I'll show 'em what I'm made of."

"I plan to drink this city drier'n an irrigation ditch in August," Nebraska said.

Jeff hoisted his glass higher.

"To Mills and Atherton," he said. "Our absent friends."

"To absent friends," Tyrell and Nebraska echoed back.

He drained the glass, dropped it to the carpet. Then smashed it with a heavy foot.

"Uh... I thought you were supposed to break them by throwing 'em in a fireplace, or something," Tyrell said.

"Greeks do that," Jeff lectured. "Jews stomp them."

"Just like they stomped them Arabs in six days flat," Nebraska said as he let his own glass fall. And gave it a satisfying crush with his foot.

"Well, hell," Tyrell said, "I don't want to be a spoilsport. Besides, I don't know any Greeks."

Smash.

The three young men looked at each other, their faces wreathed with smiles. Then the smiles faded. For a moment, all three of them felt that they were looking at strangers. Civilian strangers. Tyrell gave a nervous tug at his clothes. Then the two faces in front of him settled in. Young faces, with skin nearly as dark as his own from the blazing sun of Vietnam, but with the telltale white streak near the hairline, skin shaded by the constantly-worn steel pot.

But the eyes staring out at him somehow seemed very old. There was a look in those eyes he recognized. Far in the back of his mind he heard the pop, pop, pop of rifle fire. Someone shouting orders. Someone screaming. He almost felt the heavy wash of the chopper's blade blasting at him as the medevac settled in. Then it was gone. But from the tight look in his friends' faces something very similar had just happened to them.

One by one they each gave a sober nod. The deal was doubly done.

"Okay, I'm for the shower," Nebraska said, breaking the mood. "Then after I call my folks and let 'em know I'm safe and all, I plan to pay social call on that famous bar you been braggin' on. It may be the highest bar in San Francisco, but I tell you I plan on gettin' a whole lot higher."

"I better call my mom," Tyrell said. He headed for the phone. Then turned momentarily back to Jeff. "How about you?" He said this delicately, not wanting to offend, but worried for Jeff's folks sake. He also felt a bit uncomfortable about nagging because there was something he was also delaying. Not a call to his family. But to someone else.

"I'll phone later," Jeff said, but real flip as if it didn't matter one way or the other.

"Come on, don't do that to them," Tyrell said.

"We know you don't wanna go to that party and all," Nebraska said. "But when you don't show at the airport, they're gonna think your plane crashed someplace in the middle of the Pacific."

"My mom would have a stroke," Tyrell agreed. "You're not so mad at them you want to do something like that, are you?"

"I'm not mad at all," Jeff said. "I just want to have a good time with some friends I probably won't see the rest of my life."

"So?" Nebraska pressed.

"So, I'll call. Right now, see. Watch me get up and call."

Jeff stormed over to the phone. Picked it up and gave the switchboard operator a number. She rang it for him. He waited, tapping his feet. Tensing in growing dread. Then a big smile crossed his face as the operator came back on the line and said the number was busy.

"That's okay," he said to the operator. "I'll call back later."

"If you would like, Mr. Katz," the operator said, "I'll keep trying for you while you're out and leave a message for your father."

Vast relief flooded over Jeff as the chicken way out of his dilemma was offered.

"Would you? What a nice thing to do. Okay. Tell my father I'm spending a few days with my Army friends. And I'll be flying home immediately after that."

The operator took down the message. Jeff thanked her and hung up.

"It's all taken care of," he said. "Now. Let's get drunk!"

A little over a half hour later they were bright and clean and smelling like soap and shaving lotion and making their way to the famous Top Of the Mark.

Ten minutes after that, they were storming out the front door of the hotel.

"I can't believe it," Jeff said. "You can't get a drink in this joint without a tie."

Allan Cole & Chris Bunch

"No way am I crawlin' back in my Class A's for that," Nebraska said.

"You can see their point, though," Tyrell said in a moment of weak reasonableness. "Those are the rules. And every other guy was wearing one."

"Sure I can see their point," Jeff said. "And they can stick it in a place where the sun can't get to. I swear, from this moment on, I will never, ever wear a tie, unless I want to."

"Hear, hear," Nebraska said.

"Let's go see those naked ladies the cabbie was telling us about," Tyrell said.

"Yeah. Whiskey and naked women," Nebraska said. "And no damn ties."

"North Beach, my good man," Jeff told the cab driver. "We are seekers of truth through decadence."

The cab driver grunted and they were off.

CHAPTER FOUR

"WHAT?" TYRELL SCREAMED.

"I said... louder! I can't hear you," Jeff hollered.

"This... ain't... decadence," Tyrell tried once more.

"No shit," Jeff, having finally heard Tyrell's criticism, replied - just as the tinny recorded music blasting from speakers around the stage took a quarter-measure of blessed silence and Jeff's comment ricocheted around the infamous Big Al's nightclub.

Six middle-aged tourists who'd been staring at the stage frowned at Jeff. As did the two hulking bouncers who were appropriately dressed like Prohibition gangsters. But since none of the three young men - the only people in the club under forty besides the two dancers and one waitress - did anything, the bouncers relaxed and The Psychedelic Dance of Love continued.

Which was: One male, one female dancer, wearing pinned smiles and no more, writhed around on the small stage near the club's ceiling.

"Think they're ever gonna actually do the dirty deed?" Nebraska wanted to know. Jeff shook his head. The woman onstage was chewing gum somewhat in time to the music. Both she and the man had their eyes fixed on something just over each other's shoulder. The music itself would have been trash at any level through any sound system. Big Al's hyperdriven cheapo's did not improve it any.

The waitress reappeared. "Six more?"

Jeff shook his head.

"Set's just about over with," the woman said, semi-shouting, her mouth an inch from Jeff's ear. "Two drinks per set minimum."

"No thanks," Jeff shouted. "Our church group's leaving anyway."

"What?"

"Never mind."

The waitress left. Jeff drained his glass, and started pouring down the second drink.

"What did she want?" Nebraska asked.

"To sell us more water."

Nebraska cupped a hand to his ear. "What?"

"Never mind."

Jeff motioned... drink, drink, drink, and the three knocked back the watery contents of their glasses, got up and headed for the exit.

Big Al's - $3 to get in per person, two drink minimum per set - $2 per drink, ordered two at a time as you sat down.

The bouncers' lips mechanized smiles as they went past and out, onto the sin-riddled streets of North Beach.

"I hope you get the black syph," Jeff shouted, a smile just as mechanical and broad on his lips, and the door closed behind them, and the noise level reduced to sonic.

Just overhead, next to the shill trying to get more tourists inside, was a small speaker, echoing the music playing inside the club.

"Now *that* was a complete bust," Nebraska opined.

"No shit, Dick Tracy, Where'd you park the squad car."

"Decadence," Jeff complained, "my left testicle. No donkey. No hard-on. I've seen better stuff in Saigon."

"You buy me Saigon tea," Nebraska offered in a sing-song voice.

"Some of us," Tyrell said, "never got to Saigon. We were too busy fighting the war while guys like you were goofing off."

"Why not," Jeff said. *"Somebody's* got to be doing that, don't they? Why not the 101st? You volunteered, remember, you RA heavyduty mother, you. Airborne, airborne, all the way."

"Cool it," Tyrell said.

Then: "What're we gonna do now?"

"Good question," Jeff wondered. "Okay. Carol Doda had a hangover or maybe one of her 44's leaked or something. Bust Number One. Cheap pun intended. Then, we've got Nude College Girls. College maybe back around Roosevelt's time. Teddy Roosevelt. Bust Number Two. Bust number three..."

He jerked a thumb at Big Al's.

The three of them were shifting back and forth, trying to hold position in the heavy foot traffic that poured around them, down Columbus and across Grant.

"...back there. So far, my big idea of getting us all stewed, screwed and tattooed isn't going that far.

"Sorry, guys."

"No big thing. We'll get our shit together directly," Tyrell said. "We always do."

"Hey," Jeff said. "Hey. Look." He pointed down and across the street, at the Jazz Workshop. "Thelonious Monk."

"Now, that's just a *great* idea," Tyrell said. "Go sit and watch some spade

47

go tinkle, tinkle on a piano while some beatnik chick tries to sell us... what's that coffee that tastes like it's been condensed?"

"Espresso," Jeff said. "You're right. Next idea?"

"What about that joint over there," Nebraska wondered. "I've never seen a belly dancer."

"And you don't want to," Jeff said. "At least not over there. I was there once. It's really authentic. Just like in the Mideast."

"Which means?"

"Which means Ay-rabs like their women a little on the chubby side," Jeff said. "That's assuming that the place is authentic. Plus... I am not going in there. Staff Sergeant Applegate here made me promise to stay out of trouble. I walk in there, and what is it going to be?

"Don't think they'll buy us drinks if I start asking about where they were back in June for the Six Day War, do you?"

"Come on, Jeff," Nebraska said. "That's not your war."

The smile came off Katz's face for a moment, then reappeared, Tyrell stepped in. "Sarn't Applegate! Take charge of the men and march 'em to chow," Tyrell said.

"Now that is about a stupid an idea as we've had yet," Nebraska said.

"Yeah, Tyrell. Why mess up the high?"

"Okay. I'm easy," Tyrell said. "You're too light in the... behind for pizza... which is right down there... We don't have to eat 'til later. Or never. I'm just along for the ride."

"Pizza," Nebraska mused. "Wow. It's been... yeah. Pizza. With about two pitchers. Each. Our orders have been changed, troops. Form up, on-line, and we'll sweep straight through that joint."

"No prisoners," Tyrell agreed. "I'll take point. Put the doc back where it's safe. Where he won't get hit by flying pepperoni."

Jeff flipped him the finger for an answer, and they started down the hill.

Tyrell felt pretty good. So they hadn't connected with anybody yet. Big deal. He somehow doubted that they really would. Unless they were ready to get serious. Stop a cab driver and ask him to take them to a whorehouse. Tyrell shook his head. With his luck, they would get the only cabbie in the city who was a Methodist Reader.

"The white man's nigger looks happy," a voice came. "Pretty soon he's gonna get the banjo out and start dancing, huh?"

Tyrell jolted back and spun.

A man stood in the middle of the sidewalk. He wore a dark suit, a very thin tie and held copies of a tabloid-size newspaper. The mostly white tourist crowd ebbed around him as if he were the rocky reefs of The Farallones.

Tyrell looked the other black up and down, then moved toward him. His left hand came up... even with his ribcage... and his right fist balled.

"Who the fuck are you," Tyrell said, real quiet. "One of those Muslims I heard about?"

"No. Not anymore. But we ain't talking about me."

"Maybe we're gonna be, 'bout five seconds," Tyrell said. "Then my friend the medic over there's gonna be talkin' about you, too. Wonderin' how to get my size nine out of your asshole."

"What's that gonna change," the other black sneered. "Maybe you can whip me. Maybe I won't even fight back. Whitey loves to see us blacks kill each other. Saves them the trouble gettin' a lynch mob up of their own."

Tyrell hesitated.

"You see," the black said. "I'm speakin' the truth. You know it, don't you? I mean, who are you? Goin' out to the white man's Babylon, lookin' at his whores, drinkin' alcohol... what kind of shit is that? I'm sorry I had to call you nigger to get you to pay mind to me."

Tyrell half-lowered his stance. He glanced down the street. Jeff and Nebraska had noted he'd stopped and were waiting. Both of them looked a little puzzled.

"I'm not paying mind to you," Tyrell said to the black. "I didn't just finish fighting a war to be starting another one here in San Francisco."

"You one of the brothers come back from The Nam?"

"Never heard it called that by anybody but REMFs. Which, to the uninitiated, stands for Reach Echelon Mother Fuckers. But yeah. I was in Viet Nam."

"Fightin' the white man's war, against our brothers," the man said. "But that's all right. We all get our consciousness raised sometime that maybe is not the same as for others. Even somebody like Malcolm took awhile."

"Malcolm who?"

"Don't play dumb. Save that for the devils," the black hissed. "Go back to what we were sayin' before. You went to Viet Nam. What kind of soldiering you do?"

"101st Airborne," Tyrell said. Proud of it. Even proclaiming it to this crazy.

"So you learned," the black said, smiling. "Everything they taught you will come back around, soon. The chickens'll come home to roost once more. Like they did in Watts."

"Oh. Now I get it. What is this shit? Burn, baby burn?"

"Hell no," the man said. "Nothin's dumber than us black folks burning our own homes and businesses 'cause the white devil is persecuting us.*

"I'm talking about what's coming, not this August nor maybe next. But soon. When brothers like you come back from the war, and they start teaching. Time we went beyond empty words and got our shit straight. Better we stop talkin' and start learning how to fight The Real War. Because it's coming. I can see it, clear."

"You better hope," Tyrell said slowly, "that there's nothing there to see. You ever been in a war? A real war, not a buncha peckernecks with a couple rifles in their pickup? I'm talkin' the real shit, like with artillery and gunships and guys comin' in with more firepower than the whole Memphis Police. Each!

"You even seen that, mister? Or are you from here in California, where they don't burn a lot of crosses on your lawn.

"Not that I'm any kind of expert. I've never seen a lynching. Seen what somebody said was a burnt cross, the next day. Heard there were Klan meetings, and I stayed inside... But I've seen a war.

"And I seen who fought it. Tell you something, friend. People go to Vietnam and make it through... they ain't gonna be listening to your shit about fighting another one, real soon."

"Hey, Tyrell," Nebraska shouted. Tyrell waved -hang on a second.

"Another thing. That war... there's a lot of white boys fighting it too. They learned how to do the real shit, just like I did. So your words don't matter. Goin' in, we're outnumbered. More of them than there are of us, right?"

"That won't matter."

"Like hell it won't matter!" Tyrell said emphatically. "One of us... ten of them. That's shit odds. I went against those kind of odds a couple times. In places you never heard of... where the VeeCee let us come on their own ground.

"I've also seen what happens when the VC fucked up and came on our ground. Same thing happened to them. Ten to one, and the one gets handed his ass on a platter.

"There it is, friend. And I ain't gettin' in on the losing side from the

Allan Cole & Chris Bunch

beginning."

"Ten to one," the other man said. "How many white devils are there in the world? And how many of us? Blacks? Indians? Viet Cong? Chinese? Think about it."

"Only thing I got time to think about right now is gettin' a drink." Tyrell started away, then turned back. "Oh yeah. I have another couple of drinks, and come back up this street... don't be on it."

"If I start thinking about you callin' my friends devils and I'm liable to get me an attitude. And set about workin' it out on your nigger ass. That's no threat... that's a promise!"

Tyrell, now completely sober and his mood ruined, stomped back toward Nebraska and Jeff.

"Who was that?"

"Doesn't matter," Tyrell said. "Assholes come in all colors. Fuck the pizza. I need a drink."

Jeff started to stay something, then caught Tyrell's mood and shifted gears. "Drink. Right, drink. Speaking as your physician, *Mister* Tyrell Harris, I prescribe a double."

"Mister," Tyrell said, forcing himself to smile, and then the smile became real. "Say that one more time, Doc. I can get real used to it."

"Come on," Nebraska said, pointing. "Bar just across the street, over there."

They stepped off the curb - and an olive drab 1961 Ford Fairlane sedan squealed to a stop. It had a single red dome in its roof and, on the door, black lettering: MILITARY POLICE.

An MP first lieutenant popped out from the right door. He wore white-covered hat, MP armband, a leather belt with a nightstick, handcuffs and a holstered .45 automatic on it.

And a nametag: Sanders.

"Okay," he said briskly. "Let's see some ID and either leave papers or DA31's."

All three of them gaped. Nebraska was the first to recover. "I beg your pardon," he said politely. "Are you a police officer or something?"

"Knock off the shit, soldier. Come on. Paperwork."

"Soldier?" Nebraska asked. "You are wrong, Mister. I'm a civilian. Are you some kind of soldier-cop or something."

"The hair, jacko," Sanders snarled. "Cut the crapping around. Or you want me to just arrest you and take you to the holding cell."

Now it was Jeff's turn to apply reason.

"Lieutenant. You don't have any right to stop people, here on the streets of San Francisco, just because there's something wrong with their hair. This is a free country, isn't it?"

"You want to play it like that," the MP said, "Fine with me."

He bent and gave the driver orders: "Jenkins, call for SFPD backup. We got us some AWOL wiseasses here."

Bent over, he didn't see Nebraska reach out with his right, and grab his armband. Nebraska spun him, the black leatherette armband with the MP and the OD Sixth Army patch ripping, and then Nebraska drove a straight left, putting about 190 pounds of corn- and C-ration-fed muscle into Lt. Sander's gut.

Sanders whuffed and went double. He threw up on his spitshined combat boots.

Nebraska swung once more, a right into Sander's ear. The busman's hat crunched and his skull klonked into the sedan's rolled-up rear window.

"Haul ass!" Jeff shouted and the three pelted back up Columbus, as the square hulk who was the MP Driver came out of sedan, ripping his nightstick off its belt and lumbered - at a very fast lumber - after them.

Tyrell, Nebraska and Jeff cut right, up Grant and past Big Al's.

They did not see the black wearing the suit and skinny tie stick out a long leg as the MP rumbled past, nor the MP start a keaton-stagger, arms flailing as he tried to recover his balance and then his crashing fall as he went into and through a shabby green newspaper stand, and out into the street, where a station wagon from Iowa almost ran him down.

They were too busy running...

"Man," Tyrell breathed. "Listen to all those goddamned sirens."

"They've got to have every cop in the city out after us," Jeff agreed. "Jesus, Nebraska. You sure know how to start a party off right."

"Knock it off, you guys. What did you want me to do? Whip out our papers like we were still under his lifer thumb?"

"At least," Tyrell started, "you could've..." He broke off. Suddenly laughed. "Lord, Nebraska. You sure caught him a good one. Right in the sweetbreads."

"Thank you. I'm pretty proud of it myself."

"Hot damn," Jeff said sourly. "I've gone and cast my lot with a couple juvenile delinquents. I'm ashamed of you, Staff Sergeant. Truly

Allan Cole & Chris Bunch

ashamed."

Jeff let the moment wait. "Should of kicked the bastard! Now. What are we going to do next?"

"No way," Nebraska said, "are those cops all looking for us. Something else must have happened. Come on. Let's get back to a big street, grab a cab, head back for the hotel and try to plan what we do next."

"'Kay," Jeff agreed. "But I sort of figure we've burnt North Beach."

He stood up from behind the piled garbage cans they'd been crouched behind... and a glaring spotlight hit him.

A shout: "There's one of them! Come on!" And in a clatter of cans and garbage, the chase began again.

They came in the front door of the bar just in time to hear the protest:

"I do not *know* what a leave paper is, let alone a Duck's Ass whatever number it was. Now, either start speaking English and tell me why, if you're *really* a policeman, you're wearing a green uniform.

"Or else tell Billy and me who put you up to this camping around and then have a drink. You look like you need it, darling."

They went back out, without waiting for the response.

Now they were on Grant, in the heart of Chinatown. Jeff was in the lead. His idea, hastily muttered as they'd finally gotten across Columbus, was to follow their training and Escape and Evade their pursuers, get back to the Mark Hopkins on foot, and maybe think about having a quiet evening in.

"Back there," Nebraska muttered. "Cop just got out of a car. On foot. Coming after us."

Suddenly the situation was very surreal. Here they were, three Americans, pushing their way past other Americans, who frowned, smiled or ignored them.

But most of the people on the street were Oriental.

"Hey, Tyrell," Jeff said. "If you make believe the signs are in Vietnamese... this is pretty much what Saigon looks like. Cholon, especially."

"Thank you, my friend. I could'a lived without that skinny. Shit! Here come some more of 'em," Tyrell said.

Two police cars were pulled up at a cross-street, and cops were getting out.

"In here," Jeff said, waving them into a small store front.

"Good evening," came the voice from the back room, and a tiny man wearing a robe bowed out.

"Jesus! Uh, sorry, Mister. Uh. Good evening to you too."

"You wish?"

"I wish... do you have a back door?"

"I do." The Oriental man did not move. Jeff dug a five out of his pocket, tossed it to the man.

"Thank you." The money vanished. "And you did not come in here this night."

"Thanks, Pop. Cheap at twice the price."

"Tsk," the old man said, as he ushered them through a cluttered store-room. "I should have considered my first offer more carefully. Out here, and go up through North Beach. Too easy to get lost in Chinatown."

"He's got a point!"

"Thanks, mister... Double-time, ho!"

"Take it easy! I got a stitch in my side!"

"Christ, if I'd wanted to play run through the jungle I woulda reupped!"

They went up the alley following Tyrell's hand signals. Both Nebraska and Jeff were lost, although Jeff thought in their dartings back and forth and up and down that they were somewhere on the East of Grant, and over there - at least judging by the way the streets sloped -would be Russian Hill. Unless he was really turned around.

Tyrell brought them to a halt with an upraised hand. They wheezed for oxygen.

"You sound like a donkey engine," Tyrell told Jeff critically. "He's got an excuse," ...indicating Nebraska. "He was the Old Man's driver. But you? Thought you were combat-ready."

"Screw you," Jeff managed. "When you're short in the Big Red One, you don't hump. Least not if you've got moves."

"Quit screwin' around," Nebraska said. "How we gonna get out of this one?"

"Hell if I know," Jeff said.

"Wonder what that goddamned MP went and told the cops?" Tyrell said. "They're out and around like we're Jack the Ripper and his gang, or something."

"Whyn't you surrender, and ask them? You know. Like in the cavalry

54

movies. Save the last bullet for yourself."

"Airborne never surrenders," Tyrell said loftily. "At least, not while we still got runnin' room. Aw hell! Here they come again!"

A car nosed into the alley they were hiding in, about a block away.

"In here."

They went through a screen door, into a deserted restaurant kitchen. Pots bubbled gently on the stove.

"Smells good," Nebraska whispered. "Like the kitchen in my girlfriend's place."

Tomatoes, basil, garlic, oregano, Parmesan, meat.

"Sash. Through here."

They went through a doorway. And promptly became statues. Fearful statues.

The dining area of the restaurant was quite small. There were small tables in the center of the room and larger tables, with benches, against one wall. The tables were covered with red checkered clothes. Shelves along the walls held many, many bottles of wine.

The front window had a Venetian blind, slats closed in probably perpetuity from top to bottom and side to side. The front door stood open, and Jeff could see the lettering: *CHARLIE'S CAFE*.

Six men were looking at them.

Two of them were still seated. Those two were quite old and both of them had large moustaches. Their suits appeared inexpensive and baggy. Their shirts, worn without neckties, were buttoned at the neck. The two men were quite small - at least compared to the four who were standing.

The four men on their feet wore a uniform expression. Not very different, Jeff and Tyrell" did not realize, than the expressions they themselves would have, staked out somewhere in South Viet Nam on an ambush patrol, waiting for something to happen and coolly confident of their ability to deal with it.

The four ranged in age from their twenties to fifties. They held one other thing in common - all four of them had a hand out of sight - either in a suitcoat waistband, about to slip toward an armpit, or in the pocket of a long overcoat.

The man, Jeff noticed, who seemed to be having a suddenly-itchy armpit also was cursed with what might have been a terribly-swollen tumor in it.

Tyrell looked back at his friends. "I think we just walked into *The*

Untouchables," he whispered.

" 'Eh," one of the young men said. "You. The black kid. What're you three doing here?"

"Nothing," Jeff put in for his friend. "We, uh, were just looking for a store, and I guess we got the address wrong."

One of the four younger men went to the door, and looked out. "Lot of cops out there tonight... You three have anything to do with it?"

"Don't see how," Tyrell said, in his most innocent voice.

"Couldn't have been us," Nebraska agreed. "Anyway, like we said, wrong address, and we'll just go on back out, and—"

He started sidling backward.

"You!" It was one of the old men, speaking for the first time. Nebraska found himself at attention, as if a general were talking.

"You got short hair. All three of you. That don't match those hippie clothes. You just out of prison?"

Nossirs, in a ragged, shocked chorus.

"The Army, then?"

"Uh... yessir."

The first old man smiled in pleasure at his still-sharp eyes. The other old man took over.

"Where you come from?"

"Uh," Jeff started, "I'm from LA, and--"

"Not your homes, poco di canni! I mean in the service. You coming from or going to that Vietnam place?"

"Coming. Sir. Getting out of the Army."

"What you do to get the cops after you?"

"Uh..."

"You kill anybody?"

"Nossir!"

"Rob somebody?"

"No, sir!"

"Try to buy dope? Sell dope?"

"Nossir. Honest, sir."

"I believe you. You look like good boys. Antonio?"

The old man motioned. One of the bodyguards bobbed his head, and went out onto the street to confront the cops.

Jeff and the others could hear him shout. "Hey! You! Yeah. C'mere,

Allan Cole & Chris Bunch

McGuire. Yeah. What the hell is going on?" Some inaudible mutters. "That don't matter! You just go on! Don' argue, culo! There ain't nothin' for you here! Awright?"

Other mutters. "I don't care what you tell th' Army! This a quiet neighborhood! Mister Labella is tryin' to relax. Okay? So butt outa here, okay?"

A long pause, then a grudging: "Yeah. Okay."

The side of beef came in and spoke to the first old man in what Jeff guessed to be Italian. Or maybe Sicilian. The old man frowned and snapped something back. Jeff heard that word, culo again. The large man looked shamefaced. The old man then nodded at him, smiled, and patted the truck's hand.

"Okay," he said. "That's all. There was...a mistake."

The three ex-GI's were goggling. "Jesus, Mister, I don't know how to thank—" Jeff started.

The old man waved a finger. "Ebreo," he warned. "I don't like profanity. That's what I told Antonio. Maybe that cop is. a culo... but it ain't right, women and children might hear that. And cursin' is a bad habit to get into. Okay?"

"Uh... yessir. We've been saying the same ourselves."

The old man nodded, liking this. "Okay. Now, what're you three doin' in North Beach? Lookin' for a party? Some girls? Don't answer. I was doin' the same when I was your age. Any of you married? No? Then - it's okay to want to play around a little. But there ain't nothin' in North Beach. It's a...what's the word?"

"Tourist trap, Mister Labella."

"That's it. Don't waste your money. Maybe, you go somewhere out around State University. College girls these days, they're wild I hear. Maybe down with the hippies, over on Haight. But not here."

"Yessir. Thank you, again, sir."

"Don't thank me. You three been in Viet Nam. Fightin' for your country. All three of you... good boys. More like you, and we wouldn't have all these troubles we got now."

"You been drinking?" The other old man interrupted.

"Yessir. A couple of beers."

"Couple of beers," the old man snorted. "I am not a fool! Who ever heard of a soldier stopping at just a couple of beers. You eat anything?"

"Nossir. We were just going to—"

57

"Not smart to drink on an empty stomach."

The second old man motioned and one of his bodyguards went out, into the kitchen and they heard the clatter of his hooves going up stairs.

"Sit down, you three. Here. With us."

The old man took three tiny wineglasses and poured

them full. "You drink this. Can't get drunk on wine. To America," he toasted. "To you three. Three brave men.

"You... all of you. Get glasses. Drink. We *all* drink. To three good Americans!"

Everybody drank.

"Here comes the cab," Tyrell said. "Jesus. I'm a kinda fucked up, I mean tired, wasted, whatever."

"You and me both," Jeff said.

"I have never eaten that much in my life," Nebraska offered. He yawned in appreciation. "So what do we do now? Call it a night? Go back to the hotel, maybe phone down for a nightcap? Room Service won't make us put on a tie."

"Yeah," Jeff said.

Then: "No. Hell, no. Hey, Tyrell, you still got the card that little hippie chick gave you?"

"Next to my heart." Tyrell hiccupped from a combination of wine and good food. But it was a sincere hiccup.

"Then that's where we're going!" Jeff said. "Driver, you know how to get to Haight-Ashbury?"

Allan Cole & Chris Bunch

CHAPTER FIVE

THEY HAD THE TAXI drop them off just below Haight Street and give them instructions to The FBI Girl, which turned out to be on a sidestreet, a few blocks away. Their plans were to amble through the district looking for action. If anything that jumped out at them, that would be their party. Otherwise, they'd meander on toward this... thing... this "special party for Mulberry Street," as the lovely Sunshine had vaguely explained.

As Tyrell said, "we'll put a LURP team through, meter-meter the matter... and decide from the sitrep whether we got a hot AOR or not... and if we should run a Brigade Sweep through or just Arc-Light it."

All of them spoke in the shorthand jargon of the military. Tyrell's line translated - run a reconnaissance patrol (Lurp, or Long Range Recon) through, find out what's going on, analyze the SITuation REPort on whether the Area Of Responsibility has anything happening in it, in which case there would be large amounts of ground troops put in (a Brigade of a couple thousand men) or a B-52 airstrike.

Like soldiers in any era, they all used the military cant to apply to *any* situation, hopefully and joyfully to ones having nothing at all to do with the Mean Green Machine that was the United States Army.

They came up toward the floodlit intersection of Haight and Ashbury Streets.

"Doesn't look real special," Nebraska said, in disappointment.

"Oh yeah?" Tyrell just pointed.

Someone - someone with very long hair - danced out of the darkness and began cavorting in the center of the intersection. It was a man. A naked man.

"Uh-oh," Jeff said, and reflexively the three minor fugitives from justice drew back into the shadows as two cops strode out of the night and up to the dancer.

"They are going to rip him to pieces," Jeff predicted.

Instead, the cops talked to the dancer... who never slowed his bounding... then walked on. One of the cops waved goodbye. They laughed, and were gone.

"What did that cat say," Tyrell said. "The Haight was... interesting?"

"Follow me, gentlemen," Jeff said, eager. "Maybe we've done something right for a change."

Then the music caught them: *You gotta go where you wanna go/Do what you wanna do. .*

Music unlike anything they'd grown up listening to:

...and meanwhile, back in Penny Lane:/There is a fireman with an hour glass..

Not songs about moonlight serenades or indigo moods their parents had listened to, nor their own hound dogs or job-getting.

The roses, they can't hurt you./No, the roses, they can't hurt you...

The music crept up toward, around and through them, coming from everywhere, coming from nowhere.

I'm a caterpillar/Crawlin' for your love...

Coming like the gray wisps of fog from the Panhandle, or from Golden Gate Park at the end of the street.

Sittin' on the dock of the bav/Wastin' time...

Coming from apartment windows, from still-open businesses, from passing cars, from everywhere, from nowhere.

Come on baby light my fire/Trv to set the night on fire...

Songs that they thought were about something:

She would never say where she came from/Yesterday don't matter if it's gone...

Songs they could sense a touched meaning to, like the damp night breeze on their face:

One begins to read between/The pages of a look/The sound of sleepy music/And suddenly you're hooked...

Then the meaning would be gone.

Have you seen my wife. Mister Jones/Do you know what it's like on the outside...

And maybe, for them at least, it was not there at all:

Einstein disguised as Robin Hood/With his memories in a trunk/Passed this way an hour ago/With his friend a jealous monk...

They drifted on, listening/not listening:

Listen to my bluebird laugh/She can't tell you why...

Sober/not sober:

I read the news today, oh boy./About a lucky man who made the grade/And though the news was rather sad/Well I just had to laugh...

Through the night, through the Haight.

Guitar/snarl/man/shout Purple Haze/All 'round my brain..

Sometimes the night spoke directly to them:

60

Allan Cole & Chris Bunch

Cool cat/Lookin' for a kitty;/Gonna look in every corner of the city...
Sometimes it did not. Maybe.
She said "There is no reason/And the truth is plain to see." But I wandered through my playing cards/And would not let her be...
And again and again and always... crashing at them and through them... was the anthem of the time. The Haight and the life... building from martial-tap snake-croon to its sledgehammer finale:
When the men on the chessboard/Get up and tell you where to go/And you've just had some kind of mushroom/and your mind is moving low/Go ask Alice/I think she'll know...
Yeah, Jeff thought. Yeah. It's about time I started feeding my head...

Tyrell had never seen so many motorcycles in his life. Let alone bikes that looked like these.
"Where I come from, motorcycles, 'specially bunches of motorcycles, are a pretty good indicator for trouble."
"See," Jeff said. "Memphis and California got a "lot in common. Sameo-sameo. Except we've got the Hells' Angels. You heard about them?"
Tyrell had.
"Is any of that stuff really true?" Nebraska wondered.
"You're asking me?" Jeff said. "A nice middle-class Jewish boy from Southern California who's supposed to grow up to be a doctor? You're asking me about the Hells' Angels? Men who wear swastikas? Through their nipples? I've got to confess. Come right out and tell you what fast friends me and the Angels have become. Hang out together at the temple, just blowin' the shofa, eating our matzohs and crucifying the rabbi."
They took another look at the motorcycles - keeping at a nice, safe distance even though the bikes were unattended. All of them were Harley Davidsons. None of them looked at all like the copbikes or the touring machines they'd occasionally seen.
Gas tanks were tiny, no more than a gallon or so. Chrome exhaust pipes snaked up from the twin vee-cylinders toward the sky, or straight backward like double-barreled shotguns. Front forks were long and narrow. Some of them looked like they used chrome springs instead of the conventional hidden springs and shock absorbers.
What was not chromed was painted - candy red, green, swirls of colors. Here and there was an emblem, a leering skull, with Mercury wings coming straight back from it.

61

The bikes were lined up outside the main entrance to what they now identified as The FBI GIRL.

The building was old, post-Earthquake brick, three stories high. It stretched for half a block down the street. When it was laid out, a live theater had been the center piece of the building, reaching three stories up. The ground floor on either side of it had smaller businesses, and the second and third stories had been offices and apartments. The business on the corner had been a Laundromat, or so the rusting sign suggested. But now it had a new, psychedelically-swirling sign: FBI GIRL COMMUNITY CENTER.

The theater itself had changed over the generations: Live theater became vaudeville became hard times, and the theater became a movie house. It must have gone bankrupt some time in the past, bankrupt so quickly that the bill for its final movie had never been removed from the marquee: THE FBI GIRL.

The poster was all film noir. Titled, Woman On A Manhunt, it feature a curvaceous girl in a slinky gown, holding a guns, criminals, in slouched hats, threatening from blow. It starred, Audrey Totter, Cesar Romero and George Brent.

Nebraska scanned the poster. "Don't know anybody," he said. "But that Audrey Trotter is one fabulous chick. Wouldn't mind her hunting me down, instead of that stupid MP lieutenant."

The other two weren't paying any attention. They were laboriously deciphering the dayglo posters in the other two marquee cases. The colors and shapes were wild, seemingly nonsensical.

"Damn," Tyrell muttered. "Do these hippies *want* you not to be able to read their stuff? Or do you have to be on drugs?"

"I don't know," Jeff mumbled... then, suddenly the swirls snapped into focus and sense. "Okay. I got it. It's like that Escher cat's stuff I saw in college."

"Escher?"

"Never mind. Uh... it's for some kind of do-hickey Saturday night. Day after tomorrow. Last night of The FBI Girl. Looks like the place is going to be shut down."

He pointed to some wild looking posters, emblazoned with band names.

"And... these are the bands that are gonna play... I guess. Grateful Dead. Jefferson Airplane. Here's Mulberry Street... now we know why they're doing a party for a street... It's a band, obviously… Okay. Let's see what else... Quicksilver Messenger Service. Big Brother and the Holding Company."

"Hell," Nebraska said in some disappointment. "Never heard of any of them."

"Grand Ol' Oprey don't play San Francisco," Tyrell said.

"Screw you," Nebraska said. "And gimme a break. I'm not *that* much of a hick. But what about Peter, Paul and Mary?"

Tyrell and Jeff made mock gagging noises.

"Okay, then. Frank Sinatra. Hell, Nancy Sinatra. Uh...Diana Ross and the Supremes?"

"You got a little bit of soul, there. Not much, but some."

"What's wrong with The Four Seasons?"

They continued wrangling amiably, trying to decide if this was where they ought to be spending the rest of their first night of freedom.

Then they heard shouting from a distance and walked away from the entrance, down to the corner and looked for the action.

There was a brand new 911S Porsche pulled into the alleyway. A Porsche unlike any of them had ever dreamed. The finish had been very carefully and skillfully turned into a collage. Here was a newspaper headline: TURN ON, TUNE IN, DROP OUT. There a blown up photo of LBJ showing off his scar. On the hood four hairy Edwardians in some kind of band uniform. On one door, Lichtenstein's U-boat skipper shouting "Torpedo... los!" On the other, a bearded, turbaned black-and-white of a Mid-easterner smoking something.

"Whoever owns that thing," Tyrell said, "never learned even the basic stuff about red cars and cops' eyes."

But the owner was learning now.

Behind the Porsche was an equally-new International bobtail truck. This one was painted with flowers. From cab to drop-ramp, it looked like an advertisement for Burpee Seeds. Letters swirled across the flowers: MULBERRY STREET.

The colors from both the Porsche and the truck were brilliant. Especially since they were illuminated by the flashing red light of the San Francisco Police Department black-and-white that had the sports car pulled over.

Nebraska and the others drifted down to see what was going on.

As always on the Haight, people came out of everywhere and nowhere to watch and sometimes comment.

Zombie-eyed people standing in the shadows, others trying to get involved. Others just part of the street theater's audience.

The three ex-GIs felt safety in numbers, and certainly they were hardly the most colorful of the people wandering to the confrontation.

A very large cop, wearing a riot helmet and gauntleted gloves had a young woman's arm twisted up behind her back.

The woman had dark brown hair, combed straight and flowing nearly to her waist. The night was still warm and she wore nothing but a long-fringed leather vest for a top, insecurely tied in two places. Her pants were paisley and leotard-tight, tucked into high-top leather boots coming to just below her knees. The woman was of normal height, about nineteen and remarkably pretty.

Nebraska decided beautiful would be acceptable.

For her size, the strength of her voice was remarkable. And the rather delicate-looking beauty was using language Nebraska would have expected from a first sergeant.

"Come on, Grancell, you worthless motherfucker! Let me go!"

The cop, easily three times her size, should have been able to keep the woman under control. Maybe the crowd kept him from using more force. Or maybe he was waiting for the three longhairs standing beside the truck and evidently part of the woman's entourage, to do something.

"If you keep fighting, Miss Saint John, I am going—ouch, you bitch!"

The woman had managed to bite the cop. There were quiet cheers. The cheers became boos as the cop - Grancell, it was - managed to snap handcuffs on the woman's flailing free hand and then on her pinned wrist. Somebody oinked. Somebody else sang "Officer Krupke, you're really a drag."

"Now," he panted. "Now we're going through that purse."

He picked up the leather shoulder bag from the ground where it'd fallen and upended it on the police cruiser's hood. Quickly, expertly, he combed through the scatter.

"Here it is," Grancell announced triumphantly. "Hashish! Sorry, Miss St. John. You won't be playing tonight."

Many, many moans, boos, hisses and complaints. One of the longhairs came forward.

"Hey, man. Alexis don't play, Mulberry Street don't play, people will get uptight. Be cool."

A voice: "Shit, that ain't enough hash to fuck up anybody. Not for very long, anyway."

Another one of the longhairs - Nebraska guessed they were part of the group and the young woman was part of it - said, "Yeah. Grancell, try and be human. Just for once?"

The cop did not hear any of this. "I am required to read you the following. You have the right—"

The darkness moved. Or at least a large part stepped aside for something that did.

Nebraska hadn't noticed the man, and wondered later how that was possible. He stood easily six foot five inches. Nebraska guessed his weight at about 400 pounds, then revised upward. Hair cascaded down across his shoulders and halfway over his chest. There was a scarred face somewhere under the frothing beard.

The man wore engineer boots', now-black Levi pants with leather lacing holding the seams together, a teeshirt Nebraska was pretty sure read FUCK YOU, and a very greasy jeans jacket. The sleeves were cut off, and there were various mysterious patches sewn on it: 1%-ER; ROAD CAPTAIN; a nametag of DIRTY DOG; what looked like red pilot's wings; an Iron Cross and other even less understandable items.

He also, Nebraska noticed, had a tasteful pair of swastika earrings hanging from each lobe and, as the piece d'resistance, a twisted roofing nail through his nostrils.

The man - Nebraska guessed it to be such, since it was far too big, ugly and mean-looking to be a gorilla - spoke. "Grancell, get off her ass."

The cop let go of Alexis and did a little looming of his own. "Evans," he asked the man, "don't you have something better to be doing?"

The hulk that was a man pretended to think, scratching his chin. "Naw. Naw," he said finally. "Not unless it'd be sittin' on a cop's face."

Cheers - and Dirty Dog Evans spun. A finger that could have been used for a cannon's ramrod speared out. "Hey. You hippies. Keep outa this. This is between me an' the pig here. We don't need no fuckin' escalation."

Nebraska saw what was on the back of Evans' jacket.

Red ornate letters on white, top rocker:

HELL'S ANGELS

Device:

Red and white winged skull.

Bottom rocker:

FRISCO.

Tyrell and Jeff found it expeditious and sane to fade back into the crowd. Nebraska however, was sure this would be a confrontation to tell over and over again in Grainton. He pressed closer, until he was standing just behind the policeman right next to his cruiser.

The woman, Alexis St. John, stood to his left, hands cuffed behind her, and the monster biker to the cop's right front.

"Now," Dirty Dog started. "You say you caught the broad with some hash. She's supposed to be onstage in twenty minutes."

"Sorry about that shit," Grancell said, sounding not sorry at all.

"How much you get?"

"At least a gram."

"Gram? Gram? Shit, man. These freaks're right. You <u>are</u> a pig."

"You want to get busted too?"

Evans considered once more. "Lessee now," he thought aloud. "'M' shyster's paid current. Don't owe shit to the bailbondsman. Next cargo offloadin'll be Monday... not much happenin' tomorrow night... Yeah. Why not?

"Now. Before you'n me start swingin' out, lemme give you an estimate here. He stretched, scratched and belched. "I feel pretty dam' good tonight. So you better get on the horn for backup. I'll go six... naw, seven cars. An' get some guys from South of Market, 'kay? Not pussies like that narc behind you."

That cannon ramrod poked again... and Nebraska realized it was poking at him. He did not, really, really did not like being the center of attention as the musicians, the biker, the hippies and even the cop turned. None of the faces were friendly.

Not even Grancell's. "Him? He's no cop. Some weekend Hippie from Milpitas, maybe. Now..."

The subject of Nebraska and his non-affiliation with the forces of Truth, Justice and the American Way dismissed, the cop turned back to the biker.

"This time," he was warning, "it won't just be—"

Nebraska moved. A brown/white tie-died arm darted out, behind the cop, to

66

the hood of the cruiser. Picked up the tiny block of hash... and moving with a speed, determination and craziness that astonished him, fingers went to mouth...

...and Nebraska swallowed.

Alexis saw the blur. Her jaw dropped. Then slammed closed. She almost giggled.

Nebraska backpedalled into the crowd.

Officer Grancell was unsnapping his long riot baton, and Dirty Dog rolling his sleeves.

"All you hippies don't want to get blood all over your love an' peace, get fuckin' back," he rumbled.

"Hold it," Alexis shouted.

The biker looked disappointed. "Aw come on, Alexis," he complained. "You're taking this nonviolence too far. This pig ain't nothin' but the pain of Haight. Do him good to get a medium-size set a lumps. Somethin' for him to meditate on."

"Shut up, Dog!"

Surprisingly, the biker did just that.

"Officer Grancell, what... exactly... are you arresting me for?"

"Don't get cute," Grancell said, but his head swiveled, like a target-seeking turret, toward the hood. To the place where the hash used to be.

"God Damn It," he said in explosive realization. "Okay. Where's that bastard? That fucker wearin' the tie-dies. Come on, people! This isn't a joke, goddamit!

"Stop laughing, and somebody better..."

Nebraska, as he rounded the corner back toward The FBI Girl's entrance, heard no more. He nodded to his awestruck friends.

"Holy shit," Jeff marveled. "*This* is our friend, Steven quote Nebraska unquote Applegate? Cleancut kid who gets drafted and is such a good little boy being a colonel's driver they make him an E6?"

"First you slug a cop," Tyrell added, "then you go and steal some dope that's supposed to be evidence in a trial. Whoo. I don't know if you've got soul, like I said... But you sure have big brass balls of a size you can push around in a wheelbarrow."

"What else you got planned for the week end?" Jeff asked. "Or maybe I don't want to know."

"Oh... I thought maybe I might let that cute singer fall in love with me. Get adopted by the Hells' Angels...

Allan Cole & Chris Bunch

"Maybe walk across the Bay tomorrow.

"Long as I don't miss the rocks, I should be okay.

"Change a little water into wine on Saturday. Beat the crap out of the San Francisco cops Saturday night.

"End the war in Vietnam.

"Just the usual shit."

At this point, neither Jeff nor Tyrell would have bet Nebraska was necessarily joking.

Yeah, he might do all that. And they'd be along for the ride.

Allan Cole & Chris Bunch

CHAPTER SIX

THE MUSIC BURST out of The FBI Girl like a flash flood. It broke over the milling crowd, slammed into the buildings on the opposite side of the street, and set the old fashioned glass globes of the street lights buzzing. The undertow caught Tyrell, Jeff and Nebraska and sucked them inside.

A sign prodded for a $2 "donation," and Jeff peeled off six bucks and handed them to an outstretched hand. The hand clutched bills and Jeff heard a piercing laugh cut through the music and then the hand and its owner was gone. What the hell. If he had just been ripped off, at least no one was stopping them as the elbowed their way through the crowd jamming the lobby, past big tubs of apples and other fruit with "free food" signs pasted on the sides. Another tub was packed to the overflowing with water pistols - also free. The sign on it read: "Shoot A Pig."

The lobby was a solid cloud of incense and marijuana smoke and a tubby little teenager in a short white toga with a laurel wreath about her head was handing out fistfuls of joints. Tyrell found himself staring at four or five of them, which had suddenly appeared in his hand. He thought he heard Nebraska whoop, and three joints disappeared. As he craned about to see where they went, Nebraska shoved a lit one in his mouth. He saw Jeff with a startled look on his face and a twisted-end joint dangling from his lips, smoke curling up and biting his nostrils.

"Take a big drag," he thought he heard Nebraska shout.

The farm boy's big hand slapped him on the back and he reflexively drew in at least four lungsworth. He saw Jeff shrug and the tip of his joint glow as he, too, followed instructions. Tyrell suddenly felt wonderfully light and relaxed. He'd tried grass once or twice in Nam, but it had never done anything one way or the other. He looked up to see how it was affecting his friends. But then he felt Nebraska's hand on his shoulder again and they were being pushed deeper into the lobby, and then through the heavy, garish Indian blankets that served as the curtained door.

Just before he entered the club one of the posters on the wall to the right suddenly snapped out at him. Jolting out from all the psychedelic colors was a large circle. The painting/ poster was composed of naked men and women engaged in every imaginable sexual position, plus about maybe thirty or forty or so he never dreamed possible.

You can't put that up in a public...

Then they were inside…

The music's full volume picked them up and pasted them against the wall like a gravity experiment aboard a rocket sled in White Sands, New Mexico. Jeff felt the flesh of his cheeks flutter in the wave of sound exploding from something beyond the solid wall of light that peeled the surface moisture from his eyeballs.

He had only read about light shows in a few tattered news magazines that had made their way up to Lai Khe. Just as he had only read about just how loud music had become, including dry medical warnings concerning the dangers to vision and hearing. Jeff had learned enough about general medicine at his father's knee - plus his training as an Army medic - to know that there was a touch of truth to the conservative adult bullshit. Still. Reading and actually being there were two different things. As the wave of colored lights bathed his face, and the shriek of an electrical guitar crisped his ear drums, Jeff found himself not giving much of a damn what it did to him.

Nebraska tried to separate out the different stimulants doing battle for his brain cells. Without much luck. He couldn't make out a word or single note from the blare of music. Bodies were leaping and whirling all about him, flickering in and out of existence in the strobe lights. He took an experienced toke on his joint and held the smoke in. In his part of the world, marijuana grew wild, rope hemp in the fields and ditches. There were very few farm children who didn't take up the stuff after they had tired of sneaking out behind the barn to smoke corn silk. Hemp was a make do substitute for tobacco and drink until a kid got old enough to lie about his age and be believed.

He could see it wasn't affecting Jeff much. Nebraska leaned closer and shouted for him to hold in the smoke longer. Jeff did. Then shook his head in disappointment and gave a "nothing's happening" jerk of his shoulders. His face frogged with effort trying to do Nebraska's bidding. Smoke leaked from the corners of his mouth. Then the rest of the smoke whooshed out. Jeff giggled. There you go, boy, Nebraska thought.

For Tyrell, the light show was fantastic. Brilliant, swirling colors. Ultraviolet lights fluoresced bright, Day-Glo paints. Strobe lights flashing in hypnotic Alpha rhythms. There was a huge revolving disc covered with colored lights hanging from the high, vaulted ceiling, casting colors over hundreds of dancers, who themselves were part of an opium eater's dream. They were covered with paint, beads and feathers. They wore costumes

70

Allan Cole & Chris Bunch

ranging from clothes out of antique shops, to tie-dye jeans and blouses and shirts, to colorful thin cotton blankets imported cheap from India, to a naked boy with a scrawny beard, knotted locks, and a dick that must have hung down to his knees. Nobody noticed him - even the women - as he pranced about, so Nebraska figured the dick must be a phony. A prop bought in one of the North Beach sex shops he had seen. Maybe.

Tyrell was feeling just fine. He couldn't figure out the music yet, but the lights were starting to make some sense. Liquid projectors cast strange, colorful images on the walls of the club. He swore the blobs of color throbbed in time to the music. And around and through the blobs he could see a slide of a man and woman kissing. It was followed by colored slides of faces and flowers and seashells. A picture of a mushroom cloud. GI's marching. Missiles frozen in blastoff. Naked teenagers running across a farm field. Thirty foot portraits of the Beatles. Incredible shit. Brought to you, according to a poster he had spotted in the lobby, by the "Mighty Joe Young Light Machine."

As he somehow got his bearings, he rubbernecked his head around to see what was what. There were easily a thousand people jammed into the club. Through the flashing lights, he could make out the theater origins of *The FBI Girl*. Ceilings climbed maybe three stories with a balcony ringing three sides and people prancing and hanging from those balconies. Scattered across the floor were small oases of refreshments. Cookies, candies, cheeses, fruit. No beer, no wine, no whiskey, not even any soft drinks.

But in the middle of each table was a huge punchbowl filled with red liquid. People were dipping up gallons of the stuff. Enthusiastically chugging it down like it was spiked with 150 proof rum.

He turned to see if he could make out what was happening on the stage. The indecipherable music was blaring out from enormous banks of speakers. He could see the musicians jamming up on the stage. Bleeding through all those light show images, which also played across their equipment - which he could now see were painted white. Turning them into sort of mini-movie screens. He saw the name of the group on one of the amps: Sparrow. The guitarist twisted a knob on his amp and the reverbhowl made like hot needles on his ear drums. Another twist. Another howl. Then the drummer hit a lick, signaling the band to order and Tyrell could suddenly make out some words, as a tall, lanky blonde wearing black leather, silk and shades swaggered to the mike and manhandled it to the side...

71

...Well I seen a lotta people walkin' round with tombstones in their eyes, now... But the Pusher don't care... if they live or if they die now/God Damn The Pusher...

...and the guitar and drums slammed like incoming mortars and Tyrell felt Jeff yanking at his sleeve and Nebraska gave him a hard jab. "Look! Over there!"

...God Damn the Pusher Man...

He could barely make out what they were saying. But he turned to look. Over there...

Over there, just like they said.

As the music reached its crescendo and the crowd whooped and howled, Tyrell saw Sunshine float out of the crowd. And she was walking straight toward him.

She seemed to be swimming through all the light show images. The screen image of the man and woman kissed on her left breast. A white dove fluttered out of her golden hair. Pictures of seashells and flowers ghosted across her face. Which was lit with a smile of recognition.

As she approached him, Tyrell fumbled in his pocket and pulled out the flower she had given him that morning - or was it twenty years ago?

"Ty... Rell." She said his name as she took the flower, and tucked it in a golden lock of her hair. "Ty... Rell." She made it sound like the words to a wonderful song.

"Far out," she said in a voice so sweet it melted his knees. "You came to see me."

She gave him a quick kiss on his cheek. It felt as delicate as the butterfly game his mother used to play when he was very little. She'd lean close to him and flutter her lashes against his flesh, and say: "Butterfly kisses." Yeah. Except from now on they'd be "Sunshine kisses."

Sunshine took his hands and pulled him towards the dance floor. Snared in her magical web, Tyrell flowed out with her. Took her in his arms and danced out of sight of his amazed companions.

Jeff watched as the crowd swallowed Tyrell and Sunshine. He was glad for his friend, but he suddenly felt very lonely. Rachel's face leaped into his mind. His fiancée was rotten medicine for his malady. In his mind, the face he had once thought so lovely now seemed pinched and disapproving. She'd have left his parents' house hours ago. Gone home for an angry cry in her bed. He should feel ashamed of himself, for making Rachel feel that way.

Oddly, he didn't. A different name jumped out. Sam. The stewardess who had been kind enough, or foolish enough to give him her phone number. The slip of paper burned in his wallet. Maybe he'd call. Guilt swarmed in at this thought. He didn't know what to do.

He turned to shake his mood with a silly comment to Nebraska. But Nebraska was gone as well.

Jeff spotted the tubby girl in the toga refilling a nearby punch bowl. Stricken with a terrible thirst, he made his way toward it. It was plain old, ordinary Kool Aid. Strawberry flavored. It was a taste Jeff was more than familiar with. He and every other young soldier in Vietnam had begged their parents for CARE packages of the stuff to cut the taste of the heavily chlorinated water they had to drink to keep from getting the drizzles. Ah, well. At least this was out of a glass bowl and didn't taste like the inside of a canteen.

He downed the cup, refilled it and chugged some more. As he topped up his cup again and turned to see what kind of trouble he could get in, a big kid in tie-dye jeans and an Aussie bush hat gave him a big grin.

"You're really groovin', man," the kid said. "You're groovin'. I'm groovin'. Everybody's groovin' on the acid test."

"Say what?" Jeff said. "Acid, who?"

The kid pointed at the punch bowl. Oh, shit, Jeff thought. Now I've done it. He wondered how much LSD had been used to spike the Kool Aid. Jeff giggled. Whether from the grass or the newly ingested acid, he wasn't sure. He took another honk off the punch. Why'd it suddenly taste so much better now that he knew it was more than just umpty packets of flavored granules and another umpty cups of sugar.

Jeff drew an imaginary grenade from his belt, pulled the pin with his teeth John Wayne movie style, counted off, then tossed said imaginary grenade into the bowl. He waited a beat, then made slow motion explosive motions with his hands. Jeff and the kid watched as a whole ghostly sea of the stuff burst upward, spewing strawberry acid clear to the vaulted ceiling.

"Far fuckin' out, man" the kid said in serious awe.

"Yeah," Jeff said. " 'cept I can't say fuck or I owe Nebraska and Tyrell a bottle." He leaned closer to the kid. "It's a hard thing to do. Not using the 'F' word, I mean. Yesterday, I could say it all I wanted. Then..." he snapped his fingers, "... like that I can't say it no more... Anymore, I mean."

"Why not, man?" the kid wanted to know.

73

"We got mothers and shit," Jeff explained.

"Bummer," the kid said.

"Bummer," Jeff agreed.

"I got a father, too," Jeff said.

"No, shit?" The kid was grooving on Jeff's little tale.

"Yeah. A doctor type father. I'm a grave disappointment to him. Least he said I was. I'm not sure why. I think it's because I flunked out. An' almost got my ass shot off. Ooops. Maybe I oughtn't to say ass neither. Or maybe it is either. You won't tell Nebraska, will you?"

"No, man. I don't narc on nobody," the kid said, a bit huffy.

"I got a fiancée, too," Jeff went on. "It's hard to watch your 'F' words and your 'A' words with so many people waiting around to get pissed. Uh... you think pissed is okay?"

"Fuck no," the kid said.

"You're right. I will now also eliminate ^xpissed' from my vocabulary. You will hear it no longer from these lips." He smacked them together to illustrate his action.

"You are way too uptight, man," the kid said. "It's not a good trip to be on."

"You think so?" Jeff said. "Uptight, huh? Whadda I do about it?"

"Just get in the groove, man," the kid said. "Let it happen."

Jeff rolled his shoulders like a boxer. He shook his head back and forth. Unkinking the knots in his neck.

"Better," he said. "Thanks."

"No sweat, man," the kid said.

Jeff took another sip of his acid-laced drink. Then topped his cup off from the bowl.

"Well, I guess I better go mingle," Jeff said. "And let it happen."

"Far out," the kid said as Jeff wandered away. Jeff noticed this time the kid had left out the 'F' word. Jeff was pleased with himself. He'd obviously set a good example.

Nebraska took another toke and stared at the stage. Now it was empty. He thought for a moment. Hadn't there been a group playing last time he looked?

Come to think, when was the last time he'd looked at the stage? And what had he been doing in the meantime.

The recorded music, which sounded to Nebraska like a kitten trying to claw its way out of a git-fiddle's soundbox through supertaut strings stopped.

A mike somewhere offstage went on.

Nebraska heard a giggle.

Then a voice:

"Anybody who knows he is God, please go up onstage."

The mike went off.

Someone walked out onstage, to the mikestand, and the crowd bellowed approval. The someone was a man, wearing what looked to be, through the flashing strobes and images, the suit of a Gemini astronaut.

He waved for silence, and eventually something approximating it - give or take 70db(A) or so - arrived.

"Uh... no, man. No. I'm not God. That... that had nothing to do with this."

He giggled.

"I'm not into that Christianity shit. I mean... cannibalism? That ain't cool."

Somebody shouted at him from the wings.

"Oh. Yeah. Hey. I'm supposed to tell you cats something."

A long, very long silence.

"Oh yeah. 'Bout Mulberry Street. They got a contract. With A&M Records. Down in LA. Yeah. So I guess they'll go down and cut a record..."

He looked offstage and shouted "when you guys goin' down there?" Got an answer, and turned back.

"... maybe next week or maybe next summer, the Tripster says. Hey, so I guess this party is for them, huh?"

He stopped again, and stood smiling like an aluminum Buddha for awhile. Another shout roused him.

"Okay. So they're gonna play. You know. Hey. It's Mulberry Street, okay."

Someone came on and led the astronaut of inner space away, probably, Nebraska thought, toward the California Home for the Terminally Bewildered.

Mulberry Street ambled onstage. There were five of them - an emaciated dirty blonde lead guitarist, a short guy sporting the ever-popular Edgar Allan Poe coif and tiny moustache on rhythm guitar, a very, very longhaired bearded type on drums and the biggest black cat Nebraska had

75

ever seen, including playing pro football, on keyboards.

And Alexis.

Drumslam, and the organ took lead and Alexis had the microphone off its stand and was swaying in time, waiting and then spotting Nebraska standing close to one side of the stage and coming toward him.

She started singing.

And to Nebraska she was singing to no one but him, and making a promise to no one but him:

...I'm gonna wait 'til the midnight hour/That's when my love comes a-tumblin' down/Gonna wait 'til the midnight hour/When there's nobody else around...

Nasty dirtylick from lead guitar echoed and amplified by the organ and Alexis' body was swaying, her knees bending and it seemed to Nebraska her legs parting a little...

Gonna hold you and kiss you/Do all the things I told you/ In the Midnight Hour...

Nebraska's mouth was very, very dry...

..and Alexis smiled, spun, and body as sleek and smooth as the notes curving through the air was gliding away...

Jeff took a wrong turn coming out of the men's room and found himself puzzling along the twisted corridors and back rooms that seemed to honeycomb The FBI Girl. Jeff couldn't figure how it was possible to get lost. All he had to do was follow the sound of the music, right?

Wrong! Out here, the music came from every direction. Every wall throbbing like a bass drum. He made two more wrong guesses, and suddenly he could barely hear the music at all.

He had entered an area crammed with more rooms than there ought to be interior walls to contain. Some of them were empty, except for a few mattresses and bedrolls. Some of them had closed, unmarked doors. Other doors bore signs, or big, colorful posters ripped out of the "Oracle" – an underground newspaper - and thumbtacked into place.

One door - decorated with torn out pictures of napalmed Vietnamese children and yellowed news clippings and headlines detailing the rising casualty count in Southeast Asia - was marked "Draft Counseling." Jeff heard talking inside. He tried to bigear, curious what kind of advice was being handed out. The old, I am a committed homosexual/killer riff, maybe? Or the sugar under the fingernails for the diabetes piss test?

Allan Cole & Chris Bunch

Instead he heard what seemed to be a serious rap session on the rights of a conscientious objector. Jeff moseyed on, wishing whoever was getting the advice the best of luck.

A brand new Beatles song playing on a portable radio drew him on. At least he thought it was the Beatles...

... She's leaving home/After living alone/For so many years... bye. bye...

The room the song was coming from was filled with hippie kids. Busy hippie kids. Mostly female. They were singing with the music, and working their way through mounds of old clothing. Some were being tossed into piles for repairs. Jeff saw two girls sitting cross-legged on the floor, sewing colorful patches on ripped garments. Another big pile gave off a stale odor of old grime. Dripping dresses and dragging trouser legs, a boy staggered through an open back door where Jeff could hear the rhythm of a big industrial washing machine.

A kid with intense eyes, tousled hair and a rich, curly beard looked up. Jeff thought he looked a little like the pictures of Jesus he had seen in his Christian friends' Sunday school books. Except the kid's eyes were slightly crossed. Okay, so he was looking at a cross-eyed Jesus. Now what?

"Nice jacket, man," the kid said.

"Thanks," Jeff said, unconsciously fingering the rough material of his jacket.

"I could use a jacket like that, man," the kid went on.

"So could I," Jeff said. "That's why I bought it." Buzzed from the drink, the dope, and wondering if the LSD had cut in yet, Jeff was suspicious. A tad over protective.

"You're on a possession trip," the kid said, his upper lip sneering. "Bad Karma, man. Better watch out. Or your possessions might start possessing you!"

"A burden *you* are willing to assume for me, right?" Jeff said. He worked hard to pick just the right words - right for a sober, intelligent person, that is.

"Sarcasm, man," the kid came back. "Real downer. Why are you bumming me, man? What'd I ever do to you?"

"You tried to hustle me out of my jacket," Jeff said.

"No, that's your trip. I just said I could use a jacket like that."

"Okay. I'll bite. Why would it be better for you to have it, instead of me?"

Allan Cole & Chris Bunch

"Haven't you heard, man? There's thousands of kids out there. Hitting town every second. Runnin' away from the dogma of their materialistic parents. Tryin' to find a new way to live. To think, man. To believe."

"Well, good for them," Jeff said. "I've been doing a little of that myself, lately."

The kid shook his head... sad.

"You don't get it, man," he said. "These are kid, kids. They can't take care of themselves. Middle class types. Heads fucked up from their parents. They don't know shit about the streets. They don't have food, man. They don't have a place to sleep. Or clothes... Like that jacket."

Instant guilt descended on Jeff's wobbly brain.

"I'm sorry," he said. "Look. I'll give you the jacket. And you can give it to one of those kids you were talking about. Okay?"

He pulled off the jacket and started to hand it over. The kid just stared at it. Disdain written large in those crossed eyes.

"Go away," the kid said. "We don't want your jacket."

Jeff was aghast. "What'd I do wrong?"

"If you don't know..." the kid let it trail off, shaking his head.

"Really! Tell me."

"You can't put rules on a gift, man," the kid said. "Leave it. Or don't leave it. No one here cares, man. You do what you think's best."

Feeling like all kinds of a damn fool for probably being hustled by a college sophomore, Jeff left his jacket and got out quick before somebody admired his shoes.

The words trailed after him... ...*bye. bye...*

A slow, mechanical CACHUNKA... CACHUNKA nabbed Jeff at the next turn. He peered past a bright, white light into a small alcove. He saw a young woman with purple ink fingers intent on a mimeo machine, churning out pamphlets. There was a neat stack of the pamphlets on a rickety chair just at the door. Jeff picked one up.

SAVE THE FBI GIRL

From San Francisco Pigs & Governor Reagan's Political Game Players The Label Mongering Forces Of This City Have Ordered Your Community Center Closed! As Of **SATURDAY NIGHT** All Activities Must Cease!

To Protest This

ILLEGAL & UNCONSTITUTIONAL ACTION
A GATHERING OF THE TRIBES
Has Been Called!
Come One!
Come All!
Free Concert! Free Food! Free Freak-out!
Save The FBI Girl
SATURDAY NIGHT!

The pamphlet was suddenly ripped from his hands. Jeff whoozed back.

"What are you, a narc?" the girl snarled.

He had difficulty making out where the snarling was exactly coming from. At first it looked like the voice was coming out of furry, Yeti-like mass. Maybe it was one of those LSD illusions he had read about. Tune In, Turn On, Watch Out! Easy, boy', he thought. Beware of acid.

Then two hands came up to the furry mass and parted the hair. Peeking out at Jeff was a sliver of narrow white face with rimless glasses perched on a too small nose. The eyes behind the glasses were little blazing blue holes. Ah ha! Not a Yeti. A person. An indignant person.

"I am no narc," Jeff said with grave dignity. "I am a but a simple soldier, recently returned from the wars."

"Wasted out of your mind," the chick said, her narrow face pinching even smaller.

"I'd resent that," Jeff said, "except I think it's probably true."

"Do you always talk like that?" the girl wanted to know as she bustled back to her machine. Obviously, Jeff had been convincing.

"Talk like what?"

"A pedagogue."

"I was?"

"Just like Clark Kerr," the woman said.

Jeff was mortified. To be compared to that buttwipe - former chieftain of California's universities - was a low remark. Hadn't he, Jeffrey David Katz, demonstrated against that man's narrow-minded policies? During the final days of his flunkout senior semester, he had attended a few of the Free Speech demonstrations at UCLA. He'd even carried one of the big protest signs: "Freedom Under Clark Kerr."

"Now that, I do resent," Jeff said.

79

"Resent away," the hippie said, parting the hair again in that nervous gesture of hers. "Here, make yourself useful."

She pointed at a messy pile of newly mimeoed pamphlets that needed sorting out and stacking. Jeff did as she asked. He worked silently for a few seconds. Getting into the job. Making the edges of the stacks just so.

"What's this all about?" Jeff asked, meaning the printed call to arms.

"It says it all right there, man," the chick said. No help at all. "What are you, a drop out?"

"Yeah, I suppose you could say that," Jeff said, thinking about how the draft board had virtually made him one by snatching him into its crone arms when his grades had plummeted to "F" and beyond. One more semester to graduation, his father had warned him. Then marriage. Then medical school. Many deferments later, he could do his duty for his country as an officer and a gentleman. If a doctor from Whittier could ever be called a gentleman.

The hippie finally took pity on him. She told him about the increasing pressure on the hip community from the "Powers That Be" at City Hall. Especially in and around the Haight Ashbury district. The word had gone out to close all the dance halls and community centers.

Back around Easter, eight or nine teams of city health inspectors had swarmed all over The Haight. They" were determined to snoop out every violation in the abysmally filthy conditions that were sure to be found in all dens of drugs, sex and rock n' roll. They ferreted through nearly seven hundred buildings. But they only managed to find evidence enough to issue five-day sanitary repair warnings to less than forty. To their chagrin, only six of these were "hippie joints."

They went back to work in a holy fever. A few days later, the list of raided buildings reached nearly 1,500. Less than seventy drew warnings. Of those, maybe sixteen were homes to hippies. The city was forced to admit the problem was nowhere near as bad as they had tried to portray it.

"That made them really angry," the chick said, brushing away at her hair. A bit of purple mimeo ink clung to a strand and streaked her cheek. "All the city department heads got orders. If you can't find evidence, plant it. Or make it up. Health laws, building and safety, fire department, liquor licenses. Any trumped up excuse."

"So they got the goods on The FBI Girl, huh?" Jeff said.

"No. They *created* violations," she said. "No matter what we did, or how we fixed something, they were on us. Making us rip out walls we had

80

just put in so they could check the wiring for the fifth time. Same thing with the plumbing. Doors that opened in had to open out. And the other way around when they felt like it.

"Now, they've got an order to shut us down. Saturday night every pig in the city will be here to reinforce the inspectors. But we won't go easily. That's a promise !"

"Are you one of the owners?" Jeff asked, feeling kinship to even an uptight person like this.

"Owner ! How can you *own* something like The FBI Girl? It's a community resource! I am a volunteer."

She said it as if it were a far more important word than "owner." Jeesh! America must have changed. Had capitalism become something dirty - like that list of words he had sworn to avoid?

He found himself staring at the flame in his cigarette lighter. It towered over the body of the Zippo like the torch welded to the hand of the Statue Of Liberty. A forgotten cigarette dangled from his lips as he gaped at the blue center of the flame. The wick, damp from its home in his pocket, crackled and sparked. Wow! Like the Fourth Of July.

He looked up to tell the girl about the fireworks show going on in the palm of his hand. Her beady little eyes bored into him.

"No smoking," she said.

"Far out," Jeff said, and the phrase felt just right on his lips. He walked away, carrying the lighter before him, a seeker of truths...

...let it shine. Shine, shine, shine, let it shine on me...I said your Loveliqht, baby...

...Somehow he was back in the dance hall. Crammed up near the stage. Mulberry Street was really jamming. The girl Nebraska had saved from the cops was belting out a song. All around him, the kids were really digging it. Shouting and dancing and leaping and whirling about. Jeff's lighter had gone out. He flicked the wheel and the flame sprang into life again.

A girl ducked under Jeff's arm and leaped up on the far corner of the stage. In flash she had shed all her clothes and she was bounding about nude and spontaneously enticing. She couldn't have been more than seventeen. This was definitely *not* North Beach. She was having more fun than the crowd. Her hair, both top and bottom, was bright red. All around Jeff, other girls were shedding their blouses. Dancing topless to the beat.

The naked girl on stage caught a bump and grind in the drummer's rhythm. She worked her pelvis back and forth, in and out. Sometimes like Gypsy Rose. Sometimes like a belly dancer. She dropped to her knees and lashed the stage floor with her red hair. Then she was on her feet again, bumping and grinding, pelvis in and out. Advancing toward Jeff. A moth to his Zippo lighter flame. She had a smile a mile wide on her face. She looked him direct in the eyes and licked her lips. Her bright red bush reached for him... retreated... reached... and retreated... reached...

And then Jeff suddenly remembered the phone number in his pocket.

He shut the lid to the lighter. Put it away. And as the girl danced the last few steps to the edge of the stage, he turned on his heels and started pushing through the crowd and the topless girls. Saying excuse me when he found his hand around a perky little breast with a nipple as hard as a pencil eraser.

Jeff had to find a phone. And call Samantha.

The telephone booth was in a corner by the men's room. The light was out. So was the fluid in his lighter. The scribbled numbers on the paper were blurred in the dark hallway. Or, maybe he was the one blurring in the darkness, not the phone number. Jeff wasn't sure, but he was willing to be open minded about it. Then he got it. Plenty of light in the John. He spent ten minutes looking for something to prop the door open. Voila! One phone number of one very pretty stewardess.

Jeff plinked in a dime and dialed... 8... 3... 4... Shit! Lost his place. Start again. Faster before your fingers remember they're stoned. 8342258. Gotcha, sucker! He heard the phone ringingandringingandringing. Then he started to freak. What time was it? Had to be reallyreally late. He tried to blear at his watch. Same hand as phone. Drop phone. Phone bangs against booth wall. Bang and bang. Back and forth. Woman's voice coming out from way down near the ground. "Hello. Samantha Vaughn speaking."

"Miss Vaughn?" Jeff said. "It's me. I mean, it is I... uh..."

"Hello. Hello," the voice continued. Getting impatient.

Jeff crouched down so that his lips were near the mouthpiece. Since that part was now up and the hearing part was down, he felt a bit like an astronaut. A gravity defying phone call.

"Miss Vaughn?" he said again.

"I can barely hear you," the voice complained.

The mental light glared on like the sun coming up at Cam Rahn Bay. This would be much simpler if he picked the phone up again. He could even stand and talk if he so desired. Such was the design of those geniuses at Ma

Bell. Imagine that! Foolish me. He performed those actions. In a few seconds he was blathering on like any normal young man whose tongue had been suddenly gripped in the vise of shyness.

"You pr'bly don' member me, Sam... I mean... Miss... Uh... Vaughn."

"Who is this?" Samantha said. Jeff went for direct honesty.

"Jeff Katz," he said, fighting to speak the proper English of Whittier. "I am the individual you met on the... Uh... The... Uh…" He wanted to say the thing with wings that flies people around.

"The airplane, Jeff, the airplane," Samantha said. "I remember you, fine. Uh... Have we been out partying?"

Jeff confessed he had. He was suddenly stricken with every doubt in the world.

"I'm so sorry," he said. "I know it's too late to call, but…"

"It *is* late," Samantha said. "But I don't know about too late."

"You probably already have... " Jeff almost bit his tongue in three or four unequal parts. He had nearly fumbled out something about her having another guy sleeping over. What's the matter with you, Katz? Don't you know how to talk to an American type girl person anymore?

"No. I didn't already have a date," Samantha said. Thank God, she didn't catch what he almost blurted. "Say... Are you okay?"

"Oh, I'm jus' fine," Jeff said. "I have been out seeing the slights... I mean, sights of San Francisco. And..."

"Drunk, huh?" Samantha laughed.

"No. Not drunk. I was. Some hours past. But, I think someone slipped me just a teensy, weensy bit of Ell Ess Dee. They put it inna... in *the* ... Kool Aid. I thunk. Think."

"Where are you?" Samantha sounded worried. She was. Acid was not something to be messed with if you were alone and a virgin.

"FBI Girl," Jeff said.

"Oh, boy," Samantha said. "Get a cab and come on over."

"You sure it's not too late?" Jeff asked.

"Jeff Katz. Do you *want* to come over to my place?"

"Yes Ma'm," Jeff said. "I do... Please."

"Then come on over. I'll see you within the hour. It's close enough to walk. But it's a *long* walk. So call a cab. Okay?"

Jeff said okay. Samantha gave him the address, made him repeat it several times, so he'd remember for the cab driver. Then hung up.

Feeling like he had just won the Irish Sweepstakes, Jeff put the phone

83

back in its cradle. He got out another dime to call a taxi. Then he thought he'd be a real, low class type fool if he didn't buy something nice for such a kind, pretty lady.

Like what?

A rose. That was it.

The most perfect rose in all of San Francisco. And maybe some wine to go with that rose. Good thinking, Katz. Class act style thinking. Maturity strikes. See. The Army had been good for something. His parents would be proud of him. So would whatsherface. His fiancée. Oh, shit! That's right. He was sort of engaged. Not formally. Just a college ring party thing. Later for that. But better make that bottle of wine a *big* bottle of wine.

Jeff started simple. He went looking for the exit.

Nebraska had wandered out of FBI Girl for a moment, to clear his eyes from the stinging haze, his ears from the scream of guitars and his mind from the hashish/weed drift. And finally to maybe stop thinking about that vest with its two ties that a skilled haybaler's fingers could flip aside and the breasts be very firm against said haybaler's chest...

Two out of four wasn't bad.

He stood, breathing deeply, on the street.

The fog had closed in, and now the streetlights were haloed.

Nebraska guessed all these hippies who didn't seem to drink much had the right idea, if you were concerned about tomorrow and the hangover. But who in hell wanted to think about tomorrow, let alone anything else? That was for Sunday night and Monday morning, after he got home.

Moisture condensed on the Angels' bikes, still on line in front of the club. He ambled over, admiring them. He thought for a moment if, instead of getting that GTO with the Tri-Power he'd been saving for, what would happen if he bought a motorcycle. No, he decided. It'd be a big klunk with a windshield and saddlebags from the factory and he didn't know how to modify it the way these Harleys were.

One bike in particular caught his eye. He knelt beside it. Good Lord, he thought. Look at the work. Not that he knew a lot about motorcycles. This one was nothing but engine surrounded by the bare necessities.

Slim front forks, tiny tank, old-fashioned rigid frame, a bicycle seat for the driver, a grudging four inch by eight inch rectangle of naugahyde for a passenger's seat and a passenger backrest/rear fender support that stuck up about eight inches. Passenger footpegs? Oh yeah. Little teeny struts, way up back here by the driver's seat, just above one of the fishtailed exhausts that came up at a 4 0 degree angle from the engine. Looked uncomfortable as hell for the passenger.

Then he pictured what the driver would be leaning back against, assuming the passenger was female. Mmm, he thought. These guys arrange things strictly for their own convenience.

Rearview mirror? He spotted a dentist's mirror, tackwelded to the straight, short handlebars.

He turned his attention to the engine.

There was a lot to marvel at. He'd never seen a Harley that had two carburetors, let alone with one of them sticking out the left front of the forward head. *All* of the engine's bolts had been converted to hollow-headed hex bolts. And the valve covers ...Christ!

They'd been engraved! By a jeweler! Impossible, he thought, kneeling, his fingers moving out of themselves to touch the elaborate scrollwork.

And a voice growled, almost in his ear: "Citizen went an' touched the scooter. Citizen maybe gonna fuckin' die!"

Nebraska blurred to his feet and whirled.

It was impossible for a Hell's Angel to be larger than Dirty Dog Evans, of recent police confrontational fame. Let alone three of them. Although the circumstances may have made it impossible for Nebraska to correctly evaluate the situation, since they were all looming on him.

One of them was slipping a belt - it looked like a chromed triple-row industrial chain - out of his pants.

He looked once more - and decided he wasn't in *bad* trouble. One of them, at least, was not only smaller than Dirty Dog, but smaller than Nebraska himself.

"Uh...hey, guys. I didn't mean anything. I...was just admiring the cycle."

"We understand," one Angel said. "Now, *you* gotta understand. You didn't hurt nothin'. Least that I can see. Which is why we're talkin' first.

"But...you're gonna have to take a little punishment. Not bad, maybe just a couple punches an' Bobbie won't boot you too hard. There's a purpose, you got to appreciate. Like when you're trainin' a bird dog. You ain't too loaded up to understand what I'm saying, are you? Naw. See, if we don't whop you one, pretty soon some other bastard's gonna sit on my bike. Or one of my brothers' bikes. Pretty soon, somebody's ride gets knocked over. Scratched.

"Next time you go walking down the street, somebody's gonna ask you what happened, and you can tell 'em, and see, it's like you'll keep some other faggot from gettin' killed for real."

Shit. Nebraska looked at The FBI Girl. No friends. No backup.

"Okay," he said. "Which one of you do I fight?"

"You still ain't got it, citizen. Bylaw Number Five of our Charter says, 'When an Angel punches a non-Angel, all other Angels will participate.' You see, it's the sworn *duty* for an Angel's brothers to pitch in' and ratpack the bastard."

Nebraska couldn't help himself.

"You mean you guys got *rules?*"

"Fuck yes, man. Whatdaya think we are -barbarians?" The biker seemed offended.

Another Angel interrupted. "Hang on a shake, Indian. Ain't this the cat that smoothed up when Pig Grancell was tryin' to bust Alexis an' disappeared her stash?"

"Yeah. Yeah it is, ain't it, citizen?"

"I was there."

"Maybe we oughta cut him some slack, huh, Dick? Unless he's some kinda narc, an' runnin' a number."

"He ain't a narc - Grancell's too dam' dumb not to have blown it if this guy was."

"So what? Grancell's just a Frisco copper. He don't know *everybody* that's a pig! They got Fed narcs, too!" This from the smallest, most wild-eyed Angel.

"Bobby, bro. You gotta lighten up on that crystal. Ain't no cause to be gettin' paranoid. Yet."

Bobby looked unconvinced - or at least disappointed that the prospect of a good beating was lessening.

"See," the Hell's Angel Nebraska'd heard called Dick said. "Cast your broad upon the waters, and all that shit. You helped the broad, you keep your front teeth. There's justice in th' world, 'spite of the courts an' cops. The Angels got their own pure doctrine, like they say."

Nebraska blinked. He'd heard that term before -but not with a mind full of hashish, a stomach full of bourbon, beer and wine, standing on a crazy San Francisco street.

He passed on, however.

By rights, Nebraska should have smiled, slunk stage right with all of his

86

teeth and disappeared. However, this was a night of magic.

"Can I ask you guys something?"

"Motherfucker's pushin' his luck." This from Bobby.

"You can ask." Dick.

"This is gonna sound real dumb...but hippies preach love an' peace an' nonviolence, right?"

"Up till somebody rips off their stash, anyway."

"You people, meaning no offense, don't seem to have, well, the same ideas. So why do you hang out with them?"

Indian looked at Nebraska.

"This bastard is dumb. Even for a day tripper. Try drugs, music and free pussy, citizen. Hell, why're *you* on the Haight? Same as us, right?"

Nebraska considered. In a way...yeah. But "not exactly," he said.

"You gonna pow-wow," Dick said, "especially with a citizen, least we can do is have something to drink."

He found his own bike, dug through one pouch of a ponyexpress saddlebag, and came up with a jug of wine. Screwed the cap off, and the jug went around - yeah, give the citizen a hit.

Nebraska found a joint that he'd forgotten had been given to him in FBI Girl, lighted it and handed it around.

"Hell," he caught himself. "Sorry. I guess that isn't too bright. Out here on the street."

"Yeah," Indian agreed. "Probably bring some cops around. Probably they'd want to arrest us, Haw. Haw. Haw. Gimme that doobie."

"Sorry," Nebraska started again.

"Jesus Christ, citizen, would you stop apologizing for *everything?* If we're gonna kill you, we're gonna kill you, and 'sorry' ain't gonna have shit to do with it. Like they used to say, never complain, never explain."

Twice now. First pure doctrine, now never complain.

"Dick," Nebraska tried as politely as possible. "Only time I ever heard that never complain bit was from my CO. Sorry,' I mean, not sorry. Commanding—"

"I know," Dick said dryly, "what CO stands for. Besides Conscientious Objector.

"So that explains the hairdo. You one of those poor bastards going over...naw. I saw your eyes. Comin' back. Welcome home, bro. Give him the bottle, Bobbie.

"This is about all the fuckin' welcome you'll get. No parade, no

French kisses from the broads and no guaranteed jobs. Unless you want to be a pig or mailman."

Dick fielded the jug and lifted it.

"Salud, amigo."

"Man," Indian complained, "Another grunt. Now you and him gonna stand around all night tellin' old war stories!"

"Stop snivelin', Indian. You're just pissed 'cause you ain't run into an ex-jarhead to play your own set of Memory Lane with. Have a drink."

"Both you guys were in the service?"

"All three of us. Bobby was a swabbie for awhile, till they caught him rippin' morphine sulfate off. Don't gape, citizen. There ain't nobody more patriotic than Hell's Angels. We even volunteered once. Whole motherfuckin' gang. To be like Special Forces and fight behind the lines.

"That god damned President of ours never had the common courtesy to answer our telegram."

Nebraska may have been in an altered state of consciousness, but he didn't think it wise to say that he'd encountered another patriot earlier. The Hell's Angels *and* the Mafia. Wonderful.

"So where you from, citizen?"

"Nebraska. Little town out in the middle of nowhere."

Dick blinked, looked at Nebraska very closely.

"I thought the accent sounded familiar. Where in Nebraska?"

"Believe me, nobody's ever heard of it. Even if you come from Omaha. Place called Grainton."

"Nope. Never heard of it. What year'd you graduate from Elsie High? An' the liquor store in Grainton still sell to anybody who's tall enough to reach over the counter?"

Nebraska mouth gaped.

"Close the trap, citizen... forget that citizen shit. What's your name?"

"Steve. Steve Applegate. But I got used to being called Nebraska. Guess I better get unused to it before I get home. How the hell did you know about Grainton? I was class of '64." Nebraska was babbling.

"I," bragged Dick, "played second string end for Wallace when we beat you guys like you was drums back in '59. There was talk I coulda got a scholarship to State ...if somethin' hadn't of sorta got in the way."

Indian was looking at them both.

88

"Right now. Both of you. Stop. You expect me to believe that you and Dick the Douche come from the same goddamned town? A town that nobody's ever heard of?"

"Not exactly," Nebraska said. "About ten miles apart." Then, to Dick. "What's your last name?"

"Kreuger."

Nebraska blanched.

"You mean you're the one that, uh, well, went and..."

"That's me. So they still tell the story, huh?"

Nebraska nodded.

"Never heard how that shook out. My folks sold the farm and went off to K.C. two years later. I was long gone by then."

"The story was that they had to re-sod the football field. And that girl — "

"Abbie, it was. Suck you off like a slushpump, she could."

"Uh, yeah. She ran off to Chicago. Or at least that was the story."

"Son of a bitch," Dick mused. Then he turned to his fellow Hell's Angels.

"Brothers, I think we got a sacred duty here. Here's this guy—"

"A stinkin' citizen," Bobby grunted.

"Hey. We were *all* citizens one time. Like I said, this guy from damn' near my home town. Went off to the war, and done good. Now he's back home, lookin' for praise, glory and mostly some leg and a party.

"Are we going to deny this cat his moment in the sun? When every man has turned his back?"

"You been doin' too much acid," Indian said. "You're startin' to sound like that fag poet Ginsberg. But sure. Why not? Always room for one more.

"One thing, kid."

Kid! Under the tattoos, forehead scar, broken nose and long hair, Indian might have been a year or two older than Nebraska.

"Remember this," the Angel continued. "You're on our turf. So you play by our rules. You do that... you're our fuckin' guest. No way can you come to any harm. You got that?"

"I...I think so."

"Then that's it," Dick said in satisfaction. "Get your ass on the back of th' hawg.

"We barely begun to party!"

"He's got a new kind of lovin'... " Alexis sang in a low blues groan... *"that's what I told my girlfriend, Lou..."*

The guitar man laid on a scratch that made Tyrell's heart jump. Sunshine shimmied toward him, hips grabbing at the beat, long white arms and delicate hands parting the distance between them.

"Got a new kind of lovin..."

She closed into his arms now, fitting against him like she was born to it. Her body rocked gently against him as Alexis sang on...

"He bought him a coffee grinder... grinds my coffee fine... Bought... him... a grinder... grinds me so... fine..."

Sunshine's fingers played along the back of Tyrell's neck. The light show images streamed through her fine, blonde hair as she tilted her head up at him. Her eyes were so wide and blue he thought he'd fall in and drown. She smelled of roses and other nice things - from the floral/herbal sachet she always put in her bath. She wore no makeup, no lipstick, no perfume. Her skin was scrubbed soft and gleaming white. Now he knew what they meant about peaches and cream complexions. And those untouched lips... bursting red cherries... mouthing the words to the song... *"got a ne..www kin-da love... love... lovin'..."* All the romantic nonsense of his middle teens clutched at him.

She found the soft place at his shoulder - near the neck. Tucked her head in and crooned with Alexis. Delicious prickles as her breath stirred the small hairs of his flesh.

Tyrell's mooning eyes crossed the path of a big, redneck-looking kid with long, stringy hair. The kid's eyes stopped for just a hair on Tyrell and Sunshine. They were cold. Tyrell suddenly became very aware of his race. And Sunshine's. The kid's eyes moved on.

"... so uptight," Sunshine was whispering. "... just groove, Tyrell... just groove with your Sunshine..."

But it was no good. She was a sudden lump in his arms. He was thinking about home now. Not nice stuff. Like his mother's cooking. His sister's irritating voice, that he'd missed so much. No, he was thinking about that card in his pocket. With the name and phone number of Mister Kelly.

Mister Kelly was the white boss who owned the big lumber yard in Tyrell's town. His name and phone number was Tyrell's entire future. And his family's. "You just write me, son," the man had said. "You just write or call when you get out. I got big plans for you. Big plans." And Tyrell was standing there nervous in his new dress uniform - his mother beside him so proud of her child. Her oldest boy. Her Tyrell.

So how come he hadn't written? How come he hadn't called? But what if Mister... What's the matter big man? Whatcha scared of big time? Couldn't be worse than falling off a Huey with the VeeCee in the bushes and those kiddietroopers you were supposed to be minding off God knows where. Give Jeff a hard time for being a chickenshit and not calling home. You called home, alright. And your momma was happy. And the first thing she said after she quit blubbering, was... Did you call Mister Kelly? And you said, no momma, but you would just as soon as you got the chance. You lied Tyrell. Lied to your momma.

"Come on, baby," Sunshine soothed. "Come on home with your Sunshine. She'll make you better."

Her voice was like magic and Tyrell drifted back to the odd unreality that was The FBI Girl. Music and colored lights all around. Laughter and dancing. Sunshine was leading him off the floor, melting though the crowd of kids. He was dying of thirst and as they passed a punchbowl, Tyrell reached for a cup.

"No, baby. Uh, uh," Sunshine said. Gentle and pushing his hand away. "You're too uptight for acid. Come on, now. Sunshine's got a better trip in mind." She giggled and it was like... little Christmas bells his momma always put on the tree.

He followed his young, blonde hippie Siren out the door, thinking: Merry Christmas, Tyrell.

CHAPTER SEVEN

NEBRASKA WAS LOST.

He shouldn't have been - he could look out from the captain's walk one way and see the Golden Gate Bridge, half-right-face and see the flashing beacon atop Alcatraz, half-right face once more and see the Bay Bridge and the bulk of Oakland across San Francisco Bay.

In theory, it's impossible to be lost in San Francisco. But theory, at this moment, was meaningless to the swarm of happy chemicals, legal and illegal, tangoing through his brain- and blood-cells.

He asked the old man beside him how he'd gotten there.

"On th' back of Dick's fatbob. I thought you wasn't that messed up," the man said.

"No, I meant..." Nebraska broke off.

What he'd meant was how had he gotten from the Haight to the roof of this four story Victorian house that looked as if it belonged to and had been decorated by a more than eccentric, moderately rich man.

Nebraska had always prided himself on his map reading ability, from Cub Scout days to Land Navigation back in Basic Training. He tried, rather hazily, to replot his mad motorcycle charge using what he remembered of the tourist map he'd glanced at, back at the Mark Hopkins.

Minutes after the party invitation, Angels had begun trickling out of FBI Girl, shouting plans and intentions back and forth. Dick had hollered they were gonna go to Gramps' Place and get rowdy. Nebraska assumed that was a bar. Nebraska assumed wrong.

Dick had asked Nebraska if he'd ever been on a scoot. Nebraska didn't think the biker wanted to hear about the old Cushman he'd owned for two weeks as a kid, so he just shook his head, no.

"Hang on to the rail..." Dick indicated the tall, spear-pointed triangle that jutted almost seven feet into the air from the hog's rear fender, serving both as passenger backrest and brace for the exhaust stacks that shot skyward next to it.

"...lean when I lean... and try not to fall off. 'Cause if you do, I'll leave your ass in the middle of th' pike an' go looking for somethin' female to pack."

Pre-flight instructions complete Dick booted the kickstarter, listened to the vee-twin cough, rumble, and roar to life, waved to Nebraska to get on, put the footclutch in, reached forward to the skull-capped handshifter that rose above the gastank, almost as high as the handlebars, and then it got very confusing.

The front wheel was maybe two feet in the air, then slammed down as Dick brodied the bike down Haight. Thunder behind and beside them as other Angels gunned into the night.

Somewhere in the madness was a park, curving roads, a scream as a peacock was shocked awake by the exhaustblast, a high, very high hill. Nebraska thought they passed the Mark Hopkins, then they were going downhill, this was another street now, and just below Nebraska's foot he could see the slot for the cablecar's cable, dim sound of thrumming and what would happen if the front wheel gets into that one, and then the now-closed ripoff joints of North Beach becoming a sign saying DO NOT ENTER and up a road that curved back and forth and back and forth, Nebraska hearing the roar of laughter from Dick as he went down a gear and twisted the throttle and sparks showered up as he roadrace-leant the Harley into the exit and up, through the twists.

Fortunately, they reached their destination before Nebraska found the courage to puke.

They turned off another street just at its crest, and Dick goosed the bike up a narrow driveway. He locked up the brake - rear only, of course - and skidded to a halt.

The garage door was open. Inside were engine stands, parts of motorcycles, auto parts, welding rigs, wallracked tools and four rollaways. It was as clean as any operating room.

Oddly enough there was a ramp just lifting that evidently led to the garage's upper story. The ramp closed smoothly, flush against the ceiling. Perhaps it had never been there.

Dick looked at Nebraska. "You didn't see that."

"I didn't see that," Nebraska agreed, wishing they'd pulled in a few seconds earlier and he'd been able to see exactly where or to what that ramp led.

The man standing in the garage slid a panel over the switch activating the ramp, turned out the lights, and walked out. The garage door slid noiselessly down.

The gray-bearded man proceeded to kiss Dick. Loudly, sloppily with a great deal of tongue work.

What in God's name, Nebraska thought... The Hell's Angels weren't, uh...

"Who's the rootypoop," the man asked.

Allan Cole & Chris Bunch

Freedom Bird

"Nebraska, this is Gramps," Dick introduced. "He's been an Angel since... shit, since Christ was a corporal. Gramps, this poor bastard's just back from Nam. He's from my hometown, and needs a beer bad."

Gramps, who was just shy of 60, grunted, and stuck out a ropy-muscled arm that was tattooed like he'd once been a sideshow attraction. "C'mon inside."

Then Nebraska noticed the man, like Dick, also wore the cutoff vest of the Hell's Angels. The situation was weird, and got weirder as they entered the house. There were other Angels, other bikers. Nebraska also saw patches other than Hell's Angels: Gypsy Jokers, Satan's Slaves, Knightriders, beards, earrings, swastikas, arcane emblems. Redwings blackwings brownwings DFFL 13...

He heard singing ...*And lovers she has seen/Curve/winding, bumping, grinding./Motorcycle Irene...*

Women. Mostly young, although Nebraska saw some that looked older. Damned few of them, he thought, were anything other than pretty to beautiful. Although... he looked into the hard, hard eyes of one smiling blonde as she passed, arm in arm with an Angel monster Nebraska thought was Dog. He looked away from the both-ends-burnt candle quite rapidly.

"...The Hunchback, the Cripple./The Horseman, and the Fool..." went the song.

It *was* a party. Drinking, talking, dancing... Nebraska glanced in a room as they passed and lifted an eyebrow. Yeah. That, too. He wondered if there was any special reason for this party on a week night, but decided he'd rather think that this kind of thing happened every night of the year, here in San Francisco.

More music crashed around them, but Nebraska could see not a speaker or stereo set. Not that he looked particularly hard - the house itself was strangeness. If he had to describe it, he rather fuzzily thought, he might say that it sort of looked like where Diamond Jim Brady would have his orgies back in the olden days.

Or maybe one of those old high-class whorehouses. Red velvet hangings. Real velvet. Rooms lit by old chandeliers and lamps converted to electricity. The sheen of the reflection from waxed, ornate antique furniture. But the paintings on the wall were of twentieth-century ships. Mostly warships.

There was a billiard room - Nebraska would not have called it a poolroom, even though there were a couple of pool tables. But the centerpiece was the competition billiards table. All of the tables were in play.

Gramps led them to the bar. "What're you drinkin'?"

"Gimme a glass of wine, bro," Dick said. Gramps reached under the bar, took out a bottle, smacked its neck sharply on a galvanized tub on the floor, and passed the stirrup cup to the other biker, who used the wine to wash down a handful of pills.

"Maybe... maybe a beer," Nebraska asked. He wondered if Gramps would now rip the top off a barrel and hand it to him. Instead the man took a mug from a shelf, and filled it from a tap. "What do I owe you?"

Gramps looked at him.

Dick swallowed pills hastily so he could speak: "What can I tell you? He's a virgin."

Nebraska gathered somebody else would pay. But... "You own this bar?" he asked.

"Virgin ain't the word for it," the older man said. "This is my fuckin' *house,* boy. I live here."

Dick started laughing - and it was pretty obvious to Nebraska that this whole thing was a setup. "Your house? The whole thing?"

"Free and clear," the biker said. "Come on. You want the Grand Tour?"

Nebraska did. It may have been the effect of the hashish as it continued to filter through his system, but that was when the idea appeared that he was being given a guided tour by a profane cross between Rip van Winkle and Diamond Jim.

Except that Victorian whorehouses never had round beds, that he was aware of.

Gramps held a finger to his lips as he cat-stepped down one corridor, past a closed door. "Don't want to wake the wife," he whispered.

Nebraska didn't say anything - but thought that if anyone could sleep through this crashing music she was either deaf, dead or both.

Will you still need me/Will you still feed me/When I'm sixty-four...

The tour through this House Of An Eminent Victorian Rapscallion continued.

Except that very few Victorian Rapscallions had a double-locked room that Gramps unlocked to proudly show him a .50 caliber machinegun on its tripod.

"Uh...maybe you shouldn't be showing me something like that,"

95

Nebraska said.

Gramps smiled. "Oh, I'm not worried," he said calmly. The smile was gone as if had never been.

Another, large room had a huge Nazi flag hung on one wall. Uniforms, posters, knives, weapons were in display cases around it. There was a set of dinner plates crested with the Nazi eagle.

"Guy I got those from," Gramps said proudly, "told me they belonged to Himmler hisself."

Nebraska nodded. Fine. How interesting. Nope, never been into German stuff. Mister, you are a goddamned whacko. Let's not say that. Try: What's up these stairs?

The stairs led to the captain's walk. Nebraska sipped beer, looked out at the Berkeley Hills across the bay, mostly dark now. It was almost three in the morning.

Come on, Nebraska. Remember your manners. "Real nice place you have here."

"Used to be a whorehouse," Gramps said. "Matter of fact, that's how I first came on it. Was on my way to a different war'n the one you're in. The big one."

Nebraska wondered for a moment if Greatgrandfather Applegate would have given Nebraska's grandfather a hard way to go about The Spanish War being a helluva lot rougher than this hooraw's nest over in France you just come from, but made vague questioning noises.

"I was waitin' for my sub to get commissioned over at Mare Island," Gramps went on. "Somebody took me up here. I remember, standin' here, on this roof, lookin' over across the Golden Gate, and there was a little teeny sub, just like the one I was gonna be on in a couple of days, gettin' escorted through the nets.

"And I thought then the reverse perspective wasn't gonna be a real thrill, let alone what was likely to come after... I was right. It wasn't.

"But standin' there, back on the cigarette deck, I kept lookin' through my binoculars, lookin' back up for this house. I swore I'd own it. Some day.

"Ten years later, I did. It was kind of run down. But that didn't matter. Still the same hill, still the same house. I did a lot of the work myself."

"Oh," Nebraska said. Maybe construction guys get paid real high wages out here in California. "You a carpenter?" he ventured.

"Nope. Work with crippled kids," Gramps said. "Hospital out in Pacific Heights. Been there since '55."

96

Nazi dinner plates... Hell's Angels... machineguns... Grandfather-type outlaw bikers... restored whorehouses... handicapped children? Not very much had been logical so far in San Francisco.

What the hell, Nebraska decided. Maybe he was the one who didn't make sense.

He heard a high whine/roar, and headlights came very fast up the street toward the house. Pulled in, and Nebraska saw a psychedelically-painted Porsche 911S pull in. Alexis got out, and Nebraska free-floated, remembering *That's when my love comes a'tumblin' down*. . . until he saw the guy get out of the passenger's seat. The skinny lead guitarist.

Oh well."So much for romance. At least he could get drunk.

"Where do I go to take a whizz," he asked.

Gramps gave him instructions and they went inside.

Gramps headed for the ground floor.

Nebraska promptly got lost again.

Nebraska never got himself untwisted. But he did find a bathroom - either on the second or third floor. By the time he found it, after opening several doors and seeing curious and once a potentially life-threatening thing(s), he was hobbling with his legs crossed.

It was *some* bathroom. Multi-colored tile. Carpeted. A six-foot-tall marble urinal. Brass fixtures. The toilet tank rose almost to the ceiling. Against one wall was a monster claw-footed bathtub, its claws lacquered gold. Against another, floor-to-ceiling scrolled glass doors for the shower.

At this point, Nebraska was more than a little messed up. Possibly he thought the heavy fog hanging in the bathroom was a byproduct of the hashish. Or maybe he just had to urinate so badly he did not notice.

Regardless, he had his fly unzipped, his cock out, a hissing stream rivaling the North Platte in spring spate, and emitting a thankful sigh when the Voice spoke:

"If that's a clubber out there gettin' cute, he better be aware his next gig's gonna be tenor with the Vienna Boys Choir if he gets any cuter."

It was a woman's voice. That sounded like...

The shower door opened, and Alexis St. John stepped out.

Wet, naked, angry and reading the riot act: "Out! Just out! It has been a long day, a long show, and I do not need—well, hell!"

Nebraska was trying to stop pissing and zip up his fly.

"You're the guy who saved my ass," Alexis suddenly recognized.

"From my old fascist buddy Grancell. Aren't you?"

"Uh...yeah. Yeah, I am. And, I'm real sorry, Miss. But—"

But Alexis was staring at the heavy stream that he couldn't cut off no matter how hard he tried. "Wow. You've really got to go, don't you? You been drinking beer *all* night?"

Then somehow the floodgates slammed shut, and Nebraska was able to put it away without getting caught in his zipper.

"I'll, uh..." And he was backing toward the door.

"Hold on, bashful. This is a large sort of thank you. "

Steve Applegate had never ever been kissed by a naked woman who did not even know his name. To be more precise, with the exception of the usual GI experiences, he had *never* been kissed by a completely naked woman. Sex, in his home town, had been a few rather hasty semi-clothed fumbles in the back seat of the family sedan or grass stains on the back of a lifted skirt in spring fields.

And he never, never, never had been kissed, he thought, by anyone who knew what she was doing the way Alexis knew what she was doing.

After a moment, she let him go. "There. Was that okay?"

Nebraska managed a nod.

"If you'd hand me that towel?"

Right. The towel. That might make it a little easier to breathe. It didn't. She turban-wrapped her hair with it, then reached across him, one rose nipple brushing his arm, grabbed a much larger beach-size towel and began drying herself.

She turned away suddenly, and Nebraska thought he heard a giggle, and *did* see a quickly-suppressed grin.

She, he realized, is doing this on purpose. But somehow this, sort of the ultimate in flirting, didn't make him angry. Instead, he started laughing, and then heading for the door.

"You kiss me once or twice/And say it's kinda nice/And then you run," Alexis sang. "Do I rate an introduction, or is it," and once again she started singing, *"...just you be my backstreet girl?"*

"Nebraska," he mumbled, shy again.

Alexis looked him up and down. "Says it all, doesn't it. I'm Alexis. You gonna be hanging around for awhile?"

Yes. Yes, he would be. For the rest of the party, even if it goes for five small forevers. Hell, for the rest of his life, if she wanted.

Allan Cole & Chris Bunch

By the time Nebraska found a beer and a bit of his equanimity, his mood started changing.

Hell. What was Alexis doing, taking a shower here? She was probably living with one of these Angels. Although he didn't remember seeing what he heard biker chicks had tattooed on their butts - PROPERTY OF...

She would probably tell her old man what happened, as a Great Joke, and the biker - hell, it might even be Dirty Dog, for all he knew, which would make sense on why he was protecting her against the cop, and would hunt Nebraska down, not seeing any Great Joke here, and turn him into thin red wallpaper.

Even if she didn't, that kiss would be nothing more than a stringalong from—

Then Nebraska caught himself, and the black and stupid mood went away. Wait a minute, my friend. Think of this for a story - first you see a cop making a dope bust, and you keep that from happening... side thought, you might have, to clean that one up before telling it at the Legion Hall... then you run into a Hell's Angel from down the road, get taken to one of their parties, and get kissed by a beautiful woman who's gonna be a bigtime rock and roll star?

Hell, hell, hell, Applegate? Who'll ever believe *that* much, anyway?

What do you want? The moon? Yeah, he thought. And the sun and the stars and another beer.

He was heading down a hall - this house of Gramps had more hallways and zigging passages than a State Fair Funhouse - and he happened past an open door.

"Hey. You," came the bellow.

Nebraska obediently backpedalled.

The room was large and lined with acoustical tile. There were chairs and couches scattered around. The walls were hung with musical instruments.

Inside was Gramps and the lead guitarist for Mulberry Street. The guitarist held an instrument.

"A lute," he guessed.

"Naw," Gramps said. "Close, but no see-gar, Tripster. Called a cittern. Medieval, tuned AGDE below Middle C. Got it in a hockshop couple months ago."

The guitarist plucked a few chords.

"Twangy bastard, ain't it," said Gramps, and turned to Applegate.

Allan Cole & Chris Bunch

"Your name was... what, Iowa?"

"Nebraska."

"Sorry. Dick hadda split, but he told me to make sure you got taken care of. So you need some weed or some uppers, just gimme a shout.

"An' you wanna crash here, or go back to wherever you're staying?"

Nebraska didn't know.

"Either way, don't matter," the man said. "But if you decide to split, I'll have a prospect run you back. Oh yeah... Any chick you see catches your eye, tip me a wink. Dick said it'd be a black spot on our hospitality - they never shoulda let the sunnovabitch graduate from high school - if you end up in bed either alone or straight. "Kay?"

Uhhhhh. Nebraska wasn't sure about *this*, but didn't think it was politic to ask about how far free will went in Gramps' place.

"Here. You look thirsty." Gramps had another galvanized tub beside him. He pulled a can of beer out, opened it with the churchkey tied to his colors, and handed it to Nebraska.

Nebraska was looking at the instruments while, behind him, the guy from Alexis' group - Tripster - picked through some chords on the fatbellied instrument.

"Whoo," he admired. "You got a *lot* of gitfiddles here."

"Started as a hobby," Gramps confessed. "Looks like it kinda took over. Got strings from all over the world now. Don't understand how it worked out that way, seein' as how I'm just barely competent playin' 'Good Night, Irene.'"

Nebraska didn't recognize some of them. But one he did. "You got a *Dobro*?"

"Yeah. Won it in a poker game in Texas what... fifteen years ago? Go ahead. Haul it down."

"Maybe I better—"

"Stuff that don't get used just rots, boy. Use it or lose it, like they say."

Nebraska lifted the heavy nickel-plated metal guitar off the wall. Plucked steel strings. Tuned. Plucked more strings.

"You play?," Gramps asked.

"Most everybody in the family does," Nebraska said. "A little, anyway. Sort of tradition, actually. See, we only get one TV station clear where I live."

Fingers a little more confident, now, pushing through the rust of fourteen and more months of not practicing, not playing. He chanced a Johnny Cash

Allan Cole & Chris Bunch

tune.

"Not bad," The Voice said. "Know the words?"

Alexis now wore a green velvet dress that stopped about six yards short of where decency or the mores of the State of Nebraska would have dictated.

"Sure," he managed.

"No you don't," Alexis said, and started singing:

"I keep my pants up with a piece of twine/I keep my eyes wide open all the time/I keep the end up for the tie that binds./Because you're mine..."

...and Alexis' voice dropped to a croon... *"...Please pull the twine."*

Nebraska had to force a laugh, because quite suddenly, quite eerily, he had the feeling that he was having A Pass Made At Him. Oh shit. Oh dear.

"Keep playin' cowboy," Alexis said. "You ain't half bad."

"For a fuckin' hiller," Tripster said, near-snarling, started to slam the cittern down, caught the Deathlook from Gramps, put it gently back on the wall, and stomped out.

"What got his jaws all torqued up?" Nebraska wondered.

"It's a long story," was all Alexis said.

"Yeah," Gramps said. "Which I don't give a shit about. I'm gonna have me a chat with that lad. Straighten his attitude out a little."

"Hey. Gramps. Do me a favor," Alexis said. "Tripster's okay. He's just bummed. He'll be all right."

"A favor. 'Kay. I'll leave it. Anyway, Nebraska. Let me know if you need anything. Or maybe you don't need nothin' at all. I'll be hustlin' some pool."

He grinned, went out and closed the door behind him. Nebraska hadn't followed all of this, but he had a pretty good idea that, if Alexis hadn't of said anything, this Tripster would have gotten his head thumped for even thinking about treating one of Gramps' instruments like he was anything other than spun glass.

Angel house, Angel rules.

So how come he, Nebraska wondered, a super-straight from Bumfuck, Egypt, hadn't run into trouble? So far, anyway.

Clean living, he hoped, and touched more strings.

"So play something, Nebraska. Unless you want to get the long story about what's sauce for Tripster ain't loosey-goosey for Alexis?"

"Huh?"

"Later. I'm starting to get pissed," she said. "Gimme a honk out of your beer."

Nebraska handed the can over. Alexis drank, then reached into what must have been a hidden pocket in the dress, took out a large joint, bit off the end, and blinked up at Nebraska.

"Should a lady," she asked, deliberately husky, "offer a gentleman a Tiparillo?"

Nebraska fumbled in his shirt pocket and found his Zippo. He took it out and started to perform his one party trick: Zippo base held with two fingers, thumb on edge of lid. Pressure, and...

...and lid should flip open, and if he was super-lucky, his thumb would hit the flint and strike a light.

Instead, his fingers slipped, and the lighter went spinning across the room.

"Shit," he mortified.

Alexis laughed. "Let's go back to what it was before. Sit down. Before you fall down. Play something."

Nebraska followed orders and sat down on a chair. Alexis recovered the Zippo and walked back.

"Slide back," she commanded, and perched on his knees. She fired up the joint, took a toke, and passed the joint to Nebraska.

Confusion would be the best description of the moment, as Applegate found himself with a Dobro against his chest, a slender hand holding a joint to his lips, and what just might be the world's most beautiful woman on his lap. Who was not, he noted, wearing anything under that miniskirt except panties.

He sucked weed/air, and tried to simplify his options.

Play something, she said. Fine. Run through your *rep-ertoire*, he thought. Which is gonna take about six seconds. Try to find something that ain't too hiller. What about...oh, come on...It's your best song. "Wolverton Mountain" Naw. That's *real* hillbilly. Think of something else. You're trying to impress a musician, and you're a backporch weekend picker. Hell, why didn't you ever hear any blues, like she sings. Oh. Yeah. He remembered and...

You are being a damned fool, his backbrain said. You're the cat who just sent the Zippo airborne. Shut up, he thought. With Faith All Things Are Possible.

...and dragged dope, took the joint from Alexis' fingers, held it for her to take a hit and then impaled the jay on the end of one of the Dobro's trailing

Allan Cole & Chris Bunch

steel strings, just like he'd seen somebody do with a cigarette in some movie with was it Steve McQueen or maybe some TV show...

He remembered the chords. And was brave/dumb enough to try the lyrics, in his untrained but semi-sound tenor...

...Oh, my dear, my darlin'./I hunger for your touch/A long... lonely time...

Fourteen months of no practice and steel strings and BUZZ and his fingers slipped and Alexis, seemingly not noticing the glitch, let him not be embarrassed and recover, picked up the words...

...and time/Goes by/So slowly/And time can do so much./Are you..

His fingers/mind ran out of memory/chords.

Alexis' voice, a cappella, crawled up the register...

...still mine...I need your love/Godspeed your love...too-oo me...

"Lonely rivers do whatever they do for blue-eyed soul cats and I never learned the words to the rest of the song..."

She broke off, and kissed him briefly.

"Close enough," she said, "for rehearsals and rock 'n roll."

"We used to say," Nebraska said, "close enough for horse shoes and hand grenades."

Alexis looked at him. "Oh. Now I dig the short hair. Army?"

Nebraska nodded, waiting for the evening to suddenly come to a very hostile end. Alexis, instead, looked sympathetic.

"You still in?"

Nebraska shook his head. "Discharged today. I mean... yesterday."

"Welcome home," she said. "And I promise I won't sing Universal Soldier. Plus I think I'm setting things up to be a bummer assuming you're just back from where I think you are and maybe you don't want to talk about it. Sorry. Okay. What do I do to get out of it?"

"Uh," Nebraska said, suddenly bold once more, suddenly back to that soaring confidence he'd held walking into the FBI Girl, "you could always kiss me again."

"I could."

Alexis kissed him again. Nebraska's heart was twanging like the Dobro that was crushing his chest.

"Uh... is it okay if I get rid of this," he asked. "It's... sorta in the way."

He started to put it on the floor, but Alexis was standing.

"Hang it up. Gramps'll kill you if somebody steps on it."

Alexis stood, and Nebraska got up and replaced the guitar. Oh well.

That would be the end of that. He was used to a world where the track of seduction had certain very clear rules. One rule was that if there were one pause, glitch or hesitancy, the girl would suddenly "come to her senses," pull down her skirt and that would be that.

Correction - that would *not* be that.

Instead: "How fucked up are you?" Alexis wanted to know. "Too blown away to drive?"

"I'm *never* that ripped," Nebraska said, with just a tick of truth.

"Good," Alexis said, and headed for the door. There was a small overnight case sitting there. She unsnapped it, took out a leather-fobbed set of car keys and flipped them to Nebraska.

"Let's blow this joint," she said. "You know how to blow, don't you, Steve?"

Huh? How did Alexis know his real name? He shrugged and dismissed the matter. Some kind of hippie slang, he guessed.

There was the pooled light out of blackness of the streetlamps, the road curling through a park and the highwhine of six-cylinder/aircooled Porsche behind him and then high above the red steel stretching up, and red cables coming down from a half-circle above him and wind through the window like the clean burn of expensive brandy and the twin needles spinning past blackmarked 100 and laughter and the singing...

...So we'll go no more a-rovin'/So late into the night/Though the heart be still as loving/And the moon be still as bright...

Fog rolled low on the street as Jeff exited The FBI Girl. It was thick, billowing and glistening white from some odd trick of a barely visible moon. Jeff walked steadily through it awhile. Turning onto Haight Street and strolling in the direction of the park. He had a firm list in his mind and a vague map of San Francisco in his memory. Samantha lived in the Sunset district. He'd cut through the park to Fifth Avenue. Then over to Moraga. Down a street or four or five and there she'd be. He'd stop at some convenient place along the way for the perfect rose and bottle of wine.

He walked oh, so coolly. In absolute control. Hands in pockets. Casual. Yeah, that's me. Casual Katz.

The sounds of love making floated from a window. Low groaning and moaning and oh, baby, ohs. Music played behind the lovemaking. A song... *The days/Of Wine and Roses/Laugh and run away...* Cool shattered, Jeff laughed. He stopped at the window.

Picked up the tune. Started whistling the melody.

Jeff had always considered himself a master of the musical pucker. When he was a kid he drove his folks nuts whistling "The Poor People of Paris,"

"The Whistler And His Dog," and "Andalusia." Endlessly. He did this now with "Days of Wine and Roses." Serenading the lovers.

The lovemaking stopped. Heavy thump thump of big male feet crossing the floor. Another thump thump of feet. Also crossing the floor. Two faces peered out at him. Angry faces. Big angry faces. With weight lifter necks and biceps the size of volleyballs. Jeff looked at the necks. The biceps. The angry faces.

Casual And Hip the famous Whistler, Mister Katz saluted. Made with a sharp, military turn, and marched onwards. Whistling the "Battle Hymn Of the Republic."

He crossed to the south side of the street. Even at night, it was somehow darker here. Dingier. Dirtier. Musty odors. He also noticed this was where the fancy motorcycles were parked. He saw a young girl in a torn, dress walking barefoot toward a beat up building. She wore a tie-dyed jeans jacket over the dress. Cold air moved in a current with the fog, suddenly enveloping both of them. The girl pulled the jacket tighter.

Jeff looked at her as they passed. Her eyes were blank, and she was sniffling and wiping at her nose. Jeff could have sworn it was the same jacket he gave to the guy at The FBI Girl. The thought -true or false - made him feel good. He grooved on it awhile. Yeah... grooved... Jeff was getting the idea of the meaning of the word.

Then he forgot the girl as he came to a window. There were posters and weird boxes and objects scattered about in some sort of a jumbled display. But that's not what caught his attention. He was looking into the face of his Commander In Chief. Excuse me, Jeff thought, my former Commander In Chief. It was a handmade Lyndon Baines Johnson puppet. Complete with tiny specs drooping over that enormous Texas oil drilling nose.

Jeff gave LBJ the finger. LBJ did his best not to notice. But Jeff was ready for that. He presented him with two... count them you ass... two, fingers. He saw the slime twitch. Not much. But it hurt, he could tell. Next he gave him a single arm, Italian fuck you. LBJ reeled back. Stricken to his cold, cold heart. Then the double arm. LBJ was almost bowled over. Now that he had him good and weak, Jeff went for the kill.

He unzipped his fly and peed on the window. Take that! LBJ's face disappeared in the stream. Jeff rezipped and walked on. He didn't deign to look back at the quaking ruins of his victim.

As he got closer to the park, the street was suddenly empty windows closed against the fog. Dimly, he heard a song rattling through one of those windows ...*Secret Agent Man/They've given you a number/And taken away your name...*

Furtive white faces peered at him from alleys. Eyes blank like the poor girl with the tie dye jacket. But these were yellow and glowing like a rat's. Whispered entreaties: "Got some great speed, man..."

"I got better... give you *real* energy..." Jeff took his hands out of his pockets.

Footsteps behind him. Long, agonizingly slow, footsteps. Was he being followed? He wanted to look back. But didn't dare as paranoia crept into his soul. Jeff stopped. Sudden. Pretending to be studying some object in a window. The footsteps also stopped. Just as abrupt. Steady, boy. Just a coincidence. He walked on. The footsteps followed. His heart hammered.

Jeff wondered who was stalking him. The sound of those feet had him freaked. First one big shoe, or boot, would crunch down. Then there would be a long, very long, silence. Then the other foot would fall. Each time this happened, the sound grew closer. Amazingly closer. Oh, bullshit, Mister Studied To Be A Doctor Katz. Acid, remember? It's screwing with your head. There's nothing behind you at all. Except maybe a drug-induced hallucination. Turn around and look, if you don't believe me. Listen to your medic. Look. And it will soon be over.

He looked.

It was no hallucination. The guy coming up on him had to be ten feet tall. Draped in a long black coat that covered all ten of those feet, except the very top. Which bore a black, slouch hat.

Oh, man, are you in trouble, Jeff Katz.

He walked faster. So did his pursuer. He walked slower. Same-o, same-o. Maybe the guy wasn't after him. Maybe he was just going in the same direction. You know. That coincidence you were talking about, Jeffers.

Okay, Batman. Riddle me this: Why is a ten foot individual - dressed entirely in black - coincidentally walking exactly as you are, in the coincidentally same direction? How about: he's also going to Sam's house, right? No? Okay. Uh... I know... he's a basically shy person, being ten foot

106

tall and different from other people. Probably was teased when he was a kid. What he wants, see, is to ask directions. But he's too embarrassed to ask right out. He's waiting for the right moment.

Sure. Like that alley over there. Where the street light's busted. He'll catch me then. Rip my head off. Shit in my neck. Relieve my corpse of its valuables.

My God, Jeff Katz. You have become one bigoted individual. What have you got against tall people, anyway? You ought to apologize for what you are thinking. Right now. Go ahead. Apologize.

Jeff Katz, hero of sultry climes, stopped in his tracks and turned. A stoned out portrait of bravery. The ten foot man descended on him. Each step he took seemed to cut the distance between them by half. Then half again. And yes, indeedy, Buffalo Bob, the guy was entirely dressed in black. Looming. Closer and closer. Dreaded face hidden by the slouch hat.

"How's it goin[7], man," the ten foot man said as he passed. It was like a freighter wind blowing by. Jeff had to remind himself to turn his body with his head as he gaped at his once upon a time tormentor. He heard a loud snigger drift back.

Stalked by a guy on stilts!

Haight Street was weird.

Of course, that depends on an individual's definition of weird, don't you think, Doctor Katz? Yes, that is a very good point, indeed, young Jeff. You, for example, might find a person who chooses a height of ten feet and a costume of black, to be an oddity. A freak. I, on the other hand, might find his habit charming. Eccentric, yes. But look at all the exercise this eccentricity provides. That, with a balanced diet, moderation in liquor and tobacco intake, should guarantee him a long life. If the creek don't rise in the Spring.

Weird, to me, might be something else all together different. Such as that young woman approaching us as we speak. With the large snake about her neck. What kind of snake would you say it was, Jeff? Oh, I don't know, Doctor Katz. Either an Anaconda or a Boa Constrictor. I left my Field Guide To Man Eating Serpents Of The World back at the hotel.

The girl stopped in front of Jeff. The snake she wore draped about her was a definite Boa. Two thick bands of snake muscle encircled her neck and shoulder. She held the head with its beady eyes and flicking tongue in one hand. And the situation wasn't funny anymore.

The girl's eyes were outlined in red and shadowed with wide interior

107

bands of green. The eyebrows were black painted juts of surprise. Her hair twisted Medusa locks. She hissed at him.

Jeff fixed on that face and that hiss. The face shattered before his eyes. Pieces flying out to a point just beyond his vision. Only eyes were left. Hanging there. Staring. Then the face reformed.

The girl hissed again. Pushed the snake's head out at him. Now, Jeff found himself staring at the snake. Its tongue tasting the air, catching the scent of Jeff's hot, tasty blood. The head and neck raised away from the girl's supporting hands. Arced closer to Jeff. Closer. Tongue flicking in and out. Suddenly, Jeff was a small white mouse.

With a million-mile-a-second heartbeat. The pace of a short-lived furtive little animal. With his enemy closing in.

"Mouse," the girl said. "Come here little mouse. Come."

"This is not cool," Jeff told the girl. "This is not cool at all. If that thing eats me, I promise you my friends will come looking for you."

"Mouse," the girl said again, fighting for control over him.

"You won't like my friends," Jeff went on. "They are just back from torching villages and murdering innocent Southeast Asians. They liked their jobs. They especially liked killing women who wore snakes. Why, Nebraska alone has maybe twenty notches on his M-16. And believe me, lady, they're all for women-bearing snakes."

Jeff jumped as the girl shrieked like a banshee and ran wailing off into the fog. Trailing snake behind her.

The Slayer of Giant Serpents continued briskly on his quest for his lady fair. Mess with Jeff Katz, will she?

Still, he was spooked enough by his encounter to veer away from that planned shortcut through the park. For a short time, he got lost. He found himself wandering through a neighborhood of fine old Victorian homes, with elaborate gardens staircasing up the hillsides. It was there he discovered the Perfect Rose.

It grew out of a big red clay pot that sat on the steps at the entrance to a four-story Victorian with many windows - all of which were dark. He could not make out its color. But it had one thick, strong stem, supported by a bamboo pole. From this stem grew a single rose. He could see it was in full bloom as he crept closer to it. A cricket chirped and Jeff dropped to the pavement. He stayed absolutely still until he was sure the cricket had not been disturbed by creeping enemy feet. Then he swarmed up to the rose on his belly. Slithered behind the pot for cover. Came up to a crouch. Peered about. Nothing. Good. Very good.

Now he had time to examine the rose. It felt safe enough to flick the wheel of his Zippo. The rose was lovely. As deep and lushly red as the red velvet couch and overstuffed chairs at his grandmother's house. Each petal was well-formed and glistening from the fog. The scent was light, but lingering, like a delicate confection. He put his lighter away and got out his penknife to snip it off.

The rose pleaded with him to let it live. Jeff promised it a nice vase, clean city water, and the sunny window of a beautiful woman. The rose said it sounded so nice, why couldn't it always live there. How could Jeff argue with such impeccable logic? He tested the pot. Not too heavy. Maybe thirty pounds.

He picked up the pot and staggered down the stairs to the street. Okay, so it was maybe a little heavier than he thought. He was young. He was strong. His heart was pure with love.

Jeff Pureheart Katz slammed into a lamppost and rebounded backwards. An encounter with a parked car saved him from going ass over tea kettle. So what if had probably just snapped his spine in two? The rose was gripped safely in his arms. He lumbered onwards.

It was the Mother of all Wine Bottles. Four feet high from its basket bottom to the corked top of its long, slender neck. It sat in a window surrounded by dusty cans of Progresso Tomatoes and big nets of figs. The window was plastered with tattered cigarette signs, hand-lettered touts for fresh sandwiches and cold beer. The Coca-Cola sign on the door said the market was open. Jeff put the potted rose down and tested the handle. It turned. Good Americans that they were, the nice people at Coke did not lie.

Although the little all-night market was open, Jeff knew he was well-past the hour when booze could be sold. He got the bottle out of the window and was working up an elaborate story to beguile the owner as he approached the register.

"Twenny bucks," the little old man said. He peered at Jeff through acrid smoke drifting up from a stub of an unfiltered cigarette. The eyes were red-rimmed and bored. Jeff gave him his "twenny bucks." Disappointed that he had lost his audience for the story, he left lugging the giant bottle.

A doozy of a dilemma awaited him outside. There was no way he could carry both objects at the same time. He tried. Lord knows, he tried. But after he had nicked the edge of the pot and nearly broken the bottle, he surrendered to the physical laws of Nature. But he had not been trained by the most modern military on the face of the Earth for naught. The solution was as obvious as the nose on his face. Ooops! Where'd it go? For crying out loud, dolt, there it is between your two eyes. Oh, yeah. Sure. Knew it all the time.

Jeff picked up the potted rose and walked a precise two hundred paces down the street, looking back frequently to spot any suspicious people. At the count of two hundred, Jeff placed the rose on the pavement. Turned and marched back for the wine. Briskly now... Right shoulder... Chianti! Forrard... HARCH!

He continued this way for many blocks. Panting and puffing, drooling sweat and leaving streaks of flesh on stone walls when he cut a corner just a tad too close. But somehow he had found Moraga Street. Which he had forgotten had beaucoup formations of objects purporting to be hills. After Jeff had marched up the first one, lugging that five-hundred pound perfect goddamn rose, he was willing to give the hill theory business a slight edge.

The trip back down for the rose completed his religious conversion. It was done at a half-run. Not because he was in hurry, but because gravity beckoned so mightily. Gasping for breath, he dropped to his knees. Rested his forehead against the bottle. He'd never make it. He looked up at that hill. The potted rose at the top. Frightened and calling to him. Plaintively. Medic... Medic... Damn it! He would not give up! Failure was not a word in Jeff Katz' vocabulary. Onward, soldier. Onward.

Somehow he got to the top. Somehow he soothed the hysterical rose. Emboldened he dared the next mountain. But first he had to walk down the hill he was on to that peaceful valley waiting far, far below. It lay between a Studebaker and a Rambler station wagon. He had to do this twice. Then the mountain. Also twice.

He started down. The hill was steep. Within three steps he knew he had gotten in too deep. In fact, he had just stepped off the Continental Divide and - hurried on by the weight of the potted rose - he was sinking downward at a rate guaranteed to produce the bends. As well as a busted face, collar bone and clay pot.

Faster and faster he ran. Leaning back to keep from going over. His feet had a will of their own. Grabbing pavement for dear life. Jeff figured he was at maybe Mach Three when he entered the valley. He skillfully eightballed off the Rambler and shot for the Studebaker. But the pot had somehow got ahead of him. He ran faster to catch up. Jeff closed on the car. Then he was at the car. He lifted one foot and he was running up the bumper and across the hood. Over the roof and down the other side. Three steps more and he was at rest. Not one ding out of him or the pot.

This was gonna be duck soup. Cackling with delight at his prowess, Jeff headed for the opposite hilltop.

Then he remembered. Oh. Turned to look. Back up that hill. Where the wine awaited. Laughing and threatening to smash itself all over the street if he dared approach. Come and get me, Katz, the wine taunted.

Jeff had no choice. He'd recapture that hill, or die trying.

...Though the night was made for loving/And the day returns too soon/Still we'll go no more a-roving/by the light of the moon...

Fading away into silence.

The low splash of waves against a boat hull. Hollow footsteps on wood planks. A giggle. A chuckle.

"Careful," Alexis said.

"I never stumble/I never fall/I sober up/on wood alcohol," Nebraska sang as he stepped from the dock onto the houseboat's deck and damned near deepsixed himself.

"Haven't heard <u>that</u> since I was in Girl Sprouts," Alexis said. "Oh well. At least you can drive."

She unlocked the door, and she and Nebraska walked in. Dimness. The only illumination came from the neon lights over two enormous fish tanks on either side of the room's walls. Or, Nebraska wondered, was he supposed to use all that Navy jargon? Bulkheads and compartments and whatever? Or did any of that apply to houseboats? Hell with it.

The broadbeamed houseboat was large, nearly 50 feet long, Nebraska estimated. This room - the living room - occupied about two-thirds of the lower deck area. To Nebraska's right a door opened to the kitchen (galley?) and, he guessed, to a bathroom.

At one side of the main room stairs circled up, to possibly a sundeck or even another floor.

Framed paintings, posters and photographs hung on the paneled walls. The floor was carpeted in a weird pattern that looked like the little paramecium-critters Nebraska'd seen through the microscope in Biology class, a pattern that should have been jarring but for some reason was most easy on the eyes.

Furniture was of two types - huge, square pillows patterned with weird, Arabian Nights-looking figures and even larger, overstuffed ottoman that looked as if, should you sink into one, you'd be lucky to emerge by spring.

One wall was mostly stereo set. Nebraska had seen pictures in Playboy of various Ultimate Stereo Systems, but he'd never believed anyone, except maybe Hefner, actually *owned* one. Wrong again.

Alexis walked to the forward end of the room, and pulled drapes open, revealing sliding glass doors and San Francisco Bay. She slid the door open and the fresh, near-dawn breeze cooled them. She went out on deck, beckoning to Nebraska.

He put his arms around her waist, nuzzled her perfumed hair and looked out. There was the Golden Gate... over there, Berkeley and the beacon of Alcatraz, and... just about over there, San Francisco and where he'd been atop Gramps' house a little while ago.

"We're where?" he asked.

"Sausalito."

"Right. Can I ask you something? Why a houseboat?"

"Why not a houseboat?" she said.

Why not, indeed. But there seemed to be an answer.

"Growing up," Alexis said after a bit, "we used to take our vacations in a little town on Lake Michigan. You know. Rent the cottage for two weeks, put up the hammock, pretend to be fishing, listen to the bees buzz. Typical straight shit.

"I loved it," she said, just a bit defiantly. "Straight or not.

"Anyway, my Dad was always looking out at the lake, every time he saw a boat go past. And he'd have this look on his face, and you could tell that he wanted to be out there. I asked him one time why he never bought one. Not any kind of yacht, you know. But some kind of little trailer boat. He said Sears didn't pay him that kind of money. Besides, he had to save for my college."

She shrugged. "So... maybe, now, for me, boat equals freedom? I dunno. But it's nice, and quiet and you can get your head together just sitting here, listening to the waves. Different than the go-here, do this, play that turn those amps up regular shit."

"Personal question?" Nebraska ventured - then wondered why he was asking stuff like this when what he really wanted to do was sweep her off her feet and charge for the nearest bed. "You and your folks get along? Not that it's any of my business. But, well, what do they think about..?"

He rather vaguely made a sweeping gesture that took in the houseboat, the Porsche, the Midnight Hour and everything.

Alexis was quiet, and Nebraska thought for a moment that once again, he was asking nosey questions. But she was just considering her answer.

"Would you believe," Alexis said finally, "something like... tolerant twitching? They don't *really* like it. Probably if you asked them, they would have expected me to be some kind of music teacher or something at Normal State.

"But, see, they're the ones who said they thought I should go away to Chicago to school. And didn't go ape when I first told them I was doing my Peter Paul and Mary riff."

"Oh yeah," she grinned, looking back and up at Nebraska's expression. "I was just a helluva folkie." In a deliberately reedy voice: "We shall now perform Child's Number 83B, the original pre-Walter Scott version of the ballad of..." and her voice went to normal.

"What a joke. Oh. Sorry. I think I went and veered on you. Somebody gave me a cap of what they said was DMT before we went on back at FBI Girl, so my mind's sort of going boingo, boingo. What were we talking about?"

"Your folks."

"Oh. Yeah. There's no problem. I don't think there would've really been, ever. But it didn't hurt that I paid off their house after we started getting some fat gigs... And I bought Dad his little putt-putt."

Nebraska wondered to himself what would happen if <u>he</u> did something like this? Not that he'd join a group. But supposing he called Pa and said he was gonna stay on, here in San Francisco and maybe go to school on the GI Bill? Majoring in Agriculture and Marijuana Cultivation. What a weird thing to even consider. Good dope, he thought.

"So, what do you think of my little home for this week or year?"

"Never knew anybody who lived on a houseboat," Nebraska said. "Course, where I come from, a houseboat would have to have four wheel drive for the summertime."

Alexis laughed. Then put her hands over his, and moved them from her waist up to her breasts. Her nipples and Nebraska got hard at about the same time.

Nebraska, not wanting this to end ever ever ever, looked for something to talk about, to keep the moment going.

"You ever take this thing out sailing or motoring or whatever you call it? Houseboating?"

"Not a chance," Alexis said. "I want to go sailing, I call a friend. I wouldn't take this barge across the Bay when it's flat, let alone out through the Straits. Not only would the landlord kill me, but I think this turkey's moored solid on empty bottles of Southern Comfort and Budweiser."

She moved her breasts against his caressing fingers. "Chilly out here," she said.

They went back into the main room, and Alexis slid the glass door shut. She kneaded her neck with one free hand, stretching against it.

"Here," Nebraska offered. "You can't massage yourself. And all us Germans are born massagers."

"I thought that was Swedes," Alexis said.

"Nope," Nebraska said. "Just propaganda. It's like free love. What Swedes actually want to do is take you a Luther League meeting then show you their little tiny painted horses."

"You know," Alexis observed, "for a cat who's so straight arrow and all, you sure come up with some freaky stuff... Upstairs, Mister Masseur."

She took his hand and led him up the curving staircase into a darkened room. Alexis borrowed Nebraska's lighter. Four candles, in tripod-mounted bowls glowed into life. Alexis took two sticks of incense from a table and lit them, as well. Sandalwood filled Nebraska's nostrils.

The bed was low, and a golden, silk spread covered it. Alexis pulled the spread back.

"No silk sheets?" Nebraska joked most feebly. Again, the evening, correction morning, was moving a little too rapidly.

"All I will say," Alexis murmured, "is that in an hour or so you might be very grateful that I *don't* have silk sheets."

She stepped into the nearby bathroom and came out carrying a crystal bottle. She put that down on the nightstand. Alexis went to a panel set into one wall, and touched a button.

Music, then a voice: "This is still the Planet Earth, and this is still Larry Miller on KMPX." The voice sounded as stoned as Nebraska felt. "No more words for awhile," the voice went on. "Instead... Ravi Shankar and Yehudi Menuhin. Groove, children, groove."

Music filled the room. Very very strange music.

Alexis considered, grinned to herself and went to a dresser. Atop it stood a large candle. She lit it and the candle started flashing. Just exactly like one of the strobe lights back in FBI Girl.

Allan Cole & Chris Bunch

Then she came back to Nebraska. He started to embrace her. She stepped back, just out of his reach, then came in again. She unbuttoned his shirt... slowly... her lips touching his skin as each button came away.

Then she stepped away once more... pulled the velvet dress over her head and pitched it on a chair. She turned into profile and slid the panties down her hips... Kicked them away, image/image/image flashing in Nebraska's mind.

She knelt on the bed, then slowly lay down, face down. Nebraska managed to undress, with fingers as thick as farm sausage. He was not sure what he was supposed to do next - at least not *precisely*.

He picked up the crystal bottle, and unstoppered it. Ah. Oil.

Nebraska had never, in fact, massaged anyone in his life, let alone a naked woman on a houseboat. But he thought, in the tiny, diminishing part of his brain capable of thinking, he was going to learn. Like a baby, logic said, like Johnson's oil on a baby's butt...

Brain shut down for the remainder.

He climbed onto the bed, almost sinking into its goosedown softness and knelt over Alexis. Poured oil on his palm, and slowly started to rub... neck, lifting her hair out of the way... shoulderblades, down... stroking, smooth down back, and up, and back... then down, hand curving around buttocks... and a soft sigh becoming a woman's moan. Then back, up and around, both hands now, oil and very soft, and his cock throbbing, jutting.

More oil, and fingers gently parting her buttocks, and a finger touching, and then curving down, slipping into moistness and back out and very gently in, in with a second finger.

She pushed buttocks against him, and he lifted his weight. She rolled over. Opened her eyes and smiled up at him. She was breathing heavily.

Alexis cupped her hand. After staring at it for a moment, Nebraska realized... and poured a bit of oil into it. Her fingers found him, and began moving up and down.

His hands were back and forth, slowly and he was going to explode he knew across her breasts and the smooth flat belly and her thigh against his, pressuring, and he moved back and her legs were apart, knee curling, leg lifting, and smooth calf rested on one of his shoulders.

Fingers curling, in, out, across her clitoris. Warmth, widening under fingers. Then his cock touched and slid, momentary resistance then velvet grasp as he went into her, her other leg coming up to his shoulder, and then

115

knees on either side of his neck as he drove into her.

Her gasp became a hoarse shudder as she convulsed under him and he was in her and she was in him and there was now no music and nothing but music and no breathing and no oceanwaves and no wind and nothing but the roar, roar of interstellar space for them and ecstasyshout as the lotus blossomed.

Sunshine lived over a garage at the far end of a garden... The garden was overgrown with red bougainvillea vines, twisting and curling through dwarf lemons and oranges. A big olive spread its branches over the garage and added spiny leaves and fallen fruit to the wonderfully smelling debris in the yard. Wind chimes played a ghostly melody.

She led Tyrell up creaky stairs lined with potted plants. There was a yellow sun on the door with a curved smile for a mouth. Painted daisies edged the sun. Under the whole thing was a single hand-lettered word: Me.

Sunshine opened the door and flipped a switch. A dim light went on. It glowed through a colorful hanging shade, made of paper with bits of yarn hooked around the rim. Big overstuffed pillows, pieced together from scraps of rose-colored carpets, edged one wall. There was a small cable spool on its side in front of the pillows for a table. The rest of the room - which was very small - was taken up by a mattress, set on the floor and covered with a lovely old bedspread, purchased cheaply from a second hand shop. Sunshine had made a canopy from an India-print blanket, which hung over the whole sleeping area, creating a warm and cozy corner. A wooden Blue Goose apple crate with a big drippy rainbow candle on it served as a bed stand.

The room was cluttered with comfortable junk, both familiar and strange. There were ragged stuffed animals, obviously from Sunshine's childhood. A miniature collection of toy horses, set up on a bare plank shelf which sat on cement blocks. The horse collection flanked a battered portable record player. On top of this sprawled a great big, Raggedy Ann doll. Complete with red candy heart.

There were posters hung about, but the center decoration Sunshine had made herself. She'd glued flower and vegetable seed packets to poster board, then framed it with thin strips of wood. She told him later she had gotten the seeds free last Easter at the Festival Of Growing Things.

Sunshine pushed Tyrell into the heap of pillows and told him to wait.

The only other door in the room led into a small bathroom. He could see a hot plate set up on a shelf over the sink. Beneath it was a beat up ice chest, where Tyrell assumed she kept the perishables. He saw her open a big, old-fashioned medicine cabinet with a streaked mirror and a wooden frame that begged to be saved from termites and senility. Two mugs, decorated with flowers, came out of the cabinet. As well as a pot of honey with a wooden dipper poking out from under the lid. She got a teapot from someplace, and in a little while he heard it whistling and Sunshine was by his side again.

Sunshine fished out a small box of lacquered wood and decorated with Oriental designs. She opened it slowly with long, slender fingers as if it contained great mysteries. She said it was her treasure chest. Out of it came a stubby little pipe. Some wooden matches. And another box - about twice the size of Tyrell's thumbnail. It had three tiny blue flowers painted on the lid. From this came a sticky bit of hashish.

She curved up by his side and her mouth became a lovely red bow as she tucked the pipe between her lips, made a little frown of concentration and lit up. She took a small hit, just enough to groove on, she said, and passed the pipe to Tyrell. He drew in. Felt the sweetness coat his lungs. He let it out. Sunshine struck another match. By the time Tyrell had taken his second toke, all the tension rose from him. It evaporated and lifted away like the dismal mist it was.

"I just love hash," Sunshine said. "One time I even had enough to make brownies. Just like Alice B. Toklas."

"Did they work?" Tyrell asked.

Sunshine giggled. "Of course they worked. And if they didn't, who would say? Nobody's going to see their friends and go... She lowered her voice so that it would vaguely approximate a male's... "Yeah, I had some hash brownies on the Haight the other night. Didn't get high." She switched back to normal voice: "Bumm-Merrri." More giggling from Sunshine. "That's not a story. Who wants to lay a trip like that on people?"

"Not me," Tyrell said. "Gee. Hash brownies. With lots of fudge?"

"Lots and lots of fudge," Sunshine said. "Want to try some?"

"Just brownies? Or hash brownies?"

"There's no such thing as *just* brownies," Sunshine said. "Smoke the hash. Eat the brownies. Still get you high, baby."

She fetched a plate of brownies. Beside it she put a basket of tangerines and a couple of oranges. She poured them both some tea and stirred in thick wads of honey as dark as molasses. He had never had tea so delicious. Sunshine said she made it herself from things she got from a herbal store.

117

"I make it different every time," she said. "I think this batch has the peach leaves in it. I forget. What do you think?"

Tyrell breathed in warm tea fumes, and sipped. It smelled and tasted like... flowers... with a hint of... yes, peaches. Sunshine said she also put in hibiscus flowers, cinnamon, rose hips, a little chicory root, blackberry leaves, nutmeg and orange peel.

It sounded and tasted like... not heaven... but paradise. He bit into the brownie. Savored the fudge. Sipped Sunshine Tea to wash it down. Another hit of hash. Suddenly, his mouth burst with liquid as the scent of citrus filled the room. Sunshine was peeling one of the tangerines and arranging the slices on the edge of the brownie plate.

Tyrell popped one in his mouth. Crushed down. His mouth flooded with sweetness.

Sunshine got up to put on a record. Tyrell eased back, sipped his peach herbal tea, munched his oranges and brownies, toked on the hash pipe. Listening to the song. It was a ballad he had never heard before. The voice of the woman who sang it was scratchy, out of key. But, somehow compelling.

...Yesterday, a child came out to wonder/And caught a dragon fly inside a jar/And fearful when the skies were full of thunder/And tearful at the falling of a star...

Then, somehow his head was in Sunshine's lap. She was stroking his temples and humming the melody. She had this little smile on her lips. So innocent his heart ached. He never wanted to see that innocence leave. Or to be the cause of that smile turning bitter.

He thought of his own life... How everyone had come to count on him when his father died. A few years ago he'd only been expected to mind his manners and get good grades. And get those grades he had. Tyrell was top of the class every year at the segregated school he attended. As his father labored on the big towboats that plied the Mississippi, Tyrell studied. Dreams of college danced in his and his parents' heads. Scholarships became a real possibility. His father worked longer and harder hours, to take up the scholarship slack. He was gone for many weeks at a time. Then he died.

With him died the dreams. Tyrell quit school and went to work. Making not enough - even with his mother's wages from Mister Kelly's lumber mill. She took in white folk's washing to make up the difference. But even with the yard of their home filled front to back with dripping lines, they knew hunger.

Allan Cole & Chris Bunch

Tyrell joined the Army and sent his money home. He went for every extra penny he could wrangle. Enlist for Airborne, not because it made you the Bad Boy on the Block, but because there was an extra $55 a month jump pay (although there was more'n a bit of swagger when he went home with the bloused jump boots and glider patch on his overseas cap). Don't go to Nashville, but stay onpost at Campbell and save money. Don't drink except at the 3.2 beer EM clubs. Bust ass, stay good and get pro pay. Volunteer for Vietnam, where you didn't pay income tax? That was part of it, too, although Tyrell knew there was no damned way that a paratroop-qualified Light Infantryman could manage to avoid Nam.

And damn, he was good. The Army'd wanted him to reenlist. Promised him instant promotion to Buck Sergeant if he did. But no. He'd already taken one chance, extending for the early out. Take another? No way, Jose. That part of his life was over...along with the weird kind of security - three hots and a cot but maybe you'll get killed - the Army offered.

Tyrell was frightened of what lay ahead. Such as that lovely face just above him with its fabulous Giaconda smile.

Sunshine kept stroking his temples. Whisper-singing to the song... insistent... trying to get him to listen...

...Painted ponies go up and down/We're captive on the carousel of time/We can't return/We can only look behind from where we came/And go round and round/The Circle Game...

After a time, the song ended. Sunshine fed him a little more hash. Tyrell marveled at her. How could anyone get to be so damned nice? He asked Sunshine a little about herself. The smile widened and she shook her head.

"Don't want to talk about yesterday," she said. "Not that there's anything bad, or terrible, or... you know... Stuff. But I don't live in that time anymore, Tyrell. I live now. Listening to the music, being a little high, being a lot close to... you."

"But you don't even know who I am, Sunshine." Tyrell said.

She put a small finger to his lips. Shush, baby.

"I know who you are," Sunshine said. "You're my Ty-Rell Man. And you're very sad about something that happened. And also something you think is going to happen. But you have a lot of love in you. A lot of kindness. I saw it in your aura the second you came out of the store. All pink with bits of gold. And some red. Real angry red for the sad parts."

"You see... aura's, Sunshine?"

119

"All the time, baby," she said. "Don't you?"

Tyrell said no. He never had.

Sunshine eased him off her lap and went back to the record player. Silently, she fished through her small collection. Then she gave a firm nod as she found what she was looking for. She put the record on. She kept her back to him as the introductory bars played.

Then, as the song began, she whipped around. Dancing. Lip synching the words. Shaking her hips. Taunting him with a finger.

...Sunshine came softly/Through my window today/Coulda tripped out easy/But I've changed my ways...

Tyrell flashed on their first meeting - the flower held up to him in her soft, white hand. Sunshine sang on: *"...I'll pick up your hand/And blow your little mind/'Cause I made my mind up/You're going to be mine..."*

Tyrell laughed. This was *some* woman. Sunshine laughed with him. As the song ended she put on another record and came back to his side. Tyrell suddenly felt very shy. As if sensing this, Sunshine didn't look at him. Instead, she picked up his tea cup, drained it back into the pot, leaving only the leaves and just a bit of moisture. She did the same with her own cup. Scraped out his tea leaves on top of her own. She swirled them around then placed the flower mug down. Sunshine peered somberly into their joint futures. For a long time. Then she looked up. The smile was back.

"What does it say?" Tyrell said.

"It says... Yes," Sunshine said.

"Yes, what?" Tyrell asked.

Sunshine blushed. "Do I have to say?"

Tyrell's blood went to boil. "What if it had said, no?" His voice came thick.

Sunshine didn't answer. Instead, she put a hand on his shoulder. As light and trembling as a wounded butterfly. Tyrell put his hand on hers. It was trembling as well. She leaned close to him... lips next to his ear.

"My Ty-Rell man..." she whispered. "... been waiting for you all my life... "

The automatic changer on the record player clicked.

...Suzanne takes you down to her place by the river...

They made love in a hazy dream of music and hash. Somehow their clothes were gone. Magically. Not a fumble or false move.

...she feeds you tea and oranges that come all the way from China...

Sunshine's nipples were pink and sweet in his mouth. Her breasts small

Allan Cole & Chris Bunch

white marsh mallows that he nibbled and kissed and didn't know if he could ever leave. Her belly a soft dimpled pillow that he lost himself on for a long time. Her legs fell open at his touch and he found the tender thicket and pale blonde hair as fine as a child's. His breath was shaky as he breathed her musk. Delicate fingers curled in his hair. Coaxed him upwards.

...then she gets you on her wavelength and lets the river answer...

He heard Sunshine whispering his name and it sounded like the distant music of a choir... "Ty-Rell... My, Ty-Rell Man..." She cried out as he thrust into her. He stopped, not wanting to be the cause of any pain. Not to Sunshine. He'd stay all night and kiss her and cuddle her and pleasure her in any way he could. But, he wouldn't hurt, couldn't hurt... Sunshine...

...and you want to travel with her and you want to travel blind...

Then she arched her hips and her legs came all the way around him... And she was whispering... My man... My... beau-ti-ful... Ty... Rell... Man.

...cause she's touched your perfect body with her mind...

Sam thought she heard a thump-thump-thumping outside. She rushed to the open French doors that led out to the balcony. She leaned between the potted snapdragons to look over the wrought iron railing. Nothing. The brick sidewalk that meandered up to her apartment door was empty. Samantha was worried. It had been over an hour and a half since Jeff had called.

After she'd gotten herself ready, she'd put a record on. The new Sergeant Pepper album. After that had played through and Jeff hadn't shown, she put on Blonde on Blonde. That was soon replaced with a Herb Alpert record somebody who didn't know her real well had given her.

Finally, Samantha scritched out an old Sammy Davis Jr. album. There was a song that was just perfect for her present mood:

What kind of fool...am ...I... Sammy mocked her. *... What do I...Know of life...*

She felt like a fool for sure. Foolish for giving the guy her number in the first place. She'd never done anything like that before. But at the time, it seemed... Oh, come off it, Sam! You felt sorry for him. Sure, but how sorry would you have felt if he had been ugly? She brushed that away. The really stupid thing was to invite him over when he called... blasted on acid, or whatever. A regular Miss Do Good. Oh, bull crap... That's not it either... You've just always had a talent for picking the wrong guy.

121

Samantha determined that if Jeff Katz ever did show up, she'd freeze him with her coldest, ice dagger look. Say something so insulting, that it would destroy him for life. For Ell Eye Eff Eee, LIFE! And shut the door in his handsome face. No. Not good enough. First she'd let him have a long look at her. He'd see the filmy hostess gown she'd slipped on. It was light blue, like the satin pajamas she'd changed into after he'd called. She'd laugh, turning her head carelessly, letting her long hair spill over her shoulder just so. Peek at him with seductive eyes through the veil of mystery she knew her hair would form. Let the perfume she'd dabbed on drift up and tantalize.

Then she'd slam the door in his God damned face!

As she was about to turn away, Samantha saw something poking out from the alcove that led to her front door. A boot? Yes... A boot. Was it Jeff? If so, what the *hell* was he doing?

She raced down the stairs and flung open the door. Ready to give the errant Jeff Katz a piece of her mind.

It took a few seconds for her to recognize him in civilian dress. But he was just as handsome as she remembered. He was also asleep. Passed out was more accurate. A gentle snore came from his lips.

Across his lap was this *enormous* bottle of wine! Clutched in his embrace was a great big red clay pot. And in that clay pot was rose. A single, perfect rose.

Samantha laughed. She couldn't help it. Jeff looked so... so... She dropped to her knees and kissed him on his cheek.

Jeff stirred and murmured her name.

Upstairs, she could hear Sammy Davis Jr. winding up: *And maybe then I'll know/What kind of fool... I... am...*

And suddenly Samantha didn't feel like a fool at all.

FRIDAY: DAY TWO

"...I read the news today, oh boy/About a lucky man who made the grade..."
—Lennon/McCartney

"...Music is your only friend/Dance on fire as it intends/Music is your only friend/Until the end..."
—Jim Morrison/ The Doors

"Love needs care."
— Motto of the Haight/ Ashbury Free Clinic

CHAPTER EIGHT

JEFF CAME BACK to the hotel a bit sheepish and a lot bedraggled. He had the look of a young man who'd gone to bat with two outs and the bases loaded. And who'd then screwed himself five feet into the ground striking out. Which he felt he had. Jeff also knew that waiting for him would be two men with big smiles, not the smiles of men who had slunk away from the plate.

He was wrong on one count. Only a single smile greeted him. Tyrell's. He was lounging on the balcony, soaking up the fresh air and sucking on a cup of coffee. Nebraska was still nowhere to be seen. Tyrell started to say something. But Jeff beat him to it.

"I'm very happy for you," Jeff said. "And yes, you and Sunshine can name your first born after me. Now, shut up."

Tyrell's grin vanished. "Lousy night, huh?"

"You might say that. In fact, you can say it without *any* fear of exaggeration."

"You didn't call the stew, did you?"

"Yes," Jeff gritted out. "I called Samantha, alright."

"Ah, hell, Jeff. I'm sorry. She chickened out, huh? So what? There's zillions of girls out there. Woman doesn't know what she's missing."

"No. She didn't chicken out. Samantha invited me over."

"Uh... and you...?"

"I blew it," Jeff said. "I blew it all over the place. I was drunk, I was stoned, and I made a damned fool out of myself."

Tyrell was philosophical. "Oh, well. Shi... stuff happens. Forget it. I mean, it's not like you're ever gonna see her again, right?"

"Wrong," Jeff said.

"Wrong?"

"Yeah. I'm supposed to meet her in a couple of hours... Jesus, Tyrell! What am I going to do?"

Tyrell did a bit of gaping. "Wait a sec! I thought you said you blew it? If that's a fact, how come you have a date?"

Jeff look startled. Suddenly realizing... He did have a date, didn't he? Yeah. That's right. Jeff Katz *was* the one who woke up on the couch with a heavy case of the Jewish guilts. The one who crept around Samantha's apartment, only answering her cheery comments with

embarrassed grunts. She'd offered him breakfast. He'd said, no thanks.

She'd said, why not take a shower before you go? He'd said, thanks, but he had to split.

Then as he was about to slink out - *under* the door, for Pete's sake - she'd invited him to spend the day with her. In other words, now that he thought of it, Jeff Katz had been given a second chance. And he'd said-

"Hey! Know what? You're right. Maybe I didn't blow it. I do have a date, dammit!" He looked over at Tyrell, feeling slightly better. "I guess I don't have to ask what happened to you. Man, if they hooked that smile of yours up to a generator, they could light the whole city."

Tyrell was suddenly serious. "I really like her, Jeff," he said.

"I can tell."

"No. I mean... *really*, really like her."

"Ooops. You mean, she's not the kind you love and leave, huh?"

"No. She's not." Flat.

Jeff draped a sympathetic arm around his friend. He really didn't know what to say. But, he gave it a try.

"Why don't you worry about how the story ends when you actually get to somewhere near the ending?" Jeff said.

"Sunshine said the same thing. Same idea, anyway. Different words."

"So why aren't you listening to her?."

Tyrell thought about this for a few minutes. Maybe Jeff was right. Maybe... Down on the street, he saw a familiar looking car blast into the courtyard of the Mark Hopkins. It was a psychedelic Porsche 911S. A woman was behind the wheel. Tyrell gave Jeff an excited jab.

"Hey, is that who I think it is?"

Jeff looked in time to see Alexis give Nebraska a kiss that would melt steel. He slid out of the car. Gave his lady love a low, sweeping bow. Then threw her a kiss with both hands as the Porsche blasted away. Nebraska turned and bounded out of sight. Jeff and Tyrell looked at each other.

"It looks like number one on Nebraska's wish list just came true," Jeff said.

"You got that wrong, Jeff," Tyrell said. "The man didn't wish anything. He flat out said he was gonna do it. Oh, man! There's not going to be any living with that guy!"

"Tell you what," Jeff said, "if he brings up that walking on water business again, let's not put any money down. Not against him anyway."

"You got that right," Tyrell said as a disgustingly happy Nebraska burst into the room. Doing a badly off-key Johnny Mathis: *"The evening breeze,*

125

caressed the trees... tenderly.... The morning mist, true love has kissed... breathlessly..."

Tyrell kicked his legs out from under him while Jeff grabbed a pillow and pounded him without mercy. Nebraska rolled about, screaming in mock agony at the terrible beating. Then he saw light, broke through them and grabbed up a handful of couch cushions.

"Incoming!" He shouted, arcing the cushions into the air like mortar rounds. Everybody hit the deck as the cushions came cascading down.

At that moment, the phone rang. Nebraska bounced to his feet and grabbed.

"County morgue," he said into the phone. "You kill 'em, we chill 'em... Ooops. Uh... Sorry, sir... We were just... Ha... Ha... Kiddin' around and... Yeah... Sure he's here, sir. Wait a sec..."

A very chastened Nebraska pointed to Jeff. He had the scared, sober look that came from speaking to Authority On High... General Westmoreland... the President... the Pope...

"It's your father, Jeff... " he said in an Eddie Haskell voice. "... Doctor Katz."

"I know who my father is," Jeff said, badly frightened. "And don't kid around..." Then he got it. It really was his father.

"Uh... where..." He took the phone. False brightness. "Hi, dad. What a surprise. Me and the guys were just fooling around and... Oh... I see... Here! Like in San Francisco, here? You and Mom! Oh, boy! I mean... Isn't that great... Sure... Sure.. Come right up."

He slammed the phone down.

"Hide me," he cried. "They're on the way!"

Tyrell and Nebraska did an automatic freak. Visions of their own fathers sending them to fetch the switch for the licking they *always* deserved, spilled out of too recent memory. They looked wildly about for their own hiding places. To hell with Jeff.

While Jeff was still juggling hysteria, the two of them dashed into the adjoining room and shut the door. Jeff rushed to it just as the lock clicked. He pounded on the door.

"Come on, guys. Let me in!"

"No way," Tyrell yelled. "I'd rather tackle a battalion of NVA. Single handed."

"Ditto that," Nebraska chorused.

"You can't leave me alone with them," Jeff pleaded. "They'll make

126

mincemeat out of me!"

His mother's gentle tapping at the door saved Jeff from completely abasing himself.

"Sons of bitches!"

"What was that, son?" came his father's voice.

"Be right there... sir," Jeff shouted back. He went to the door of the suite as if he were approaching a hangman's scaffold. Pressed a smile of innocence on his mush and opened the door.

"Hi mom! Hi dad!" Then his false cheeriness was buried by the rush of his mother into his arms and much loud wailing and weeping and a burble of Thank God, He sent you back to me.

His father stood tall in the background. Face dark with emotion. A big surgeon's paw came up to knuckle a tear from a corner of his eye. There was a large gold ring with a fat diamond on his pinkie finger. A gift from his own father - also a doctor - who gave it to Katz when he completed medical school. When Jeff had his bar mitzvah at thirteen, his father had drunkenly promised to bequeath the ring to him when Jeff completed medical school. Six years later he had repeated the promise - cold sober. Jeff didn't have the nerve to tell him he'd always hated that ring.

Finally, when he had gently peeled his dampish mother away and gotten a big fatherly hug and clap on the back, they settled down to talk. They asked about his friends and Jeff said they were getting dressed to go out. He heard soft scurrying from the other room, so it wasn't much of a fib. They were probably tying bedsheets together right now, getting ready to make their escape out the window. Oh, man, what was he going to do?

The talk was awkward, as his folks tried to steer clear of controversy. This was difficult. Because there was a lot for them to be pissed about. From their point of view. And Jeff really could see their point of view. That was his trouble. It made it nearly impossible for him to stick up for himself.

It had always been assumed Jeff would be a doctor like his father. That he'd get his BS and medical education at USC - his father's alma mater. And join his dad's rich practice in general surgery and internal medicine. There would be no problem, his father always said, in Jeff getting into USC. The old man was on the board, best pals with the Dean, and a prized guest lecturer.

For three years, Jeff had performed like an undergraduate champ. Then he had met Rachel. Young lust. Of the super heated unconsummated variety. It was Rachel's freshman year. She also came from a wealthy, prominent Jewish family. They pledged their troth at a sorority ring party. This was an engagement made in heaven, they then told their astonished parents. They said they planned to wed immediately.

Anguished parental cries all around: what about school? No problem. We're both going to stay in school. Besides, two can live cheaper than one.

"But not three," Jeff's mother said.

Rachel's mother said much the same. "If you really love each other," the argument went, "you'll be able to wait. If your love can't stand this small test of time, then maybe the whole thing is a mistake."

A one-and-a-half year delay was agreed upon. Time for Jeff to get his degree and progress into medical school. In return for the wait, massive parental support was offered. A honeymoon in Europe. An underwritten home. Nice car for each of them. And much more. Rachel thought all this was swell. But as time progressed, Jeff did not. If I do this thing, he had thought, I'll be bought and paid for the rest of my life. Then he felt young and stupid and went along with the program.

From that moment on, Jeff started questioning his life and goals. Then his parents' as well. His father's glittering Whittier practice seemed tawdry with so much poverty and misery in the world. His grades plummeted along with his mood. Then the draft came knock, knock, knocking on Jeff Katz's door. And the Army had him in its olive drab grip.

The only odd thing about Jeff's service experience as that, for once, the Army didn't look at this Nearly-Trained Round Peg and decide to make him into a Army-Trained Squarepeg Baker. After Basic (all the way across the country at Fort Dix, of course rather than California's Fort Ord), he'd gone to Fort Sam Houston, Texas. To be trained as a Medic.

His mother was frightened out of her wits. With good reason, he realized, when he got his orders for Vietnam. She believed what was happening was unnecessary. And Jeff's fault. Both were true. His father had similar views. With the added speech on how if he had only at least finished his senior year, he could have gone into the Army as an officer, instead as an enlisted man.

Doctor Katz had been an officer during the "Big War." Although he didn't say so, Jeff had never envied his father's WWII rank. Telling people what to do had never been his life's ambition. Especially when he later saw orders result in things worse than mere death - which he had previously, and falsely as it turned out - believed was the physician's greatest enemy.

128

Allan Cole & Chris Bunch

Now it was a shrapnel airburst, blinding a man Jeff had just stabilized after the guy'd lost both legs and his balls to a bouncing betty. A guy that was a friend of Jeff's and someone that unfortunately still might live.

At last all the empty safe ground talk was gone and they were reduced to mentions by his mother of people he had never heard of who had been divorced, or stricken with some dread carving away kind of disease since his absence. One of those long silences followed. No physicist had ever charted the infinity that falls between parent and child in such a circumstance. Experience, wisdom and absolute Tightness on one side. The world has changed and you don't know what you are talking about - I *think* - on the other.

Jeff's father cleared his throat. He lit up a cigarette. Offered Jeff one. It was a conscious, man to man thing. His father disapproved of Jeff smoking.

"About the party, Jeff... " his father began.

"I'm really sorry about that... " Jeff began.

"Nothing to be sorry about," his father interrupted, but without enormous conviction.

"No, Jeffrey. Not at all," his mother joined in. "Of course, it was a real coup to get Art's Catering on such short notice. And I spent four solid days phoning all our friends... who canceled their own plans... And I had to fire the gardener, because he wouldn't... "

"... Your mother worked very hard on your welcome home party," his father broke in.

"It was nothing... no trouble at all," she said. "I had to buy new china anyway."

"Sorry," Jeff said again.

Damn. He was always saying that.

"We're the ones to blame," his father said. "We've spent the last twenty four hours talking about this, son. A hard twenty four hours. And you know what? We realized that we had forgotten what it was like to be young. With a war on."

"We had a pretty rough war ourselves, Jeffrey," his mother said. "Of course, in those days, we all knew what it was like to sacrifice. There was simply no place for decent people to live in Washington D.C., even those who were assigned to important advisory posts like your father was. But I made do.

"Goodness, gracious, the flat we lived in was filthy. It had..." Jeff knew she was going to say "... roaches so big the DDT wouldn't kill them... and

129

once..." Jeff knew she was going to say "... I saw a rat! In the alley right behind the building, if you can imagine such a disgusting thing."

The last time Jeff had seen a rat, it was breakfasting on a dead American's face. But he didn't think it was wise to get into rat comparison stories with his mother.

"So, dismiss the party from your thoughts, son," his father said. "I remember what it was like when I was mustered out. The pressure is suddenly off. You're confused. You need time to get your thoughts straightened out. To set your goals fresh in your mind again.

"Son. We're going to give you that time. Kick up your heels a little. Take all seventy two hours, if you like. Heck, take four days!"

"Thanks," Jeff said. Dry. Sorry again soon as he caught the tone in his own voice. But they didn't notice.

"All this has been our fault," his mother said. Jeff was wary. His mother never took blame. "We pushed you too hard in school... I told your father that at the time..." Jeff's mind eased as she shifted blame.

"We should have let you get married, son," his father said. "Oh, I suppose everything we discussed then was correct - in its way. But, like I said, we weren't remembering what it was like to be young, with a war on."

"We were in a hurry ourselves," his mother giggled.

"So, we talked all night," his father continued, "and we came up with a new plan. One we know you're going to like."

"Oh?" Jeff was afraid to say more.

"You and Rachel can get married right away," his mother gushed. "Her parents agree. We talked last night."

"What about..."

"School? No difficulty there. I've pulled some strings, son. I have you signed up for the Fall semester. And... a real victory, here... the Dean says you can challenge any course you like. Hit the books hard this summer... "

"After the honeymoon..." his mother said, blushing.

"Yes... after the honeymoon, " his father said. "And you can probably do the entire year in one semester. Then it's on to medical school and never look back."

They were both beaming at him. Love and kindness shining through their eyes. Jeff stomach lurched. He felt ill. They had seen to his every need. He was pinned. Nailed to the floor of the fancy hooch they called the Mark Hopkins Hotel. What could he say? What could he do? Hell, right now, he couldn't even remember what his home looked like. Even Rachel's face was a fuzzy memory.

"There's one other surprise," his mother said.

Jeff stifled a groan. What more could they do to him?

"Rachel's waiting downstairs," his mother said.

"Say fu... I mean, who... Uh..."

"I told you he'd be surprised," his mother said to his father. "Tell your father how surprised you are, Jeffrey."

"I'm surprised, father," Jeff, the obedient son, croaked. Actually, he thought he was having a heart attack. A band tightened across his chest and it was difficult to draw a breath.

"I reserved a room for her at the hotel," his father said.

"For appearances," his mother giggled, "see how modern we really are, Jeffrey, dear? We understand what you're both thinking. And what's wrong with it, I say? What's wrong? You're engaged to be married, after all. It's only human to have... feelings. Rachel's mother... you know what a sensible woman Sal is... sends her blessings."

His father checked his watch. "Your mother and I have a flight to catch home," he said.

"We'll leave you two lovebirds alone," his mother said, wiping an eye and touching a sniffle at her nose with a lace kerchief.

"Don't worry about the expense," his father went on. "The whole weekend is on us. For both you and Rachel... *and* your friends!"

"Although I don't think he'll be seeing much of them, will he, dear?" his mother giggled.

"Not if I know my son," his father said, giving Jeff a knowing, manly wink."

"Wait a second," Jeff said. It was almost a strangled shout. His startled parents looked at him. So stunned, that Jeff's anger balled itself tighter into guilt.

"Uh, sorry, Mom and Dad. Uh... I'm just not used to…" his voice trailed off.

The kind smiles reappeared. His parents rose to depart. Hugs and kisses from his weepy mother. Hugs and claps on the back from his father. In a minute they were going to be gone and Jeff would be stuck with all those decisions in his behalf.

"About Rachel," Jeff began.

"She's waiting for you downstairs in the cocktail lounge, son," his father said.

131

"Go to her, Jeff," his mother said. "Sweep her off her feet. That's what a woman wants in times like this... But be gentle. Be gentle."

"But not that gentle, Jeff." His father made with another knowing wink.

They were gone. Jeff slumped on the couch. His emotions as flat as if he had just been run over by a tank.

Nearby, a door creaked.

Tyrell and Nebraska crept into the room.

Jeff looked up at them. If someone made a joke, they were dead. But the faces staring down at him were full of sympathy.

"You heard?"

"Most of it," Tyrell said. "Except what you were saying... didn't hear much of that."

"Nobody ever does," Jeff said.

"I take it you don't hold with every bitty thing they got in mind for you," Nebraska said.

"You got that right."

"You shoulda asked for a last cigarette and a blindfold," Nebraska said. "Old son, they tore you every which way but loose. But, look on the plus side... "

Nebraska's wave took in the posh surroundings... "at least we'll be doin' it on your old man's tab."

"No damn way," Jeff said. Firm.

"But... " Tyrell tried to but...

"Nope. Not a penny will I take from my father."

Nebraska sighed. "If that's the way it's gotta be. Still, Jeff. Sure would be a whole lot... "

But Jeff suddenly remembered... "Oh, my God. Rachel! She's... downstairs... Waiting for me... Guys, you just got to help me out."

Very dubious looks greeted this announcement.

"Like what?" from Tyrell.

"Like... come with me... I mean, how mad can she get at me in front of two perfect strangers?"

"Whatcha got in mind?" Nebraska asked.

"The marriage is off," Jeff said. "I mean, we were real young when all this started. And maybe our folks were right the first time... And I've been thinking that I really ought to see more of the world, before I... "

"If that's what you plan to say to that woman..." Tyrell said, "... who

132

Allan Cole & Chris Bunch

happens to be a fiancée type female person... with probably her nightie packed and such... count me out. And don't give me any garbage about not getting mad in front of two strangers."

"She'll tear the roof off, man," Nebraska said. "No way. You got your sights set on twister territory... Fine. But me and Tyrell are headin' for the storm cellar."

"So, what am I supposed to say?"

"Same thing you told us," Tyrell said.

"Except, not so direct, like," Nebraska said. "You know, hit it from the side. Give your wheel a jiggle afore you go over the hump. Otherwise, she'll throw ya."

"Gee. Thanks, guys. Give me a damn break! What do you mean, don't hit it direct? Give my wheel a jiggle... What kind of advice is that?"

"Best we got," Nebraska said as he slid out the door.

"Good luck," Tyrell said. "Meet you at the FBI Girl later - if you survive."

"Cowards!" Jeff railed. But Tyrell had already slammed the door.

Rachel sat in the far corner of the lounge. It was nearly empty, except for the bartender and a few morning lushes who kept their thoughts to the glasses in front of them.

She was small, dark and dazzling pretty in a pink mini outfit cut just above the knees and hugging the round little figure he now remembered very well. It was what had gotten him in this trouble in the first place. He had been barred from anything more than some torrid groping until the night of the ring party. And she hadn't disappointed. Even inexperienced, Rachel fairly sizzled in bed. The first few times, that is. Until her mother discovered the birth control pills during the big debate about their engagement.

Out of guilt Rachel had cut them both off until the week before Jeff went into the Army.

Jeff flashed on a song from last night - maybe it was last night: *...Days of wine and roses/Laugh and run away...* It was a melancholy throbbing in his head. Distant string instruments that darkened the mood.

Rachel gave him a wan, tentative smile that was so out of character, Jeff found his nerve dissolving. In the past, she would have made a great public display, squealing like a little girl, running across the room to fling herself into his arms. Apparently skipping the party and their Whittier reunion yesterday didn't go down as easily with Rachel as it did with his folks.

"Hi, Jeff, " she said... but so shyly. What was going on?

"Hi, Rach," Jeff said, feeling like he had just entered the Twilight Zone.

He leaned over to kiss her. Their lips touched. Then, Rachel suddenly grabbed his head and gave him a hard, long kiss. She pulled away just as abruptly. Turned her head to cover emotion. Feeling weirder and weirder, Jeff sat.

He flashed on the chaos that had been his favorite bazaar hangout until a few days ago - a shack with blaring stereo, tin roof, guys half naked in the heat, swilling beer that was warm all too often when the ice didn't get through and grab assing. Others that sat silent in their thoughts and filth caked fatigues.... brooding out through tunnel eyes to nightmare distances. Whores working the crowd. Distant thunder of guns softening up some jungle that would probably be air assaulted by the Big Red One tomorrow. Where more Grunts would go down, screaming and bleeding and Jeff would be darting through the madness with his aid pack, trying to save a few of the lives America seemed determined to throw away.

Then he was back with Rachel again, in the cool dark bar. With only rich drunks, a bored bartender, and a girl he could barely remember. Hell, Jeff wasn't sure who he was himself at this minute, acid flashbacking to last night... ".. given you a number... taken away your name..." ... and back to the present again.

This was a homecoming he had never imagined. And Jeff had many months to imagine a whole lot of different things.

The bartender wandered over and took his order. Jeff had a Bloody Mary. Rachel kept nursing her coffee and Tia Maria. She looked up after his drink came and made with another of those wan smiles.

"Well... here we are," she said.

"Yeah... I guess we are," Jeff managed.

"You talked to your parents?" she asked.

"Yes I did." Non committal. Very good, Jeff. Progress. Sure, it's only tone of voice. But a guy had to start some place.

"They really are doing the best they can for us, Jeff," she said. "Both of our parents."

"I suppose they are," Jeff said. The image of the ten foot man stalking him down the midnight streets blew past him in black frock coat and

134

mocking laughter.

Without warning, Rachel suddenly sobbed an excuse me and bolted from the table for the Ladies. Leaving Jeff sucking much wind and gaping after her. He'd figured she might be pissed over this current little adventure, but jeesh. He must have really broken her up. You are one big damn heel, Jeff Katz. Quit screwing with the poor girl. Leading her on.

You've got to tell her right now:. I'm sorry, Rachel, but it's over. It can't work... blah, blah, blah. No, too heavy.

Leave a tad of hope. Like: I need time to get my head straight... Maybe you ought to see other people... Not fair of me, otherwise... No, too wishy washy.

How about: I'm not the same person, Rachel, dear. Neither of us are. I'm not sure what I want to do with my life. I have strong doubts about being a doctor, as my father wishes. And it wouldn't be fair to you after all this time and agony waiting for my return... Yeah. Mucho better. Mature. To the point. And, omigod, here she comes again.

Rachel's eyes were red and she sniffled a little, saying she was sorry under her breath. Then, the dreaded silence. Twin to the one that had afflicted Jeff and his folks a short time back. Speak to her, man, Jeff shouted at himself. Speak to her! His vocal chords even flexed for the words. Hummed with the thought of sound like a guitar string picking up a low vibration.

Then: "We have to talk!" the four words came out so suddenly, that for a moment, Jeff didn't realize he had said it in chorus with Rachel. Weak laughter from both of them.

"You go first," Rachel said.

"No, no, you," Jeff - ever the gentleman - Katz said.

"Okay. Maybe I better," Rachel said, and the moment went so fast Jeff only dimly realized he just might have lost his only chance. It didn't stay dim long.

"I have a confession to make," Rachel said. "This is very hard for me to do. And I'm so very sorry I even have to say it. I honestly never thought of myself as the kind of person who would find herself in this situation."

She kept her head down and her eyes hidden as she talked. Jeff listened as she went on. Confused, at first. Then joy ringing in his heart.

Rachel had spent the last two months in Mexico. A college exchange program kind of thing. Yeah. Jeff remembered something about that a few letters back. So?

So, it seemed Rachel had met this Mexican university student - the son of a very good family, Rachel assured him. Oh, yes. Of course. He would be. Yes, indeedy boys and girls in the Peanut Gallery, he would, he wouldhewould. Oh joy, oh, bliss, Rachel had an affair an she was dear johnning his former olive drab behind in goddamned person!

You're free, Jeffrey Katz! You're free! As soon as she gets to the end of this convoluted explanation, you are once again a free man. But Rachel went on and on. She told him everything about the guy and all the places they went and what he looked like and how he sounded and would she ever just shut up and tell Jeff to get the hell out of her sight, her heart belongs to another.

It took several small forevers. Jeff wondered why she thought he needed every tiny detail. If it would have been him, he would have just... Well, at least he wouldn't have told her how tall the guy was and what were the color of his eyes. Maybe a Rachel type woman honestly believed he deserved to know all this. That she would wrong him terribly by not revealing All. Somehow, this would relieve his pain. Don't worry, Rachel, his mind pleaded. And, frankly, my dear, I don't give a fat... hoot. But he kept the deeply concerned expression sutured to his face.

"... and so, I really think under the circumstances, it would be wrong of us to continue seeing each other. Much less, get married."

You are absolutely right, Jeff thought. This Mexican guy is obviously a far better person. Dump me, baby! Dump me, now.

Then she went and spoiled it.

"Oh, Jeffrey," she wailed and tears that would humble a rainforest drenched. "I am such a terrible person. Such a slut! Oh, what you must think of me! I am so... so... sorr...eee...."

Jeff found himself sitting beside her, patting her as she wept in his shoulder saying there, there. There, there. He felt like an absolute shit. So big deal she falls into bed with a guy. Once. Like he had kept it in his pants the whole fourteen months.

"I know I'll never see you again, Jeff," Rachel sobbed, "But can you ever find it in your heart to at least forgive me?"

Freedom crept unnoticed out the door.

"Wait a second, Rachel," he said. "What's there to forgive? So you had an affair. Big deal. You were lonely. You are also a human being, for crying out loud. It happens. Especially in such a screwed up world."

Rachel looked up at him, her eyes filled with tears. Big, black, beautiful, how could you ever hurt me eyes.

"So... you... do forgive me?"

"If it makes you feel better, of course I do. But I still say there's nothing to forgive."

"Really?" Jeff missed the tone here.

"Really."

She threw her arms around him, burbling nonsense about how she really loved only him and the other guy didn't mean a thing... and she would never do anything like it again... she swore on their unborn children... and....

Ooops.

Children!

Leftover acid throbbed in his veins and visions of fetuses swam in his head. With great big eyes buds as dark as Rachel's. Oh, boy. There was Jeff getting married again.

How it happened, he would never know, but soon the table was covered with pictures of this darling little house her parents and Jeff's were buying for them and how she had picked out the furniture and hoped he liked the silver pattern... and, wow, do I have an idea... how about a pool...

"Mouse, mouse, mouse," the lady with the boa said, holding the head out at him with its beady eyes and flickering tongue. "Come here, mouse..."

"Rachel, listen to me," Jeff finally blurted. "I have to go. "

She looked up at him. Stunned. "Go? Go where?"

"Honey, I'm really sorry, but I promised some friends... "

Jeff used all the weasel words at his command. How important these guys were to him. How confused he was. Just getting home and all. Culture shock.

And really, he just needed these three days with his buddies and all would be well... Just give him these three days... please, understand... and so on and chicken out so forth.

Actually, what could she say? How could she object under this onslaught. Except make some meaningful hints about the delights that awaited them in the room upstairs. The one his father had rented them.

Still... unspoken between them was the affair with the Mexican student and Jeff's magnanimous to her, disaster to him, reaction.

So, instead of freedom, Rachel's affair only won Jeff a reprieve. He grabbed it like a drowning man. Put her in a taxi for the airport.

He sprinted through the shower, threw on his clothes and rushed off to meet Samantha as if he had hellhounds on his trail. Perhaps there were.

Jeff had no idea what would happen next. The song on the cab radio went: *We're Sgt. Pepper's Lonely Hearts Club Band/We hope that you enjoy the show/... Sgt. Pepper's Lonely/Sgt. Pepper's Lonely.../*Sat. Pepper's Lonely Hearts Club Band..."

CHAPTER NINE

NEBRASKA YAWNED LUXURIOUSLY. "I could learn to like this real easy," he said.

"Don't flake out on me, you hulk," Alexis said. "It's not even noon yet."

"A wicked, wicked lady kept me out past my bedtime last night." Nebraska turned his head on her lap and kissed Alexis' breasts through the thin dashiki top. Alexis squirmed, enjoying it.

"... If you're real lucky," she said, voice husky, "... I might do the same tonight. Assuming you're still up to it."

She slid one hand under the waistband of Nebraska Levis. "And that's no pencil in your pocket," she murmured.

"You keep doing that," Nebraska said, "and that Jesus-shouter is in for one hell of a surprise." He waved idly up at Beach Street, where the distant figure of a wild-eyed preacher held forth. They could just dimly hear him damning all the sinners in the world.

"Hey, Mister Preacher Man," Nebraska suggested. "Best you flee them works of the flesh like fornication that appear to be coming up." The lay preacher kept on. "He's not listening."

"That's all right," Alexis said. "He's there with his soapbox, unrighteousness, sickness, maliciousness, covetousness, envy, murder, debate and a bunch of other nesses I can live without, like it says in Romans... "I guess I can hang tough with a little fornication."

"Not bad," Nebraska said. "Knowing your Bible that well. Bet you started singin' in the choir."

"Sure. And then I got old enough to figure out what the preacher was saying between hymns, and then listened to all that judging in the hymns themselves. Better a little balling between friends," she said, "than all that jive about killing folks who don't pray the same way you do."

"Lady," Nebraska complained gently. "Not only are you getting uptight and taking it out on me... but I've already been circumcised."

"Sorry." Alexis looked a little sheepish.

Nebraska sat up, and looked around. They were lying on the grass in Aquatic Park. The water of the Bay was very blue, as blue as the cloud-flecked, sunny sky overhead. There was flute music floating through the air - coming from a longhaired young man sitting in a tree, happily playing for his own and the great god Pan's pleasure.

The remains of an early picnic lunch was nearby. Nebraska started cleaning up.

"Police up your brass and ammo, and move to the break area," he said. "You know, you've sure spoiled me for Good ol' American Legion Nebraska burnt hotdogs and yellow potato salad picnics."

Their meal had consisted of a Dungeness crab purchased live on nearby Fisherman's Wharf and steamed on the spot, then cracked and cleaned. While it was steaming, they'd hurried down a few blocks and scored a large loaf of sourdough French bread, fresh from the oven. Butter, some mayonnaise, paper napkins and a bottle of Wente Brothers Gray Riesling completed the menu.

"Didn't think you'd like crab," Alexis said. "Most folks from the Midwest get a little freaky, presented with something that wasn't on their menu growing up."

"I," Nebraska bragged, "will eat anything that isn't trying to eat me."

Alexis looked ostentatiously innocent.

"Even then, there's some exceptions I can think of," he said, trying to Groucho his eyebrows.

Alexis kept ignoring that and helped him gather debris, lug it to a trashcan and they started back toward her car.

They passed an entwined couple, who were as oblivious of the Jesus freak as anyone. Next to the couple's blanket, a transistor radio played softly:

... *Did you ever have to make your mind/ To pick up with one and leave the other behind...*

"Kind of nice down here," Nebraska said. "Not too crowded."

"Today's only Friday," Alexis said. "So all we've got are the summer tourists. Tomorrow, we'll get the weekenders. Wait till you see what the Haight will look like then.

"Speaking of which," she said, "anything you especially want to do? I've decided... I'm your self-appointed Gray Line Tour Guide."

"I *had* plans yesterday," Nebraska said, "... and I ended up getting chased by cops and fed by gangsters. Then I quit making plans... and look what happened to me."

He put an arm around Alexis. "What've you got in mind?"

"Hang out," she said. "Down on the Haight. I've got to run by the Dead

140

House and pick up a power lead for Mister Funk. We're gigging tomorrow night at The FBI Girl. And I'm supposed to do some kind of interview at the Underground. Maybe see if there's a party. Or what's going down in the Park. Just generally groove."

"Sounds great to me," Nebraska said. "I'm nothing but your sex slave, anyway."

"Kind of a shame," Alexis said, "that you've got to go back on Sunday."

Nebraska shrugged. "You'd get tired of me," he said with a grin. "Besides, it'll be nice to get home," he said. "It's been a long fourteen months."

"I thought the way the song went was, *'How You Gonna Keep ^xEm Down on the Farm/After They've Seen Paree.'* Or something like that."

"Not me. I'm just a shitkicker, Alexis, not a city boy. The family farm... my great grandfather homesteaded it, way back when. A hundred sixty acres the government sold him... and we built from there.

"Beneath this sophisticated, dee-bonair, definitely Cary Grant type exterior..." and Nebraska deliberately stumbled, "...is Jethro Bo-deen, Boy Hillbilly!"

He recovered his balance after some mock arm windmilling.

"You're trying to get somebody to stay on," Nebraska continued, "Work on poor Jeff. Now *there's* a cat that maybe oughta stay here in San Francisco."

"I'm not sleeping with him," Alexis said. ""Besides... I still haven't met your friends. Are they going to be on the Haight?"

"Probably," Nebraska said. "Tyrell for sure. Jeff after he gets through with his fiancée."

Alexis' expression was an unqualified Huh? Nebraska explained as much as he knew about Rachel and Jeff's family, and the more that he'd guessed. When he was done, Alexis shook her head.

"Wow," she said. "You never think of somebody... your friend's what, about the same age we are... somebody getting trapped this young. But... How much is he trapping himself?" She frowned, thinking about Jeff's dilemma. Then: "Sorry... I didn't mean that like it sounded."

"I don't know if you're not right," Nebraska said. "Hell. How much do we *all* trap ourselves? For all I know, maybe I ought to say screw the farm, drop out like those posters say, and try to get a job here... maybe driving the band's truck or something."

Allan Cole & Chris Bunch

Alexis' smile disappeared. "Something to think about, farmboy. Isn't it?" she said seriously.

No, it hadn't been a dream, but Tyrell still had to pinch himself as Sunshine saw him and called out his name. She wore a pure white tunic cut just above midthigh, belted at the waist with a black cord - Grecian style - and a black headband held her golden hair. Sunshine floated off the landing, down the steps and into his arms. She didn't weigh a thing and he swung her off her feet and held her close as she covered his face with kisses.

Then Tyrell heard a little groan and felt dampness on his shoulder. Sunshine was crying. He put her down and she turned away.

"What's wrong, Sunshine?" he asked. "What'd I do?"

She turned back to him, weeping, trying to stop and shaking her head because she couldn't.

"Nothing's wrong," she said, finally sniffling to a stop. "I just get that way sometimes. You know, so full of stuff you... just get... overcome..."

Sunshine stepped into his arms again and he held her.

"See... I was watering the plants," she explained to his chest, not wanting to look him in the eyes and start the faucet going again, "... waiting for you to come... and then I thought... what if he doesn't... I don't know what I was thinking... Stupid stuff. Then you came after all and..." She straightened herself. Squared her shoulders.

"I'm okay, now. See. No big deal." She flashed him a big Sunshine smile.

"Don't feel so weird," Tyrell said. "I was worrying about the same kind of thing. I thought, okay, you got real lucky last night, Tyrell. Met a woman who happened to be in this great mood that included you... But, this morning, she's gonna think a second' time and probably hide in the closet until you go away."

"Ha! Fat chance," Sunshine said. "See, before I started thinking that stupid stuff I told you about, I was remembering... " she leaned close to him... a shy whisper... "what we were... doing last night."

Tyrell grinned. "Like what?" he teased.

"You know," Sunshine blushed... but he could tell she was teasing back.

"No I don't. Tell me." Tyrell was feeling better and better.

She leaned to whisper in his ear again, the few words came so fast he could hardly make them out, but the hot rush of perfumed air stirred him

142

powerfully.

"Uh... say, Sunshine, honey?"

She felt his hardon pressing against her and giggled.

"Why, whatever could you have on your mind, Sirrah?" She murmured.

"Oh, I was sort of thinking... maybe we might just get held up for a little bit. I thought I saw something needed fixing up in your apartment."

"Oh, you *did*, Tyrell," Sunshine laughed. "You most certainly did."

She spun and ran up the stairs, Tyrell laughing and stumbling after her.

...*your debutante has what you need/But I have what you want*...

Samantha came strolling down the street to meet him. She had one of those unintentional hip rolling walks that make strong men weep. Behind him, the outside speaker of Tracy's Doughnuts blared:

...Lil' Red Ridin' Hood/ You sure are lookin' good/ To me....Ahhooooo!....

She wore a sheer white blouse with twin pockets decorated with blue embroidered daisies. The shirt tails were tied up snug into a halter. Her breasts moved freely -dark nipples doing a peek-a-boo dance behind the flowers. Beneath those tantalizing breasts was a dazzling expanse of bare flesh, tucking into a miniscule waist and flaring into painted-on hip hugging jeans. A big white Panama hat with a beaded Indian head band framed her face.

What's more, the eyes that looked out from that face were full of fun and delight at seeing him.

He knew he was gaping at her, but he couldn't help himself. Just as he couldn't help being struck suddenly and massively dumb by the image of Rachel's sad face staring out at him from the cab window, superimposed over all this loveliness greeting him.

It was remorse that gripped his heart, not lust. Some stud you are, Jeff Katz, came the bitter thought.

She gave him a wicked little grin as she came up to him and without saying a word, she went up on her toes and gave him a long and decidedly unchaste kiss. Unbound breasts and slender form crushing against him. Then she stepped back to review the results.

"That," she said, "was to start the day off right. When you left this morning I decided to skip the whole first date, second date fumbling around and feeling stupid... I have plans for you, Jeffrey Katz."

The little wicked grin flashed again. "Unless you have some objection?"

Confession rose in his gorge and spewed out: "I can't do this, Samantha."

"Do what?"

It all came out in a tumble.

"To lead you on like this... Look, my whole life's a big twisted mess right now. Everybody wants some kind of decision from me. My father with the doctor business. ... my mother with the she was young once, stuff... Rachel and the Mexican and the house our folks are gonna buy without ever even asking me and... hell, there's probably folks I never even *heard* waiting in line to tell me to get my butt on track... except it's always their track... And I don't know what I'm going to do... So why don't you be real smart and tell me to turn around and kick me in the behind like I deserve and don't waste your time on a dope like me."

Samantha peered up at him, an eyebrow raised. "If that was the short version," she said, "boy is this going to be a long day."

"You... mean... you're not mad?" Jeff was confused.

"First, I have to understand what you're trying to say," she laughed. "When I get that far, believe me, you'll know if I'm mad."

"So, I shouldn't... just go?"

"Not after that, you don't. I know a good soap opera when I hear one. Come on. Let's hear the rest... But first, buy me a cup of coffee and a jelly doughnut. Come to think of it, this sounds like a *two* jelly doughnut problem."

He bought the coffee and the doughnuts and they sat on the curb and Jeff spilled his guts. It wasn't as hard as he thought it would be. As he talked, he couldn't help but compare Samantha's intelligent interest and sympathetic questions, to Rachel's constant obsession with her own problems. Also, Samantha seemed so confident about everything. Steady. But with a sense of adventure, which Rachel had always certainly lacked.

Before he knew it, he was done. He looked shyly over at Samantha, awaiting her verdict.

It was quick. "To start with, Jeff, what do you think all that has to do with me?"

This jolted him. "Uh... well... Rachel and I... "

Allan Cole & Chris Bunch

"... Are going to do whatever it is you decide to do. Frankly, I think you behaved admirably. If you had said something else to her about the affair, I'd have spit in your eye and taken you up on that ass kicking offer.

"Next question, before we go back to the first, how betrothed do you feel?"

"Not very," Jeff confessed. "In fact I feel kind of..."

"Manipulated?" she broke in.

"I don't know... yeah... maybe I do."

"Boy am I glad that light bulb finally went on, buster," Samantha said.

"What light bulb?"

"The GE 150 Watt guaranteed a lifetime of manipulation, kind. Got a special this week, didn't you hear. With ten percent off that low low price for guys just off the plane from Vietnam.

"As far as I can tell, you had about fifty or more people waiting at that welcome home party just begging to help your parents and poor, little defenseless Rachel hogtie you and haul you off to suburban paradise. The smartest thing you did was run like blazes."

"Really?"

"Trust me... So, they followed you. Surprised you in your room. Put the girl with the sad story downstairs to back them up."

Jeff thought about this a minute. Then he realized how right she was. Oddly, he wasn't angry. He could see it was behavior none of the people in question could help... or change. Little pearls of victory shone at her lips when Jeff finally nodded, getting it.

"But, I still don't know what to do," he said. "... What I want to do, that is."

Samantha stuck out a hand. "Welcome to the club," she said. "When you figure it out, let me know."

"I can't really believe that," Jeff said. "You seem so... "

Samantha giggled. "Sure of myself? Wow, do I have you fooled! Now, let's get back to my first question. What does any of this have to do with me... and you... right now?"

"But... I'm sort of... entangled... "

"Will being with me make it worse?"

Jeff had to be honest: "I don't think so. But... "

"Stop it with the buts. One thing at a time. Now, let me tell you my situation. I wasn't looking for a steady boyfriend when I met you. Heck, I

145

wasn't looking for <u>any</u> kind of boyfriend."

"Don't you want to get married someday?" Jeff asked.

"Let's put it this way," Samantha said. "I never saw myself married. On the other hand, I never saw myself <u>not</u> married, either. I'm not all that interested in motherhood and children, although I suppose I could be persuaded.

"I have my own set of stupid confusions. Like what I want to be when I'm grown up. I found out I was good at languages at college. I got my degree, with some kind of vague idea of working for world peace... and if that isn't a joke, I don't know what is. Besides, there's not much you can do with a degree in modern languages. If you're a woman, anyway.

"So right now, I'm more or less contented being a stewardess, seeing the world and meeting all kinds of odd people. Sometimes I think of quitting and joining the Peace Corps. Sometimes I want to say to hell with the whole thing and just drop out and go with the flow, as they say.

"The only thing that keeps me from going quite mad, when I'm in those moods, is remembering when I was a little girl that I wanted to be rodeo rider and my father and mother gave me a toy nurse kit instead of a pony. I threw such a tantrum, they hid the kit. I still never got that pony, but believe me, brother, nobody ever asked me to be Florence Nightingale again."

"I believe," Jeff said, fervent. This was not a woman people told what to do. But Samantha was just getting warmed up and veered back to the subject of boys and girls together.

"To be perfectly honest," she said, "I've learned over the last year or so that I'm quite content to be alone. I'm not a hermit, but I enjoy my own company. I like doing what I want, when I want. I don't mean to sound like I'm boasting, but a few men have asked me to marry them. And so far, I've not been sorry I said no."

"I'm sure not," Jeff couldn't help but say.

"So here we are," she went on, "on a bright summer morning in San Francisco... And if you think you've been manipulated before, watch what's going to happen next.

"... Because I want you to look at me right now, Jeffrey Katz. Look at me. And tell me that if you leave this minute - no matter what happens later - you won't regret it the rest of your life."

Jeff looked. Saw the delicate little bridge of freckles across her nose. He could not lie.

"I would never forgive myself," he said.

Allan Cole & Chris Bunch

"And I'd never forgive you either," Samantha said.

The way she laid her hand across his arm, fingers warm and curling slightly on his bicep, he knew she meant every word she said.

... Wild thing... the music blared from Tracy's... *You make my heart sing... You make everything... Groovy...*

....Just get a guitar/That's what you do...

Nebraska turned the volume down on the car radio. "I forgot to congratulate you."

"On what?" Alexis was concentrating on the suddenly-heavy traffic around them.

"Your record deal. Or was that guy last night just tripping?" Nebraska was proud of himself for this last - the new words were coming easily, just as easily as the old ones - shortimer, ETS, lifer - were falling away.

"I guess we're gonna be rock 'n' roll stars like the song says... Assuming the group holds together."

"Why wouldn't it? Oh. Is *that* what you were saying, about that guy with the cittern back at Gramps?"

"Tripster is what he calls himself. Christened Xavier Aloysius Murphy, so maybe it's better like that. Yes... and no. Me and him, well, we. used to live together. He's a guy who likes to get it on with just about anything that comes along.

"That's okay. I guess. Then he gives me the clap, which is very much *not* okay... And the last bit is when we were playing LA a few weeks ago. He comes bustin' in the hotel room screaming and shouting and throwing shit."

"Was he stoned?"

"Of course. But that wasn't why he was freaking out. I had... company. Which I figure is none of his business."

Once again, Nebraska was reminded that Alexis was not defined by his hometown's rules, and if he tried to apply them he would end up with some very ugly, very false labels. The second reminder was of what Alexis had said about the jesus-jumper, back at Aquatic Park. Nebraska had never had much truck with preachers or churches either, primarily because of all those labels they wanted to put on people who maybe were doing things a little different. And why hadn't he said as much to Alexis? Hell, they had to have *something* in common.

Alexis glanced at him, as if waiting for some kind of response. Oops. He'd been on his own trip there.

"Sorry," he apologized, quickly and creatively coming up with a lie. "I was just sort of being amazed that this guy would screw up something like a record deal... Which I don't know much about music, but it's gotta be important, because... because you two aren't... uh, together anymore."

"If he does, he does," Alexis said. "A&M signed all of us, not just him. There's only about a zillion blues guitarists walking the streets looking for a gig. But maybe they think *he's* the star, and that'll blow the deal. Then the deal's blown. Things happen that way. I walked away from that folkie group that brought me here... and there'd been talk that Vanguard was interested in us.

"If Mulberry Street breaks up, that's karma. It wasn't meant to be. So I'll cast the coins and try again."

She broke into a staccato song/chant:

...Ring bell, hard to tell/If anything is goin' to sell/...Join the army if you fail/Look out kid, you're gonna get hit...

"Like that," she said.

Nebraska did not understand that kind of thinking at all. To him, it would be like seeing cornborers hit an entire field, shrugging and say okay, we'll grow tomatoes next year.

"Why, if you don't mind the stupid question, did you name the group Mulberry Street?"

"Not necessarily stupid at all," Alexis said. "There's a pseudo doper's group floating around right now that calls itself Strawberry Alarm Clock, which is Pu-sy-ka-del-ic, and all they're really playing is Paul Revere and the Raiders kind of teenybop shit. No way can you tell me that group came up with the name with any better reason than wanting to sound like they're serious acidheads.

"Mulberry Street is named quite logically. Remember Doctor Seuss? The kid's writer?"

"Oh. Yeah," Nebraska did remember. "So it's "...and to think that I saw it on Mulberry Street.'"

"You mean you *do understand*." Alexis marveled. "Hell, we came up with the dumb name fried on Owsley White Lightning because it was better than White Trash, One Spade, Ripping Off Boogies' Blues.

"You sure," she questioned, "you aren't some kinda closet ex-beatnik hipster freak?"

"I'll never tell," Nebraska said, smiling in a mock superior manner. He looked out the window. Beautiful, beautiful day.

Allan Cole & Chris Bunch

A face was looking at him from the next lane. Tightassed, angry glower. A woman, in her 50's. Sitting next to her, at the wheel of a five year old Rambler, was what had to be her husband, who was giving Applegate an equally baleful eyeball blast.

What'd I do, Nebraska wondered? Then he got it. It wasn't him. It was the Porsche. His mind listed several Instant Pissoff Factors:

1. A brand new, very expensive car.

2. A brand new, very expensive car, being driven by someone under the age of senility.

3. A brand new, very expensive car being driven by someone *female* under the age of senility.

4. A brand new, very expensive car being driven by someone female under the age of senility who not only obviously owned this car, but had so little respect for Private Property that she or someone painted the car with flowers, swirls, sunbeams and all the rest.

"Hey, Alexis," Nebraska said. "Don't take this car to Texas anytime soon, okay?"

"What are you talking about?"

"Never mind."

Nebraska started noticing other expressions - pissoff from the straight, older types. Grins and waves from longhaired or semi-longhaired kids. Shorthairs driving American iron, however, didn't see anything funny about the 911S, he noted as a Olds 442 gunned around them, passing as close as it could without taking off paint... Or maybe nothing funny about a car that could whip their Detroit iron asses off the line, through a curve or on a mindbend blast for top end.

Nebraska was suddenly not at all sure he was going to go ahead and buy that Pontiac Goat when he came home. Not if assholes like that ran around in musclecars.

Speaking of assholes, he thought, seeing Presidio San Francisco off to the left and a squad of fatigue-wearing soldiers marching along, and his hand came out of the window and the Automatic Finger sent a burst of six in their direction.

"Eat it, lifers!" he shouted.

None of the GI's bothered to look. They must be used to this kind of thing so close to the Haight Ashbury, Nebraska thought. He laughed.

"You know, day before yesterday, I was just like those guys and would've kicked my ass if I'd have gone and done something like that."

149

"That's San Francisco for you," Alexis said. "One way or another it's guaranteed to blow your mind,."

They were a few blocks away from The Haight when the red light went on. Alexis swore, and pulled the Porsche over.

She stared in the mirror as the cop got out. "Oh whoopie. Let's do the Hallelujah Chorus."

Nebraska turned to peer at the cop, trying to look unobtrusive. Fuck! It was the same one who'd been about to bust Alexis the previous night. Grancell? Something like that.

"May I see your license, please?"

"You ought to have it memorized by now," Alexis growled.

"And the registration, please."

Alexis, steaming, dug out paperwork.

"Afraid you made too close a lane change, Miss Saint John. Car behind you had to hit his brakes."

"For Christ's sakes," Alexis snapped. "We're doing five miles an hour stop and go, Grancell! Everybody's hitting their brakes!"

"You can mention that to the judge."

"Yeah," Alexis said.

Grancell walked back to his squadcar.

"Now he's gonna run me for outstanding warrants," Alexis said. "Which he did on Monday... the last time I got unlucky."

They sat. The interior of the Porsche got hot, and so did Nebraska. "Look," he said. "This is bullshit."

"No shit, Batman. Which my lawyer will straighten out. You wanna get out and go toe-to-toe with him?"

Nebraska knew better, of course. There'd never been a farmer, let alone a farmer's kid, who didn't think the Boys In Blue were on the Other Side.

Eventually Grancell came back, returned Alexis' license and registration. The he leaned in and pointed at Nebraska.

"You," he ordered. "Out."

Nebraska swallowed. But followed orders.

"Let's see some ID."

Nebraska took out his license, sweat and water stained from a year in his "elephant hide" wallet overseas.

"It's expired."

Allan Cole & Chris Bunch

"I know. I'll get it renewed when I get back home."

"Let's see something current."

Reluctantly, Nebraska took out his military ID.

"You in the service, huh?"

"No. Just got out." Nebraska tried to put himself on the cop's side. "Just back from Viet Nam."

Grancell didn't even flicker.

"You got any proof you're not AWOL? Or a deserter?"

Nebraska felt very much like thanking God for being a bit of a worrywart. He'd taken one copy of his separation orders and tucked it into his wallet... Along with his DD214, Release from Active Duty. He gave them to Grancell.

Grancell seemed more interested in Nebraska's very full wallet. "You're carryin' a lot of money, aren't you?"

Nebraska did not find it necessary to answer. Grancell gave the papers back. He returned to the Porsche, and extended his ticket book for Alexis to sign. She did. He tore off the ticket and handed it to her.

"Piece of advice," he told her. "You wanna be careful who you're hangin' out with." He shifted his gaze to Nebraska, then back to Alexis. "Accessory ain't hard to prove. And it's a hard fall... Consider yourself warned."

He walked back to the cruiser, got in, started the engine, and gunned away, leaving his red lights on for almost a block. Nebraska got back into the Porsche.

"What was that all about?" Alexis asked. "You got some dirty dark secret maybe I ought to know about?"

"Hell if I know what he meant," Nebraska said. "And I don't think I want to find out, either."

..Gonna be your chauffeur, baby/Goin' ride your little machine...

They pulled up near a large, gaudily psychedelicized Victorian mansion on Ashbury.

"The Dead House," Nebraska theorized. "Called that because The Grateful Dead live here. Right?"

"A couple more days, and you'll be the Gray Line Tour Guide," Alexis said.

"What is it? Some kind of commune?"

"Sometimes that, sometimes a crashpad, sometimes a party pad. Depends on the day, depends on the Dead, depends on the mood."

There were a couple of dogs and a naked child on the sidewalk in front of the house. Nebraska swore that all three of them were trying to dance to the wailing harmonic being played by the biker sitting on the steps.

The man wore cowboy boots, suede pants, and a button-decked cutoff Levi jacket. Nebraska noted the boots were snakeskin. The biker lowered the harp, rewarded himself with a shot of Jack Daniels from the open fifth beside him and eyed the pair approaching.

Without preamble: "Who's the citizen?"

"My current squeeze," Alexis said. "Calls himself Nebraska."

"Good handle," the biker type said, and sang gently, "Little boxes, fulla ticky-tack...'"

"He thinks his shit is together, Pigpen." Pigpen looked thoughtful. "Went an' jumped too fast, didn't I? Sorry, friend. Whatcha need, Alexis? Or you just come by to pass the time?"

"Mister Funk said you had a spare power cord."

"Yeah. C'mon in. Got it in the back."

The man stood, wobbled a little, and shoved the bottle of bourbon in Nebraska's direction. "Here, man. Settles out the rush."

It was a little early - and Nebraska wasn't that much of a hard boozer anyway, but he took the bottle and swallowed. Managed to suppress the cough. Pigpen led them inside.

The house was a swirl of paintings, skulls, skeletons and posters. On one wall W.C. Fields scowled over a tightly-held poker hand across a corridor at Winston Churchill, who seemed unworried by the scowl, probably because he was armed with a cigar and Tommy gun.

Music was at groundzero level. It was a sound unlike anything Nebraska had heard. An assemblage of raw noise, seemingly chosen at random.

Alexis shouted over it, to Pigpen: "Phil's awake, hey?"

"Yeah. Him an' his fuckin' Stockhausen."

Alexis noted Nebraska's bewilderment. "Electronic music. Phil Lesh... he's the bassman... writes it."

This was music, too. Nebraska disagreed, as, evidently did Pigpen: "Gonna run some Ma Rainey up his ass soon's I get control of my horizontal an' vertical," he announced.

Pigpen led them to a storeroom, filled with cased instruments,

Allan Cole & Chris Bunch

amplifiers and all the rest. He started sorting through stuff. He and Alexis carried on a shouted conversation, seemingly having no trouble communicating over the sonic caterwaul from the stereo. But Nebraska could only pick out a word here and there:

"... bummer of a... go."

"... last set, anyway. What... hurt?"

"Yeah... community... that shit."

"Well... they say," Pigpen was shouting, when suddenly somebody stopped slaughtering the pig and there was silence but his shout went on:

"... or anyway Freewheelin' Frank says, either they practice peace an' love or we'll go into a fit of fuckin' destruction., right?"

"*You* go into anything you want to," Alexis advised. "You've got Owsley bankrolling your ass. Me, there's any destruction, I'm gonna grab my amp and boogey out the back."

Another series of sounds began: This was overamplified breathing. Screaming. Echoed shouts.

The biker and Alexis finished their conversation, and Nebraska followed them out.

"Thanks, Ron," Alexis said.

"No problem," Pigpen - Ron? - said. "Oh. yeah. Tell Tripster to get his head out, or I'm gonna whop him."

Then, most courteously to Nebraska, "pleased to make your acquaintance. Guess I'll see you at The FBI Girl tomorrow. For the brawl."

Uh. Yeah.

They stashed the power lead in the Porsche's trunk, and went on foot on to Haight Street.

"What was all that about destruction?"

"Tomorrow's the last night for The FBI Girl," Alexis explained. "The pigs and the City have been fucking with them since they opened. Worse, even, than the Straight Theater scene. So the owners just finally said screw it, and they're gonna pack it in. Go grow dope in Nepal, or maybe smuggle pre-Columbian shit up from Yucatan.

"Saturday night'11 be finite But some people - like the Angels, like the politicos, like the Berkeley radicals, don't think we should roll over for the pigs... Some people want a confrontation."

This jolted Nebraska. It also confused him. "But how? With what? You mean... like a riot? Like Watts or something?"

"Or something."

"And you're gonna be playing there?"

"Promised. Matt and Flamingo have done us a lot of favors."

"Go back to this riot. You mean with guns?"

"Christ, I hope not. But if so... the Angels have more of them than the cops. Also, there's the Panthers from over in Oakland, although I don't think they give much of a shit what happens to hippies. Dealers. Freelance crazies... Nobody knows what could happen."

Alexis seemed slightly fascinated by the possibility of chaos.

Wonderful, Nebraska thought. Absofuckingwonderful. I get out of Vietnam with my young ass intact, go and fall in love with some singer who's gonna be doing the Main Theme From Combat, Live On Our Really Big Stage.

On the other hand, maybe there wasn't that much to worry about. To the City Fathers, The FBI Girl was probably just another dump dive. And, if they didn't bust heads at the really awful dives down on North Beach, why would they bother with a joint full of kids?

Still... He had to think on this.

And then they were on the Haight and he stopped thinking.

.

..chased our pleasures here/Dug our treasures there/Can't you still recall/The time we cried/Break on through to the other side...

They touristed along in the sunlight, with no particular place to go and no one in particular to see...

"Hey, Mister. Wanna buy an Oracle? Got the Barb, Trib. Oh. Hey, Alexis. Didn't know he was with you....

"You cats wanna score some really good skag? Army-issue?"

Alexis shook her head, and they went on, through the semi-crowds that flowed up and down, and back and forth across the street, darting or wandering between cars.

Brownian movement, Nebraska thought. Just like in physics class. Random movement among particles suspended in a fluid medium.

Correct, he thought. But the medium was not fluid, but smoke, he realized, incense/carbon monoxide exhaust/marijuana floating into his nostrils.

Shouted greetings. Excited waves. Underwater gestures with ragged claws in stoner recognition drifting in dope silence past the colored seaweed reaching up into the sky...

Allan Cole & Chris Bunch

Even the business names were Out There: I/Thou Coffee Shop. The Blushing Peony. The Print Mint. The Phoenix. Love Burgers. The Drogstore Cafe. In Gear. The...

"... howinhell do you pronounce that one?" Nebraska asked. "Mnasid... nasic... masidka?"

"Try Minsidika," Alexis advised. "And slur it a lot."

...Well the dealer is a man/With the lovegrass in his hand...

Two young men, a little younger than Nebraska, were just short of swinging out on each other.

"...You can't be doin' this," the first said. "Price of dope is ten dollars a lid, right?"

"Hey, man. Th' guy was a *straight*!!"

"I don't give a shit. Nobody said one price for freaks, one price for citizens. Hey, you were a shorthair once."

"I'm just doing my thing. So, back off."

"Okay. Okay. You do your thing. Charge whatever you dam' well want. But next time you wanna score off me, I'm gonna be doin' my thing. Which is twenny bucks a bag, an' you better plan on spaghetti, 'cause it's just likely to be oregano."

The second young man slumped. "Okay, man. Okay. You don't have to get *radical…*"

"…Speed. . .acid. . .grass? I got Simple Simon…

...And if you go chasing rabbits/And you know you're going to fall/Tell 'em a hookah-smoking caterpillar/Has given you the call...

Yeah. The Haight.

Tyrell found himself admiring the dancing young woman. She was not, he thought, pretty by any means. But graceful... he'd never seen a ballet, but thought this woman lithe enough to be partnered with that Nureyev cat.

She danced on a street corner, smiling in joy.

She had no partner and there was no music.

Passersby smiled, frowned, ignored and went on.

Sunshine looked on approvingly. "Dance is a fundamental human need," she said. "To deny that need is to become hostile, neurotic and menopausal."

Tyrell gaped at her. Was Sunshine really a 30 year old college

155

professor, or had she somehow memorized this from somewhere.

"Dance in your living room," she went on. "Dance in bed. Stick flowers in your typewriter and dance at the office. Dance at the supermarket with a smoking banana in your teeth. Dance in the streets.

"Dance beneath a diamond sky with one hand waving free."

She leaned her head against Tyrell's shoulder, smiled up at him, and they went on.

Across the street Tyrell spotted Nebraska and that singer chick. He waved. Looked for a way across. But the traffic was too thick... and Nebraska didn't spot them... and then he lost sight of his friend.

A shout echoed through the music and growl of engines:

"Hey! You a fuckin' boy or a girl with that hair?" Forced, hysterical laughter, buried under the angry gunning of a car engine.

Nebraska, trying to spot where the bummer shout had come from, wasn't watching where he walked.

"Hey," came the mild protest from below.

Nebraska looked down and felt like hell. He'd just stepped right into the middle of a masterpiece. Done in chalk on the cement sidewalk, was an immaculate rendering of the Golden Gate. Floating over it, haloed and sainted Beatles. Now with a large Footsmear as the Fifth Beatle. The bearded, scraggle-haired artist was looking up at him.

"Aw, shit, man. I'm sorry. Here, maybe we—"

An unconcerned wave. "Oh no, brother. That..." indicating the smear, "... is now part of my picture. All it needs..."

...and a hand gently went out, swirling, smearing, and moving across the Beatles' faces and now there were just ghostly figures above the bridge...

"... fog, maybe. Far out, man," the artist said. "Thanks."

"Tranks. Rainbows. STP. Yellowjackets. Grass."

The fat tourist scratched, and complained. "Ain't there nowhere around these hippies you can find a drink?"

"Pall Mall bar," a longhair said. "They pour doubles."

"Whyn't you get a fuckin' haircut?"

The longhair smiled. "Peace," he said, and drifted on.

Allan Cole & Chris Bunch

Alexis picked up a couple of fingerbells and chimed them in Nebraska's ear.

"Naw," he said. "You need something like that." He indicated a huge gong, in the back of the store, which was aptly named The Psychedelic Shop.

"Sure," Alexis agreed. "Just like in those old British movies. We hire you, get you to strip to the waist, and clang that bastard just before we go on... Eat your heart out, Grace with your goddamned tambourine!"

Nebraska bigeared a conversation between a very intense-looking, in a desperately mind-altered way, girl and the shop's manager.

"These are so groovy," the girl said, holding up beads.

"Yeah," the man agreed. "They're Indian. Just got them in last night."

"Far out. You know, maybe sort of string them... seashells between each one... use blue-dyed string. Wouldn't that look far out?"

Her expression changed, and she seemed to touch down on Planet Earth. "Yeah," she said. "Groovy."

But she put the beads down. She looked downcast, and turned away.

"Hey, wait a second, " the man behind the counter said. "Could you pay me tomorrow? Or Monday at the latest?"

The girl's expression brightened. "Yeah. Yeah. Petey's gettin' a money order from his folks. I could get them finished before the love in. Thanks, Ron. You're a groovy cat."

"A broke, groovy cat," the man said quietly. But gave the girl the beads.

...If you're qoin'/To San Francisco/Be sure to wear some flowers...

"Hey, man. You got a buck for some Night Train?"

The man scowled at Jeff. Looking, he thought, very much like the pictures he'd seen in Life Magazine of Syrians... just before the Israeli Army beat their ass for six days running.

At first he took it personally, then realized, the scowl was generic and seemed to include anyone passing on Haight Street, even those who entered his tiny storefront... a joint Samantha called a "head shop."

Interestingly, hanging just behind his head were four posters: One said **LOVE,** the second showed happy hippy nude dancers, the third was a couple making love captioned with **YOU GOT TO GIMME SOME LOVIN'** and the fourth was a picture of a nude teenager with an inviting

157

smile, with the swirling caption of **DON'T YOU WANT SOMEBODY TO LOVE...**

This man, Jeff thought, is really getting the message.

"Grass? It's Acapulco Gold, I swear."

"Yeah. A Love In, man! Sometime this afternoon. Up near Hippie Hill. Maybe the Airplane. Charlatans. Somebody said the Dead are back in town.

"An' the Diggers got lucky. Free Food. In the Panhandle."

"All right!"

A frantic young man bellowed at Tyrell as he sprinted past: "The narcs! They're coming! The narcs!"

Tyrell and Sunshine stepped out of his way and the young man and ran on, shouting his warning. Ripples of alarm... movement. Somebody ran across the street toward imagined safety... almost getting run down by a delivery truck.

Tyrell took Sunshine's arm, ready to pull her out of the way of these narcs, whoever they were. He looked around for danger: Nothing. There was nobody pursuing the man. At least, no one Tyrell could see.

There was laughter, tension breaking and then he saw two women in whiteface makeup, having trouble opening an invisible door, and very eager to explore the mimed joys waiting within.

....Summertime/Will be a love-in there...

A sign in a storefront: TAKE A COP TO DINNER. Somebody had crayoned next to it, on the white wooden wall: ONLY IF THE FUCKER PROMISES TO BE THE MAIN COURSE.

Enginegrowl and a shout: "Hey! Nebraska!" Nebraska turned and saw Angel Dick on his fatbob. Dick gunned the engine and glowered at the car in front of him. The driver suddenly decided to turn right before this iron monster behind him Did Something.

Dick pulled up next to Nebraska, put the shifter into neutral and shut down. Dick looked worried. "Hey. I heard some shit about you at Tracy's."

"About me?"

158

"Yeah. You know that fucker Grancell? Th' one who was tryin' to bust Alexis for the hash last night?"

"Yeah," Nebraska said. "He just pulled Alexis over, wrote her up and then warned her about keepin' bad company. Meanin' me. Why the hell's he on my case?"

"Who know? That bastard's just sort of floatin' around. Askin' questions. But weird kind of stuff. Like... askin' people if you've said anything about expecting some shit from Viet Nam... Or if you've been asking about Army AWOLs an' deserters."

"Huh?"

Alexis got it. "Just exactly the kind of shit that'll start rumors," she said. "Rumors that'll flash down the Haight in a couple of seconds.... This is not good... Sounds like Grancell's playing Lone Ranger on you, Nebraska."

"Man, that ain't right," he said. And got bitter, knowing laughter from the Angel and the singer. "Sorry," he said. "What's the matter with this Grancell guy, anyway?"

"There's stories," Dick said. "That his kid ran off with a spade. Or OD'd. Or his old lady got gangbanged. I figure all the stories are bullcrap. People don't need a reason to be pigfuckers, y'know?

"Grancell maybe thinks it's the Old West and he's Matt Fuckin' Dillon... gonna clean up Dodge single-handed. Or some kinda Bull Connors don't let the sun set on your ass here nigger kinda pimp. Not that it matters, really.

"It's like Kipling said," the biker continued. "Bullies are bullies 'cause they get off on it. They spend their free time thinkin' about it, an' their duty time practicin' it."

Nebraska was a little too concerned about his own ass to admire or even realize Dick's literacy. "What do you think I should do?"

"Get off the Haight'd be easiest," Dick suggested, watching Nebraska very closely. "Grancell's like a goddamned fightin' bulldog, once he decides he's gonna shaft somebody."

"Fuck that!" Nebraska blurted. "This is my party, an' I only got two more days till I gotta go home, anyway!"

Dick nodded. "Okay. You're gonna hold your mud. That's righteous. But if you're gonna be on the street, try to walk small. Keep an couple extra eyes in the back of your head. And don't be holdin', don't get planted, an' don't go in any front door that ain't got a back one close by.

"Grancell's real trash. He'll do anything to mess with you. Even if his cheap lies get you ripped off by some dealer or shanked by a punk.

"We'll listen for stories, an' if anybody starts runnin' shit down on you, we'll make 'em, like the reporters say, check their sources... Alexis, you know how to keep him straight."

"Yeah," she said.

"Dick... why you willin' to do this?" Nebraska wanted to know. "I mean, you aren't hot for my bod or anything."

The biker laughed. "It's summer time, man. Time to kick back, get loose an' see if you can't fuck with the squares' minds a little bit. 'Sides. Maybe you won't end up goin' back to the farm. Or you might come back to San Francisco.

"You might make acceptable-type scooter trash... Anyway. I gotta run an' pick the kid up from summer school... Hang loose."

He thumbed the kickstarter out, bashed it through, put the hog in gear and waited for a break in the traffic. It came - followed by a patrolling SFPD car. Dick flipped the cops the finger, gassed it as he took his foot off the clutch, and disappeared between two cars and was gone before the red light could come on.

"That cat," Alexis observed, "has a certain style about him."

Nebraska felt a flash of jealousy, then went back to his previous worries.

"Hell," he mourned. "Sometimes it seems as if just when things are going perfect, something's gotta come out of nowhere and rain all over your parade."

Alexis hugged him. "Come on, baby. Don't let yourself get bummed out. We'll figure out some way to fuck with ol' Grancell's head."

Nebraska knew she was just trying to cheer him up. But he privately decided she was telling the truth- Somehow, someway, Grancell's head *was* due for some rearrangement.

Come on, he thought. He's a cop! Stop playing games with yourself. Still...

He caught Alexis looking at him, a little concerned. Nebraska forced a smile and a laugh, put an arm around her, and they continued on, heading rather vaguely for Alexis' interview.

..The killer awoke before dawn/...He put his boots on/....He took a face from the ancient gallery./And he walked on down the hall...

Someone passed Tyrell a mimeoed leaflet: FREE FREE FREE FREE FREE FREE FREE FREE FREE FREE

CRASH PADS FOR TONIGHT
(A list of addresses followed)
Bring Love
Bring Food If You Have It
Please
No Drugs
The Crashpad You Protect
Might Be Your Home For Tomorrow
com/co

Jeff looked at a sign: IF SOMEONE ASKS TO SEE THE MANAGER TELL HIM HE'S THE MANAGER.

"This," Samantha explained, "is The Diggers' Free Store."

"Diggers?"

"Strange people," she whispered. "Real easy to not like. Arrogant. Play a lot of mind games on people. But they're some of the few people really doing something to feed all these kids who're coming here this summer. The Diggers, the Free Clinic, a couple of ministers."

Samantha spoke worriedly and loftily about the new arrivals on the Haight... almost all of whom were less than ten years younger than she was. And her attitude was right.

"Diggers, huh." Jeff thought about the guy who'd conned him - or helped him con himself - out of his jacket last night.

There was a basket. FREE MONEY. It was empty.

Jeff wandered down a clothing rack hung with everything from war surplus uniforms to bowling shirts to flowering Hawaiian nightmares.

At one end he saw what he was pretty sure was his old tie-dye jacket. He took it off the rack. Sure looked like it. It was a little dirty, the rivets a bit tarnished and greasy, but otherwise still brand new.

He wondered what had happened to the orphanannie he'd seen - or thought he'd seen - wearing it the night before. He hoped that if his memory was correct, she'd sold it rather than lost it or had it ripped off. He also hoped to hell she hadn't sold it for something other than what appeared to be the most common commodity.

"That's kind of nice," Samantha said of the jacket. "And it's in better shape than most of the other things here. Say! This sort of matches what you were wearing this morning. When I found you... napping on my doorstep."

Jeff thought he'd explain later.

The problem was how to reacquire his jacket. Between the way the kid had behaved last night, the sign and Samantha's warning, he was pretty sure he couldn't just make a contribution to the Diggers and walk out.

Sure enough:

Someone was holding up a book in front of the only longhair in the store who looked like he might be interested in being in charge.

"How much?"

"How much do you think it's worth?"

"Uh..."

"Come on. If you want it, you've got to have some idea."

"Seventy-five cents."

"That's the price, then."

Money exchanged hands.

"Hey. Anybody here need seventy-five cents?"

Mind games, indeed. Jeff pondered. He didn't know shit about these Diggers, but he suddenly remembered his brief infatuation with Zen back as a junior in high school, which had included wading through Professor Suzuki's introductory work.

He took out a ten dollar bill. He twisted it up like a spill. Walked up to the store's "clerk." Took out his Zippo.

He lit the money and handed the bill to the man.

The man examined it as the flames started to build. Unhurriedly then, he blew the fire out, and pocketed the tenspot.

Jeff slung the coat over his shoulder and, satisfied, left the store.

"Grass? Acid? I got real Sandoz, man."

Nebraska sipped his coffee and admired The Drogstore. Paisley tabletops, with very very antiquey-looking pharmacist's stuff around the walls.

Then he noticed the looks... They were coming from four longhairs in peacoats, lounging at a nearby table.

Alexis caught the glares, too. "Dealers," she whispered.

"So? How'd I shit in their messkit?"

Alexis had what was probably the answer: "I wonder if maybe Grancell dropped the black marble with them?" she said. "You know, the rumor spreading business I was mentioning?"

Allan Cole & Chris Bunch

"Oh. Yeah." Nebraska's mood deflated a little. But he refused to let it happen. He drained his cup and stood. "Come on. Let's split."

"Sure," Alexis said. "Besides, we're running late for my interview."

Jeff saw the olive drab sedan with the red light and the white lettering, and decided to stay well behind the two yellow-robed chanters while the MP car went past.

It couldn't be...

He chanced a look as the car passed.

Shit. It *was*. That goddamned lieutenant Nebraska had suckerpunched.

What the hell was he doing on the Haight?

CHAPTER TEN

*...Dandelion won't tell no lies/Dandelion will make you wise/Blow away
dandelion...*

SUNSHINE AND TYRELL lay curled around each other enjoying the
sun's warmth. They were lying about twenty yards from Haight, about
halfway up the hill that made up the vest pocket Buena Vista Park.

"Happy?" Sunshine whispered.

Mmmm, Tyrell mmmmed.

Wouldn't it be nice, he was thinking, if summer went on forever, and
somehow his wallet would never get empty and winter would never come
and it'd be real nice if his momma and brothers somehow had money and
sunlight all their own and no crackers and rent to worry about.

Come on, he thought. Straighten up. Like Sunshine's been trying to
teach you. You've got to groove on the moment... and let the rest go on
by.

"Hey, Sunshine," came the voice. "Who's the new brother?"

Tyrell opened his eyes. Standing over them, a Major Spectacle.
The dude was stone gorgeous, from his high, leg-fitting custom
made flowered boots to the multi-colored pants to the silk shirt that
looked to be styled after the flags of the United Nations to his scarf
to his handworked leather vest to the Afro blooming out to frame his
smiling face.

Sunshine bounced up and hugged the man. "This is Ty...Rell,"
she introduced. "Isn't he beautiful?"

Tyrell had never thought of, let alone heard himself described
that way. He sat up.

The other black grinned at Tyrell's expression. "M'man."

He knelt and held up his palm. Tyrell remembered the gesture,
and held his own out, flat.

"I," the fashion plate announced, "am Supersplib."

"No shit," Tyrell managed.

"Yeah," the man agreed. "Really freaks the straights and the
peckernecks out. Good for them to get a little out of their rabid-ass
head. Show 'em an' profile 'em."

"You are doing that, brother," Tyrell agreed.

Supersplib sat down, legs crossing and folding into almost a yoga stance. Sunshine curled up again, this time with her head in Tyrell's lap.

"Nice lady you have there," Supersplib said. "Just in case you haven't noticed."

Tyrell looked at him. How would he know?

"How long you been in town?"

"Since last night."

"Where you crashin'?"

"Mark Hopkins."

Supersplib goggled, then recovered.

"Well lah-de-dah-de-dah! Here I thought you was just a broke hippie like everybody else. Instead of bein' a richbitch."

"He's just stopped being a soldier," Sunshine explained... sort of. "And he needed to mellow out before he goes home."

"Ah," Supersplib said. "From Nam?"

"Yeah."

"You don't agree with Mister Ali? The Viet Cong called you nigger a lot? You kill a lotta gooks for Whitey?"

"Hey, man. I want to talk politics. I dig Ali... mostly. But I dig him as a boxer."

"Yeah," Sunshine said. "Don't bum us out, man."

Supersplib held up a hand. "You are right, you are right my brother and sister, and I am wrong and abusing your fine courtesy."

He dug into an inner pocket, and produced a large joint. "As a token of my wrongheadedness," and he fired it up.

"Uh... there's cops down there on the street."

"Fuck 'em," Supersplib said. "I am the wind. I am Mercury. I have wings at my heels. By the time they can climb that wall, lumber up here, puffin' an' pantin' like rhinoceroses, I am gone, gone, color me gone."

That sounded rational to Tyrell. He toked, handed the jay to Sunshine. "Whooo," he eventually admired.

"Not bad," Supersplib said. "Comes in from Kona. Might I ask, without offending, what form of servitude you just completed?"

Tyrell thought he understood.

"I was a paratrooper," he said, a bit proudly.

Supersplib's eyes widened. "I was not only being discourteous, but in desperate danger of being obliterated. I must learn to dance my dance more softly. And so you are going home. Which is where?"

Allan Cole & Chris Bunch

"Memphis."

Supersplib suddenly got very serious. "You goin' back to the *South*?"

"Where I'm from."

"Which you been *away* from," Supersplib corrected. "But I guess bein' in the Army's not much different than bein' in Klan Kountry."

Tyrell could have said yeah. But thought for a second. "No, man. Not where I was. Maybe... back in the rear, back where there's Rear Echelon Motherfuckers an' brass that's got time to mess with you... I hear they even got the Klan in some places. But not up with us line doggies. Not with the grunts."

"What?" Supersplib scoffed. "They give paratroopers sensitivity training? Give them a magic pill that turns them colorblind."

"Hell no. And we've got as many rednecks from Possum Corners Georgia as anybody else. But they ain't *that* dumb. They ain't gonna be callin' me a nigger, remembering next time out... beyond the wire... I'll be walking behind their white asses, cocked and locked and finger on the trigger."

"Ah. Of course. The sun is scrambling what little remains of my gray cells. Those that I have not scrambled with glee and that good Doctor Leary's chemicals."

"You're the first black hippy I've seen," Tyrell said. "I was starting to think there was some kind of weird color bar."

"There is, actually," Supersplib said. "See, if you're black like you and me, you are *born* with your back against the wall. Is that not correct? We don't need to grow our hair long or wear freaky costumes to get the straight world, which is a white world, thinking that we are dropping out. Just by being alive, we are dropouts of their so-ciety.

"That's what everybody here is doing," Supersplib said, "here on the Haight. Turning themselves into white niggers."

"Hey," Sunshine protested. "Not me. I'm just making a better world. Change my head, change my world. Can you dig that? You know... love? What nobody seems to doing now... with the bomb and hating people like the Russians... and all these wars all over the planet... and uptight people and all."

That was just about the longest speech Tyrell'd heard Sunshine make. It was also straight from her beautiful soul, so he was sort of disappointed that Supersplib didn't answer her. Just absently patted her, and took another hit... intent on his point with Tyrell.

"So I am not a hippie," he said. "I am a dealer."

Allan Cole & Chris Bunch

Tyrell should have guessed it. And it should not have bothered him. *Somebody* had to sell the stuff he'd been smoking.

"A very good dealer," Supersplib continued. "A fair price and a fair amount. No shuck, no jive, no burns. I don't deal pills, skag or meth... although I can usually score a cap or two if a good customer really wants to get amped.

"How else you think I pay the rent? I am not nearly as beautiful nor trusting as our friend Sunshine here, nor do I trust the gods and fates to put beans on my plate each day. And I certainly do not fancy stumbling from corner to corner like some of those poor folks down there, barefoot, ragged, half-starving, dogshit on their Levis and no place to sleep at night except the street.

"Let me inform you of a fact, Mister Tyrell, of which you may be unaware. You sit here... absorbing the rays and the soft wind of summer. But in the winter, San Francisco has been known to become fierce. Winds, storm and rain, all of which arrive directly from the Arctic Circle. Sleeping outdoors in such a time I find stressful.

"I would not deserve the title of Supersplib if I accepted any of that."

"You talk like dealing's the only gig you can find," Tyrell said.

"For a person of color, it just about is. Most straight jobs, at least those that pay more than a pittance, seem very interested in the degree of one's tan.

"Civil Service? They do not seem much interested. Especially with all these fine young white boys and girls showing up, with their college educations and their fine ability to fill out paperwork and take tests.

"I could probably get a little testy," he went on, "at the entire concept of hippie, since it has hardly helped black people advance. My fellow freaks have gotten themselves first in line for the jobs, the welfare checks, the charity beds at the hospitals, even the niggerwork of pushing a broom, all too often.

"I could, as I said, become irate. But fortunately, I have cast my fate with a new culture. Win, lose or draw, I'll travel with this love generation. Until I see better on the horizon.

"So, my friend... if you decide to come back to San Francisco, after you have returned to Memphis - and remember that even on Beale Street blacks go in through the back door - think about what I have said.

"Sunshine is an old, old friend of mine... Should you return, and should you be interested, you might want to look me up.

"You would not be the first, nor the last, I have fronted. I consider it my own version of what our beloved Lyndon Baines calls a War On Poverty.

"... Speaking of horizons... I see someone on mine. Beckoning frantically. Forgive me... here. Keep the joint. Mercy, mercy, have mercy. Little more than a roach. Here, then. Accept its big brother."

And, without touching the ground with his hands, Supersplib was on his feet and ambling down the hill... grinning that crazy grin of his at the hopeful-looking customer.

"You must understand," the man went on. "All this is but a moment. One single instance, where the colors swirl together, and those on the path meet... "But only for this instant, and only because this is the first waystation.

"Beyond this gray concrete city lies a world that we must embrace, a world where we need no drugs, where we eat no meat, where we practice ahimsa, and honor and venerate all our fellow creatures and do not interfere nor intersect with their lives."

"Even pigs?" was the skeptical question.

"Even the police," came the calm answer.

Jeff was having a bit of trouble understanding the lecturer. He had a very British accent. He looked, Jeff suddenly thought, very much like that actor in "The Great Escape." Donald... Donald Pleasence. Yeah. Same meek look. Same thick glasses. Same balding fringe.

Except that he didn't remember Pleasence ever playing Gandhi. The man wore only a beatific expression and a loincloth that kept unraveling itself every few minutes.

He was holding forth to a small crowd. Some tourists, some hippies, some winos, some dropouts, and Jeff and Samantha.

The skeptic, a young man with hair just starting to wave down toward his shoulders and a beard wisping out, wasn't satisfied.

"Look, man. I ain't out to hassle the pigs. They go their way... and I go mine. On the other side of the street. But they keep crossin' over! And beatin' on me!"

"You must pray for them," the mystic said. "I shall do the same. Their karma shall be just that. But perhaps I may help you further."

"How?"

"You must learn to sense their rhythm... and when it is not the Joy-dance."

"An' haul ass."

Allan Cole & Chris Bunch

The Englishman sighed. "Sometimes... withdrawal of your physical self from their asat is the only answer. But this should not lead to anger... nor to a stirring in the blood. So you must soothe the atman, and warn your brothers and sisters.

"So you chant. Chant *ikimasho, ikimasho*. which means 'Let's go.' For those who do not understand Japanese, a more understandable chant that will also maintain the karmic flow *is Ikimasho, ikimasho. ikimasho. go, go; ikimasho. go. go. ikimasho. ikimasho."*

"Meditate on that, my children. For there lies wisdom."

"Thanks, pops. But I'd rather have a shotgun."

The offices of the Haight-Ashbury Underground were in a former "beatnik" coffeehouse, a coffeehouse that, Nebraska thought, probably went bankrupt because there weren't that many black-white colorblind people who could live with the paint scheme.

The steps that up to the editor's office were alternately red, white and blue. The banister was zebra-striped black. Someone had collaged one wall and somebody else had done what Nebraska thought was probably pop art (he read Time magazine every now and then) on the other. Anyway, he guessed that endlessly repeated paintings of a jackhammer qualified.

The ceiling was done in realistic style. Just like Norman Rockwell's covers on the *Post*. Nebraska thought. But somehow he didn't think Mister Rockwell'd appreciate what all of his mid-American people were doing to each other, whether they were naked or not.

Back home, Nebraska had been in the local weekly's office once or twice. So he sort of recognized some of what was going on. But not very well. It looked like - instead of a big chuffing linotype - somebody'd figured out how to set type using a larger-than-normal IBM typewriter. And instead of those big metal plates that were used to print the pages the paper's artists were just pasting things on heavy paper sheets.

The place was a babble of rumors, stoners, artists, photographers, and blasting rock.

Toward the back - where "it's quieter" - Alexis was being interviewed by a very hairy man who called himself Mojo. He wasn't taking notes. Instead, a large Akai tapedeck whirred noisily on the rickety desk between them. Nebraska wondered how anybody'd be able to transcribe the interview through the extraneous din.

But this wasn't his scene, nor his place. He listened in the background as the interview "progressed."

Q: Wouldn't you agree, Alexis, that rock is primarily 'head' music?

A: Giving or getting?

Q: I don't... Oh. You were making a joke. No. I meant that rock is inherently psychedelic.

A: You mean you gotta be fucked up to get off on it? It helps... but it doesn't have to be on acid. Or even weed. Beer and a shot'll get you out there, too.

Remember, Mulberry Street plays the blues. We're doing music that black cats came up with down in the Delta, to keep 'em from thinking how whitey was poundin' on them. I never heard there was much dope, except maybe red dirt marijuana, down there.

And just because we run twelve-measure AAB through an amp doesn't mean psychedelia's there. Or not there, come to think about it.

Q: (a nervous laugh). I... I see. What about baroque being the direct ancestor of rock?

A: Huh? Baroque? You mean like... Antonio Vivaldi. And... who was that other guy. Hayden? Shit, I thought I had some good dope. Let think about that one. (background noises). We got a bass line... we got, at least most of the time if Tripster remembers to show up some implied harmonies. But polyphony? Guess that's 'cause we don't always remember the words at the same time.

Q: Isn't rock truly the wave of the future? I mean that it's a regenerative art and we can see the shape of tomorrow in its structure?

Alexis looked for some help from Nebraska. He shook his head, thinking about saying "Hell yes. I give it a 74, good lyrics an' you can dance to it," but it was her interview and her problem.

So, instead, he mimed hoisting a glass... Meet you at the Pall Mall. I need a beer. Alexis quick-flashed... five minutes. It was going to be a very, very short interview...

...There's a man with a gun over there/Telling me I got to beware...

Sunshine spotted the cop first. She tugged at Tyrell's sleeve and hissed for him to be extra cool. Tyrell had no intention of doing otherwise. Especially when he saw the cop was Grancell.

Tyrell shot a look down the side street and saw the front entrance of The

170

FBI Girl. So could Grancell. Tyrell also saw Nebraska and Alexis chatting amiably, killing time until Tyrell and Jeff joined them with their ladies.

Grancell was talking heatedly to someone whose identity was partially hidden by a slow-moving tourist bus. As Grancell talked, he made violent pointing motions in Nebraska's direction. Ooops. Guess he was still pissed at Nebraska for scoffing the evidence last night. Oh, well, tough on Grancell.

Then the bus pulled away and Tyrell's heart skittered. Grancell was talking to Lieutenant Sanders! The MP creep who had harassed them last night. He was leaning against that olive drab MP sedan, nodding as Grancell talked and glaring at Nebraska and Alexis.

Now it was Grancell's turn to listen as Sanders began flapping his jaw, obviously adding to Nebraska's list of imagined sins.

"There's your other friend," Sunshine said. "Jeff, right?"

Tyrell said right as he turned to see Jeff and the stewardess join Nebraska. Grancell and Sanders spotted them at the same time.

"I don't like how they're looking at them," Sunshine said.

"Me neither."

"What do we do?"

Tyrell knew what he wanted to do. He wanted to run and hide from those baleful coplooks. Get you in a corner of a cell and put the stick to you. But it wasn't jail, or physical abuse he feared.

He looked at the girl beside him. Young, blonde, white, and beautiful. Tyrell suspected that even in San Francisco, Sanders and Grancell would not take it well if he was seen in Sunshine's company.

Sunshine's eyes were wide and waiting for his decision. From her expression, he thought she knew what was going around in his mind. More importantly, Sunshine was prepared to go with the flow, as the hippy kids said. No matter what he decided, she wouldn't judge him one way or the other.

Tyrell lifted an arm, elbow crooked formally to receive her hand. "Shall we join our friends, m'lady?"

Sunshine's smile would have diminished the sun. She took his arm. "Far out," she laughed.

Arm-in-arm, the two of them stepped off the curb and were spotted by Grancell and Sanders.

Tyrell ignored the startled, angry looks from the cop and the MP as he steered Sunshine toward The FBI Girl and his friends. Sunshine gave his arm an appreciative squeeze against a tender breast.

He thought this was a far better reward for heroism than a measly ass Silver Star.

...Young girls are comin' through the canyon/And in the morning I can see them laughing...

"This calls for Solidarity, Sisters," Alexis was saying. "United we stand.... divided we're back on the meat market."

"I never thought someone like... uh... you... would have that kind of trouble," Samantha said, as delicately as she could.

"It's probably worse for her," Sunshine put in for Alexis. "Just because she's pretty, and famous... "

"I'm not pretty," Alexis broke in. "I call me acceptable. *You're* pretty. And I'm sure not famous... Although I hope to be."

"Well, you're sure a lot more famous than me, or Samantha," Sunshine said. "I mean... we don't have men mobbing the stage and drooling all over us. Right? But that just makes the meat market bigger for you. Right? Tougher too. Right? Because there's so many it's hard to see who's nice and... who's not. Right?"

There were too many rights for Alexis to deal with. However, naive child that she have been, Sunshine had hit the mark first go. The more she got to know her, the more Alexis saw big spots of maturity in the little hippie chick.

"You win on all counts," Alexis finally said. "I thought my head was screwed up about men when I was a kid. But now I've had a little experience, I know I was a hopeless optimist.

"My mother blames it all on the pill. Of course, she also blames Communist aggression and the decline of Western Morality on the pill. Turned her only child into a slut. According to her, the only man she ever went to bed with was my father."

"Mine's sort of the same," Sunshine said, solemn. "But we can't blame our mothers. No matter what they say, we just have to love them. That's what will win out, someday. We just have to keep loving... until all the hate is gone."

There is rarely an answer to that kind of idealism, so they walked on for a few minutes in silence. They were wandering through the Haight in the general direction of the Panhandle. Just ahead of the women were their three

172

new boyfriends - in a deep discussion about Grancell and the MP lieutenant.

"Back to the ways and means business..." Alexis said, returning to the subject at hand, "I am definitely smitten by that damned farmboy. I'd like to keep him around. Why should some woman from place called Grainton, for crying out loud, luck out?"

"I've got the same sort of the same problem," Samantha said, thinking of the manipulating Rachel. "Although, just how smitten I am and how long it's likely to last... I'm not sure. Yet. Still, I think it would be a lot better for Jeff if he did stay in San Francisco. Solo... Or, otherwise."

"We'll always be together, Ty-Rell and me," Sunshine said. "But it doesn't have to be an actual physical presence, kind of thing. Although that's very nice. It's our karma to be together. And you know what?" Sunshine lowered her voice. "I think we've been together before. You know, like in a previous life?"

"That's one way to beat the first date blues," Alexis said. "Instead of all that does she, or doesn't she/ would he, or wouldn't he...' Christ, by the time the night's over you're both a nervous wreck. Past dates in past lives. I like that, Sunshine.

"Maybe that's why the farmboy got to me. Maybe we were star-crossed lovers in another life. He was Rhett. And I was that bitch, Scarlett."

"The only time I identified with Scarlett," Samantha said, "is when Rhett swept her off the floor and carried her to the bed. But then there wouldn't have been a movie or a book with me as the heroine, anyway. Believe me, there would have been very little resistance before that big sweep off the floor into bed scene."

"You've got *that* right," Alexis laughed. "Except he'd never have got me off the floor. Not with the leg lock I 'd put 'on him!"

Samantha was amused, but Sunshine was silent. Her face was serious... lost in thought.

"We have to watch out for Grancell," she suddenly said. "He likes to hurt things... Maybe somebody hurt him once, and that's why... But, he won't just wait around for a chance... He's a lurker... He's *always* lurking on people.

"You ever notice how he comes up out of nowhere?"

"I sure do," Alexis groaned. "And I've got the tickets to prove it."

"Grancell's the shadow in the corner," Sunshine said. "You watch him some time. He likes to swagger down the street, so everybody can see him.

173

Then he ducks into a doorway, or an alley or something. Until you forget you didn't see him split.

"I saw him once. He was sliding down the street like he was the Invisible Man, or something. He went from shadow to shadow... like this old orange cat I used to have, going after the jays in the back yard. Nobody even saw him.

Then he was all of a sudden there and people were really freaked, man. It was like a total bummer!"

"You're forgetting one thing," Samantha said. "There's three of us and only one - thank God - Officer Grancell."

"Pretty good odds," Alexis grinned.

"Look out Grancell," Sunshine laughed.

"I've been workin' on this theory," Nebraska said. "Maybe the plane never really got past Guam. Instead, that old Freedom Bird busted a wing on Pacific lightnin' and right now we're all dead."

"What brought on that flight of metaphysics?" Jeff asked.

"An attempt at pure reason, college boy," Nebraska prodded back. "I was just tryin' to account for the three angels walkin' behind our ugly asses."

"You've got that right, my friend," Tyrell said, with feeling. "ˣCept I was leaning toward one of those time-warp thingies. Like on Outer Limits... " Tyrell's voice dropped dramatic-deep: "We now take control of your television sets... We control the horizontal... We control the vertical... "

Jeff saw a boy and a girl, costumed in streaming red ribbons covered with tiny jangling bells, dance across the street.

"It sure isn't the same, world I left fourteen months and ten small forevers ago," Jeff said. He looked behind him and saw Samantha laughing at something Alexis was saying. Thought about what she had to say to him on the curb outside Tracy's Doughnuts... wisdom through jelly-specked lips... Yeah... Big difference.

"I hate to be Captain Bringdown," Tyrell said, "But what about Grancell? And that MP lieutenant?"

"One thing I learned haulin' the Old Man around," Nebraska said, "is not to jump soon as somethin' worrisome goes boo. I'll get my shot... by and by."

...Now at midnight all the agents/And the super human crew/Come out

Allan Cole & Chris Bunch

and round everyone/That knows more than they do...

Crosseyed Jesus of the Diggers had a cop's nightstick across his throat. And was undaunted.

"Go ahead," he croaked. "It's your free food too. Take what you want, officer."

The cop didn't answer.

But the crowd did... starting a chant of PIGS, PIGS, PIGS as the Public Health workers hurled bags of day old bread from the Ukrainian Bakery into city trucks. Then it growled angrily, as a cop kicked over the huge tureen, and steaming food splashed into the street.

A firehose from a nearby pumper crashed on, and the Digger Stew was washed into a storm drain.

There was an angry growl and the five cops guarding the health workers fingered their weapons. "Fascist motherfuckers," somebody shouted.

Nebraska and the others pushed their way through to the edge of the crowd. Five or six Hell's Angels, including Dick, watched - impassive.

"What the hell?"

"City health," Dick explained briefly. "Peter over there..." and he waved at cross-eyed Jesus... "an' the rest of the Diggers think food is free. City don't agree."

Another Angel Nebraska didn't recognize snorted. "Hard thing," he said, "is anybody even figgerin' that's food, no matter what's the cost."

"The Diggers call it Stew," Dick went on. "Whatever they can scrounge. Outa dumpsters at the Safeway. Other stores. Stuff they can steal. Stuff nobody wants. They're real big on lamb shanks an' turkey necks.

"Stuff white folk'd have to be starvin' to eat. Or else be a busted-out hippy who ain't got the balls to just grab what he needs and say come an' get me."

"Wouldn't catch me scoffin' any of that," the other biker agreed. "Doin' these pukes a favor, washin' it away. Keepin' 'em from gettin' ptomaine an' the drizzles."

"True... maybe," Dick said, not happily. "But still... Dumpin' folks food into the street... seems fucked, you know?"

175

Nebraska was watching the last of the FREE FOOD go down the storm drain, and the doors of the city truck slam shut.

"Where I come from," Nebraska said, "you don't ever throw food away."

"Yeah," Dick agreed. "We was raised the same."

Nebraska turned to the others. Tyrell had heard the "white folk" line, and was keeping both a deadpan and away from the bikers.

"You remember," Jeff said, trying to change the subject, "just how much shit got wasted in Nam?"

Tyrell took the change. "Not by me, man. And not by anybody else in the Pukin' Buzzard. 'Cause we never *had* enough shit to begin with. Always got ripped by the REMFs before it got up to us field animals."

"Yeah," Nebraska agreed. "I remember the stuff that got tossed out of the Battalion Officer's Mess. I drove the garbage detail once... when the Old Man was assed at me. The dump was covered with gooks, and that was *their* ration point.

"I guess," he said, thoughtful, "the Haight's got more'n something in common with Vietnam. This ain't right."

Nobody, not even the Angels could argue that one.

The show was more or less over. The cop turned Digger Peter loose, and the city trucks, copcars and pumper pulled away.

Nebraska was still upset. "Dick," he asked, "how many of these people ain't gonna eat tonight, because of them grabbing that food?"

Dick thought for a moment. "Some. Not all. There's some weekend hippies here that'll go home when the love in's over. Some more got money. Others'll sell their asses for a meal an' a crashpad. But some... yeah, some'll be goin' through garbage cans, like they was stray-cats or listenin' to their stomach growl."

"Fuck 'em," the other Angel said. "Damned kids go an' decide they don't wanna be sheep, come out here an' figger that God's gonna provide? Shit. God ain't dead, he just don't wanna get involved. Only thing He ever give me was puttin' me in that bar down in Berdoo when The Club happened to drop by. An' he ain't givin' these squids nothin' at all!"

Not that anybody seemed worried about the next meal or the pillow just then. The sun was bright, the sky was blue and there was the tingle of a thousand songs floating through the Haight. Darkness

Allan Cole & Chris Bunch

and hunger were long hours away. Right now, the crowd was looking for the next Haight Happening.

As usual, it was only seconds in coming, as a screaming runner hurtled around a corner. He wore only pants and a wild expression. Tyrell thought he recognized him - oh yeah, the frantic narc-shouter of a few hours ago. But this time, the pursuer was real, as that green MP sedan broadied nearly across Fell Street to a halt. The runner went over the median strip, onto Oak, and gone.

Out of the MP car sailed Nebraska's nemesis, Lieutenant Sanders and his hulk of a driver, Jenkins. Jenkins had the ignition keys to the sedan and a bandaged nose from his newspaper-dive back in North Beach.

"What in blazes?" Samantha wanted to know.

Any of the three ex-GI's could have told her what was going on, but instead the answer came from a fairly pretty, sunken-eyed teenager who wore ringed bells on her toes, a vastly oversized prison work shirt and very filthy chinos.

"That's Max," a Hippie chick explained. "He's a deserter. From you know, the Army? Or maybe the Coast Guard?"

The momentary interest opened the floodgates.

"Yeah, me an' him, we were shooting speed all last week, just runnin', up at the Jeffrey-Haight, that's where he ended up when they threw him out of that crashpad but they were lying about what he took and it was kinda groovy with him except sometimes he got so hyper about things, and didn't know about letting the flash take over your mind and keep it from scheming on you. It's like an explosion in your skull, like a monster bomb in your whole body, warm like fire. Your head gets so big you can't imagine how big it is, then you get into a trance, spaced out, making plans.

"Me and him were gonna get back together if one of us scored, and maybe we could score enough for one big rush, just swoop on up there, the big rush into the clouds when it all takes over and it's all over."

She stopped. Seemed to listen to what she'd just said, then giggled. "But I guess that ain't gonna happen, huh? I guess he'll go to jail. Or maybe a hospital. Too bad. Too bad, too bad, too bad, Max, max, maxie..."

And she wandered away.

Samantha looked after her. "If I ever, ever take another diet pill," she said, "I hope somebody speaks to me harshly."

Sunshine nodded solemnly. "Speed kills."

Nebraska was not listening. "Dick," he asked. "Can I ask you for a favor?"

"Maybe."

"I got a real strange idea. And I need that MP car. "

"You want me to hotwire it?" the Angel asked. "Right here in daylight? Uh-uh, Nebraska. Neighbors ain't brothers."

"No," Nebraska said. "At least, not yet. But can you keep those MP's from moving it... when they come back."

"Oh hell," Dick said. "That ain't even a favor."

The huge man was suddenly not beside them, but across the street and at the door-open Ford Fairlane. The hood was popped, Dick bent over the engine, tinker tinker, then slammed the hood down and was beside Nebraska once more.

"Here. Ain't goin' nowhere without th' rotor." He handed it to Nebraska.

"Thanks. Now, look. Me, Tyrell and Jeff gotta go back to our hotel. Where you gonna be in... thirty minutes?"

"Down to Golden Gate. For the Love-In. Unless somebody comes up with another idea."

"No. Okay, you said that getting the distributor rotor wasn't a favor. So lemme ask another one. Can you meet us here? Half an hour?"

Dick examined Nebraska closely. "Maybe. Maybe. If you let on to what your scheme is. I'm assuming you got one, and you aren't just fucked up and bein' a trickbag on me."

"Oh yeah," Nebraska said slowly. "I got me a plan, all right. A real fine plan...

"A plan I been workin' on back when I decided to roll the dice in Vietnam for an early out. Just didn't know it at the time."

Allan Cole & Chris Bunch

CHAPTER ELEVEN

THE TRIBES HAD had gathered at Hippy Hill. Thousands of young people danced, sang, toked, and generally grooved. The park was a wild sea of noise and color; a riotous confusion of beads, bells, bangles and bota bags of wine. The air was a profusion of incense and marijuana smoke.

It was a warm July day - made for costumes revealing glowing acres of young flesh. Samantha and Sunshine sidestepped a young, freckle faced boy, dancing naked except for a jock strap that had been covered with glitter dust and bells. His only other article of clothing was a beaded leather band around his biceps. He grinned and waggled his pelvis.

"Not today," Samantha said with a giggle. "But thanks for the thought."

She started to push on, but Sunshine recognized the kid. "What's the haps, Robbie?"

"Just groovin', Sunshine, until the real fun starts," Robbie said, twirling and stomping to the canned music that blared from the makeshift stage at one corner of the park.

"We miss anything?" Sunshine asked.

"Leary was up there awhile," the boy said, never missing a step. "Did his usual turn on, drop out riff. Shit, who's he think's here, man? We all did that number, already. Then there were some political types from Berkeley. Kept goin' on about Vietnam and world peace. Which is groovy and very cool... but everybody I know's already got their head into that stuff. We're here for music, man. Not preachin'."

"Sounds like you're bummed," Sunshine said.

"No way," Robbie said. "I'm here to commune, man. Nobody's gonna spoil my trip today. Besides, the bands oughta start pretty soon. First, we got Mulberry Street. Then the Dead says they'll play 'til the dope and beer run out. Then... who knows?"

"Far out," Sunshine said. "Say, Robbie. You do us a favor?"

"Sorry, Sunshine," Robbie said. "I'm tapped out. Was gonna sit down maybe tomorrow and write my folks. Hustle up a little..."

"This is not about bread, Robbie," Sunshine gently chided. "This is about making sure everybody has a groovy day."

"Whatcha want me to do?"

"Have you seen Grancell?"

"Who hasn't? That fucker's been snoopin' all over the place. Lookin' for somebody to bust. But we just shine him, man. What's he gonna do? Nobody's bustin' nobody in this crowd."

Samantha could see this was true. The Love-in was working itself into a frenzy of bliss and brotherhood. But, it could turn ugly just as quickly. Even Grancell wouldn't be so dumb as to try to cuff one of these kids with so many of their friends about.

"Where did you see him last?" Sunshine asked.

Robbie was getting bored with all the questioning. He vagued a hand in the general direction of the stage. Sunshine and Samantha both spotted him at once. Grancell was moving to the edge of the woods - about thirty yards beyond the stage. They saw him take station under a clump of trees. He wasn't wearing his uniform, which in a way made it even easier to pick him out for what he was.

Grancell had "gone under cover." He was wearing brand new dungarees and a white shirt with the sleeves rolled up and the tail hanging out like a dog's tongue. You could see the lump under the shirt and the dip in his jeans from the gun he had hidden there. Grancell had ruffed up his short hair, until it was maybe one tenth of an inch long. And he wore black socks and brown leather shoes - $9.99 at Kinney's "Summer Casual Sale." He also had minimum ten years on most of the other people in the crowd.

The kids mostly ignored him... treating him as if he were the invisible man. If a newish hippie wandered by, the others made oinking noises in Grancell's direction... although you'd have to be blind not to know that Grancell was a narc.

"Listen, Robbie," Samantha said. "Maybe you could help us out with Grancell and the other cops a little later. We might need a sort of diversion. You know, screw with his head?"

Robbie looked Samantha up and down, his boredom vanishing at the prospects of impressing a very lovely "older" woman.

"Far Fuckin' Out," he said. "You got it, Sunshine... Just ask."

Armed with that first of many promises to come, Sunshine and Samantha said goodbye to Robbie and moved on.

They edged along the outskirts of the crowd, generally circling the stage, keeping Grancell firmly in sight.

Suddenly, the noise level kicked up. The crowd was cheering and pushing. Sunshine and Samantha saw Alexis and the other members of Mulberry Street bound onstage. Drums rolled. Strings twanged.

Allan Cole & Chris Bunch

Alexis approached the mike. The cheers became deafening, setting off a reverb howl from the sound system. Alexis held up her hands to hush the crowd. They quieted for a moment. Then a new eruption set Alexis laughing. Finally, the din lessened.

"You ready for some lovin'?" Alexis' voice boomed through the speakers. The crowd shouted back that it was ready. "I mean, *real* lovin'! The kind that chases the blues away." They were ready for that too.

Alexis held a hand up again to hold back the shouts and cheers.

"I want to dedicate my first song to a brand new love of my own," she said. There were friendly catcalls from the crowd. Behind her, Tripster's face darkened in jealous fury. But even if Alexis had seen it, she would have paid no mind.

"He's out there right now listenin'. I want all of you to be real friendly to him, now, because this guy is somethin' special... All you ladies know what I mean by special... right?"

Feminine howls pierced the air in agreement.

"His name is Nebraska. Where are you, Nebraska honey?'

She shaded her eyes and peered around the crowd. Samantha and Sunshine saw Grancell's interest perk up like the ears of an excited bloodhound. He was scanning the crowd along with Alexis.

Suddenly, the singer yelled. "There you are, baby." She pointed deep into the crowd. "Say hello to everybody, Nebraska."

There were several waves from the direction she was pointing in. Then she threw a big sloppy kiss. From Grancell's reaction, it looked as if he had spotted Nebraska as well. He started edging along the tree and brush line, getting closer. Sunshine burst into laughter, and Samantha shushed her and pulled her close. But she was laughing too hard herself at Alexis' trick to make the shushing stick.

Up on the stage, Alexis was getting ready to deliver.

"This is for you, honey," she said. "From Bessie Smith. It's called, 'Gimme A Pigfoot.'"

The song began, Alexis delivering the first few lines in a growl:

Twen-ty five cents? Hah! No! No!... I wouldn't pay twenty-five cents to go in no-where... 'Cause lis-ten here;

And the band joined in...

...*Up in Harlem every Saturday night/When the highbrows git together it's just too tight...*

"Just a hit or two wouldn't hurt, would it?"

Jeff read the expression on his friend's face correctly and put the joint away.

"You only get your mind messed," Tyrell told him in the command voice of an experienced combat leader, "*after* the shootin', shittin' and shoutin' dies away."

"Okay, okay," Jeff moaned. "Here I am, in this big high-rolling expensive suite at the Mark goddamned Hopkins.

Excavating through my stupid duffelbag for some stupid fatigues. That we're gonna try to use for some stupid-ass Errol Flynn moves... here we go.

"Look at these vines, my man. Brand new.

"Not tailored, not faded, no patch, no stripes, no nothing. Just the way they were issued when I turned in the jungle suits.

"You know what I'm going to closely resemble when I put these on? Besides Private Doberman, I mean?"

Nebraska, who'd had the phone receiver into one ear, brightened. "Sergeant Kerley, right? K. .,E...R...L...E...Y? Yeah. Put me through."

He hung up the phone. "Okay, that's the mess sergeant over at Fort Mason. Now, Jeffie-poo, what're you gonna look like?

"You're gonna look like a cherry trooper," Nebraska said. "A 'cruit. Both of you guys will, which is what you are. Tyrell, I want you in a set of Jeff's fatigues.

Tyrell started to protest - the baggy look was not in this decade. Nebraska shut him up with a wave.

"Exactly, my man," he said. "The baggier you look, the better. Right now, you look too goddamned experienced. This is a disguise, you idiots. You're on a shit detail under the command of an experienced non-commissioned officer. Which is, kaff-kaff, me."

He examined his own tailored, faded, stripe-equipped fatigues, frowned and tore the MACV patch off his right shoulder, the patch that showed he'd been in a combat zone.

"Nope," he explained. "I don't wanna look *that* experienced. Hey, Jeff. You got a Sixth Army patch?"

"Yeah," Jeff said. "They sewed one on my new greens over at Oakland."

Nebraska not only had a sewing kit, but knew how to use it. He razored the olive drab six-starred patch of the San Francisco-based unit off Jeff's

Allan Cole & Chris Bunch

dress uniform, and quickly sewed it on the left sleeve of his fatigues.

"Anyway, like I was saying. You two E-l-Type Privates are on a detail... and you don't like it... and you don't want to have anything to do with it."

"We are going to get busted," Jeff said.

"So what?" Tyrell said. He was starting to like this idea. If it worked, he'd be a hero, wouldn't he? Not one who'd killed people, which he knew damned well was a cold shudder to Sunshine... and a thought she did not want to consider.

"What are the charges?" he asked. "You tell me what the Army could come up with."

"Oh they'll come up with something," Jeff said. "They've got years and years of coming up with laws that cover anything and everything when they want to crucify you. "

"Oh hell," Tyrell said, "What're they gonna do? Send us to Vietnam?"

The suite was very silent, and Tyrell played back what he'd just said, the automatic bluff-retort of the veteran.

"Hell, guys," he realized. "I guess that line's only funny when you're somewhere west of Vung Tau, huh?"

"What they'll get us on," Nebraska said, "Is Article 134. Bein' ugly in a public place."

"That's it," Jeff said. "That's what they'll get us on."

"So what," Tyrell said. "If they do nail us you won't have to get married, will you? At least not until they let us out of the stockade, right?"

"Hmm," Jeff W-C-Fielded. "Yaaas. Yaaas indeed, my little chickadee. This has suddenly become a most interesting proposition...."

"Let's do it," Nebraska said. "We can change in the cab."

...Runnin' out of money. Lord, I need more pay//Gonna wake up in the mornin'. Lord, gonna pack my bags/I'm gonna beat it on down the line/I'm goin' down the line, goin' down the line...

The Grateful Dead was whooping it up on stage now, and the whole crowd was in constant motion. Like some weird alien creature, with thousands of moving parts barely under the control of a single brain.

A straight-looking boy in pegged jeans, an oversized white-on-white tee shirt, and a short curly mob of hair gave a sudden shout of joy. He ripped the straight-job wig from his head and a shock of hair that would shame a St. Bernard tumbled down. The boy grabbed a passing bota bag...

Allan Cole & Chris Bunch

held it up... and a thin stream of wine gushed out. Filling his mouth, spilling over and spattering his companions.

His girlfriend caught the spirit and came up with a squeal. If there was anything straight about her, it was gone in a flash as she pulled her tee shirt off and began dancing topless. Her small, hard breasts bouncing to the beat, while her hips swiveled to a slower, more primitive rhythm. Her boyfriend held the bota bag up and let loose. Wine streamed all over her firm young body.

The fever caught and all over tops were being peeled off, pants shed, and girls climbing half-naked on their similarly clad boyfriends' shoulders.

A hundred voices shouted "Look."

Hundreds of other people were pointing. Up in the sky. Three small figures plummeted out of an airplane. Red, blue and gold smoke torched from their heels, marking the path of the skydivers as they freefell over the park. It was a magnificent sight and everybody oohed and ahhed at the smoke and bravery. Then there was a long crowd intake of breath as first one, then the second, and finally a third chute opened. The parachutes were all paisley printed,

They drifted down and down to a clear space in the park. A few uniformed cops burst out and ran toward the landing area. There would be hell to pay - in jail - for these permitless jumps.

The three long hairs hit the ground standup, collapsed and started hauling in their chutes, hoping to make a hasty, bust-free exit. But the cops were going to beat them to it.

Then the kids saw what was happening, and ran to the rescue. A screaming mob enveloped the skydivers before the cops could reach them. By the time things were sorted out, the jumpers had disappeared.

...they all congregates at an all-night strut/ And what they do is tut-tut-tut...

"It worked pretty much like you thought it would," Dick said.

"Yeah," the other Angel, who'd now been introduced as Monkey, said. "You ain't got too shabby a way of casin' a job. For a citizen."

"They come back... without that runner I might add," Dick said. "Climbed in. Grind, grind, grind, no joy. Got out. Had the fuckin' balls to ask if we'd give 'em a push. We said sure. An' told 'em where, too.

"Figured you wouldn't mind if we had 'em stacked safe in a garbage can somewhere. But they didn't wanna play, an' hiked off toward the

Allan Cole & Chris Bunch

Presidio."

"Lessee," Nebraska thought. "Friday. Three o'clock. How long'11 it take to get some kinda towtruck over here?"

"Hey, babe. You think I remember Army time?"

Nebraska grinned. "Okay, Dick. Now, if you'll show me how to hotwire the sucker."

"Already taken care of, my boy. All you got to do is turn the switch. Even found an old key on the street, an' busted it off short, so if anybody looks close there'll be a real key in the ignition."

"Damn," the Angel said... suddenly *really* noticing the three men, who now wore those green-brown work uniforms and somehow-disproportionate baseball caps. "I forgot just how donkey-dumb people look in fatigues. You think I ever looked that dopey when I was a buck private in the rear rank?"

Not even Jeff was willing to pick up that straight line.

... I thought I heard a young man mourn this morning/I thought I heard a young man mourn today...

                                        "

Hey. Hey, Grancell," came the voice.

Grancell ignored it, pissed that his cover had been blown, but determined to stick it out.

"Yo, Grancell. You deaf, man?"

Stifling a groan, Grancell turned. He was being confronted with a little freak in some kinda weird jock strap. Robbie Something or other.

"Fuck off, Robbie."

"You workin', Grancell? Or did they stiff you for the uniform at the cleaners?"

"I said, fuck off."

"How come you skipped the action?" Robbie said, pointing at the place where the skydivers and cops used to be. "You lookin' for somebody special to bust?"

"If you don't get outa my face, it's gonna be you." Grancell was peering around desperately. He'd lost sight of his quarry.

"What for? Just tryin' to help."

"Sure, you are." He'd just seen Alexis, he thought. And where she was, was sure to be Nebraska. Grancell was determined to keep tabs on the sonofabitch.

"See you later, Grancell."

The cop turned, and saw Robbie strolling away. Then he saw him wave at somebody. A female somebody. Way, way over. Hot shit, it was Alexis! Casually, he started strolling in the same direction.

But a chorus of oink oinks blew his cool, and he nearly went sky ground over a stump.

...A fine little girl/She wait for me/Me catch the ship/Across the sea/I sailed the ship/All alone/I never think/I'll make it home/Louie... Louie...

A woman in a fishnet sarong hip-strolled along, trailing three or four guys behind her, like bees mesmerized by a fruit cart. She had a lush, Earth momma's body stretching that net, wide, dark eyes and a haughty nose.

A shriek of fear cut over the music and crowd noise and the fishnet woman stepped aside as a half-naked blonde girl ran past. The blonde collapsed in a tumble by a water fountain. Sobbing and calling out.

"Bad acid," one of Fishnet's followers guessed.

"Bummer," said another.

Fishnet went straight to the girl. She found a rag and wet it at the fountain, then crouched over her, rubbing the cooling cloth over the blonde's forehead and making soothing whispers.

A little later, the blonde was calmed and asleep and Fishnet's followers were gone. The girl's lips fluttered in a gentle snore - an odd contrast to frantic screaming all around them.

...Old Hannah Brown from 'cross town gets full of corn and starts breakin' 'em down...

The Presidio. Sixth Army Headquarters. Home of Letterman General Hospital where the worst casualties of the escalating war were brought. The facility sat calm, peaceful and eucalyptus-wooded, overlooking San Francisco and the Golden Gate Bridge. There was no barbed wire closing off the post, nor were there hostile military policemen, guardshacks or roadblocks.

The MP sedan, Nebraska driving, sleazed onto the post without nary a glance. The three started laughing as they drove past the onward-trudging sweating forms of Jenkins and Lieutenant Sanders.

"Man," Tyrell marveled. "Them legs are slow-moving cats. Maybe I

186

oughta holler a Jodie or two at 'em. Airborne... airborne... all the way..."

"Okay, troops," Nebraska announced. "Duck on down. We're coming up on the motorpool."

Obediently Tyrell and Jeff flattened on the back seat. It wouldn't have mattered. The solitary guard at the motor pool's entrance didn't glance up from his copy of *The Love Book* longer than to make sure there wasn't a salute-crazy officer in the car as the MP sedan breezed through.

They parked the sedan behind a five-ton truck and got out. Now, they were inside the enemy's gates. None of the drivers or wrenches busting butt to finish their jobs before the weekend started even noticed them.

"Why do I feel so weird dressed like this," Tyrell wondered. "Day before yesterday, these kind of threads were all there was."

"It is because," Jeff explained, draping a tender arm about Tyrell's shoulders, "you have seen the light."

"I have seen the light?"

"You have seen the light."

"I see the lights/I see the lights/I see the party lights/Shining red and blue/And green... man, that song ain't nothing but white folks shit. No soul a-tall."

"Shaddup, you two. What we want is 6A HQ 36. Don't forget."

Nebraska was pointing to a truck which had, like all the other vehicles in the motor pool, identifying numbers painted in white on its front and rear bumpers. In this case 6A meant Sixth Army, HQ meant Headquarters, and 3 6 was the number (and assigned section) of that individual vehicle. It was, like everything else in the Army, very organized but making no real sense whatsoever.

"Yessir, sergeant, sir. Head Thirty Six. Helluva fine looking three-quarter ton it is. Brand new. In maybe... 1948."

They found the dispatch shack and entered. There was one dispatcher/clerk inside, intent on filling out some piece of bureaucratic gibberish. Nebraska studied the nail-studded walls. Each nail had a piece of masking tape above it, with numbers scrawled on... from HQ 1 on up... over a hundred numbers. Each number representing a vehicle. Some had keys and a clipboard with paper sheets attached to it, others did not. If a clipboard hung on the nail below a number, that meant the vehicle was in the motor pool. Otherwise, it'd been checked out.

"Whaddaya need, Sarge?" The SP/4 clerk finally noticed.

"Pickup for Colonel Libnoski," Nebraska said briskly. The clerk frowned.

"Who?"

"Colonel Libnoski. Told me to grab a deuce and a half... Headquarters 58, I think... and report to his quarters. He's getting reassigned."

"Nobody called. And Head 58's out. See?" The clerk pointed to the blank nail. "Gone."

"Shit," Nebraska said. "Now that bastard'11 have my butt."

"Who's this Libnoski?" the clerk finally asked.

"You ain't met him yet? Lucky you. Fuckin' airborne ranger son of a bitch, thinks he's still STRACK with the 82nd Airhose. Thank God they're shipping his ass out!"

"Never heard of him," the clerk said. "Guess he ain't been on post long."

"Long enough to make some real serious enemies," Nebraska said. "Which is why I got told by... you know who..." and he jerked a thumb in the general direction of the most palatial officer's residence he'd seen driving onpost, "...to expedite."

"Nice way to ruin a Friday," the clerk sympathized. "How much stuff's he got?"

"A whole goddamned household," Nebraska said. "Which is why I got these two guys to help, plus I was supposed to use a 2 1/2 ton truck. And from what the guy at S-1 said, we won't get everything loaded 'til midnight.

"Man," he continued. "When things go in the shitter, they never come out. First I get this detail... then I guess somebody forgot to call you... and now you tell me I can't have a deuce and a half."

"Wait a minute," the clerk said. "I can't help it if—"

"Hey, nobody's picking on you," Nebraska said. "But... look. You got any ideas? I mean, I'm just thinking about that friggin' Libnoski, and how he's gonna go apeshit when I go doubletiming up with my two privates sayin' we're gonna right shoulder household goods to help you move. I can see some kinda Article 15 and I don't need that shit, coming fresh on a new post my own self."

"Yeah," the clerk said. "Didn't think I'd seen you around the company area. Lemme think."

"Any ideas you can come up with..."

The clerk subconsciously looked at his own eagle of rank, Nebraska's three stripes plus rocker, probably thought this proves that an E4's got twice the brains of an E6, and Cogitated Hard.

188

Nebraska kicked Tyrell.

"What about that 3/4 ton," Tyrell asked, on cue. "That clean-looking one over there? Headquarters, uh, 36."

"Hey, knock it off," Nebraska ordered. "The guy's trying to help us."

Jeff could see the logic of the clerk's thinking as the man bristled: I'm just a Speedy Four temporary Soldier... as is this poor goddamned black recruit. So me and him together are gonna have the idea that'll save this blonde lifer staff sergeant's ass.

"Sarge," the clerk said. "That ain't a bad idea. Look. I give you that 3/4 ton..."

"And I'll have to make two trips across the Bay," Nebraska gloomed. "In Friday traffic."

"Hey," the clerk said, smiling as he got a chance to twist it a little in a Regular Army asshole. "Best I can do."

Nebraska grimaced. Then nodded slowly... resigned to his fate. "Okay. You got it. I know when to cut my losses and save my stripes."

Ten minutes later they gunned out of the motorpool with Sixth Army Headquarters 36, a 3/4 ton four-wheel-drive truck with canvas cover all their very own. At no time in the confusion had the clerk asked for authorization, identification, orders nor had he checked with any higher authority, thanks to them having first been inside the apparatus talking the appropriate jive; the razzle-dazzle of an unknown colonel who the motor pool clerk certainly didn't want to encounter ever, let alone piss off; a harried sergeant; Downtrodden Recruits and the chance to Show Bureaucratic Superiority in handling Life's Little Problems.

"We blew it," Jeff mourned as the 3/4 ton rocked through the curves. "We should have politely requested that tank they had parked over in the corner. We could have sold it for Big Bucks to your buddies in the Angels."

"Don't get cocky," Nebraska said. "And you wanna wave at our MP buddies? They're just coming toward the hill now. Wonder how long it'll take 'em to figure out how their sedan went and levitated from the Haight to the motor pool?"

Jeff wasn't the only one who was getting a little self-confident. . .

...Well I ain't superstitious/But a black cat crossed my trail./Don't brush me with my broom, Babe/I just might land in jail...

The kite fighters were out in force at the far end of the park. Graceful paper and balsa creatures swooped and dipped and struck out across the sky. Down below, hippies worked the strings, zooming painted kites toward their enemies. Some tried to tangle lines, others went for a paper-ripping blow that would knock the enemy out of the sky.

A few, however, stood well away from the action. Letting their big, colorful giant kites drift at will. Grooving with the winds and the sky.

"See that young man over there?" Supersplib was saying to Sunshine. He pointed at a tall, gangly hippy, dressed in a patched shit of twenty or thirty colors. He looked like a court jester, or:

"Cat says his name is Alan O'Dale," Supersplib said.

"Like Robin Hood's, Alan O'Dale?" Sunshine said.

"You are aware, sweetheart. Anyway, he's one of my special customers. A real favorite."

"What's so neat about him?"

"I like how the man thinks, if you get my drift. "See how he grooves with that kite? Man, he does not rush around like he is playing crazy cars or something. Nor does he try to humiliate the other cat. No, he stays cool and easy. Lets his kite go where it wants. Smokes some of my best dope, and just goes along with that old kite.

"Says he used to be a worrying man. Busted his behind in school... and later on the job. Said he got so uptight his folks tried to put him in the nut house."

"Poor man," Sunshine said. "What'd he do?"

"He discovered marijuana, sweet child. And split. That was his salvation. At least, that's what he tells me. He said smoking grass was like plugging a breast into your mind. I like that. I like that a lot. He has learned to commune with his Neolithic substance."

He got no argument from Sunshine. "Far out," she said. "If breasts are his trip. Although, what's to be mystical about breasts? They're just sweat glands. Personally, I like what that Chronicle reporter said the other day. You know, that undercover with the hippies story?"

Supersplib nodded. The piece was famous all over the Haight. But Sunshine told him anyway.

"He said: 'Get high... stay high... Closer to God... and the real you."

Sunshine watched Alan 0'Dale's kite climb higher and then seem to touch a small cloud hovering over the park. She turned back to Supersplib.

"So, what about Grancell? I don't mean to, like, push you, or anything.

Allan Cole & Chris Bunch

But I kind of need to know."

Supersplib gave her a hug.

"Don't fret, Sunshine. Old Supersplib is at your service."

...Take a vacation/Fall out for awhile/Summer's comin' in/And it's qoin' out in style/Well, like down smokin'/honey have yourself a ball/'Cause your mother's in Memphis/won't be back 'til the fall...

The Dead was really smoking now. The crowd was pressed tight and sweating against the stage.

Love-in volunteers worked the edges of the stage... hurling cooling buckets of water onto the cheering crowd. More buckets and tattered cardboard boxes were passed up to them. They were all filled with flowers.

The crowd moaned in ecstasy as thousands and thousands of perfumed buds rained down.

...Just at the break of day/You can hear old Hannah say...

There was nobody in the rear of the messhall's kitchen. Everybody was up front, getting the line ready for Friday's supper.

A shadow moved through the screen door, letting it close silently behind him, and went into the deserted number-ten-can-stacked office.

The shadow went to the desk, found the stacks of forms. Sorted through it, and found the correct pad. Tore two of them off.

"Who knows what weevil/Creeps in the hearts of men," Jeff whispered, and lamont-cranstoned back out to the waiting 3/4 ton truck.

....Mississippi River so big and wide/blond haired woman on the other side/Now she's gone, gone, gone I don't worry/'Cause I'm sittin' on top of the world...

A

bubble rivaling the size of the Hindenburg bumped along the ground. It was one of a gigantic stream being created by a half-a-dozen Street Theater kids. They were costumed straight from Tolkien... wizard's robes and tunics with mystical crystals twirling about on colored threads.

They were dipping huge wire hoops in buckets of soapy water and running through the crowd, leaving a trail of bubbles... colors shimmering on

191

tight surfaces... until the bright summer sky was filled with them.

"They're free, mommy, free!" A five-year-old shouted to his young mother.

The crowd picked up the chant: "Free! Free!"

People batted at the bubbles. Some burst, raining color. Others proved sturdier and kids knocked them back and forth like big volley balls.

"Free... Free... Turn on the world!" The crowd shouted. "Turn on the world!."

...Gimme a piafoot and a bottle of beer...

"Sarge? I'm Sarn't Appleyard. Here to pick up the B-rats for Fort Mason."

The mess sergeant sat in solitary splendor at a messtable - a cold, cream-heavy cup of coffee in front of him, chewing on the ruins of a very cheap cigar, and holding open on the stained teeshirt that semi-corseted his gut, a copy of *Morphv On Openings*. Ten minutes had passed since Jeff's solitary slither.

The sergeant looked Nebraska up and down. "You're outa Fort Mason, huh?"

"Yeah. I guess OARTS is full, 'cause we got some green beanies outa Bragg we gotta put up."

"And of course you've got paperwork."

"Sure do. Plus Sergeant Kerley said he talked to you. "

"You got the name right," the obese one grudged. "What kinda B-rations?"

"You mean..."

"I mean I ain't talked to Kerley since Christ was a corporal. Not that I'm callin' you a liar. Yet. Whaddaya after?"

Nebraska frowned in puzzlement at the mess sergeant, then passed over the hastily-filled-out requisition form Jeff had filched moments earlier from the back of the mess hall.

"Basic stuff," he said, and handed over the list.

Orations were the individual field meals issued to soldiers. B-rations were non-perishable canned or dry food given to mess halls as staples in big mamoo tins.

The mess sergeant scanned the list. Noodles. Spaghetti. Canned hamburger. Canned pears. Some cases of individual-serving breakfast

Allan Cole & Chris Bunch

cereal. Peas. Beats. Wax beans. Fruit cocktail. Wrapped slabs of what somebody'd convinced the Army was cheese. Canned bologna.

At which point the sergeant looked up. "Can't let you have any horsecock," he said. "Low ourselves, an' I'm puttin' what I got out on the line so my people can get cleaned up and outa here early."

"We can live without the bologna," Nebraska said agreeably.

"Where's your truck?"

Nebraska pointed, and the mess sergeant looked out a side window. Military vehicle. Two detail-type soldiers waiting, looking miserable.

..

.Send me. gate. I don't care/I feel just like I wanna clown...

The mess sergeant looked a little less suspicious, started to look agreeable, and then a Cunning Yet Subtle Expression wallowed across his poland-china-like features. He was going to Test Nebraska...

"Officers, you said you got? Green Berets?"

"Yep."

"Maybe you wanna take some steaks with you, huh? Since these poor bastards'll prob'ly get themselves killed over there."

Nebraska shook his head. "We got freezers full of steaks, Sarge. Matter of fact, if you ever need any t-bones, give us a shout."

The mess sergeant grinned. "Okay. Take whatever you want outa the store room. But if you'd wanted any steaks, I woulda hadda check up on you. No offense, but everybody's tryin' to steal from me these days."

Nebraska pointedly did not look at the sergeant's bulging gut nor at the diamond-studded wrist watch he wore.

"Pure hell bein' an honest man these days," Nebraska said.

"You play," the mess sergeant asked, indicating the chess book.

"Chess? Not me," Nebraska said. "Don't have the brains or education."

The fat man looked smugly superior. Nebraska turned to go. "Thanks a lot, sarge. We'll get right...shit!"

"What's the matter?"

"Nothing. Nothing. Just remembered I gotta dry cleaning down town, and I went and left the slip with my wife. Thanks again," and Nebraska was motivating toward the side door.

Check all your razors/And your guns./We gonna be rasslin' when

193

the wagon comes...

The Shit started coming down when he saw two disgruntled people walk into the mess hall and pick up trays, after the commissioned one signed a register. Both of them wore green dress uniforms... plus white-covered busman's caps under one arm.

And MP armbands.

Jenkins and Lieutenant Sanders.

Perhaps they were now off-shift or else Higher Authority had told them to chow down before retrieving the dead car from the Panhandle. Nebraska didn't care - he just wanted to be suddenly invisible. But they didn't spot him, and were intent on loading their trays with coldcuts, dead bread, yellowing potato salad and Jello salad.

No longer cocky, Nebraska moved the truck around to the rear of the messhall and started loading up as quickly as he could, before the two MP's could finish their meal and exit the messhall.

Finally the truck was loaded with enough rations to feed every starving runaway on the Haight for a day or so and gunning away, down the hill, out of the Presidio toward Golden Gate Park.

"Whoo, that was a little close," Nebraska said.

"Yeah, but the mother... oops. Sorry about the language. You know, you put on the uniform again, and right away, you spin right back into bein' a garbagemouth," Jeff observed. "Which suggests the only reason we're getting away with it is because of our Constant Clean Living and Religious Thoughts. And can I have a toke now?"

"Not until we're back behind the wire," Tyrell said firmly, "That damned Grancell might still be waiting to swoop on us."

...I was born in the desert/Raised in a lion's den/And my number one occupation/Is stealing women from their men...

Crafts booths delighted the eye at one end of the park. There were glass blowers, bead stringers, leather workers, candle makers and women turning out tie-dye sheets and scarves from big washtubs of every color dye imaginable.

There were buttons for sale and for giveaways: Supersex. Don't Mess With Mesc. CIA Off Campus. Power To Powell. Ruby Was Murdered.

Allan Cole & Chris Bunch

Fortunes were read, I Ching stalks cast, and a lady in a tent painted bright, swirling designs on people's bodies.

The crowd was as exotic as the booths.

There were jugglers and clowns and a team of acrobats hurling themselves aloft on a trampoline, their bodies were covered in beautiful designs painted on by the lady in the tent.

Archers twanged makeshift toy bows. Magicians pulled ankh necklaces from the ears of surprised kids.

And there were all kinds of musicians. Jamming with the Dead. Or communing with some inner listener. They competed with whistles and flutes, tambourines, conch shells and toy slide trombones. Some played Chinese oboes, or six-foot-long trumpets... chanting Tibetan wisdom all the while.

New and old copies of underground newspapers were passed about. A popular favorite was the Oracle. The cover displayed a snow-topped mountain with the words "San Francisco" inscribed on its peak. Three flying saucers hovered over the mountain.

Purple rays formed the face of Chief Joseph of the Nez Pierce Indians.

The newspaper smelled of Jasmine mist perfume.

...Well. can't you see that you're killing each other's soul/Well, you're both out in the streets and you got no place to go...

A

young woman in a see-thru plastic minidress and boots led a band of war protesters through the park.

She wore nothing under the dress, which was covered with little white symbols of peace. She hoisted a sign that read: "Make Love, Not War."

Her helpers passed out a raft of banners and posters. One had a picture of a sweating LBJ, trying to charm some GI's in his recent visit to Vietnam. "Why Is This Man Sweating?" The caption said.

There were others: "War Is Unhealthy To Children And Other Living Things." This beneath a picture of a napalmed Vietnamese girl. "Bomb Washington... Not Hanoi," went another. "Gold Star Mothers Go To War," chided one more. And finally: "17,000 Americans Dead... And Counting."

Samantha watched all the signs and people push by. She thought about Jeff and the gut-churning turmoil he faced coming home. What waited in LA seemed so trivial and pointless after what he and his friends had been through. What did it matter what kind of a life he chose? At least he was

195

alive to do some choosing.

Then Sunshine was at her side. "It's time... right?"

Samantha came back to reality. Yes. It was time. Now... Where was Grancell?

...Gimme a reefer and a gang o'gin/Slay me, 'cause I'm in my sin/Slay me 'cause I'm full of gin...

But there were no problems. Samantha's decoy operation had sucked the heat far away from where they cross-countried with the 3/4 ton. They unloaded the truck's supplies back of Hippie Hill and waited. Now, if Sunshine had been able to con somebody into giving them a working party...

But first they had to get rid of the truck.

Jeff thought there would be no problem, jumped inside, and gunned away, leaving four-wheel-drive cleat marks across the summer grass.

...The Judge decreed it/The clerk he wrote it down/Clerk he wrote indeed-o/Judge decreed it/clerk he wrote it down/Give you this jail sentence/You'll be Nashville bound...

The big cop smelled an even bigger rat. He'd spotted some husky-looking youths disappearing over a hill. It was their purposefulness that roused his suspicions. All seriousness. No hippy grab-assing or dope sharing. He also caught the swift, sidelong glances at him and his uniformed brothers who were monitoring the crowd.

Something was up.

"Hey. Hey, Grancell."

"You again, Robbie. Thought I told ya to get lost!"

"I tried, man," Robbie said, a touch mournful. "Honest, I did. But some sucker went and found me again."

"Yeah... Well keep tryin' you little creep. Now, get out of my way."

Grancell started by, intending to check out the hippy-dippy types doing the disappearing act. To his amazement, he found his way barred. It was his least favorite little creep in the dazzling jockstrap.

"What is this? You wanna get busted?"

"No, man," Robbie protested, face glowing with innocence. "I wantcha to bust that other guy."

Allan Cole & Chris Bunch

"What other guy?"

"The one that keeps finding me, man. You gotta stop him, Grancell. It's hard gettin' lost, you know. I mean, this is America, right? Cop tells you to get lost, you do what you're told. Momma raised me like that. So, there I was, loster'n shit, and this big guy comes up and says... 'Aha! Found ya!' You can't let 'em get away with that, Grancell."

He pulled at Grancell's sleeve. "Come on. This is a good bust, man. I fuckin' promise."

It was the hand on the material that did it. Grancell blew. Pulled back a fat ham fist and struck out.

He blinked in surprise.

Robbie wasn't there. He'd done a double back flip and was now standing maybe fifteen feet away. Laughing.

"Hey... No violence, man," came another voice.

Grancell whirled to see Supersplib doing his permanent lounge.

"You want some too?" Grancell threatened.

Supersplib acted like he was offended. Taken aback. He gave a sad shake of his head.

"Definitely not my bag, sir," Supersplib said with great dignity. "Nor is it welcome among all the peace loving young people you find here."

An elegant wave of his hand took in the whole crowd.

"If you don't cease, this instant," Supersplib warned, "that young man over there and I shall be forced to seek assistance from the law."

Another elegant wave indicated a few uniforms.

Grancell gaped. "I am the god damned law!"

"You have identification, I suppose?" Supersplib pressed.

"Knock it off, asshole. You know who I am, dammit. Grancell. Officer Grancell, to you! Tell him, Robbie."

The only reaction from Robbie was another wild laugh.

"The way I see this situation," Supersplib said, "is that two distinct possibilities have just presented themselves. One: If you are an officer of law... as you maintain... then your language to a citizen is deplorable. Second: I know of this Grancell you speak of... And he tends to be hard on imposters."

Grancell had enough. "Arrggh!" he shouted. But as the growl burst from his lips, and his hand went to the hidden gun, badge and cuffs, it suddenly occurred to him that he was being messed with. Shit! where'd those kids...he saw a final party of them disappear. Screw these two clowns!

197

Grancell broke into a sloppy run.

"Hey. Hey, Grancell. Wait up, man!" A second later, Robbie was jogging easily beside him. Just out of reach. He'd stripped off the jock strap and was completely naked, except for that leather band around his biceps. To Grancell, it looked oddly obscene. But he had no time for nonsense. He'd deal with Robbie later.

There was a wild cry of fright, and Grancell's nose met the ground. Tears spurted out as he rolled over to get up. The pain was fierce. What the hell happened?

"Why don't you look where you're going," came the woman's voice. Grancell startled at the vision climbing to her feet and rubbing a sore spot on her haunches. Haunches covered only by a fishnet sarong.

Grancell gaped at all the pulchritude.

"Yeah, what's the matter with you?" Came another voice. This from an all-over champagne blonde, hand on her naked hip.

"What's the cat in such a hurry for?" Asked a girl in a see-through plastic mini.

"I don't know," said another nude person. This one a man in white-face. "Maybe it's something over the hill? Is that it, buddy?"

Now people were appearing from nowhere and everywhere. Naked people. Curious people. Crowding around and asking stupid questions. Private parts hanging out in front of God and everybody.

Grancell's blood hit the boiling point again. He stormed to his feet. "I'm gonna bust every one of you assholes!"

"Bust us? Is he crazy, or what?"

"Claims he's a pig," came Supersplib's soft voice. He was the only dressed person in the crowd. But just as cool as ever.

"I told you... I am a pig... Shit! I mean cop."

"Well, I guess we're all arrested than," said a naked young woman. "We better go with him, Sam."

"You're right, Sunshine" said the woman next to her. "Okay, everybody. We're arrested."

There were many, many oh, darns, and jimminy beeswax, and, aw, please, Mister Policeman, can't we stay and play?

Before he could take a second breath, there were minimum twenty volunteers, holding out their hands for cuffs. All wearing birthday suits.

Grancell could just imagine himself conducting these freaks to the station. He'd be a laughing-stock. Shit! It was worse. He'd be lucky to get to

198

Allan Cole & Chris Bunch

the station alive.

"Fuck all of ya," Grancell snarled.

He started for that damned hill again. But the naked types crowded around him. He raised his arms to fend off blows, but all that was threatened was a shower of kisses.

A sloppy one hit his cheek. He whirled to find the offender, and got a tongue in his ear. A hand went to his zipper. Grancell was frightened because he didn't know what sex the hand was.

"You can't do this," Grancell shouted. "All of you are going to..."

A bota bag was upended from someplace and warm red wine streamed all over Grancell. He tried to fight, but gentle hands were coming in from everywhere. Pulling him down. Softness everywhere... the belt came loose, the shirt buttons popped away... the gorgeous casuals from Kinney's were tugged off... Grancell wanted to scream for help... His brother officers would drive these freaks away in an instant... but he felt his trousers pull away from his ankles... fresh air shriveled his nuts as the boxer shorts went the way of the trousers... and all thoughts of shouts for help went out of him.

Instead, he redoubled his efforts. Hurling against the naked weight pressing down.

Suddenly, he was wrestling nothing. Lashing at emptiness. Grancell looked up, bewildered. The naked kids were staring. Humiliation washed over him. Grancell tried to cover his balls with a hand, not doing a very good job.

He looked wildly about for his clothes... And, oh, fuck his gun and... He saw them passed from hand to hand and then rolled up like a football, tied with his belt... and hurled into a dense clump of thorny brush.

"This isn't right," Robbie was saying. "I mean, the man wants to go over the hill... we should let him. Right?"

"Right," said the woman in the fishnet sarong. "It's a free country."

"We're sorry, Mister," said the all over blonde. "You go do what you have to."

She turned, displaying the loveliest behind this side of the Rockies. But Grancell was not into appreciation. He was into helpless pissoff as the crowd chorused apologies and drifted away.

Grancell looked at the brush, where his clothes and gun were. Then up the hill.

"You ought to be ashamed of yourself, young man," came a quavery voice.

Allan Cole & Chris Bunch

An old woman was blinking down at Grancell's nakedness.

"Behaving like this... in front of all these innocent children."

Scorn and venom dripped from her lips. Grancell had visions of many lost years of seniority. How would he explain this? Especially losing his gun. He scrambled to his feet and ran like the blazes toward the dubious safety of the thorny brush.

The old woman laughed at such a sight. Fingering the silver peace sign dangling from her neck.

...Could have been a spoonful of coffee/Could have been a spoonful of tea...

By the time Jeff trotted back, the work gang had showed up, a disorganized giggle of stoners, but being ramrodded by Hell's Angel Dick and Digger Peter. Cases and cans were vanishing over the hill and out of sight.

Tyrell was admiring a huge can of fruit cocktail.

"You remember," he asked Jeff, "How you'd kill somebody, anybody, three days in the field for that little C-rat can of fruit cocktail. And now, look at this mother."

"Yeah," Jeff agreed. "Guess we really <u>are</u> back in the world, aren't we?"

"Guess so," Tyrell said. "An' you know, I just realized something. I never liked fruit cocktail much, anyway."

He turned and pitched the can to a particularly hungry-looking young man. "Oh yeah," he asked. "Where'd you ditch the 3/4?"

"I didn't. I gave it away."

"You what?"

"Pulled up alongside a couple of guys on... Masonic, I think it was. Said I thought their karma needed a free truck. They thought so, too. Jumped in, and drove right off."

Tyrell started laughing. He sank back onto the grass. "Okay, Doc. Here. You deserve it." And he fired up the boomer and passed it to Jeff. Then he started laughing again, and his laughter chopped.

"Oh my...would you look at that?"

Jeff spun and saw Nebraska standing on top of the rapidly-dwindling stack of supplies. In one hand he held a can of bread, in the other a monster oval tin of Del Monte sardines.

"Yeah," Jeff wondered. "So?"

"Oh yeah," Tyrell remembered. "We didn't go to the same church, did we. Uh... it's in Matthew. And goes something like, uh, [x]...And He commanded the multitudes to sit and took the five loaves and three fishes and they all did eat and there were twelve baskets left over.'"

"Oh come on," Jeff protested.

"Let's take him on down to that model ship pond and see how far he hikes, hey?"

"Shut up. Gimme back the joint. Before ol' Nebraska realizes who he is, and whomps us with the old lightnin' bolt.

"We got some party catch-upping to do!"

...Check all your razors and your guns/Do the shim-sham-shimmy till the rising sun./Gimme a pigfoot and a bottle of beer.. .

...Just a little spoon of your precious love/Is good enough for me/Man lies about that/Man cries about that/Man dies about that/Spoonful. spoonful, spoonful...

"You mean... *all* **of you were naked,"** Tyrell said, gazing in amazement at his lovely Sunshine. She was fully clothed now.

"If that don't beat all... Wish I coulda seen his face," Nebraska drawled.

"We got a better look than that," Sunshine laughed.

"Wasn't much of a winker, honey," Alexis said. "I wasn't there, you understand. But all reports from women I respect... say you got no competition at all." Alexis gave Nebraska a big kiss.

Jeff laughed and pulled Samantha closer to him. He took a well-deserved toke. Not that he needed it. He was already high from excitement and the hero's welcome they had received. And he was getting higher still by the minute. A contact high from all the bizarre sights and sounds and smells of the Love In.

"Look out!" Samantha shouted, pulling at him.

Jeff found himself gaping at a long dragon, snaking through the crowd. Its head stood two stories high, and he couldn't see the end of its long body.

The dragon was green and red, with dangling ribbons for teeth in its gaping maw.

Samantha pulled again. Just in time, they both stepped aside and the dragon cut between them and their friends. The people under the dragon decided to do their dragony dance right there.

"Had enough?" Samantha asked, a gleam of promise in her eyes.

Jeff's answer was a squeeze of her slender waist and a wave at Tyrell and Nebraska.

"See ya later," he shouted.

Nebraska shouted something back. Tyrell hoisted a thumbs up sign.

Jeff and Samantha turned away, and in a blink, had disappeared into the crowd.

Allan Cole & Chris Bunch

CHAPTER TWELVE

....They'll be laughing, singing, music swinging and dancing in the street...

…WHICH WAS AS FAR as far as The Dead got into "Dancing in the Street" when the screaming started.

Jeff started to roll flat and scrabble for his M16 - the screaming was exactly that of somebody who'd just lost his kneecap to a boobytrap. Now they spring the ambush, he thought, caught himself and looked around for his backup.

But Nebraska and Tyrell were nowhere in sight.

He heard the shouts over the music: "Freakin' out... swallowed... tongue... Jesus Christ!" And he was darting through the crowd as the song chopped and somebody onstage had the mike:

"Uh... we've got somebody on a bummer... is there anybody from the Free Clinic here? Do we have a doctor..."

Jeff, trailing a more-than-a-little startled Samantha, shoved his way through the ring of gapers standing around the thrashing body.

The kid was maybe fifteen or so. Pudgy. He was in the process of growing his short hair long and wore clean clothes, now vomit-spattered. He was coiling and rolling about, and Jeff was on his knees as the boy puked again.

"Somebody hold him," Jeff said. But nobody moved. Jeff forced the boy over on his side... fingers automatically prying his jaws... holding his mouth open, while three careful fingers slipped inside... caught the slippery eel of a tongue... pulled it free, vomit gushing.

"Water," he shouted again, and somebody handed him something - a jug of sweet wine - which would have to do - and he sluiced it into the kid's mouth, not letting him swallow any and there was an Angel thudding down on the kid's chest and the boy was pinned flat.

"Goddamit," Jeff swore, "we're not wrestling! Just keep him still! Somebody get some water," He pegged the emergency-only wine bottle back into the crowd. Then, somehow there was an old boy scout canteen in his hands, and he sluiced the kid's mouth again, and again... rasped breathing becoming normal.

The boy began moaning and the thrashing started again. Jeff didn't know what the hell was going on.

The boy rasped words: "Too big... sun coming down... and my father's got a brand new jag... Poppa's got a brand new bag..." shrill hysteric giggle.

Epilepsy, he wondered.

"Aw, he's just on a bad trip," somebody above him said. "Whaddaya expect... weekend hippie."

Bad trip? Acid? How do you treat this? Where the hell was a *real* doctor anyway? Jeff was nothing more than a Clear the Airway/Stop the Bleeding/Protect the Wound/Treat for Shock grunt medic.

Samantha was kneeling beside him.

"Get a cop," Jeff said. "I dunno what's the matter... but we gotta get an ambulance in."

The Angel broke in: "Naw, man. You don't know what you're sayin'. They'll just bust him down to Park Station... or else put him in Frisco General which'll really fuck his mind."

"So what do we do?"

What was this? Some kind of overdose? All Jeff knew about overdoses was he'd heard that some REMF'd banged six syrettes of morphine in his arm once. But he'd supposedly been trying to suicide after getting Dear Johnned anyway... and oh yeah that movie he'd seen with The Rifleman in it about Synanon.

"The Free Clinic," both the biker and Samantha said in near-unison. Wonderful, Jeff thought. I get a chance to see a real live love-in, the only one I'll ever get too, and miss the first part stealing food for kids who oughta be told to go home before they get in real trouble and now we got this fattie...

"Son of a bitch," he swore... and his fingers scooped into the kid's mouth again, pulling his tongue back out as the boy tried to strangle himself once more.

"We better get going," Samantha said. "Pretty soon the cops will stroll down this way... and then he's going to be put in a straight jacket for sure."

The three of them lugged the boy to his feet.

"Oh, I can walk, I can walk," the boy suddenly said. "But where oh where are we going... going... gone..." And the laugh was maniacal once more.

"We're going," Samantha's voice soothed, "to a bridge by a fountain... where rocking horse people eat marshmallow pie."

The boy giggled - a happy laugh - and they moved off. Jeff guessed that the way to keep the young man calm was to *sound* calm

- just like you did when you had somebody as stable as you were going to get them, and they probably weren't going to make it, but the dustoff was on the way and they deserved a chance.

So he awkwardly parroted Samantha's phrases for a bit, then shut up when he realized that the tripper was reacting far better to a woman's voice.

He was starting to get pissed - they'd walked past half a dozen cops, all of whom had looked at them, looked at the stumbling young man, and ignored everything. Instead, he saw two heavy-set cops beefing a puzzled girl who had a backpack and sleeping bag: "Told you hippies once, told you a thousand times, you can come in the park all you wanna. But not with a sleeping bag. This ain't no crashpad, this is a *park!*"

Jeff had never liked cops much anyway. Now he was starting to see them as real enemies.

He shut off that train of thought as unproductive, and concentrated on helping the freaker toward this Free Clinic place.

At the Free Clinic Jeff realized in seconds that Free was more important than Clinic, because this lashup resembled no clinic he'd ever seen, least of all that air-conditioned, plush series of modern-art-decorated suites his father based his practice from.

It was at the corner of Haight and Clayton Street, upstairs in a yellow building that probably had been a dentist's office at one time.

Outside there was a sign: **David E. Smith. M.D. and Associates: Haight-Ashbury Free Medical Clinic and Happening House.**

Inside, an emblem, a white peace dove on a blue cross and a slogan: Love Needs Care.

At the top of the stairs were posters with the House Rules:

No Holding. No Dealing. No Using Dope, No Pets. Any of These Can Close The Clinic. We Love You.

Another poster:

No Smoking Except Tobacco.

A third, rather grim one: A nude girl, crouched in a rocky cafe in fetal position; with an inscription: **RETURN.**

Jeff glanced at the boy they were half-carrying upstairs. He'd started moaning again.

Wonderful. And they were bringing him into:

Allan Cole & Chris Bunch

Chaos - Somebody trying to slam herself through a wall... another young girl prancing naked through the room.. yet another quietly drawing pictures in the air.

The waiting room itself was threadbare carpeting, some battered chairs, posters on the wall, a mattress on the floor, no curtains. There were four people waiting on the bed, paying no attention to the prancing dopers. These four, Jeff hastily diagnosed with a gulp of disbelief, looked just like he did when he'd had the measles. Except that they were sixteen or more, and he'd had the disease when he was seven.

He was just thinking that perhaps both Samantha and the Hell's Angel were full of hops - even a rubber room at the local charity hospital would be better for this guy than this Free Clinic dump when a bearded man - about five years older than Jeff - wandered up. He looked at the three of them:

"All three of you tripping?" he asked in a pronounced San Joaquin Valley drawl.

"No," Samantha said. "Just him." She patted the boy.

"Do you know what he's on?"

"No," Jeff said. "We were over at the park... the Love-in... and somebody started screaming about a freakout. We went over... he was in a convulsive state. He'd managed to swallow his tongue, which I pulled out. Panic state... I noticed some pupillary distortion... Reflexive vomiting. I washed his mouth out."

"With what?"

"Somebody handed me some wine."

"Mmm."

"He didn't swallow any... or anyway not much. Then I sluiced his mouth out with water."

"Okay. Hi, son."

The young boy started crying.

"My name's Daniel," the doctor said, conversationally. "Who're you?"

"I... I thought my new name was Rocky," the boy sobbed. "But I'm not. I'm just a big fat blob... and the sun was melting me."

"Of course, you're a Rocky. That's a good name. And we're inside, and the sun's back of a cloud, so you can't melt here. Come on. Feel like maybe a little orange juice? I can handle a glass of it myself."

"Mmm. Orange juice. Okay... Daniel."

The doctor put an arm gently around the boy, and started leading him

Allan Cole & Chris Bunch

away.

"Everything is cool, everything is calm," Daniel said. "We have a place where you can just sit and be mellow... and no one can ever, ever bother you."

The boy's tears had stopped, and he went through the door. The doctor looked back at Jeff and Samantha.

"If you don't mind... Hang around for a little bit. I'd like to talk."

"He'll be all right," Daniel said. "At least till he comes down. Then he'll have to deal with whatever set him up for this bummer in the first place. Family... friends...just being an adolescent. Whatever."

"I sure wouldn't want to be a teenager these days," he said. "I had enough trouble with beer and bennies."

"What was he stoned on?" Samantha asked.

"He said Blue Dot acid, which means probably some LSD, plus conceivably some methamphetamine to give it a boot plus if he bought it as a heavy dose anything up to and including a little strychnine."

"That's just great," Jeff shuddered.

"It's interesting," Daniel went on, "how folks roll into the Haight, full of being on the natural and eating brown rice and being vegetarian... which is cool, of course.

"But they'll go ahead and dump anything... and I mean anything... that somebody says will get them stoned into their system without wondering what just might happen.

"Oh well. If I'd wanted consistency I could gone to Johns Hopkins."

"How'd do you treat someone like this?" Jeff wanted to know.

"Easy... even if those straights at the hospital don't want to know or don't care. Get them inside, get them to a calm, non-threatening atmosphere.

"Orange juice seems to cool them out a little bit. As a quick fix, thorazine will bring them down... somewhat.

"When we've got it, though, we'll use 50 milligrams chlorpromazine intramuscularly every couple of hours. If the reaction's prolonged, then we get serious."

"What did you mean, when you've got it?" Jeff asked.

"We're Free," Daniel said, a note of bitterness in his voice. "Which means the fair city of San Francisco doesn't give us diddly but what we can poor mouth them out of. And sometimes we run

207

out. Hell of a summer it's been, and so far it's only July."

"Oh well," he said, crossing to the coffee machine, and pouring three cups. "I've just been up too long," he said, handing the cups to Jeff and Samantha. "We operate on volunteer help... and sometimes volunteers can be hard to find."

He turned and looked out a window, pretending not to notice as both Jeff and Samantha slipped bills into the donations can next to the coffee machine.

Then he turned back, and asked, very directly: "Where'd you take your premed before you dropped out?"

Jeff eyed him. "My dad once told me," he said, "you could get about half your diagnosis just filling out the information sheet. You've got moves on him.

"I flunked out of USC when I was a senior," he said. Then the Army grabbed me for a medic."

"Very interesting," Daniel said. "Proof that I don't <u>really</u> have moves. Otherwise I would have tagged you as being a serviceman from the haircut.

"Are you going to or coming from Vietnam? Or have you... decided you don't want to participate in the war?"

"Coming back," Jeff said. "I'm a slow learner."

"So what are you doing on the Haight?"

Jeff stammered a bit - hell, he wasn't really sure, and just having a good time sounded thin.

Samantha stepped in: "He was supposed to go home and get right back in the same trap that got him flunked and drafted. I'm saving him from himself."

Jeff blinked... yeah, he knew Samantha went straight for the truth, and yeah, that was pretty close to the truth, but damn, did she have to tell everybody everything? Not that it really mattered, he realized.

"Going back," Daniel quizzed. "Med school again?"

"That's what the family wants."

Daniel and Samantha exchanged looks.

"There are lots of doctors," the bearded man said, most obliquely, "... and some of them didn't go to the University of Southern California."

There was the thunder of feet up the stairs - more emergencies? Instead,

208

it was a black couple, both wearing medical tunics.

"What're you still doing here, Doctor?"

"Miller didn't show up to replace me," Daniel said. "Guess he's still on-call."

"Would you go the hell home?"

"Maybe, after—"

"After nothing," the woman said. "We can handle the farm. You two. You look respectable. Take him somewhere and buy him a scotch or something. Something strong, so his peckerneck conscience won't let him come back and try to help out because he's Been Drinking."

"But—"

"But me buts, Doctor. The Love-In is breaking up... there's no riots... no murders... and just the usual amount of walking wounded on the Haight.

"So out, out, outsky!"

Samantha and Jeff looked at each other - why not? Buy a doctor a drink...

·

..And the only sound that's left/After the ambulances go/Is Cinderella sweeping up/On Desolation Row...

"Back there," Samantha prodded, as they wove their way through the building near-dusk foot traffic along Haight, "you said something about lots of kinds of doctors."

"I said, to quote myself exactly, that there are lots of doctors. But lots of kinds also applies."

"I don't understand."

"Well, me for instance. My folks are dirt farmers. So I had to work. First the grades, so Cal would take a look at me, and maybe give me a scholarship. But that wasn't enough.

"So I waited tables at fraternities. I hope neither of you happened to Go Greek as those over privileged idiots would call it."

"Not a chance," Jeff said. "I'm a Jew."

"Good," Daniel said. "Just don't lose sight of that - none of us who've been on the bottom have any business hanging out with the elite. Unless we're after a donation."

"Anyway. Kinds of doctors. So I'm a pathologist. Doctor Edwards and his wife - the Afro couple you met back there - are both psychiatrists."

He sighed. "What we really need at this zoo we call a Free Clinic... besides a Sugar Daddy... is an emergency surgeon... But all of them I've hit on seem more interested in other things."

"Like money?"

"They aren't quite that bad," Daniel said. "Or at least not that blatant. But it's always... after I'm established... hem, hem... I'll have plenty of time for charity work. Call me then, Doctor."

Daniel's weary temper sparked: "Charity! As if being a doctor entitles you to—"

"Stop frothing, Doctor," Samantha said.

"Was I? Sorry." Daniel stared out at the bumper-to-bumper traffic on Haight, then changed the subject. "You were a medic, you said? Doing what?"

"Just the usual," Jeff said, casual. "Blisters. Sunstroke. Crabs. Mosquito bites. Once or twice something a little different."

"In other words, you were in combat. What I've heard called a line medic."

Jeff didn't respond.

"I wonder how long it will take," Daniel mused, "before America realizes what a resource it's developing in Vietnam?"

Both Jeff and Samantha looked at him askance.

"You don't understand, either," Daniel said, with some amusement. "But let me ask you a question: If someone happened to get hit in that tropical paradise, and survived the immediate shock long enough for one of those helicopter ambulances—"

"Medevacs," Jeff said automatically.

"Medevacs... to pick them up, what were their chances of living?"

"Good."

"Very good, to be exact," Daniel said. "Well above 80%, according to some things I've read. That is unlike any other war. Remember the Civil War, where half of all battle casualties died, and most of that half were those who were lucky enough to avoid the man with the saw?"

"You've lost me."

"What I'm saying is—"

Whatever point the Free Clinic doctor had been planning to make went unmade as:

Allan Cole & Chris Bunch

BRAKESCREAM

WOMANSCREAM

The long grate of metal.

The completely hollow THUUD of the impact.

Shouts and Daniel was running toward the nearby intersection, where traffic suddenly locked solid and the Haight crowd swarmed. Jeff and Samantha dashed after him.

Part of Jeff's mind was being a lookyloo - the bus would just have been pulling out, and the bike cop, probably angry at the trudge through traffic, gunned it, just as the light went yellow and the El Camino gunned it, trying to make the left on the light.

If it'd been a car instead of small pickup the big Harley'd gone into, the motorcycle policeman would either have been dead of a broken neck or lucked out and suffered only minor lacerations.

Instead, he'd gone airborne, over the rear of the truck, spun in midair and then ground his way down Haight Street on his chest.

The bus driver was out of his bus, shouting. The man driving the El Camino was out of his truck... puking. The Haight freaks were surging back and forth.

"He's dead...Jesus, he's gotta be... no, I saw him move..." and Jeff elbowed through, behind Daniel. Who stood there for a moment, trying to figure out, it appeared, what the steps were to take with no medical tools for a man without much of a face any more.

Jeff pushed him away, and was on automatic pilot. Pull that stupid dishpan helmet off, and get him turned over, and somebody pulling at him:

"Hey, he might have a broken neck—"

Jeff came up, straight punch into the officious bus driver's gut as he snarled the cop wasn't fucking breathing and who cared about his damned neck! Ripping the cop's leather jacket and uniform shirt open, pen knife snapped open cutting the necktie off, and listening to his chest.

Even through the crowdboom around him, he could hear. Or not hear. No heart at all. He could feel no pulse.

How nice. Jeff appeared to have both cardiac arrest and, thanks to the crash itself, respiratory arrest from an airway obstruction on his hands.

Jeff's eyes were scanning. There. In the back of the El Camino.

211

Toolbox. Three big steps, and he was at the truck.

He ripped the toolbox open, praying the Camino's owner was a real working guy, not somebody who wore greasy mechanic's uniform because that was his trip.

Jumper cables.

The car that'd skidded to a stop just in front of the dying - technically dead - bike cop was an old Plymouth. Its driver, a little old lady, sat frozen behind the wheel.

"Sam! Get her out!"

Jeff had the hood of the Plymouth popped, and was hooking the jumper cables up. One to the ignition coil's hot . side, the other cable to ground. You don't know what you're doing, do you, he thought, quite collectedly, having the cool to notice that his breathing was about normal. But didn't somebody say something once about some green beanie medic who'd done this with cleaning rods?

The old lady came tottering out from the driver's seat.

"Sam! Hit the starter when I holler! Just a twitch - don't give it any gas."

Kneeling again... next to the cop grounded jumper cable in his right armpit... live one in the left. "Do it!"

The Plymouth's starter ground, and the body convulsed! But that was all.

Again. Another jolt.

Damn.

A third time.

Damn, damn! But this time, cursing in pure surprise:

"It worked," Jeff muttered, checking, and feeling that slow tump... tump... tump as the policeman's heart tentatively beat... beat... and then caught.

From here on out it was easy.

Jeff flipped the jumper cables away. Now he had all the time in the world - hell, somebody could handle not breathing for four to six minutes before there was brain damage.

And we *are* talking about a cop, aren't we? So how can you tell brain damage, anyway?

He picked up his pen knife again. His other hand pulled the skin tight over the cop's windpipe, and then he slit, straight down, cutting through several of the tracheal rings.

212

Allan Cole & Chris Bunch

"Daniel?" Jeff called.

"Right here."

"If you got a ballpoint, you want to bust it in half? Pull the guts out and give me the tube."

Daniel obeyed, and slapped the busted pen into his palm, OR-style. Jeff gently tucked the tube into the cop's windpipe to keep the incision open. Blood - and air -bubbled back and forth as he breathed.

Jeff peeled back an eyelid, then checked the cop's pulse and his gums. The son of a bitch would live. Jeff then looked to make sure there weren't any blood-pumping wounds he might have missed amid the gore. There weren't. The cop'd need a new face, but at least he wasn't going to bleed to death here on Haight Street.

Far down Haight, he could hear and then see the siren/red light of an ambulance. Fine. These guys - *real* medics - could handle the rest of the emergency procedure.

Jeff muttered "Take it, Tommy," to himself, and stood up, to suddenly-perceived crowd/awe.

Not bad, Katz, he thought. Bet even the old man'd be surprised.

The crowd may or may not have been shouting or talking. He couldn't hear anything. He turned.

Both Samantha and Daniel were looking at him. Considerable respect. Okay now, Jeffrey, for once, don't blow it Think Doctor Kildare. Hell, think Lionel Barrymore. But the best he could come up with was:

"Okay," he said. "Now, weren't we talking about a drink?"

Daniel, after a very long moment, just pointed.

Jeff looked at himself.

His brand new, hippie-mod, high-dollar vines were sodden with blood. Hell. And it wasn't till later that he came up with three sick jokes about Bloody Marys.

It didn't matter.

Samantha took him by the arm.

"Come on. You need a bath before you have a drink.

"Doctor."

CHAPTER THIRTEEN

JEFF LIFTED AN aching leg, gripped the tap with his toes and twisted. The hot water thundered into the tub. He let it run until his skin was about to blister, then tiredly twisted the tap off. He eased back, stifling a groan of aching muscles. He scraped his blood-encrusted nails across a bar of soap and then wearily scrubbed them with a brush. Dried flakes came away, turning bright red in the water. Diluting to pink. Then vanishing.

He heard Samantha singing along to the stereo:

... The celebrated Mr. K/ Performs his feat on Saturday at/ Bishopsqate...

Jeff sighed... feeling better, feeling better all the time... Hummed along with her as he scrubbed up a good lather all over. Then he started noticing some of the comforts Samantha had laid out for his bath. There was a tall, cold glass of wine. Beside it, several fat, handrolled joints waited in the ashtray on the edge of the tub.

He sipped the wine, then lit up. Inhaled like a pro... kept that smoke in until his head swam... then eased it out in a fine hiss of Mexican brown, just like Nebraska had taught him.

This wasn't exactly how he had planned on ending the day. He'd had serious ideas about Samantha. Identical, he was sure, to her own. But after being up to their elbows in bad trips and blood, he doubted she was still in the mood. What about you, Jeff? Me? I'm whipped brother, but... he took another toke ... I could get there... Definitely get there.

What about Rachel? Okay, bud, what about her? Nothing. Just asking. Jeff snarled his conscience back into the shadows, drank some wine to kick start the blood machine, and considered some tried and true methods of sleazing Samantha back into the mood.

Then he flashed on Atherton and Mills. Wouldn't they be diggin' this scene right now. He raised the wine glass to two permanently absent friends and promised: whatever happened next was for them. He drained the glass.

Elvis was singing out in the living room now: *One night with you... Is all I'm praying for...* Jeff took a super heavy toke.

"You're getting pretty good at that, Doctor," came Samantha's voice.

Jeff turned hazily to see her standing in the doorway with a jug of wine. Then he did a doubletake - his breath whooshing out a fat cloud of marijuana smoke.

Samantha was wearing this a nightie whose only description was Incredible. Sinfully brief with these amazing little panties and the whole outfit the color of... well, Samantha. It was so sheer she might as well have been starkers.

Samantha giggled, then did a slow showoff whirl.

"Well... what do you think?"

"Amazing," was the best Jeff could come up with. Except for the sudden surge underwater as his groin got the message. "Only thing is... uh. . . you wouldn't be cold, would you? Because if you are, I could sort of... "

"I wasn't cold at all," Samantha laughed. "Actually, I was feeling kind of warm. Flushed, here... and here... and..."

She let her fingers trail across some wonderful places of possible affliction.

"I thought maybe... I ought to get a doctor to... you know... look into it..."

"Yeah," Jeff said. "You should. I know just the guy. He's not in the book, but I guarantee he'll give you rapt attention."

"Give him a call," Samantha said, turning away to go, giving a purposeful wiggle to show off that incredible behind. "I'll be waiting... in my bedroom..." she was gone, her voice trailing in her wake. "... You know where my bedroom is, don't you Jeff?"

Jeff didn't answer. He came boiling out of the tub and in a flash there was nothing in the bathroom except the big puddles of his footprints.

The day ended like it began. Unexpectedly.

They never did make it to the bedroom.

SATURDAY: DAY THREE

"...This is the end/My only friend, the end./It hurts to set you free/But you'll never follow me..."

—Jim Morrison/ The Doors

"...Do your own thing. Be whatever you are. If you don't know, find out..."

—Chester Anderson Communication Company

"...If I'd been out till quarter to three/Would you lock the door,/Will you still need me, will you still feed me/When I'm sixty-four..."

—Lennon/McCartney

CHAPTER FOURTEEN

...an' I was made to love her...

TYRELL TOLD HIS singing-along mind to shut up, told Stevie to do the same, and focused on this bright shining morning.

This is the morning of the last day. No time to be fooling around with thoughts of love. Just hang your hat on what is, my friend:

Above them was a white-flecked dome. Over there was the knife-edge blue of the Bay. San Francisco's patented morning wind that cuts through hangovers, regrets and logic whisked past them.

Ahead stretched Haight Street, a street beckoning them into a new day full of endless promises.

Tyrell stepped over a wino.

The Haight was deserted at this hour. Only a few windows blew music down the street, and even these songs were sharded, mixed and then they vanished:

...You came to stay and/Live my way/Scatter my love like/Leaves in the wind...

Find another song, Tyrell.

...Everything is all right/Up-tight/Clean out of sight...

It is, dammit.

A ragged poster blew past them. Tyrell saw some words: SAVE THE FBI... and then it was gone.

Sunshine squeezed his arm. "You're the first boyfriend I've ever had, Ty-rell, who liked to get up early like me."

Tyrell gave her a hug, but just smiled. No, beautiful lady. I don't like to roll out of the sack any more than anybody else does. But the gooks had their own set of rules - mostly they'd hit us either at midnight or just around dawn. Fourteen months now, from false dawn on, the kid's been wide awake and bushytailed and would you for Christ's sake stop being such a bringdown.

Tyrell sipped at the paper cup of tea he held, and choked a little.

"Uh," he said, "I'm sorry. But... this herb tea isn't doing it. Guess it's meant for the nighttime. I gotta have some caffeine in me before my heart works right."

Sunshine looked a little disappointed - her beau ideal was human after all - but just smiled, and moved on, toward the Bob's Big Boy at the end of

Haight.

...If you feel like loving me/If you've got the motion/I second that emotion...

...There is a barber taking photographs/Of every head he's had the pleasure to know...

Supersplib looked at them through eyes that glowed like a tiger's in the night jungle. In the booth in front of him was a coffee cup and a ashtray full of half-smoked Kool butts.

"What are *you* doing out of bed," Sunshine wondered. And Tyrell was proud of himself for not having even a flickerthought of *how would you know*.

"Forgive me," he began, talking quite rapidly, "if I do not make a great deal of sense... or if I am not my usual jovial, witty self.

"Because I am amped. I am overamped, to be perfectly honest with you, and honesty I have found to be a virtue beyond all possible comprehension... although comprehension and understanding is something that I am just a tiny bit short of... being as how I am methed to my proverbial eyebrows not out of any desire to see how buzzed I can be or how much of a boring motormouth I am, but out of pure necessity, necessity being the mother *and* a mother... and at any rate I was supposed to meet a young man shortly after midnight who was coming up from South of the Border down Mexico way with a consignment of goods which he felt I might have a slight interest in Sunshine, do you want a donut?"

"Sure. Jelly, please."

"And you, young hero-type paratrooper?"

"Just coffee."

Supersplib waved to the waitress, who hurried to their booth - Supersplib evidently being, in the truest sense of the word, a longtime customer. Supersplib ordered including another refill for himself. "Although the Good Lord knows this is carrying coals to Pelion. I shall not sleep before doomsday, I fear.

"If I had known my... possible business source would be encountering some kind of delay, I most certainly would have caught some winks rather than hitting this expressway. Which has a most unfortunate effect on me. Not only does my complexion suffer, but I tend to become cranky. Irritable.

Allan Cole & Chris Bunch

"Which is not the most efficient way to conduct business," Supersplib went on, in his mad methadrine run.

"Oh well, oh well," he said. "This is but part of the parcel that comes with my chosen profession. One that they do not present with the glamour of the fast life, young Tyrell."

Tyrell had never thought that dealing drugs was very romantic... but what the hell did he know? The way America was now, maybe they were putting up recruiting posters in high school, the way the Army'd done.

"Oh well, oh well," Supersplib said once more. "There is a broken heart for every light on Broadway.

"And I may be unhappy with the state of the world... but I am nowhere near as unhappy as him!"

Supersplib waved out the window street... Tyrell and Sunshine turned, then ducked back, not wanting to be spotted.

An unmarked car drove slowly down Haight Street. Unmarked or maybe civilian. Behind the wheel was a bleary, unshaven Grancell. His eyes were as bloodshot and burning as Supersplib's. He passed without seeing them - or maybe he wasn't looking for them.

"Now there goes a man with a problem," Supersplib explained.

"Why," Sunshine wanted to know. "Just 'cause he got pantsed at the lovein yesterday? Man, the dude is *really* sexually uptight!"

Supersplib took another cigarette from the pack on the table, lit it, took three puffs, then stubbed it out. "He is that, he is that without a question, but his problems go farther, deeper and more sonorous... No, that isn't the correct word. What I'm looking for is..." Supersplib stopped and thought. Then shook his head.

"No. It's not there. My mind is behaving like a tropic cyclone."

"We were talking about ol' Grancell?" Tyrell prodded.

"Right you are, my friend. Grancell. He's looking for his badge and his gun."

"Whaat?"

"Yes. They were pitched into some bushes... and by the time he reached those bushes, they were gone, gone, gone/and I don't worry/'Cause I'm sittin' on top of the world."

Tyrell and Sunshine started laughing. Supersplib smiled. "As a matter of fact, someone asked if I wanted to purchase them, not an hour ago."

Supersplib shuddered. "I told ...this person... I thought not. This ticket agent is not interested. Try one of the hoodies or street spades. I preferred not to imagine what would happen if, say, I were rousted by one of San Francisco's finest, and not only happened to be holding, but was in possession of a badge and a gun. I assume that guns have numbers on them, and can be traced, yes? Ah. I was correct. Yes.

"It would not be fun to be a black, an arrested black hauled down to Park Station and to be found in possession of a police officer... a police officer who probably thinks George Lincoln Rockwell was a liberal... what was I saying?"

"About Grancell's gun," Sunshine said. Worried. "You're right, Super. Guns are bad, bad, karma."

The idea floated through Tyrell's mind like a big, happy, pink cloud. He smiled. "Bad karma," he said. "There was a guy in my company, back at Campbell. Lost a machinegun."

"Good for him," Sunshine approved.

"Maybe... but the Army didn't think so. Said the gun cost $973.00, or something like that, and he was gonna have to stay in the Army, I heard, until it was all paid for."

"Ah," Supersplib nodded. Even wired, he was not slow.

"You think whoever was trying to sell the gun might still have it?"

"I do. I would appear to be the only dealing man awake at this less-than-godly hour. And he wasn't interested in money. It was your friend, Sunshine. Robbie."

Sunshine startled. Stood. "A gun? Robbie, you can't do that. I'll talk to him. See if I can't get him off this bad trip."

"He'll be down at the crystal palace," Supersplib said. "Do have a word with him, you two. I fear he's in danger of falling into bad company."

Tyrell started to get up, then sat back down. "Supersplib," he said, "are you holding?"

"You have learned the vernacular quickly," the dealer approved. "I am. And I assume you are interested in... thirty dollars worth of lysergic acid diethylamide?"

Tyrell grinned, and dug bills from his pocket.

"Across the street," Supersplib said. "The trashcan? Reach underneath it. The bag is taped to the bottom. Sunshine will know what thirty dollars buys.

"Wait," Supersplib said. "I sense a jape. Yes. Yes, I do. Just take the acid, Tyrell. Consider this my contribution to a proper Summer of Love."

Allan Cole & Chris Bunch

Sunshine, not sure what was going on, but impressed at the gift, kissed Supersplib. Who looked just a taste uncomfortable, then recovered. "Go with God, my children. And I shall, no doubt, see you later. After I have a chance to crash for a few hours behind some reds, or at least stabilize out, when and if my connection ever materializes.

"In any event, I certainly shall be at The FBI Girl tonight. For the closing ceremonies... It should be... quite a reverberation."

Supersplib went back to endlessly stirring his cold coffee and waiting for his own Man...

...he's mighty handy/With a gun and a knife... the radio blared from the passing car. Tyrell and Sunshine paid no mind. They were intently watching the entrance to the police station.

"Suppose they bust Robbie," Sunshine asked.

"For what? He's being a good citizen."

"These days," Sunshine said, "policemen don't seem to need much of an excuse to arrest somebody. I sure will be glad when they get their head straight and just learn to groove with things."

Tyrell might have said something on the likelihood of that happening before the Second or Third Coming, but he spotted Robbie. The skinny young man strolled out of the station, looking Very Innocent. Then darted across the street and down the block to where Tyrell and Sunshine waited.

"Sunshine. Hey, Sunshine."

"What happened?" Sunshine asked, eager.

"Man," Robbie chortled. "They ate it up with a spoon! I come in, looking as stoner as I know how to, and the maincop sitting there growls something at me, and I just smile.

" 'I say, 'I was just trippin' through the park, Officer, an' I happens on this... is this a real gun, officer?'"

Tyrell snickered. "I don't say 'Hey, pig. Found this piece, and figured only a dumbass plainclothesman would pack something as worthless as this Smith .38 Centennial Airweight and thought I'd return it.' Figured it's always best to play dumb.

"Made sure I held it by the barrel, so the cop wouldn't think I was gonna shoot him or anything. Cop grabs it, right off. He's about to say something, and then I reach in, and hand over the shield case.

"Cop flips it open, goes oh shit, and tries to pretend he didn't say

221

Allan Cole & Chris Bunch

anything and so that's groovy, I go along with the show.

"He checks some kind of roster, and goes oh shit again, and then gets this *real* nasty grin. I guess ol' Grancell doesn't have a friend in him.

"The cat thanks me for bein' a good citizen, and not like them other freaks out here, and slips me ten bucks.

"You see," Robbie said, posing nobly. "I shoulda figured I was doing wrong, wrong, wrong, being an evil hippy and like that. I shoulda kept my hair short and taken ROTC, just like my uncle wanted.

"Anyway, so my blessings are now laid up in Heaven, right?" He looked rather pointedly at Tyrell. Tyrell walked over to a nearby bush, fished the plastic bag of acid tabs out, and gave it to Robbie.

"And like they say in the movie," Robbie said, making an elaborate bow, "a nation lifts its grateful eyes to you.. Peace. "

He bounded away.

"That guy should be an actor," Tyrell said.

"Or something," Sunshine said. "You know... I don't usually wish bad things on anyone... but I *really* hope they do something mean to Officer Grancell."

"They will," Tyrell promised, hoping that the incident wouldn't just get ignored... like so many other police "mistakes" had been around Memphis.

"Now. What say we motivate over to the hotel, wake up Nebraska and tell him that the Weed of Crime bears Bitter Fruit... The Shadow Knows...

"Heh. Heh. Heh.

CHAPTER FIFTEEN

ALEX WOKE WITH a song in her head *"...And the bulldogs all have rubber teeth/And the hens lay softboiled eggs/The farmers' trees are full of fruit/And the barns are full of hay..."* and ravening hunger in her gut.

Ridiculous, she thought... fuzzy. I am *never* hungry in the mornings. A: I was out too late the night before, and probably ate something in the wee hours; B: I usually have a hangover and food is right up there with Top 40 Music on my fave-rave list; and C: I can't stand the weightgain, so it's black coffee and dry toast max because my high school health teacher said you're supposed to put something in your stomach in the morning.

But she smelled bacon cooking. Heard it crisping. She was starving.

Ludicrous. This was Saturday. Nobody in Sausalito got up before noon. And it was only... her eyes opening, reading Babyben clock... eight in the stupid morning for Pete's sake... eyes closing again... and nobody on the houseboats was into breakfast, anyway.

Mmmm. Potatoes! Cooking in some of that bacon fat. Good god, woman. Do you know what'll it to your body? Where do you come up with these dreams?

Sausage.

A steak.

Now she could smell strawberry preserves. No way!

Her fingers crept out, toward Nebraska. That was it - just being around this farmboy made her think of Big Farm Breakfasts. Next, her brain freewheeled, there'll be a triangle chime, and somebody shouting:

Her fingers found nothing on Nebraska's pillow.

"Come and get it!"

And the hell with you, Aunt Bee, you're probably some kind of whacko with the hots for Barney Fife anyway. Plus that was a man's voice.

Come on, Alexis. You haven't taken acid for a month, at least - and why not came the flash - so there's no particular reason that you should be:

Smelling fresh-squeezed orange juice.

"Soo-ee, soo-ee, pig-pig-pig!"

Alexis snapped awake and up in bed.

"You gonna lay in bed all damn' day, woman?" Nebraska asked. "I already got the pigs milked, the cows slopped and the south forty harrowed, disced and planted with Acapulco Gold, not to mention all kinds other good clodhopper-type duties."

He was standing there, wearing a pair of trunks that had been left by some long-forgotten guest of Alexis', and holding a spatula. "Damn, woman, don't you *ever* do any cooking? All you got in the kitchen is a can opener and the phone numbers for pizza delivery places.

"Good morning."

Alexis managed a good morning. Nebraska knelt on the bed... and kissed her. She kissed him back.

"This has gotta be true love," she said. "You didn't even tell me to brush my teeth first."

Her hand stretched out, under the swim trunks.

"Ah-ah-ah," Nebraska said. "Fool around with the cook and breakfast'll burn and the combine hands we picked up for the harvest'll move on to the next spread, 'thout threshin' our fields first."

"Whatever that means," Alexis said. "The hell with those combine hands anyway. I suddenly went and joined the boss class."

But, obediently, she quit fondling, rolled out of bed, and found a short robe.

"You cook?" she marveled.

"Some," Nebraska admitted. "Mom's idea."

"Huh?"

"Well, she always wanted me to go off to college. You know, like away? She said I'd best know how to sew, and wash and iron and cook.

"Else there'll be some lady who'll start doing all those things for me, and I'll get all confused and think I'm in love, and then there'll be real trouble.

"Needless to say," Nebraska went on, "I didn't go bragging on my new skills back of the gym after school... But yeah, I cook. Basics, anyway."

"One of these days," Alexis said, "you're going to make someone very, very happy." She grinned. "Me... I'd always call down for room service... Come on, farmboy. Let's eat.

"Although there's no way I'll manage more than a few bites... assuming my nose hasn't been lying and you really have been cooking for the King Ranch roundup crew or whatever it was you called it."

Alexis was lying. Between the two of them, they devoured the steak, the hashbrowns, the fried ham, the bacon, the country sausage, the biscuits

224

with gravy and the rest.

Finally: "I am destroyed," she moaned, pushing away from the table. "I'll never eat again. Jesus, I'm starting to look like Janis!"

"Good for you," Nebraska said. "Ah laks a woman with meat to her bones!"

He turned, hearing a loud engineblast outside, on the water. Speeding past was an old, immaculately-restored wooden speedboat that looked as it would be right at home running rum to thirsty San Franciscan Prohibition throats. A few seconds later, the wake gently rocked the houseboat.

"Now maybe I could live with that," Nebraska said. "I guess there's other ways of going fast besides a GTO."

"Thought you didn't have any water in Nebraska?"

"We don't. To speak of, anyway."

Alexis looked at him, peculiarly.

"Damndest thing happened," he said slowly. "When I was over at the store, getting the groceries, this guy went and offered me a job. Said I looked like I had good muscles."

"Was he straight?"

"He didn't appear to be drunk or loaded."

"That wasn't what I... never mind," Alexis said. She'd explain some of the cultural phenomenon's of San Francisco later.

"Asked if I knew how to swing a hammer. I said surely. Asked if I was afraid of work.

"I told him hell, no. I could lay right down and go to sleep beside it without flickerin' an eyelid.

"He said he had a job if I wanted it. Eight dollars an hour. He said there's always a call for construction around here.

"Damn. Eight dollars an hour's rich man's wages, compared to what farmin' would work out to... if you put it on some kind of hourly scale.

"Eight dollars. Damn!" Nebraska sat quietly for awhile, looking out at that same white-patterned blue sky and blue bay. The breeze kicked whitecaps up in the water.

"You thinking about staying on?" Alexis said, breaking the silence.

Nebraska started to answer, then turned to her and considered. "No," he finally said. "...No. But it's an idea, isn't it?"

"I don't know," Alexis said. "I think... I mean, I think you're about seven kinds of wonderful, at least from what I've seen... And I'll you the truth. I never was one of those people who got off playing stupid hard to get games.

"I told Jeff's friend, Samantha, that I wouldn't mind if you stuck around for awhile. I mean, Monday's coming up fast. And I still think I could stand to see your face next to me, come Tuesday morning.

"But... speaking personally," she said, confused, "sometimes I've gotten a wild idea, and done something before I thought it through. Now, sometimes it worked out just fine. But then again, ...oh hell," she broke off. "I don't have the foggiest God damned idea what I'm talking about or even thinking."

"Good," Nebraska said. "Because I do."

He slid around the low table, left hand going around Alexis' shoulders, right unerringly going under the robe, and finding the dampening warmth, and her legs parting as they moved together.

"Oh come on," Alexis said. *Nobody's* that horny! We just finished fooling around a little bit ago. And it's almost ten! We've got to meet your friends! And we've got a baseball game to go to!"

"I'm not horny," Nebraska protested, grinning. "I'm just standing here, taking a shower, and this nice looking young stranger pops in, and says, mind if I share?

"Bein' the easy-goin' sort I am, and coming from a water-conserving state like I do, I said not 'tall, ma'am.

"Next thing I know, is somebody's playing with my tally whacker, getting it all soapy and slippery.

"I can't help it if strange things start happening," and his strong hands were under her arms, lifting her, her legs coming up and coiling around his hips and one hand came down, guiding his cock into her and Alexis' head contorted back, her nails digging his shoulders as she moaned and thrust against him.

Neither one of them noticed the shower curtain had pulled off its rack, water was spraying across the carpeted bathroom and there would be a hell of a mess to clean up later.

If they had - they wouldn't have cared...

Halfway across the Golden Gate Bridge, Nebraska broke the dreamy silence eyes unsafely creeping off the road up the red lead cables and spires of the bridge toward heaven:

Allan Cole & Chris Bunch

"Uh..." he started, "what was this about a baseball game?"

"Old San Francisco tradition," Alexis non-explained. "Which we started next week."

"That didn't tell me squat."

"Wasn't supposed to."

"Okay. Are we playing or watching?"

"Depends," Alexis said, cryptic.

"Okay. Next," Nebraska said, "about this thing tonight? At The FBI Girl?"

"Thing... yeah. That's probably the best way to label it," Alexis agreed. "Maybe a party, maybe a concert, maybe a riot."

"If you want," Nebraska said, "Me and the others could maybe hang around. Backstage? So if anything happens, like what you and that guy Pigpen were worried about, at least you'll have somebody who can help."

"Help how?"

"Carrying equipment out the back door... if things get rowdy," Nebraska suggested. "All that gear looks real expensive, and hard to replace."

"We've got roadies," Alexis said. "And there's no problem getting volunteers. If worst comes to worst, we can bail on the amps and let the insurance company sort it out. Or maybe stick our brand new record company with the bill.

"But I think I'd like at least you around. I might feel like some casual rescuing. I mean, I'm at least as expensive as any Fender."

"And one helluva lot harder to replace," Nebraska said. He took her free hand and squeezed it.

"Which brings me to the last thing," he said. "I don't think I thanked you. For... for saying what you did. That you wouldn't mind if I decided to stick around."

"Farmboy, you thanked me," Alexis said. "I feel like a sore ex-virgin the morning after."

"I'm serious," Nebraska said.

"I know," the woman said. "And it's a little scary. Which is why I'm trying not to be. But... thanks for the thanks.

"And I meant it."

Nebraska half-smiled, then turned and looked out, earnestly studying a sailboat far below, tacking near Fort Point.

CHAPTER SIXTEEN

"R-E-S-P-E-C-T/FIND OUT what it means to me/R-E-S-P-E-C-T/ Take care of pleasin'..."

Click! Jeff shut off the hotel radio. He turned back to Samantha, a crumpled sheet of paper in his hand. It was covered with many scratched out words and phrases. The few remaining were a jumble of sweat-stained agony.

Samantha sat poised on the couch. Scattered about were the remains of a large room-service breakfast. The door to Jeff's own room stood ajar, revealing a much rumpled bed.

Jeff's eyes strayed from the paper in his hand to the long thighs stretching out from under Samantha's recently-donned miniskirt, and started thinking about how that bed got so rumpled. Samantha caught the look, laughed and tugged at her hem.

"You better keep your mind on business, buster," she warned. "Now, go on. I'm all ears."

"Right," Jeff said. "I've got to hit them with it now. Get them on my side. Or at least off my back. And I think I finally figured where I've been going wrong."

"That's as good a start as any," Samantha said. She glanced at her watch. "But maybe you better get moving. Didn't you say your father has a golf date with his buddies every Saturday morning?"

Jeff glanced at the phone. Then at the scrawled notes in his hand. It was getting time to piss or get off the pot.

"Okay... Here's my new way in. I call... My Dad answers..."

"What if someone else answers?" Samantha asked. "Like your mother?"

"My mother? Shit! I mean... yeah... she could... That could be a problem. No way could I say this stuff to mom. She'd freak out. And if I say... Hi, mom, can I talk to dad... she'll know something is up and freak double."

"So fake it," Samantha said. "Tell her you love her and say you want to talk to your father so you can tell him the same."

Jeff considered this. Not bad. "Great idea," Jeff said.

Samantha shook her head. "Steady. Now... What do you say to your father?"

"I say..." Jeff consulted his notes... "Dad... There's something I have to get off my chest.

"I'm sorry to do this on the phone, but it's too important to let wait until I get home."

"Good," Samantha said. "That's very good."

Jeff took heart. Plunged on, his voice firmer... deeper: "Times have changed, father... I have changed..."

"Damn," Jeff said, breaking off as the door to the suite slammed open and Tyrell strolled in.

"Sorry, guys," Tyrell said, a little embarrassed, figuring he had been responsible for a little coitus interruptus. "I didn't know you were..." He started to back out of the room.

"Wait," Samantha called out.

"That's okay," Tyrell said. He was a little rattled and motormouthed on. "I just stopped by to check in with everybody. I'm supposed to keep Sunshine company. She borrowed some wheels so she could go across the Bay and pick up some stuff. She'll be along any minute."

"Will you come back in here," Samantha said. "There's nothing going on. Really."

Jeff held up the scrawlings. "I was just rehearsing," he said. "I have to call my Dad. Tell him what's what."

Tyrell sat right down, interested. "Good for you," he said. "About time you kicked some butt." Brave words. But he was a little squirmy inside. He had a phone call of his own he had to make. But, later. Later. He gave Jeff a bland smile. "Go ahead."

Jeff got himself ready again. "Try this on," he said. "I get my father on the phone, see,? Then I say-"

"Wait up," Tyrell said. "What if your momma answers?"

"We've been through that already," Jeff said. Gritting his teeth.

"Sorry about that," Tyrell said. "My lips are glued."

"So... I get him on the phone," Jeff said, glaring at Tyrell to make sure there was no further interruption. "Then I say: Dad, there's something I have to get off my-"

There came a tapping at the door. Jeff stopped again. Tyrell gave him an apologetic smile. "Must be Sunshine," he said.

It was. A few minutes later Sunshine was perched on the couch beside Samantha. Listening. This time, Jeff got past the part about his father answering the phone. Also the getting things off his chest business.

Allan Cole & Chris Bunch

"... Times have changed, father," Jeff said. *"I have-"*

Slam! And Nebraska trooped in.

"For crying out loud," Jeff protested. "What is this, Grand Central Goddam Station?"

Nebraska ignored him. He was in a hurry of his own.

"I gotta talk quick," Nebraska said. "Alexis'll be up any second."

Tyrell asked him what was up.

"You remember that FBI Girl deal comin' down tonight?"

Everybody did.

"Well, she and the band are gonna play. Even though there might be some trouble. If there is, they're gonna have to get while the gettin' is good!"

"What do you want us to do?" Tyrell said. "Toss a couple of grenades to buy 'em some time?"

"Naw. I was thinkin' more of a rear guard, type action. Give me a hand with their equipment. Get the instruments and stuff off the stage before they get busted up. Which'd put her out of business."

Tyrell and Jeff said that would be no problem at all. General chatter followed. For a few minutes, Jeff almost let it continue. Let busy circumstances be his excuse for not making that call home. Then he gave himself a mental swift kick. He'd do it, dammit. Jeff looked over to Samantha, and he could see that although she was talking up a storm with the rest, that she was waiting too. To see what Jeff would do. He signaled for help. Samantha caught it right off.

"Gentle people..." she broke in. "Remember Jeff? And his little problem?"

"Oh, yeah," Tyrell said.

"Poor Jeff," Sunshine said.

"What bitty problem?" Nebraska asked.

Samantha brought him up to speed. In brief seconds, Nebraska joined the audience.

"I get my father on the phone," Jeff said. "And if you give me any crap about maybe he won't answer, Nebraska, I swear I'll kill you."

"Why wouldn't he answer?" Nebraska said. "Oh, I gotcha. Maybe your momma'll pick up. No sweat. You can bee ess something. I got every confidence in you, kid."

"Thanks," Jeff said. Dry.

"Don't mention it. Geesh! A body'd think I had no class at all. Fellah wants to talk, I say jaw away all you like. Shoot. You can take all day, if you want. You can talk 'till..."

"Nebraska!" A warning from Jeff. Nebraska quit teasing and started listening... again.

"So then I say... Dad, there's something I have to get off my chest. Times have changed, fa—"

Bang, bang, bang on the door. Jeff threw the notes on the ground. "To hell with it!" I'm just going to pick up the damn phone and call. Right now!"

"Wait up," Nebraska said. "I gotta let Alexis in."

"Oh, no problem. No problem at all," Jeff said. "Invite everybody. Get the whole hotel up here! See if I care!"

"What's the matter with Jeff?" Alexis wanted to know. She had entered in mid rail and was getting comfortable.

"Supposed to call his folks," Nebraska said.

Alexis saw the crumpled paper on the floor. She picked it up and glanced at it... squinting at the scriggles.

"I like this," she said. Then she read aloud: "'... Times have changed, father... *I* have changed...' Pretty good start, Jeff. Let me hear the rest."

Alexis handed Jeff the notes. Then leaned back and closed her eyes. As if ready to concentrate.

"Don't ask him about his mother," Sunshine warned. "He freaks out."

Alexis' eyes snapped open. "What's he got? Some kinda complex, or something?"

Jeff groaned, but nobody heard him.

"Nothin' like that," Tyrell said. "He and his momma get on fine. Although she's probably gonna have kittens when she finds out he's dumpin' Rachel."

"Hot damn!" Nebraska said. "Do we get to listen in?"

"You are not..." Jeff roared, "... I repeat... you are definitely not helping."

The phone rang. Disgusted,. Jeff grabbed it off its cradle and growled into the receiver: "Who the hell is this?" Then his eyes jolted to saucer size. And his voice cracked: "Uh... Dad! Is that you?"

At the mention of the magic dad word, the room plunged into silence. Except for a few "Oh, shits."

"Ha, ha. We were screw— I mean, fooling around again... uh, Dad... No, I'm not surprised you... uh... called. In fact... I was just going to call you... What about? Uh... Yeah... Good question. It was about..."

He looked frantically around for his notes. Then realized he had them in his hand. Jeff's eyes darted over the scrawling.

"See... the reason I was calling... Yeah, I know you called first. But... Look... Times have changed, father... What do you mean, *how* have they changed? Lot's of ways. Like it's... a different date and all and then there's... Forget it, Dad. The times haven't changed, okay? We'll leave them alone. But, see... *I've* changed... and... Hold on a minute, Dad. Let me get on the other phone."

He held his hand over the receiver until Samantha rescued him. She took the phone... kissed his confused face... pointed toward the bedroom. Jeff went. Walking as if he were a condemned man. Everybody made cheering gestures, but none of them changed Jeff's last mile expression. He closed the door. Samantha listened on the phone until she heard him pick up. Then she gently set the phone down in its cradle.

"I'd rather face bullets," Nebraska said. Youthful empathy over a peer facing the parental enemy had cut in.

Tyrell nodded reflexively. Thinking of Mister Kelly at the mill back home. Nebraska was right.

"Jeff, before you tell me what you have to say, I'd appreciate it if you'd give your old man the floor for a little while."

That was the last thing Jeff wanted. He needed to blurt out the whole thing right now. The words were swarming at the back of his throat, his speech mechanism itching to be put to work.

"Sure, dad," he said. "Go ahead."

"Thank you, son," his father continued. "To be frank, your mother is very worried. You know how she is."

"Yeah, I know, sir."

"I think I have an idea of what's going on in your mind, son" his father said.

"You do?" Jeff was amazed. Maybe this wouldn't be as hard as he thought. I Hope, I hope, Ihopelhopehopehope.

"Of course, I do. How could I miss it? When you sent Rachel home on the plane with us... Instead of... Well, I know my son. A real mensch. If he chose to stay on in San Francisco alone instead of being in the willing company of a beautiful young woman... A woman, I might note, whom he loves more than life..."

Allan Cole & Chris Bunch

"Wait up, Dad," Jeff broke in. Here was the first nut to crack. "Rachel was one of the things I was going to call you about. You see..."

"You promised me the floor, remember, son?" His father said. "Be careful now. You don't want to say something you'll later regret. As matter of fact, Rachel is here right now. In the kitchen with your mother."

"Oh," was all Jeff said. Shit oh dear is what twitched at his lips.

"Do you want to talk to her?"

"No sir."

"I didn't think so. Now, don't think I've taken sides. It's your mother that's worried. And Rachel."

"Yes sir. I know sir."

"So, here's how I see the situation. Stop me if I get anything wrong. You're confused about Rachel. Is that right?"

"Yes sir. I mean, no sir. I *was* confused. But now. . . "

"Don't say it, son. You've made promises to that girl. Sacred promises."

"But, not—"

"Son?"

"Yes sir?"

"You did promise, didn't you? You weren't toying with that girl, were you?"

"Of course not, Dad. I..."

"That's good enough for me, Jeff. And I'll tell her you said just that."

"But—"

"So you're a little confused at the moment. This is not unusual, Jeff. It's quite normal, in fact.

Considering the terrible experience you just went through.... I was speaking to Wally Bishop just yesterday... You remember Wally, don't you."

"Yes sir. He's the psychiatrist, right?"

"That's him. We were on the debate team together at SC. Hell of a competitor, that Wally. Although he believed he was a lot better than he really was. Good thing for him we were on the same team, I always said."

"About Rachel, Dad," Jeff said, with new determination. "I don't think it's going to-"

"Of course it will work, son," his father said. "And you'll be glad to know that Wally is convinced it will as well."

"But, Dad..."

"Wally says you're just going through a minor shock, Jeff. Nothing worrisome. Or pathological. Nothing that needs treatment."

Jeff was silent.

"Are you there, son?"

"Yes, sir. I'm here."

"Time is the cure, son. Wally predicts everything will be back to normal in just a few weeks. A month and a half at the most. How about that for a diagnosis?"

"I don't know what to say, Dad."

"Didn't think you would. Basically, all we have to do is pitch in together. Wally says you should keep yourself real busy. That way you won't dwell on your experiences. He thought the best thing in the world you could do is plunge right back into life. Maybe even think about you and Rachel having a child right away. New life as a healing force, if you will.

"Don't worry about the money, if you and Rachel decide to do that. Your mother and I will always be here for you."

More silence from Jeff.

"Son?"

"Yes, sir."

"You don't sound too pleased."

"It's just that-"

"I don't want you to think I'm pressuring you. I have every faith. It's your mother who's worried. You know how she gets."

"Yes, sir."

"But that's all emotional business. It'll be water over the dam before you know it. The most important thing ahead - as I view it - is to get your loins girded for the battle ahead. The professional battle.

"Because, to be honest with you, it mostly doesn't matter who you marry. As long as she's from a good family...

"A man learns to... Oh, well... We'll talk after you and Rachel have a few years of wedded bliss behind you.

"No. The bullet that has to be bitten immediately is your future. Your career. Enough time has been wasted.

But you know that better than I do. It's your mother who's worried. About medical school. You know how she gets."

"Yes, sir. I know, sir."

"So I promised I'd talk to you. To tell you what a great calling the

Allan Cole & Chris Bunch

medical profession is."

"Yes, sir," Jeff said. But what he wanted to say was: I saved a man's life last night, father.

"It is the most ancient, most honorable endeavor in human history. But those are just words. Words I heard when I was a young man contemplating many years of hard study ahead of me. But I didn't really understand their meaning until I laid my hands on my first real patient."

He was a cop, Dad, Jeff thought. And he had no face and there was blood all over the street.

"It was an old woman. She was afraid at first, when she saw how young I was. But no more afraid than I was. I didn't dare let her see how my hands were shaking. There wasn't much I could do. She was very old. Very ill. But I never let on. I gave her the most professional examination I could. And I made sure that I explained carefully everything I was doing. After awhile, she wasn't so afraid anymore."

I started the cop's heart with jumper cables, Dad, Jeff thought. Then I used a pen knife on him. And a broken off hunk of a ball point pen. Which I jammed into the bubble of blood in his neck.

"She died, of course," his father went on. "A few days later. But that was an important a lesson for me as well. Overcoming my fear. A doctor has to learn about death, Jeff. He has to learn about failure."

It wasn't the first life I saved, Dad, Jeff thought. Back in Vietnam... but it was the memory of the street that kept grabbing at him. Car horns and screams. Lights flashing every which way. The sudden heave of the chest lurching for life. Air whistling out of the hole he had cut with the pen knife.

"So, I urge you, son, that if you are having any doubts about being a doctor, put them aside for now. You won't regret it. I promise you."

The cop made it, Dad, Jeff wanted so badly to say. Daniel thinks I'm a damned genius. But I think I was just damned lucky.

"Besides," his father went on, "if it turns out to be the wrong track for you, why you can always take up law. My God, do you realize how much lawyers are making off of medical malpractice? It's a national scandal. The really rich ones have gone to the trouble of getting their MD's. Like my old classmate Bill Weisner. God, is he raking in the dough. Just like you would if you chose that route.

"Why, before you know it, you and Rachel will have a house that will have your mother and I grinding our teeth in envy. Maybe you can put an add-on for our old age. Ha, ha... Are you there, Jeff?"

"Yes, sir. I'm still here."

"Do you understand what I'm saying, son?"

"Yes, Dad. I understand."

"So, I can tell your mother that you'll seriously think on it? You know how she worries."

"Sure, Dad."

"See you tomorrow at LAX, then?"

"Yeah, Dad. Tomorrow."

"Goodbye, son... I love you."

"I love you too, Dad. And tell mom... you know."

"I'll give her your love, Jeff. Goodbye, now."

"Goodbye, Dad," Jeff said and the phone went click and he was listening to the dial tone.

He carefully set the phone down. Then went into the bathroom and threw up. Jeff brushed his teeth and washed his face. Sprinkled on some after shave. And went into the other room to join his friends.

Nobody had to ask how it went. They saw the fishbelly paleness of failure on his face.

"He blew me out of the water," Jeff said.

Nebraska pulled his long, lanky frame up and went over to Jeff. Draped an arm around his shoulders.

"Naw, he just tickled your ribs with some tracer rounds," Nebraska said. "You'll get him next go-round."

Jeff looked at Tyrell. Who gave him a thumbs up sign. Then, reluctantly, at Samantha. She looked worried, but oddly enough, not disappointed.

"It was just bad timing, Jeff," she said. "He caught you off guard."

"You can say *that* again," Jeff said. "Can you believe my luck? Next time I go to answer a phone, somebody please bust my fingers. All eleven of them."

"If you really need cheering up," Sunshine said, "you have to get Tyrell to tell you about what he did to Grancell. Wow, was it far out!"

Jeff needed cheering up. So he asked. Within a short time, he was definitely jolly. Especially with a room service double screwdriver warming his stomach and joint from Sunshine easing his spirits.

Soon it was time to go. They all agreed to meet later at The FBI Girl.

236

Sunshine suggested they make it at 4 p.m.

"That's high tea time," she said with a giggle.

"High tea... At The FBI Girl?" Jeff couldn't believe that.

"Really, really high tea," she laughed. "You Know... Have A Little Tea With Goldie?"

"Who's Goldie?" Tyrell wanted to know.

"The lady on the Smothers Brothers, silly."

"We been kinda outa town," Nebraska drawled. "In a place where they don't have a whole lot of tee vee. But if your friend Goldie is for it, Sunshine, why I'm ready to tuck right in."

"Groovy," Sunshine said.

As they all trooped out, Jeff thought once more about his conversation with his father. Of all the things Jeff hadn't told him, the one that disturbed him the most was the incident with the cop. Why had he held back on that? Then it came to him that maybe he was afraid his father would have been jealous. The thought held there for a tantalizing instant: A solution to something he had long puzzled over.

Then he thought it was the stupidest idea he'd ever had.

He put his arm around Samantha's soft waist and gave her a squeeze for comfort.

His father jealous? What a dimwit, Katz!

CHAPTER SEVENTEEN

"... WE SHALL SCRIMP and save..." Sunshine crooned along with the Beatles on the van's radio... *"Grandchildren on your knee... "* She sang on, giving Tyrell's knee a firm squeeze... *"Vera, Chuck and Dave..."*

He liked the way she said "Chuck." Ch-uu-uk. Pulling on the name like taffy to make it sound British.

The beat-to-shit, dayglo spattered van coughed its foul lungs into the rich air of San Francisco Bay. They were chugging along the Bay Bridge, high over the water, and he could see in every direction. It gave him a giddy sense of freedom, as he steered with one hand, toked on the joint with the other, and rubber-necked the spectacular view.

On the other side of the bridge was Oakland. Beyond that, Berkeley. Where Sunshine's folks lived.

He'd been startled when she'd asked him to come along. More than a little nervous. A black cat meeting a white girl's folks? Wow! He'd tried to stutter his way out, but Sunshine had this way of flowing over every difficulty like honey.

"I just need to run in for a second," she'd said. "You can come in if you want. They'll have friends there. For the barbecue they throw most every weekend. I grew up thinking everything tasted like charcoal. Especially beef. Yech. Or, any kind of meat. Double yech. I told them they were poisoning themselves, but they just got all uptight.

"They never *say* anything, when they get uptight, you understand. Dad frowns a lot. My mother gets all worried looking. Anyway, there's always plenty of food if you want to come in with me."

"Uh... wouldn't it be better... uh.. back to the Haight..." Tyrell'd stumbled, "to... uh... you know... be with just each other..."

"If you didn't want to come in and be bored and stuff, we'd be back a whole lot quicker," Sunshine untangled the thought for him.

So, Tyrell had said that would be the best way, of course. The most practical. Slipping through the crack she had left him.

Now, as he looked over at her, humming and singing along with the radio, he had this dreamy view of the two of them. On the Isle of Wight, like the song said. Where ever Wight was. Didn't matter. On an island, the whole world is shut out. There'd just be the two of them, along with a few very interesting, and very open people. Color blind people.

He could see himself and Sunshine strolling along a solitary beach on this Isle of Wight place. Maybe fooling around among some big dunes... or maybe even while they were swimming.

"... Will you still need me," Sunshine sang, "Will you still feed me... When I'm sixty four?"

She gave his knee another squeeze, let her hand tease a little trail up his knee... just a way of letting him know she'd need him and feed him forever;

Sunshine's errand involved money. To Tyrell, this was almost as weird as the notion of meeting her parents. Sunshine was definitely not into material things. She was almost an ethereal creature, capable of living on air and love. But, every few weeks or so she went to her folks' house to pick up a thickish sheaf of cash.

"They call it my allowance," she said with a shrug. "I let them, because it makes them happy."

"It makes them happy to *give* you money? Which you also *give them your permission* to call an allowance? No offense, baby, but isn't that a little weird?"

"I don't see why," Sunshine said. "I don't want money. I don't need money. Well, maybe a little bit once in awhile... but I don't need *their* money. I give most of it away. To other kids. But don't tell them, okay?"

"No worry there," Tyrell said. "Besides, I'm not gonna actually meet them, remember?"

"Uh, huh... But back to the silly money thing... I hate that word: Allowance. A person has no right to ' allow' people things.. Or, not 'allow' people things. But, they're my parents, okay? So I let 'em say it and they're not so uptight when they say it and it makes them think they're keeping their little girl sort of safe when they give it and they don't like go around freaking and calling the cops and hospitals to look for me and if calling something an allowance takes care of all that... then it doesn't make any sense for me to be all uptight about them using it. If you understand what I mean?" All this was said in one long breath.

Tyrell kinda did understand. Maybe. Maybe not. And as he sorted the confusion between the two he oddly got Sunshine's drift. If it made Sunshine happy, then he understood. Whether he did or not.

"What's your father do?".

"He's sort of a professor."

"Sort of a professor of what?" Tyrell was surprised at this. He didn't know Sunshine came from such a high falutin' family.

239

"English, or something to do with English. At least that's what he's got his doctorate in. But mostly he bosses other professors around. I love my dad, I really do. But he gets off on that bossing stuff. Not me, or mother. He wouldn't dare boss mother. He just likes to tell the other teachers what to do. How to run their life. Their classes. But he works real hard at it. Always tired when he gets home. I guess that's why he's the head of his department. ˃Cause he works so hard. At everything... except..."

... Except teaching, Tyrell thought, filling in the uncomfortable phrase for her.

She was quiet for awhile as they pushed their way through Oakland traffic.

"So how did you convince them? I mean, you said they called the cops and all when you quit school and ran away. "

"I've never quit anything in my life, Ty-rell Harris," Sunshine said, a touch miffed. "I had no *need* for school anymore... That part of my life was over. So, I guess that means I finished, right? And I didn't run away. Why would I do that? I wasn't afraid of anything. It was like school. Home, I mean. My parents' home. It wasn't my trip anymore. So, I left."

"And they dragged you back," Tyrell said.

"It was a bummer," Sunshine agreed.

"But you kept run- I mean, leaving, huh?"

"Sure. They were really pretty thick for awhile. It was their karma to be thick. Still is, although I keep hoping... But, that's their life, right? And this is my life, okay? It took awhile, but now they understand. Sort of. Except for the money part. And that's their trip and not mine, so nobody's hurt and everything's groovy after all."

The house was set in the hills at the end of a long, curving, tree-lined street. The house was expensively old. Just the arched front door would easily eat a year of a GI's pay.

Sunshine shouted she'd be right back. Leaped out of the van before it came to a full stop, and was heading around the side of the house to the backyard, where she said the barbecue was. Her long blonde hair flowed behind her as she ran. She wore sandals, tight, bleached to pure white jeans, and a long, white, tunic top - tied in the middle with a beaded belt.

Tyrell shut off the engine and settled back to wait. As the van fumes wisped away, he could smell the charred, acrid odor of tormented meat.

240

And a hot, musty smell - sorta like mushy potatoes being burned in their jackets. Naw, couldn't be. Must be some kinda luxurious white folks dish with a French name. He could hear music -just barely. A tinkly piano, maybe and an uptight horn. And a no imagination steady thum thum of bass. White jazz, he guessed. If so, this was real, real white, brother. People who were hip when it was hep to be hip.

Listen to you, Tyrell Harris. You sound like a peckerneck yourself. A black peckerneck. He heard Sunshine call his name and looked over to see her coming back around through the side yard.

There was somebody with her. A matronly, blonde somebody. Who vaguely looked like - holy shit, it must be... Mrs.... Mrs... Mrs. Sunshine? Oh, no, her freakin' mother! Oh, why, oh, why are you doing this, baby. Man, they are goin' to eat us alive.

...We gotta get outa this place/If it's the last thing we ever do/We gotta get outa this place/Girl there's a better place/For me and you...

But then Sunshine was at the van and pulling open the door and her mother was standing there with this big, frozen grin on her face like she'd just seen The Creature From The Black Lagoon emerge and Tyrell wanted to say it's only me, Tyrell Harris, and I got good grades in school and went to church regular and sang in the school choir and my prospects with Mister Kelly at the Mill are pretty good.

"It's cool, don't worry," Sunshine whispered as she looped a proprietary arm through his and turned to introduce him to her mother.

"I'm very *very* glad to meet one of Sunshine's little friends," Mrs. Sunshine said. He'd missed the last name clean was there was no way he could tell Sunshine he didn't remember something so basic. Give it time, Tyrell, somebody's sure to use it in conversation. And he was so worried about forgetting his true love's last name that he shook the cold, limp hand he was offered, and forgot about matters of complexion. For a minute.

"He's not so little, mother," Sunshine giggled, squeezing his biceps.

"No... I suppose he isn't," Mrs. Sunshine said. She painted the welcoming smile back on. "You really *must* have a bite with us, Tyrell. My husband will so want to meet you."

"Gee... thanks a lot Mrs... Uh... But we'd better get-"

"Nonsense," the woman broke in. "Please. I insist."

He could tell she didn't mean it one damned bit, but she was forcing the issue because that's what she thought Sunshine wanted... The woman was afraid. Of him... maybe. Mostly she seemed afraid of spooking her

241

daughter.

"Come on, Ty-Rell," Sunshine pleaded. "It'd just be for a minute."

Tyrell had no other choice but to follow.

"See? I told you everything would be fine," Sunshine whispered. She was so happy that he was meeting her parents that Tyrell bit his tongue to keep himself from spoiling it all. And saying, let's git! Quick!

The backyard was controlled mass confusion. People filtered back and forth, or stood, balancing drinks and paper plates of food. The uptight jazz was playing from hi fi speakers spotted around the garden. Sunshine kept pulling him along - towards the far end of the sprawling landscaped yard. There was a portable bar there. It was tended by a slender, aesthetic-looking man. He was middle aged and Tyrell guessed it was Mr. Sunshine, himself.

Meanwhile, snips of conversation swirled all around him.

"I wouldn't call the *Love Book* obscene per se," said a ditzy older woman with cat eye frames on her glasses. "But as I told my. students, the jury system is inherently flawed..."

"I say the union movement has lost sight of its goals," said a tweedy guy with a stubborn purple look about him. "Hoffa is in prison because he is a thief of the worst sort. And the union still supports him. How shortsighted..."

"... Great things ahead in communication. One hundred million telephones! Can you imagine? That's one for every second household in America! Add that to at least two radios per, a television, a daily..."

"... I realize he is Jack Nicklaus. But paying a golfer nearly two hundred thousand dollars a year? Aren't we letting things get out of hand?"

"Of course, we all *sympathize* with the protesters. The war is wrong. My views are well known on the subject of Vietnam. But must the young people look so... scroungy?"

"They were blind to let the movie theater owners block pay television. California lost a significant chance in that vote, mark my words. A significant chance..."

"Congress was quite right in barring Mister Powell from office," a distinguished-looking man was saying. He was one of the few blacks Tyrell could see at the party. He was boring a matched pair of very short white folks. "Adam Clayton Powell has humiliated every single educated member of my race..."

242

Allan Cole & Chris Bunch

Tyrell was almost relieved when he finally approached the dreaded portable bar. Sunshine's father was talking in anxious hushed tones to his wife. Who was obviously apprising him of the situation. The man looked up as Tyrell approached. Bland.

"Excuse me just a moment, young man," her father said. "I have to turn over the record album."

Tyrell saw the portable Hi Fi system behind the bar and a jumble of records. Mister Sunshine lifted the arm of the player and flipped the record over. There was an album sleeve beside the Hi Fi. The jacket read: Bernstein Plays Brubeck Plays _Bernstein._

Oh, maannn, Tyrell thought. You are in the shitter.

"So... You're just out of the Army, Tyrell," Sunshine's father was saying.

"Yes, sir, I am," was the best Tyrell could manage. His brain had gone on hold along with his tongue.

This had everything to do with the fact he and Sunshine had been hustled off to a quieter corner of the garden. To be grilled by her father.

They were partly screened by some willows, but Tyrell was in plain view of Sunshine's mother, who had taken over her husband's bartending duties. Every once in awhile, he saw her throw a worried look his way.

"What was that, sir?" He'd missed the next question from Sunshine's father.

"What kind of work were you considering?"

"Oh... I have some prospects back home. In the... uh... building ... uh... supply... business. But... I'm sort of still keeping my eyes open."

"In this area?"

Tyrell was stumped. "Well... uh... gee.. I'm not..."

"You could help, couldn't you, Daddy?" Sunshine was saying, and what the hell was she talking about?

"Now, how could I do that, Princess?" her father said. He seemed honestly puzzled. Then he forced laughter. "As a professor," he said, "One is more suited preparing young people for jobs. Finding them is not my line at all."

"He could get the GI Bill, couldn't he?" Sunshine insisted. "Then he'd be making money. So, that's kind of a job, right? And maybe you could help him get accepted to the University."

This really startled her father. "I suppose he qualifies for the GI Bill...

243

Yes... Doesn't really need my help there... But... I'd certainly do what I could."

He looked at Tyrell. "I don't know about college, however. No rudeness implied, but the academic standards are quite high."

"But Ty-rell did great in school, Daddy," Sunshine said. "Scholarship great."

"Oh... uh... Very good, young man. What sort of an athlete were you? Track and Field?

"No, silly," Sunshine said. "Not jock scholarships. Scholarships for smart people. You were honor roll all the way, right, Ty-Rell?"

Tyrell was embarrassed. But he'd have lied if he hadn't mumbled that it was true.

"See, Daddy!" Sunshine gushed. "You will help, won't you?"

Her father hemmed and hawed and hesitated. He was damned if he did and double damned if he didn't. Tyrell almost felt sorry for him.

"Still... May not be quite good enough... But we shall see... I can't promise... We'd have to peruse your academic records... Uh, where did you say you were from?"

"Memphis, sir."

"Well, there you go then," her father said, visibly relieved. "The standards there might not match up to California. So don't hope too much. Wouldn't want to disappoint."

He turned to his daughter. "But I'll help the best I can, Princess."

Tyrell watched the light dying in Sunshine's eyes. He understood now that this meeting had been her goal all along. She'd wanted to get him together with her father. Find some way, somehow, for him to remain in San Francisco. With her. And now her father was letting her down. But in more ways than he could ever imagine.

He looked over at Sunshine's mother again. Saw the fearful look of hurt crisping the edges of her eyes. Bigotry? Certainly. But an odd sort. Because Tyrell knew that look very well. It would be the same hurtfulness his mother would feel if he brought Sunshine home.

"I know you love her, son," his mother would say. "And there's no denyin' the girl loves you... But..."

And after that "but" she would go on about the children that were sure to come... and their miserable future in a racist world. She would preach to him about the difficulties of any marriage. Much less one where the people are from different races or religion. Then she would say she was

244

sorry and she would cry.

So, there was really not a lot of difference between how his mother would react, and the way Sunshine's was right now. His father would probably behave the same. If he were alive.

But, who was talking marriage and kids, anyway? It was summer and he and Sunshine were in love.

He looked at Sunshine's father. No way could he say something like that. You don't tell a girl's dad – any girl's dad - that marriage is not necessarily anybody's intention. Just fucking for now, sir. Not to worry.

Riiight!

Instead, Tyrell took him off the immediate hook.

"I don't know, Sunshine," Tyrell said. "The GI Bill doesn't pay much. And although, I think I'd like to go back to school someday... Right now, I have to help out at home."

"No big deal, right Daddy?" Sunshine said. "There's lots of jobs in San Francisco. That pay good money."

"Yes... there are..." her father said, but so hesitantly that Tyrell knew those high paying jobs were not for guys who emigrated to America in slave ships.

Suddenly, the looks from Sunshine's mother and the hesitation crab-waltz from her father combined to curdle just at the back of his throat. He felt suddenly very cold, as if he had lost a great deal of blood. Then the piss off kicked in and his heart trip hammered so hard he thought the big artery in his neck was going to blow out like a worn inner tube.

It wasn't them he was mad at. What would be the fucking point?

But the anger was charging through his veins and he knew if he didn't get out quick, he'd blow. Really blow. Rip off some honkey heads and...

He got to his feet.

"It was a pleasure meeting you, sir" Tyrell said, as controlled as he could. "And thank you for the great meal."

He looked down at Sunshine. She was just staring at him... Realizing... Aw, shit... Somebody like Sunshine should never have to realize fucking anything. And he could tell she was so sorry and blaming herself.

He gave her the best smile he could manage. Trying to shout through his eyes that it was okay... he loved her... don't be upset... it doesn't make a damn bit of difference.

But what he said out loud was: "I don't mean to be rude and rush you,

Sunshine... But I got to get back to the hotel. There's a phone call I have to make...

"It won't take very long..."

The Sloop John B. was mournful on the radio: *...send for the captain ashore/ I want to go home...:* But Tyrell had a little smile back on Sunshine's face... or maybe she was just trying to make him happy... Either way he'd done his best to soothe her and stroke her all the drive back to the hotel.

He kissed a smudged spot where a tear had been.

"This is gonna take a little while, honey," he said. "So why don't you meet everybody at The FBI Girl and tell them I'll be by directly."

She nodded, taking his word for it, and she didn't ask what this urgent business was about, but leaned out the window for him to kiss her.

He did. Then she forced the van into first gear and it shuddered away.

Tyrell looked up to where the suite was. And the telephone. A thousand foot-dragging miles away. He started off on his right foot. Then the left. They hit the pavement like mortar rounds.

"... I'm just tickled pink to hear you're back, Tyrell. Safe and sound to boot. We been real worried about ya at the mill. But I told the boys... Don't y'all fear for Tyrell Harris. He'll do Memphis proud. Wax the ploughs of those Vee Ett Cong."

"Thank you kindly, Mr. Kelly. And I'm real pleased folks've had me in their thoughts and prayers." Tyrell had his best booster voice on although his guts were crawling.

The only thing he had going for him in this conversation was that Mr. Kelly was a well-brought up Southern man. Polite to a fault. Especially to black folk who provided him with a small but healthy percentage of his milling business. In short, he was an experienced racist.

"And I did I hear your momma say somethin' about you gettin' a medal?"

"It wasn't any big thing, Mr. Kelly," Tyrell said. "Lot of guys who didn't one deserve it a bunch more."

"Well, the Army says you're a hero, son, so that's good enough for me... Now, whatcha got on your mind? Don't mean to push you, boy, but it's Saturday and I gotta close up real soon get home to my Lucy or she'll give me all kinds of. . . you know what blasphemy I got in mind.

"Although, she probably won't be too mad, on account of I'm talkin' to you. She'll be tickled as I am to hear from y'all. You know how high Mrs. Kelly's opinion is of your momma?" His mother had been taking in the Kelly laundry since his father died. Lucy Kelly was a tight-fisted, over-critical harpy of a woman.

"My momma's real proud of that, sir, and I know for a fact she feels just the same about Mrs. Kelly...

"What I was callin' about, sir, was that last time I saw you in your office. Before I was shipped out?"

"I remember it like it was yesterday, boy. What about it?"

"Well... It was about that job you sort of promised me. I was real flattered, sir, I don't mind sayin', especially with you goin' on about havin' big plans for me and all...

"So, now I'm comin' home, sir... And... I'm askin' about that job."

There. He'd said it, dammit. Got it out. Then he realized that Mr. Kelly hadn't answered. The phone was agonizingly silent.

"Did you hear me, Mr. Kelly? Maybe there's something wrong with the connection..."

"No, Tyrell. I hear just fine. I'm sorry not to answer right off. But, I'm thinkin' to myself... Kelly, didn't you tell that boy to write?"

"Yes, sir. You did, sir. But... Well writin' was pretty hard sometimes... places I was at."

"Now, isn't that what I told myself right off. I said, Kelly, you blind fool. Boy was off bein' a hero for his country and his god and his race. How could he possibly write? Real shame, son. Real shame."

"Shame for what, Mr. Kelly?"

"That it's gonna come as a blow like this. See, if you'd been able to write and ask about that job we were discussin'... Well, I'd a had a chance to let you down easier. Life can be real unfair, can't it? The Lord works in mysterious ways, they say, and isn't this livin' proof?

"See, it's like this, Tyrell. You remember my youngest boy, Harold, don't you, son."

"Yes... sir. I... do..." Harold was as notoriously stupid as he was lazy. Mr. Kelly usually kept him busy screwing up the guys in loading. Paid him a handsome salary for it, too.

"My Harold's been comin' along real fine. Fact is, he's doin' so well, I had to go and give him the job I was hopin' to give to you. I mean, he's

247

family, son. Knew you'd understand."

"Yessir." Tyrell said it quick so he wouldn't scream into the phone that Mr. Kelly was a lying... Get off it, Tyrell. You could hurt your momma real bad. Besides... he had to keep trying.

"What about another job, Mr. Kelly? There's got to be all kinds of things I could do at the mill."

"There you go again, Tyrell! Why, you can read my mind. Kinda spooky when one of you boys has that ability. Makes you wonder what the Good Lord has in mind, don't it? .

"Anyway... I was just thinkin' to myself. Kelly... You must have another job you can give that boy. But that was no help at all. Business has been real tight out here. Barely keepin' my doors open. Howsomeever... I can maybe throw you a little part time. Minimum wage, you understand. Dollar sixty an hour. Can't be helped. And then maybe in a couple... maybe six months... we could squeeze in a few more hours. Maybe even get real, close to full time.

"How's that, Tyrell? How's that suit cha? You can see I'm doin' the best I can. But my hands, as they say, are tied, boy. Tied real tight."

"I really appreciate you going to all that trouble, Mr. Kelly," Tyrell found himself saying. Wondering how in hell he was keeping his voice from shaking. "But my family just couldn't make ends meet on part time, minimum wage work, sir."

"I *told* you I was doin' the best I could, boy." Mr. Kelly's voice was suddenly and dangerously frosty.

"Don't you think I was complainin', Mr. Kelly," Tyrell soothed. "It's just that I guess I'll have to... make other plans, sir. And thank you kindly for goin' to so much bother on my account."

A long, long silence from Mr. Kelly. Then: "Whatcha goin' to do, Tyrell?" The frost was gone. You could almost hear a little touch of sympathy. Like scratchin' the ears of a beat up old dog and never mind the fleas, poor fella.

"I'm not real sure, Mr. Kelly. But I'll do fine. You don't fret. But, I'd sort of like to ask you a favor, sir. If I got call to ask?"

"You got call, boy," Mr. Kelly said. And Tyrell did. Just not much of one.

"You'll watch out for my momma, won't you sir?"

"I'll do that, Tyrell... That mean you're not comin' home, son?"

"I'm not sure, sir," Tyrell answered. "I gotta figure out what's best...

248

For my family and all."

"You thinkin' of stayin' on in San Francisco?"

"I don't know, Mr. Kelly... I might."

"Real hard, cold town, I hear. Especially for a boy from Memphis."

"I don't know, sir. Folks have been real friendly."

"Your home's gonna miss you, son," Mr. Kelly said.

"And I'm gonna miss home, sir."

And that was the end of the call.

Tyrell was absolutely calm as he hung up. He mixed himself a drink with some leftover bottles. Chewed on some stale salted nuts. Stared out the window for a long time.

Then the solution came to him. Dawning bright and clear and hot like the Southern sun.

He felt remarkably better. Downright cheery, in fact.

Tyrell did a little dance as he exited the room. His feet as light as feathers.

Allan Cole & Chris Bunch

CHAPTER EIGHTEEN

WELL, EVERYBODY'D DANCIN' in a ring around the sun/Nobody's finished, we ain't even begun,/So take off your shoes, child, and take off your hat./Try on your wings and find out where it's at...

"Jesus Christ! Why'd you wanna go and do something like that," Nebraska gasped.

Hell's Angel Dick had yodeled at them when he saw Alexis' psychedelic Porsche pull in. Bounded across the parking lot. Then he'd kissed Nebraska. With lots of tongue action.

Dick tasted like sour wine, and Nebraska'd never been smooched by anybody with a beard. He spat... and Dick helpfully handed Nebraska a cold bottle of Rainier Ale. Nebraska gurgled it empty.

"Congrats," Alexis said. "You've just been welcomed like a brother."

"Yeesh! I'd rather be an orphan!"

Dick chortled. "That kinda shit sure blows the straights' minds." Sure enough a couple of family-types, unloading their cars for a picnic turned delicate shades of green, decided they'd much rather spend Saturday at Golden Gate Park instead of Park Merced, and started restuffing children into station wagons.

Dick fired a joint and passed it to Alexis as they headed for the ball game. He could see from the size of the ball and the pitcher's underhanded throw, that actually the game was softball.

"One big advantage, bein' an Angel," Dick observed, "is that most times you don't have to worry about findin' campgrounds or places to picnic when you hit some park.

"Take those guys," and he jerked a thumb at a group of shorthaired men playing softball across the open field. "They was all set to bogart this field, which is where we <u>always</u> play, until I went and reasoned with them.

"They saw the light real fast. Not bad guys, for a buncha Reserve-type Cops."

Nebraska damned near swallowed the joint. "Isn't it kinda risky to be smoking," he finally managed.

"Nebraska," Alexis chided. "Would *you* want to be the pig that busted a Hell's Angel game?"

Nebraska would not. Not without some backup. Such as the 82nd

Airborne Division and every damned one of Patton's tanks.

The game was just getting started as they fell into the shade of some trees.

This game, this instant tradition was: The Hell's Angels and their friends (bikers, dealers, cons just out on parole, bartenders, whomever) vs. The Rockers. Today that meant Mulberry Street, some backup singers from a soul group touring through, a couple of guys from Johnny Cash's road group, a Fish or two; two somewhat puzzled-looking but interested jazz guys who were gigging North Beach, and various roadies and groupies.

"Which side you wanna play on," Dick asked.

Nebraska felt suddenly honored, in a weird, weird, weird way.

"Remember, before you pick a team, you're not sleeping with Dick," Alexis said. "Or at least, I hope not."

That decided that. Dick bellowed laughter. "Prospect," he shouted. "Get this guy with the skinny legs a beer."

The on field team - the bikers had lost the toss -were more or less in some kind of playing formation. Under the trees were the hangers-on, the Rockers, and general rabble. The "prospect," Nebraska astutely guessed a prospective member of the Angels, ran to a cooler, grabbed a bottle, ripped the cap off with his teeth and in seconds had it in Dick's hand.

Nebraska was uncomfortably reminded of what little he knew about fraternities, pledges and hazing.

The prospect, sporting jail tattoos, was a bulging-muscled man in his late 20's, with the beginnings of a goatee, his long blonde hair combed into a ducktail. He wore the sleeveless Levi jacket of the other clubbers, but instead of having a top rocker and emblem the back was vacant, except for a bottom rocker that read CALIFORNIA.

"Watch this cat close," Dick advised. "He'll be comin' up for his patch in a month or so. He'll get it. Maybe. If his shit stays straight. Right, Zero?"

The Angel-to-be flashed a grin full of hope.

"Maybe," Dick said. "How deep's the Lake over there, prospect?"

Zero didn't answer, but spun and started to run toward it.

"'Sawright," Dick said, stopping him. "Maybe you'll go skindivin' later. Just wanted to see if you were payin' attention. Oh yeah. You know those arrow tank emblems you wanted? I scored 'em last week down in Berdoo.

"Give 'em to you tonight." Dick helpfully added an explanation to Nebraska - "th' prospect's restorin' a 61 knuckle fulldresser."

Nebraska wasn't sure what all that jargon meant -but he had a vague idea that maybe prospecting wasn't quite as one-way a servitude as pledging a fraternity. Made sense, he thought. Guy'd have to be a <u>real</u> loser if he couldn't see some bennies from being a fieldhand for the others.

"How long," Nebraska wondered, "do you ride prospect?"

Alexis looked vaguely alarmed at Nebraska's seeming interest in becoming a biker.

"You hang around first... for awhile. We make sure you can hold your mud. Then you get voted on. Then you're a prospect. Sooner or later, anywhere from six months to a couple of years, we decide whether you've got your shit together enough to get the patch... It's real simple."

Nebraska somehow thought it wouldn't be so simple at all, but didn't say anything. Instead, he asked about another set of rules - the rules for this game.

"It's siiiimple," Alexis drawled, winking at Dick. "We made a few improvements. But the game's just like you used to play in a vacant lot. More or less.

"We just added some things. You get a hit, get to first, you gotta drink a beer before you can run to second. Second base... see that ashtray with the doobie on it? One good hit, and then you can go for third... Third's that gallon jug of Red Mountain."

"You hit a homer," Dick broke in, "which is anything beyond the fielders or if they're too fucked up to run for it or if it goes into the pigs' game or if it happens to bounce through those citizens havin' picnics, then everybody on the other team has to chug a beer and toke."

"How many innings?" Nebraska asked.

"Who the hell knows," Alexis said. "We've never made it that far. The only rule is, there are no rules. Just like it doesn't matter how many on each side."

Somebody shouted PLAY FRIGGIN' BALL.

It was the Umpire.

Ron (Pigpen) McKernan. Sitting in the tree, with a bottle of Southern Comfort. No drunker - nor more sober -than he'd appeared to Nebraska the day... hell, it was only 24 hours, not half a lifetime..., ago. He was barefoot and there was a banjo on his lap.

Nebraska watched the players take the field. He noticed there was an

Allan Cole & Chris Bunch

extra shortstop positioned between first and second - good idea for folks so intent on getting fucked up-. And maybe seven or eight types wanderin' around the outfield. No rules, is right!

"Come on," Alexis said. "You got some people to meet."

She led him to a big, big, very big Indian-print bedspread, where sprawled the members of Mulberry Street. Less, Nebraska was quite happy to note, the jealous, pain-in-the-ass lead guitar, Tripster.

The incredibly longhaired drummer was Flip. He seemed more intent on filling a tiny hashpipe than anything else, but took a moment to stick out a hand and bonecrackingly shake. "Nice to meet you," he said. "You gonna sit in with us tonight?"

"Uh... I'm not much of a musician," Nebraska said.

For some reason that inspired roaring laughter from the group. "Welcome to Second-rate City," Flip managed. "And I ain't Louis Bellson, either."

The E.A. Poe lookalike, rhythm guitar, Harold, smiled politely, but didn't stop humming a very elaborate melody to himself.

"Harold," Flip explained, "is flyin'. But he'll come in for a landing in a while. With luck, it'll be before it's his turn at bat. Speaking of that," he murmured, "it looks like you two got an unfair advantage."

He lit the pipe, passed it to Nebraska, who toked deep like he'd learned and like he'd taught Jeff, and his lungs damned near came out. Eventually the spasmodic coughing subsided. Alexis had rescued the pipe from being flung, and was trying to hold her own hit down.

"Hash takes getting used to." This from the final member of the group - the black keyboardist who looked like he was better suited playing line for Green Bay - was Mister Funk.

He had the deepest voice since... since - who was that guy who sang *Old Man River*? Nebraska couldn't remember his name for a minute. Then he had it. Robeson. The guy everybody said was a Communist. Who cared, he suddenly wondered. Since when do politics and good music have much in common?

"Hard going down," Mister Funk said, "but it *will* hit you with a hammer."

Nebraska, running through his thought-pattern of seconds earlier, figured it already had. He was thirsty, now. Before he could lift his beer, Mister Funk handed him his own bottle.

It was Mumm's Cordon Rouge champagne. Nebraska had tasted

champagne exactly twice in his life - both times at relatives[7] weddings. All he knew was it was bubbly and expensive, so he sipped cautiously.

"Go ahead," Mister Funk said. "I got a whole case iced down in the back of the Jag."

"Like hell go ahead," Alexis said. "Nebraska's the closest thing to a jock we got, compared to those tree-swingin' Angels. He's gonna win the game for us."

Nebraska somehow doubted he was going to suddenly turn into Ty Cobb or even Bo Belinsky - but he <u>had</u> better go light, considering he didn't want to be too wasted before his possible Emergency Rescue Plan might be needed at The FBI Girl that night.

But the Mumms did disappear painlessly.

The batter - some guy Alexis said was named Cippolina or Cioppina or something, Nebraska thought - got a good, solid hit. The ball rose high into the sky. High enough for the batter to reach first, and pop a beer open with the churchkey around his neck before it descended.

Shouts:

"Mine!"

"Screw you! I got it!"

BODYSLAM as two bikers, eyes intent on the descending ball, crashed into each other. They instantly rolled to their feet, softball dropping unnoticed nearby, and were swinging.

Shouts... and outlaws began running toward the building rumble. Then a shout:

"Naw! They're both brothers'"

The two Hell's Angels - one, Dick said from Vallejo, the other from Oakland - slammed at each other a couple of times before stopping. The other HA members, denied the chance for a cheery Saturday ratpack, went back to the game.

Nebraska wondered what would happen if a non-Angel base runner tried to break up a double play? Would that .50 caliber he'd seen at Gramps be used to arbitrate. • No.

Pigpen, still in his tree, came back to officiating:

"Any more fightin'," he shouted, "between brothers or not, an' the whole team don't get any weed for an inning."

That produced pacifism, and the game continued.

The musician, unnoticed, had time for two tokes at second, then zigged on to third where he glugged cheap wine and went for home. For

Allan Cole & Chris Bunch

some unknown reason - the catcher was still watching the fight-turned-shoving match and the ball was still in the outfield - he decided to slide home. His slide stopped about ten feet short of the plate. The catcher came back to the game, and started shouting for the ball. Somebody remembered where it was, and threw for home. But by that time the musician had crawled the last few feet to safety.

Even a little stoned and drunk, the Angels were far better at any sports than the Rockers. With a score of Rockers 2, Bikers 0, one musician struck out, another got a little confused and ran the bases backward - he doesn't drink much, Alexis whispered - and a third lofted a pop fly into a biker's waiting paws.

Somehow Nebraska found himself playing first base. Mister Funk was nearby, playing the extra shortstop position.

"I guess you know we're goin' down to LA next week," the black called. "You think you'll be going with us?"

"No," Nebraska said, "I got to go home tomorrow."

He suddenly got busy as an biker hit a grounder down the baseline, and Nebraska grabbed it, swore as it skidded out of his ungloved fingers, and the ball spun through the air where somehow Mister Funk waited. Mister Funk had the ball, and tossed underhand to Nebraska.

The biker was barely halfway to base. "But I get the beer anyway. Right?" he asked.

"You surely do," Nebraska said, handing the man an Olympia from the nearby cooler.

The next batter decided he stood twice as much chance of getting a hit if he swung twice at each pitch. That produced an argument, settled by Pigpen and more weed, over whether two swings on one pitch produced two strikes.

"Alexis said," Mister Funk went on, "that she thought you were okay. You got any particular reason to go . back to... where you from? Kansas or somewhere?"

Nebraska corrected him. And no, he had no particular reason to hurry home. Except he missed his family. But, Mister Funk asked, if they heard you had a chance to be on a record, wouldn't they understand?

"Come on," Nebraska said.

"I'm not bullshittin'," the keyboardist said. "Hell, maybe you're just bangin'[7] a tambourine in the background. Or whompin' on a gong for an intro.

255

"It ain't like we're all experts - you think I look like James Brown? Or E. Power Biggs, either?

"You think about it," Mister Funk advised. "It'd be something you'd end up telling your grand-kids about.

"Assuming," he went on slyly, "you decided you still wanted to go back to Center City or wherever and farm. This is an interesting time, Nebraska.

"There's all <u>kinds</u> of options out there," he said, mysterious.

At that point an Angel knocked it out of the park and into a citizen's potato salad. The citizen was cleaned up, pacified with a sixpack, the Rockers drank the penalty brew, smoked the penalty joint, and the game went on.

The next biker hit a double.

Then, after hitting on the joint at second, he decided to steal third. While the second baseman was holding the ball.

As he came in off the field, Nebraska was starting to think maybe this new style of America's Favorite Sport was a helluva lot better than watching the Yankees when a voice sneered at him:

"Well, so the studhorse decided to make his appearance."

It was, of course, Tripster.

Nebraska, raised polite, was looking for something civil to say. But Alexis beat him to it, and was backed up by a scowl from Angel Dick.

"He is that," she said. "And where've you been?"

"Takin' care of business," the blonde said. "While everybody else was out playin'."

"Which means?"

"I been down at The FBI Girl. And we gotta be ready for tonight."

"You don't mean... *practice*," Harold said, sounding shocked and emerging from the ether.

"Don't be funny. I mean the shit is going to happen!"

"Like how?"

Tripster took out a copy of a poster: SAVE THE FBI GIRL it was headed. He waved the poster.

"Like they say, this has *got* to be a Gathering of the Tribes! But it's gonna do no damned good," he near-shouted. "Everybody's gonna show up, groove on the music, chow down on whatever the Diggers score, get stoned, and then go far fuckin' out that's karma when the pigs padlock the joint. And they'll have *won*, dammit! Just like they always do!"

"They got the guns, don't they, kid?" Mister Funk said. "We just got to learn not to play their game by their rules."

"That's bullshit, man! Don't you listen to the Panthers? They got it right! Power grows out of the barrel of a gun."

"Now wait a minute," Harold said, back once more to Lake Merced. "You want us to get guns? To do what? Some kind of Gary Cooper sorta trampas walk High Noon stuff? Hey, Tripster. I'm not Matt Dillon!"

"Hey, look, Harold," Tripster near-snarled. "You're stoned. Don't be saying anything if you can't be positive."

"So he's stoned. Since when has being high had anything at all to do with whether or not you're making sense? Saying Hell No We Won't Go is pretty positive to me," Flip argued. "Which is what Harold's saying to you. Man, we aren't playing political head games like you want to do. We're just musicians."

"That's everybody," Tripster said intensely, almost in tears. "We're just musicians, we're just beatniks, we're just hippies and the pigs are rollin' us over every day!"

Alexis held out calming hands. "Hey. Guys. We are starting to get a little bit loud, and just a little bit shrill around the edges. Tripster. Take a couple of deep breaths, okay?"

The guitarist glowered, but followed instructions. "Now. Real simple," she said. "We are playing at The FBI Girl tonight, right? I mean, that's what you want us to do. Right?"

Tripster nodded.

"Then I'm not tracking," she said. "What else is there?"

Tripster, in between spates of getting excited and getting calmed, did. He wanted to take and hold The FBI Girl. Barricade the doors. Make them come and get us. Call the TV stations and the Chronicle.

"Somebody get a hold of Herb Caen," he suggested. "First time he sees some cop break a teeniebop's head, we'll get us some good stories."

Take and hold, the phrase whispered through Nebraska's mind.

"I got a question," he said. "You want everybody to sit there in that club, and wait for the cops to come in after you? Which is sort of like what we're doing in Vietnam, isn't it? Just sitting there waiting for the bad guys to make a move."

"Oh, for Christ's sake," Tripster said. "I am talking, my big dumb farmboy friend, about the politics of confrontation. Like Selma, Alabama? I guess you've heard of that, right?"

Allan Cole & Chris Bunch

Nebraska bristled. Mister Funk held up a great paw. "Not like Selma, man. No way. I was *there,* boy. Gettin' firehosed for my troubles. And the Haight ain't got any similarities. First, Reverend King marched with more'n a few thousand people from Selma to Montgomery.

"Which, even before the shit came down, got some national attention. Which meant Cronkite and CBS TV, just for openers.

"That ain't us. Look around, Tripster. We're freaks in the eyes of America. People who want to grow their hair long, who don't want to work the straight job, who want to hang out, explorin' their minds instead of the Great Society.

"A few dozen of us get roughed up by the San Fran pigs... you think anybody's gonna give a shit? "Believe me, they won't. Not yet. Not this summer. Maybe never."

The man was warming to his passion.

"Remember, couple weeks ago, that Russian ballet guy... I don't remember his name... was at some pot party when the cops raided the place? Charges got dropped right away. Just 'cause there was a Big Name Highroller around.

"That was the first time I ever heard of any pig losin' interest in prosecutin' everybody they could for smoke. There's a lesson there. Ain't none of us names to nobody. Not yet, anyway. Not this summer," he said once more. "Maybe never."

Nebraska suddenly thought of who Mister Funk *really* reminded him of. Not Paul Robeson, but a black tent preacher he'd heard once... when his folks went to Omaha. A guy who had them coming forward for Jesus like they were driven cattle. Mister Funk might, Nebraska thought, have been trained in another school besides rock 'n' roll.

"Not to mention three people got killed at Selma. You remember *that*? Didn't think you did.

"You think somebody can't get killed playin' games with the cops? You think there aren't some serious freaks here on the Haight? People who might've split with Daddy's deer rifle instead of his credit card? And they've been runnin' on speed long enough to get crank bugs and start thinkin' that guy down in Texas... that guy up in the tower with the rifle... had his shit together and maybe he's a good example for them?

"But you want us to go out there, and fort up The FBI Girl, like we're in some episode of Wagon Train and the Indians are ridin' around whoopin'? Got a flash for you brother. Harold says he ain't Gary Cooper.

Allan Cole & Chris Bunch

Well I ain't Reverend King, nor Ward Bond, either.

"We're just a rock and roll band, Tripster. A *hippy* rock and roll band. So don't be expecting no *Marseillaise* outa my young ass !"

Thirsty after his soliloquy, Mister Funk reached for another bottle of champagne, then came back with another thought. "Something else we ain't," he said, "is badass Marines. So when the cops come chargin' your tender young body, Tripster, who's gonna jump in to save you?

"Ain't gonna be me, I can promise. I'm going out the back, an amp in each hand, mix panel between my teeth and my track shoes on!"

"I can take care of myself," Tripster said. Which did a lot to lighten the increasingly angry mood. "Plus," he went on, "we've got the Angels."

Angel Dick, who'd been standing beside Alexis was abruptly came across the Indian spread. Had Tripster held clear of the ground by his flowered short robe.

"I am gonna say this once," he hissed. "And I ain't gifted like the splib over there is. So you listen close.

"Ain't fuckin' nobody's got the Angels. Except the Angels. We aren't some kind of fruitcake Flying Squad for you freaks. We'll hang out with you. And try to keep the shit off your back as long as it don't conflict with our own interests. Maybe. But that's it.

"Some of us'll be at FBI Girl tonight, sure. And maybe, if the shit comes down, we'll do what we can. But don't you fuckin' <u>ever</u> go trying to speak for the club. Especially not like that. We ain't gonna be out there on Haight Street, bein' smilin' targets.

"Most of us got records. A lot of us are on probation or parole. Which means we can't stand for no bust, unless it's by our own doin'. We'll be the first to get busted, and the first to get thumped. Not to mention what'll happen to our scooters.

"You fuck, maybe you don't care, somebody goes and busts your guitar over your head. Maybe you think you're fuckin' Hendrix down at Monterey last month.

"But you ain't a biker, and you ain't an Angel, and you ain't a brother and you ain't *never ever* gonna be none of 'em."

Dick started to hit Tripster, then thought better of it, and dropped him. Tripster had the brains to stay on the ground. Dick, breathing hard, stared down at him.

"Fuckin' Commie," he snarled. Then blinked, as if aware that he'd blown his own climax. He looked around at the musicians, to see if anybody was anything other than blank-faced. No one, including Nebraska, showed expression one.

"Now, let's knock off all this politics shit and get our heads bad and play some ball," he said, and stomped away, shouting for somebody to give him a Serious Drink.

After a moment, Tripster got up. "Fuck him," he said, but fairly softly. "He doesn't speak for the Haight. And there's a lot of people who think the same as I do. Tonight... what'll come down, will come down."

Then he, too, stalked away.

Mister Funk was looking after-him. He shook his head, not unsympathetically. "Alexis, you think Tripster'll <u>ever</u> get the message?"

"I don't know," Alexis said, tired from the hot talk. "Before he dropped outta college, he joined SDS. Told me he did it 'cause it really blew his parents minds."

"I would suppose," Harold added, now sounding very much like Nebraska imagined that Raven of Poe's might sound like, once he got off the nevermore schtick, "being a general's kid doesn't help any."

Nebraska blinked at him. Alexis nodded.

"Yeah. His old man's some muckety somewhere. In the Pentagon. Tripster doesn't want anybody to know about it. Darned if I know why - it's not like he's responsible for his father or anything.

"But that's our Tripster. I guess he's just gonna keep on with this rabblerousing until something real, real serious happens, one of these days."

Nebraska had a very large, very real Premonition Of Doom...

Quite warranted. It was his turn at bat.

The pitch came in, low, slow and hovering like an old H13 bubblefront helicopter. Nebraska swung, just like his coach had taught him, back in Little League. From his shoulders, from his gut, from his hips, from his ankles, hell from his bootheels!

He connected with a solid crack he'd only heard in sports movies, and the ball disappeared!

Flat started vanishing.

Nebraska's perception warped, as he watched the ball. It was traveling. Look at how much smaller it's getting, he thought, ignoring the WANG WANG WANG like George Harris' sitar coming from somewhere.

Boy it's getting smaller, and boy, I guess those trees at the far end of the field are a lot farther away than they look.

He realized:

The ball *was* getting smaller. And it was not from any changing perspective.

His hit had ripped the ball's cover entirely away, and, as it flew, it unraveled. The elastic string making that Ravi-raga-ringing as it went.

And so they stole the ball from the Reserve Cops so the game could continue...

.

..Hey hey, hey, come right away/Come and join the party every day...

Allan Cole & Chris Bunch

CHAPTER NINETEEN

"... I SAY, HEY! You! Off of my cloud/ Don't hang around ' cause two's a crowd...

Saturday afternoon on the Haight: Incense and engine fumes. Sweat and marijuana. Angry horns bitching. Music taunting. Everywhere an insane babble of American tongues: "What a trip, man... blew her mind!" ... "Get away from that hippie, Melissa. I'm warning you!" ... "And the little children shall lead them, Praise the Lord." ... "Lookit that fag in beads." ... "El primo STP, man, El fuckin' primo." ... "What was Gandhi's sign?"

Jeff and Samantha drifted with the human tide that flooded the Haight every weekend. There were so many people and vehicles Jeff could barely make out the surface of the street or pavement. Cars made progress by inches. People flowed in and out of any spaces they could find.

He craned an ear at Samantha, who was shouting something over the confusion Jeff was mentally comparing to a medieval market place that'd discovered the internal combustion engine.

"What was that?"

"... Day trippers, I said... Welcome to weekend hippieland!"

She said something else, but Jeff lost it as a middle-aged woman wearing a "Love Power" tee shirt elbowed him in the breadbasket to get by. She had blue, spangle-sprinkled eye shadow and a blue-rinsed bubble hairdo.

"Gotcha," Jeff shouted at Samantha.

"What?"

"Never mind... Ooof!"

The ooof was the air whooshing out as his already tender abdomen encountered a hand barring his way. A guy in a golf hat and flowered shirt, complete with camera and fat wife in a mu mu.

"Stand over there," the guy shouted. He was pointing at a big "Summer Of Love Poster" pasted to a blank wall. "You too, cutie," he urged Samantha.

"Oh, Harold... real hippies," his wife was cooing. "They're so... quaint."

Jeff had to laugh.

"Whatsa matter with you?" the guy said, getting pissed.

Jeff couldn't help him, he was laughing too hard.

"Say... You *are* a hippy, ain'tcha?" The man's tone was accusing. As if Jeff had been trying to pull a con.

"Why, this is the most famous hippy in San Francisco, Mister," Samantha broke in.

The guy peered at him. Suspicious. "What's your name, bud?"

Jeff shook his head, going along with Samantha's act.

"He refuses to have a name," Samantha said. "That's how *groovy* he is!"

"Oh, Harold. She said groovy. Take her picture. Quick!"

So Jeff and Samantha stood under the poster and had their picture taken. Just before the camera snapped Jeff felt Samantha's hand grope his crotch. This was going to be one hell of a picture! Flashbulb pop. Her hand was snatched away.

Mission accomplished, the couple turned away as if Jeff and Samantha didn't exist. Not a thank you or bugger off.

"Hey, buddy!" Jeff shouted at the guy. Three steps and he had him by the elbow.

Squinty eyes looking at him again. "What's your problem?"

"Five bucks," Jeff said. His tone mean. His palm outstretched.

"Get outa here!"

Jeff snatched the camera away and held it aloft, dangling over the guy's head. Displaying it to the passing crowd. "Free camera! Free camera, here!"

"Alright! Alright!" Jeff had five bucks in his hand and the tourist and his wife were storming away, swearing at such rude behavior.

A ragged boy with dark eyes and hollow cheeks zombied by and Jeff stuck the fiver in the kid's hand. Turned away before the boy could see where the money came from.

Samantha grabbed his head, pulled him down, and gave him a fat, sloppy kiss.

"What was that for?" Jeff said in pleased amazement."

"For learning so quick," Samantha said. She gave him another.

Wild hormone giggles and grab assing squeals and a gang of junior high day trippers blew through and past them.

Jeff and Samantha came unstuck and moved on.

263

...and though the holes were rather small/They had to count them all/Now they know how many holes it takes to fill the Albert Hall...

Steam and water geysered out of a stalled 20-passenger bus. It was old and yellow and the lettering on the side read: BIBLE TABERNACLE DAY CAMP.

The hood was popped and a harried driver was swathing his hands in rags. Getting ready to complete the fuckup by removing the radiator cap.

Aboard the bus were two frantic adults - one each, male and female - and a pint-sized horde of Sunday schoolers. They were shouting and yelling and hanging out the window to check out the latest fashion in adolescent sinning. The adults scurried back and forth, peeling kids off windows, jamming them back in their seats. Then doing it all over again as the little kids kept popping back up.

Peace signs were flashed from the street. The Sunday school kids caught on fast and started waving peace signs back.

A frizzed-hair freak pounded on the side of the bus. "Free the children," he laughed. "Free them."

The Sunday school kids took up the cry: "Free the children. Freefreefree..."

Chang. Rattle. Chang. Rattle. Chang. A line of white-robed Buddha worshipers trooped past, banging on bells and tambourines. They pushed fistfuls of flowers through the bus windows to the excited children. The adults flailed at the hands poking through. Trying to beat back all that evil intent.

.

..Everybody's talkin' at me/But I can't hear a word they're sayin'/Only the ripples of my mind...

"George Harris! George Harris!"

"Where? Where?"

"I just saw him get out of a limo, man. He was so coooolll, man. Had outasight shades."

"Blow me away, man. Wow!... You sure it was George Harris?."

"Fuck yes! 'Less it was Bob Dylan, man... But it *had* to be one or the other."

Allan Cole & Chris Bunch

···

You better stop/Look around/Here it comes/Here it comes/Here it comes...

Lee Harvey Oswald sneak-bobbed across the stage. Abraham Lincoln waited, bearded and brooding on his stick.

The puppeteer brought Lee Harvey within inches of the Lincoln puppet's back. A pistol-wielding hand pushed aside the curtains to the theater box.

The Oswald puppet hesitated. Losing its nerve. Started to fade back.

"Shoot, you fool!" Came an angry scream.

Out bopped J. Edgar Hoover. He beat Oswald over the head with a club. Drove him back to the box.

Bang. Bang. Two firecrackers went off and Lincoln was dead.

...I'm free to do what I want/Any old time...

A clown with ankh-painted eyes plucked objects from people's hands and pockets. Tossed them into the air. Feeding purses and wallets, half a melon, a beaded bracelet, and a lit joint into his juggling act. Hands moving up and down and to the side. Grabbing and hurling. A constantly changing array of objects - ordinary and bizarre - twirling through the air.

A day tripper threw a hot dog. The clown fielded it without a hitch. A pair of jockey shorts sailed out of nowhere. Up and down it went... the hot dog now poking out of the fly.

The clown lost it when somebody tossed a box of rubbers.

.

..Thinking each trip/Was sent by the dove/Off on a trip/Accompanied by love...

"My parents are such... such... hypocrites," the girl said. She was Ohio straight and just out of mary janes and training bra. "Medicine cabinet full of uppers and downers. Two pitchers of martinis every night."

"Same here, baby," the boy in the sharp-looking leathers said. He was 17. Max.

"I smoke a little grass," the girl went on. "Drop a few whites and they freak out. It is definitely not fair. Why is it wrong for me and right for

265

them?"

"You wanna come up to my pad?" the boy asked. "I got some heavy tunes. And somebody laid some MDA on me. You like MDA?"

"I'll try anything once," the girl said. "That's my motto."

"Groovy chick!" the boy said. And he led her away.

A rival teenage pimp flashed him the finger. The guy just grinned. The girl would be turned out by a gangbang part before the day was through.

...And in the naked light I saw/Ten thousand people maybe more/People talking without speaking/People hearing without listening...

"... LA's like a total bummer. Nothin' happenin' there. Except, maybe Venice. Lot of freaks in Venice. Or the Canyon. But the rest... Shit. You can have it, man. Smog. Thought I'd choke my lungs out..."

"... I hear it's against the law to like, walk in LA. Pigs'll stop you if you're like not in a car. You gotta drive like every place, or they like harass you... Bust you for like walking across the street, man!"

"... Ronald Reagan! My father voted for that asshole! Can you believe his act? 'Seen one redwood,' Ronnie says, 'and you've seen them all.' And I'm weird and immature 'cause I ran away from home."

"…They came to where I worked, is what they did. The FBI! Three big dudes in suits. And this is after my parents had already spent ten thousand dollars on lawyers. Beefing the draft board every time it beefed me.

"I told 'em I had a hearing all set up. To go CO. I told 'em they had no right to arrest me. Jesus, did they throw a shit fit. Screaming names at me. In front of my boss and friends and all. I mean, I was standing there on the damned shop floor. And they put me up against the wall. Almost smashed my nuts searchin' me. Christ, that hurt. Swelled* up the size of basketballs.

"Then they handcuff me and put like chains around my legs... and they haul me out of there like I was some kind of dancing bear, or something."

"So you split?"

"Shit, yeah, I split. Thinkin' of heading up to Canada soon as my folks send me some more money..."

"Get a job, you fuckin' hippie!"

"Turn on...Tune In...Drop fuckin' dead!"

Allan Cole & Chris Bunch

> *...The Spanish bulls are beaten/The crowd is soon*
> *beguiled/The matador is beautiful/A symphony of style...*

Jeff and Samantha dined on lamb shish ka bob and a mound of savory-tinted rice. They passed a quart bottle of beer back and forth to wash it down.

They were tucked into a miniature haven from the Haight madness. It was a scant angle formed by a fortune teller's booth and a car somebody had skew-parked right up on the sidewalk.

"Some fun, huh, kid?" Samantha said. "It gets worse every weekend. Twenty straights for every hippie. And eighty percent of *them* are just day trippers."

Jeff watched two big, lumbering tourists buses edging their way down the street in tandem. They were filled with middle-aged people gawking at the crowd. One particular couple caught his eye. They were peering out the window with frightened eyes. Clearly intimidated, the man put a protective arm around his wife.

"You'd never catch my parents on that thing," Jeff said, indicating the bus.

"Maybe that should tell you something," Samantha said.

Jeff looked at her, surprised. "What do you mean?"

"I'm sorry. I shouldn't have said anything."

"Oh, come on. You just can't leave it there. I won't get mad. Honest."

"It's just that... Stupid as those people are... Maybe it's better to look out the window and see something... Anything. Than not look at all."

"Wouldn't make any difference," Jeff said. "They'd be without a clue no matter how hard they looked... Like those tourists." A small laugh. At himself. "Big talk, GI. Try saying something like that to their face... Hell, I can't even do it on the phone."

"If you don't quit talking like that about yourself, Jeff Katz, I am going to... to... I don't know what. But you'd better stop."

"Well, it's true," Jeff said.

"It certainly is not. To begin with... you were caught off guard."

"Boy, *was* I."

"Also, I don't think you really have any idea what you really want to say."

"Sure I do."

"What, then?"

"Oh... The thing about me and Rachel. For starters."

"What does your father have to do with Rachel?"

"Oh, for crying out loud. He has everything to do with it. *And* my mother."

"I see. Your father and your mother have proposed marriage to Rachel. How strange."

"No. Of course, they didn't."

"So why are you talking to your father about Rachel?"

"Because I'm stupid, that's why."

"Not stupid, Jeff. Buffaloed. If you and Rachel have a problem, maybe she's the one you ought to discussing it with. Maybe that's one of the reasons you keep going round and round. Your folks keep getting in the way. Of course, it's easy for me to say all this, because I'm not involved.."

"Okay. So I whittle it down to the core. I'm still chicken for not telling him right out how I feel about medical school."

"What business is it of his? It's *your* life."

"Yeah, I know. But I sort of owe him an explanation."

"Great. But you have to figure it out first."

"I don't get you."

"That's because you haven't the faintest idea what you want. Although I could guess, after watching you last night... With that... poor policeman."

"That had nothing to do with anything at all. It was an accident. The Array trained me. And I was there at the right time."

"You loved every minute of it, Jeffrey Katz. Don't lie to me!"

"No way. You got me wrong. I told you it just happened..."

"So, I'll shut up."

"You mean... you think I ought to go to SC? Like my father wants?"

"Is that the only medical school in the world?"

"Of course not. But-"

"And is the only way you can make it is if your parents' subsidize you?"

"I can take care of myself," Jeff said. Stiff. A little insulted.

"Certainly you can, Jeff, dear. I was only trying to point that out. Now. I will shut up. Forever more."

"Come on. I'm sorry. I really want your opinion. Please?"

Allan Cole & Chris Bunch

"You don't need it," she said. Firm. "Quit looking at things from everybody's viewpoint but your own. I don't want to sound like Sunshine... but if you open your mind... you'll see."

"Thanks a lot," Jeff said. "That's a big help."

"You're welcome," Samantha said. She stole the last piece of ka bob and Jeff had to tickle her and kiss her to get it back.

Angry horns and shouting blared from the streets.

"Get out of my way, you little creeps."

A straight with oak barrel arms and a beer belly was bracing four hippie kids. He was accusing them of blocking his pickup. The man was in his 40's. Over the hill and mean about it.

"Fuck you. It's not your street." One of the kids screamed back. His face was painted with lipstick. He wore baggy fatigue pants. And a torn, frilly woman's top. The shoulders straining that frilly material, Jeff happened to notice, were of the size one measured in axe handles.

"Hey, freak!" Another straight shouted. "He's not speakin' just for himself. Get outta the fuckin' way!"

Beer Belly took nerve from this. Gave Frilly-Blouse a shove. Frilly Blouse did not budge. Shoved back. And bang, Beer Belly was on the ground, looking up. Frilly Blouse taunted him and danced back a step.

Beer Belly huffed up to one knee. Jeff could see he was about to come up. Swinging. For half the block, straights and hippie kids were ready to go to fist city. Normally gentle young people were shouting obscenities into the faces of the motorists. The motorists were shouting back.

Chang. Rattle. Chang. Rattle Chang. Out of nowhere came the line of white robed worshipers. Whipping in and out of the crowd. Hurling flowers in every direction.

Beer Belly looked up in amazement, finding himself covered with sweet smelling petals.

The ugly mood suddenly broke and Frilly Blouse laughed and reached out a hand to help him up.

Beer Belly grinned and took it.

The white robed line sucked in people like a wrecking yard magnet. Scores of hippies, day trippers and finally, even straights were joining in.

Singing and snake dancing down the street. Weaving in and out of traffic. Carrying away Beer Belly and Frilly Blouse and all the hot afternoon pissoff.

Even the tourists on the bus were smiling.

"I like a happy ending," Jeff said.

"The day's not over, yet," Samantha said, worried. "Wow, are people uptight." But the final sight of Beer Belly's pendulous gut bouncing to the beat of the snake dancing made her laugh.

They took their restored good moods with them to The FBI Girl.

CHAPTER TWENTY

...Sha da da da da,/Yip yip yip yip/Yip yip yip yip/Mum mum mum mum/Mum mum/Get a job...

As they walked under the marquee of The FBI Girl, a bit of rhyme heard somewhere rolled through Jeff's mind: When in question or in doubt/Run in circles, scream and shout...

There seemed to be a lot of questioning and doubting in the club, because almost everyone was darting around, less in circles than ziggety like drunk ants, and there was a plethora of screaming and shouting going on.

With four exceptions:

Alexis was on a pay phone. Shouting only because of the racket. Otherwise, she appeared fairly calm.

Nebraska, unsurprisingly, had put on his I Know Exactly What's Happening expression the Army'd issued him at the same time they gave him sergeant's stripes.

Sunshine sat huddled in a corner, looking worried, not saying anything.

And in the center:

Digger Peter, beaming as if this madness was just exactly what he'd wanted in his Christmas stocking.

He looked as beatific as Allen Ginsberg, and was chanting. But his words, dimly heard over the hooting and hollering were hardly a mantra for peace:

"...Reclaim the territory... through spirit... focus street attention... an audience for an event. Release of crowd spirit can accomplish social facts. Riots are a reaction to police theaters... and overturned cars are responses to a dull heavy-fisted... deathly show... People fill the street to express special public feelings...hold human communion... The alternative to death is a joyous funeral in company with the living."

He was ripped to the tits.

Alexis screamed for silence, got the decibel level cut by one quarter and listened. From her expression the news was not good. She slammed the receiver down and said, quite loudly:

"Shit!"

That started the chaos all over again. Jeff and Samantha fought their way through the mess to their friends.

"What inhell's going on?"

"That was Air India," Alexis non-explained. "Bill and Teddy just hopped a plane for Calcutta, connections to Kashmir, change flights to Air Nepali"

"Huh?"

"They're the bastards that *own*. ... owned this place!"

Alexis then explained. The FBI Girl's manager had showed up around noon to open the joint and get ready for this night's farewell performance. Instead, the doors had been left unlocked and there was a huge note, scrawled on butcher paper hanging from a chandelier:

> **THE FBI GIRL IS FREE**
> **TAKE**
> **WE'RE LOOKING FOR A NEW FOOL**
> **DON'T FOLLOW LEADERS**
> **WATCH THE PARKING METERS**
> *love, Teddy and Bill*

"Which means?"

"Which means the Last Night at The FBI Girl is gonna be BYOB," Nebraska broke in. "Peter thinks it's great. Anarchy rules, he keeps shouting."

"Uh... so what's going to happen?"

"Hell if anybody knows... Not that that's slowing the action down," Nebraska said, indicating:

People were passing out pamphlets: DEFEND YOURSELF AGAINST POLICE BRUTALITY. There were some tables over in a corner, and some Diggers were preparing food - a lot of it stuff that Nebraska, Tyrell and Jeff had ripped off from Fort Mason. Somebody stood in a corner, intent on his cello and soloing through a Villa-Lobos concerto. Two mimes were busy amusing themselves and almost no one else. A couple of six year olds were tossing a frisbee across the room, barely-overhead. Roadies were busy schlepping equipment into the auditorium. Feedback SCRAWKED as somebody started a soundcheck. Two women carried a liquid projector inside.

"I have it, boys and girls," Nebraska said. "We're going to put on a show!"

"Go to hell, Nebraska. Go rapidly to hell. Do not pass go, do not collect $200," Jeff said. "Come to think about it, take Andy Hardy with

272

you. What happened to my straight, shit-kicking buddy from Nebraska? You're getting weird on me, son."

"It's a dirty job, sarge. But somebody's gotta do it."

"This is going to be a trip without a ticket," Alexis said. "A block party without any host. Because come hell or high water, everybody on the Haight, plus about half of San Francisco, is gonna show up here come dark. And we better be ready for them."

A young man, wearing only a dirty pair of jockey shorts, boiled through the door, shouting: "The cops! The cops are coming!"

Panic started to spread, and Nebraska flashed through the crowd. He had the boy by the arm and muscled back to the "sane" corner where the others waited.

"The cops are coming?"

"I saw 'em," the boy panted. "They're up in the Presidio, man! And they've got shotguns and helmets and some kinda shields! Honest, man! I mean, I'm straight! And I saw them! Must've been hunnerds and hunnerds of 'em.!"

"Yeah. Fine. Thanks. Now, look. Don't go freakin' everybody. It's just some kind of cop-type ceremony," Jeff lied.

"You sure, man?"

"Read it in the Chronicle. Got nothing to do with the Haight."

The young man calmed down. Collected himself. "Just thought I oughta tell somebody," he said, looking a little shamefaced, and then slunk out.

The four looked at each other.

"Wonderful," Alexis said.

"And the riot squad they're restless/They need somewhere to go/As lady and I look out tonight/From Desolation Row," Samantha quoted.

So every hippie, freak, rock and roller and curious tourist was going to descend on them, Nebraska thought. And the cops'll run a search and destroy mission right down our throats.

Jeff was looking around. "Where's Tyrell, Sunshine?"

"I left him at the hotel. He said... he had a phone call to make. And it'd take awhile. He wasn't happy. But he said he'd be here in an hour or so."

She shook her head, sad. Jeff, under normal circumstances, would have asked if she had any idea what had happened to his friend - Tyrell'd been pretty chipper at the Mark that morning. But there were more immediate concerns. Such as:

"Okay," Jeff said. "Uh, Alexis, you don't know this, but Nebraska volunteered us to go an emergency type extraction on the band's stuff.

"I have a minor suggestion. If the cops are gonna rock and roll on us - and maybe we can find somebody to take a walk up to the Presidio and make sure that kid was telling the truth - why do we have to participate? It takes two to tango, right?

"I mean, suppose they gave a riot and nobody came?"

"Uh-uh," Alexis said. "We've *got* to play. So do the other bands. You ever been to a concert where the main act opens late?"

"Yeah. Like James Brown? Or Ray Charles?"

"Or the Stones," she agreed. "The theory is to get the audience worked up, and a little angry. Then when you bop onstage, the crowd lets it all hang out, in one big orgasm.

"But if you <u>never</u> show up..."

Jeff got it. That crowd - especially since this last night was FREE, FREE, FREE - would be looking for blood. Without being terribly particular about whose. Up'd show the cops, looking like medieval knights ready to scrag a Saracen or six. They'd loudspeaker something about this is AN ILLEGAL GATHERING. Somebody would shout like hell and somebody else would peg a bottle and...

They'd take out the first cop, maybe. Then the forces of Truth, Justice and the American Way would strike back. And the bodycount would start.

"Shit," he said. "So that won't work."

Another problem occurred to him. "So there's going to be a riot, no way around it," he said glumly. "And the cops will show up. And among them is gonna be that fucking Grancell. Looking for us... especially looking for you."

Nebraska grinned. "Don't go creating problems where there aren't any," he said. "Forgot to tell you, but it looks like Tyrell's little scam this morning paid off right handsome.

"Grancell's sitting down at the Pall Mall right now. Drinkin' double brandy and chasing them with ginger ale. The sucker's suspended from the force until there's a hearing about that lost gun and badge. One of the Angels saw him there, not twenty minutes ago."

"Whew," Jeff managed.

"Course we still got to worry about that damned MP Sanders, but since we're civilians now, he can't get too rowdy on us, right?"

Allan Cole & Chris Bunch

"Double whew."

"What do we learn from this reading, my flock?" Nebraska said. "We learn that behind every cloud lies a big goddam storm! That every problem has a solution..."

He stopped, and a look of radiance crossed his eyes.

Sunshine managed a smile. "Nebraska... you look like you've just had a real Zen experience. You've been enlightened."

"I have, I have, oh lordy I have," Nebraska beamed. He kissed Sunshine and hugged Alexis. "Doctor Katz, if you weren't hog-ugly, I'd even kiss you once or twice."

"Why? What'd I do? I didn't have any ideas. Did I?"

"A riot...and nobody came? That'd work. All we need is for no audience. Like you said, it takes two to riot. The cops'd have to beat each other up."

"It won't work," Alexis said. "There's been leaflets. Com/Co's had stuff on the street for a week. Plus the rumor mill. And Larry Miller and Tom Donahue been talking about nothing else on KMPX for days."

But Sunshine was shaking her head. "Nebraska knows something," she said wisely. "He was a soldier. The Government knows how to make things invisible, but they're keeping it a secret. Just like the UFO's."

"Sorry, Sunshine. But my security clearance didn't go that high. But I do have an idea... "We'll just head for a pay phone and call in a phony bomb scare.

"Everybody freaks, and splits and by the time they realize it's a hoax it'll be three o'clock in the morning and everybody'11 be ready for bed.... naw. Won't work."

"Naw is right," Samantha agreed. "I'm not a fulltime freak... at least not yet... but I bet most of the people on the Haight would think it was some bullshit the cops made up just to jinx The FBI Girl... And they'd get even madder."

Nebraska's second look of enlightenment auraed across the room. "Not," he said slowly, "if there was a *real* bomb."

"Come on," Jeff said. "I know you were an engineer. But you were a driver kinda engineer. And maybe you know how to set off dynamite... I heard you plowboys do things like that to get rid of stumps and stuff.

"The only people I could think of that'd have some real stuff that goes bang is the United States Goddamned Army. But if you think I'm going to climb back into my Ree-cruit drag, and pull *another* commando raid on

275

the Presidio... uh-uh.

"Stealing food's one thing. But ripping off explosives?" Jeff looked around, abruptly feeling real fear crawl through him, and making sure nobody was eavesdropping on this rapidly-becoming-criminal discussion. "I bet the FBI... and not any FBI Girls ... come after you for that one."

"Sorry, Nebraska. I don't want to make Mister Hoover's acquaintance. He's an ugly mother, at best."

"Are you through," Nebraska asked.

"Uh... yes."

"Bomb, you dummie. Think bomb. Bright blue type bomb. Two dollar type bomb."

The light dawned for Jeff: "Oh. Yeah. *That* bomb!"

The plan unreeled in Jeff's mind. "Samantha, if you'll excuse me... I've got to go make a small purchase. As for you, Nebraska, you're a fucking genius!"

"Hey... the language. Remember?"

Jeff just gave him the finger and sprinted away, looking for a taxi.

...All around/People looking half-dead/Walkin' on the sidewalk hotter than a matchhead...

Jeff was too excited to notice at first - but then both he and the cab driver realized they weren't strangers.

The cabbie was the merchant seaman/beatnik with the long gray hair who'd picked them up at Oakland Army Terminal a century ago.

"So you took my advice, huh?"

"Yeah," Jeff said.

"Well?"

"Hell if I know what to think."

"Good," the cabbie said. "A mind blown is a mind shown. Where you want to go?"

"Uh... you forgot to put the flag down."

"No, I didn't."

"Oh. Thanks. I want to go over to Market Street. There's a surplus store there..."

"There's a *lot* of surplus stores on Market."

"I'll know the one when I see it."

The cab pulled out, into the heavy Saturday tourist traffic. Somebody

Allan Cole & Chris Bunch

swore at the cabbie. He smiled at them.

"None of these squares realize," he said. "They don't look around and see, man. It's like Eliot said, 'our only health is the disease/If we obey the dying nurse/Whose constant care is not to please/But to remind of our, and Adam's curse/And that, to be restored, our sickness must grow worse.'

"Wonder how much worse it'll get - they'll get -before they change?"

Jeff blinked. Was about to ask. But there was no time, no time at all, as his mind began to elaborate on Nebraska's plot. "Hey, do you know where there's a model store?"

"You mean... where they give you a camera without any film, and you sit and whack off when the girls bump and grind? I think there's some down in LA, but none around here, yet. If you want to get laid, I know some part-time ladies who'll—"

"Hell, no! I mean, you know, like models? Model airplanes? Hobby shop, that's the word."

"You got it, chief."

"Yessir. And I'd like that little electric motor..."

"This?"

"Yeah. That's the one. It runs on batteries, right?"

"Standard flashlight type. They're over in that rack, there."

"Yeah. Gimme six... no, eight of the big D-cell guys. And a roll of wire, and you got some electrician's tape?"

"You won't need batteries that big for such little motor, sir. Normally most boat builders use these little penlight cells."

"I'm not building a boat. Now, I need some decals. Something that looks real military. Maybe... an airplane kit?"

"If you're doing a custom model," the clerk suggested, "you'd be better off buying these sheets. Any letter, almost any size."

"All right! Okay, ring 'em up. And do you know where there's a good paint store around here?"

The cabbie helped Jeff wedge that large, electric-blue aerial bomb into the back seat of the cab.

"You've set a record, man."

"What do you mean?"

"Hey, I've had other fares I turned onto the Haight. Most of them took

277

two, three weeks to turn freaky-deaky."

"And what," Jeff said, "is strange about a man wanting to own a bomb? I have quite a collection at home."

"Uh-huh. Where's the next stop?"

"That's it. Back to the Haight. And...could you pull in the alley? Just as soon nobody see me unloading La Bamba here."

"Mmm. 'By the prickling of my thumbs/Something wicked this way comes.'"

That one, Jeff knew:

"^{X}'A deed without a name,'" he agreed. Then the smile vanished from his face:

He saw Tyrell walk out of the Army recruiting station down the street.

He was in deep conversation with another black - a Sergeant First Class in dress greens. A recruiting sergeant.

Tyrell said something. The sergeant laughed.

Tyrell did not.

Then the sergeant stuck out his hand. Tyrell shook it.

As if they had just struck a bargain.

"Hey," the cabbie said. "Isn't that your buddy?"

"Yeah."

The cabbie started to hit his horn - and Jeff caught his arm. "No, man. I don't think he wants anybody to see him right now... And I hope I'm full of shit.

"Let's get back to the Haight, okay? I got a dark and bloody deed to get started on."

...And the good Samaritan he's dressing/He's getting ready for the show/He's going to the carnival/Tonight on Desolation Row...

Allan Cole & Chris Bunch

CHAPTER TWENTY-ONE

"...WHO'S DRIVING YOUR plane?/ Are you in control. or is it driving you insane..?"

The group on stage was blasted to the eyebrows and warbling a weak imitation of the Rolling Stones.

No one seemed to mind.

The FBI Girl was packed to overflowing and there were still freaks and hipsters pouring in from all over. The house lights were full on and shockingly bright. There were solo dancers shaking to an unheard beat. Sprinkled among tight knots of arguing, pissed off young people. There were abrupt breakouts of snake dancers weaving through the hot debate. Whipping up the simmering broth.

The woman in the fish net sarong was there. Dancing alone in a small, clear space. Eyes closed tight. Hands graceful above her head. Body wriggling, wriggling in a sensuous dance. Shimmying from ankles to fingertips. Building to a violent climax.

... I said, "my, my." like the spider to the fly/"jump right ahead in my web"...

"The FBI Girl's for the people, man," one boy said. He had a purple ankh tattooed on one cheek. "Let 'em *try* to take it away!"

"They're calling in the National Guard," a wild-haired young woman said. "Aria's friend Joe heard it on the radio..."

"Fuck 'em. Can't bust us all. There's too many of us!"

"... It was in the Barb, man. They got all these camps left over from World War Two, see? Where they used to keep the Japanese. So guess who's goin' this time, baby?"

"Chickenshit city. Chickenshit pigs..."

"They hate us, man! ' Cause we're young. That's why they're sendin' us all to Viet Nam, man!"

"Capitalist cocksuckers. Fat-assed martini swillin' Rotary Club joinin', steak eatin' sonsofbitches! All they give a shit about is profits."

"Fuck their clubs. Fuck their guns. Fuck their tear gas. We're gonna fuckin'.... fuckin'... you know... Fuck 'em back, man."

"... Chicks up front soon as we hit the street, got it?"

"... I'll tell you why. 'Cause The FBI Girl's a symbol, that's why! A symbol of all that is good and healthy. It's love, people. Love is freedom. Freedom is love... "

"I thought we'd have a little more time," Jeff said, wiping a drip of gray paint. "Listen to them out there! And it's only eight *o'*clock."

"Don't get your bowels in an uproar," Tyrell said. "We'll make it. Now... you just keep a steady bead with that spray can like I showed you."

Tyrell cocked his head. Studying the metal surface in front of him for a second, then he started spraying again.

"I don't know why everybody says you're so dumb, Jeff," Tyrell said. "This idea is pure genius."

He kept at his work. Cheerier than hell. Humming "Time is on my side... yes it is..." as he worked.

Jeff shot him a fast look. His friend didn't seem to have a care in the world. As happy as if he'd just won the Irish Sweepstakes.

Weird.

Then he saw Sunshine giggle something into Tyrell's ear. Tyrell laughed and gave her a squeeze.

Weirder still.

He went back to work.

Down the hall, Jeff's old girlfriend - she of the rimless glasses and skrinched face - staggered out of the mimeo room with a big bundle of freshly printed pamphlets.

Nebraska, a bustle with his own plans, was rushing down the hallway. He nearly knocked her over.

"Watch it!" came the angry voice.

"Uh... Sorry, m'am... I didn't-"

"Don't call me m'am. It stands for madam. And I do not supervise whorehouses!"

"No, ma- I mean... uh... I 'spec not," Nebraska stuttered, thinking, the Queen of England is addressed as madam and last he heard she wasn't running any cat houses. But he kept his yap shut. Jesus, this woman would intimidate a bull in heat.

He eyed the bundle. A big red banner peered out: "OUR DEMANDS."

"What's this demand business?" Nebraska asked.

"For when the pigs come, of course," the woman said, getting one hand free from the pamphlets and parting her hair. So she could properly glare at Nebraska. "Now... take these, and pass them out."

Nebraska woofed as she dumped the heavy bundle into his arms.

"One per person," she ordered. "And be quick about it. We don't have all night!"

She hurried back into the mimeo room before Nebraska could get the nerve up to tell her to get lost.

He looked down at the demand list: (1) Amnesty for The FBI Girl Freedom Fighters. (2) Repeal of all business license laws. (3) Legalization of marijuana. (4) The bombing of Hanoi must cease...

There were sixteen more. All of them nonnegotiable.

Nebraska got out of Skrinched Face's range before he dumped the whole thing into the trash.

"Hmmm. Your problem, m'lady, dawns bright and clear," Supersplib was saying. "You require an asshole of noble dimensions. Wherein two trains might pass in complete safety."

"Exactly," Samantha said. "We have to have somebody the police will listen to when this person calls. And they have to live as close as possible to The FBI Girl," Samantha said.

"We've got five or six possibilities so far. But, for one reason or another... nothing
quite fits the bill."

"I have just the gentleman in mind," Supersplib said, teeth gleaming. "I'm speaking of the
Ultimate Straight, you understand. A man who would turn in his dear, sainted grandma-mere, for addiction to Geritol."

"I knew we could count on you," Samantha said. "... Now, I have one other little problem you might be able to help me with. A very personal favor, please.

"I am, as they say, all ears, my dear," Supersplib murmured.

Jeff was sliding the big letter "L" into position. "Damn!" he swore as the "L" folded over into a blob of nothing.

"I feel like a human paste pot," he said. "Not a very good paste pot, either."

"Piss pot is more like it," Tyrell said. "You've got no talent at all, son.

Here. Let me. You are looking at the champeen Booker T. Elementary School paster upper ."

"Riiight!"

Tyrell ignored Jeff. He soaked the sheet of half-inch letters until the proper ones started sliding free. Lifted off a letter. Angled it toward its intended home between the rear fins of La Bomba.

"Ooops. Aw, shit!"

"Piss pot yourself," Jeff said, dismissing Tyrell's handiwork with a sniff.

"Oh, here, let me," Sunshine said. "Your fingers are too fat."

"I thought I was the love of your life," Tyrell said.

"You are. But your fingers are still too fat."

She laid the "L" in place first go. Then added the next letter... "C."

"What's the LC stand for?" she wanted to know.

"The cow, honey," Tyrell said.

"The what?"

"The cow! You know... Elsie? Borden's milk?"

"Not very military," Sunshine said. Then: "I always felt sorry for Elsie," she said, serious. "Like she's just a cow, right? And cows like to always be surrounded by other cows. So they don't get lonely, right? But, poor Elsie. They're always dragging her out all by her lonesome to be in some stupid advertisement. Making her into some kinda television star. That's no life for a cow!"

"Sunshine, you are a certified nut," Tyrell said.

"At least I don't have fat fingers," Sunshine said, quickly adding a colon after the word, "Warning." And started the next group of letters.

"... and the cry rang out across the land: Come to San Francisco. Where the power of love reigns supreme!"

"Right on, man!" Tripster shouted, banging on a tambourine. He'd turned the stage mike over to a bearded youth from Berkeley.

"But the political toadies at City Hall grovel before the fat cats and war mongering mobsters. The Summer of Love is over, they say. We've taken all your money, now. There's nothing left.

"And soon, the pigs will be upon us."

"NO! NO! NO!" the crowd screamed back.

"And what will we do when they come? With their tear gas and fire

282

Allan Cole & Chris Bunch

hoses?"

"Fight them," Tripster shouted, wracking that tambourine back and forth.

"FIGHT THEM!" the crowd screamed back.

Tripster started leading them in a chant. Bang bang banging on the tambourine.

"Power to the people! Power to the people! Power to the-"

A fifteen year-old meth freak was perched by the stage. He had an old revolver in his hand. He spun the cylinder and Snap dry fired it in the air. Snap. Spin. Snap. Spin. Snap.

The pistol was empty.

For now.

The batteries broke free of the tape and scattered all over the floor.

"Why're you bein' so persnickety with the tape?" Nebraska growled at Jeff. "We got enough to tape a B52 to the ground."

"Am I, or am I not the supervisor, here?" Jeff said.

Nebraska ostentatiously looked around the room. It was empty. The other four were out scheming and plotting.

"Took a vote, huh?"

"Yep," Jeff said, fumbling the batteries off the floor. "They bowed before my superior qualifications."

"Oh, yeah, I remember," Nebraska said. "Somethin' about you gettin' an erector set for your tenth birthday."

"The big one," Jeff said. "With wheels and gears and the ever popular electric motor."

He held up the one he had scored at the hobby shop by way of illustration.

"Gimme that!" Nebraska said, ripping it from Jeff's hands.

"Hey! That's my job."

"Tell me this, Mister Erector Set Owner. How many gizmos did you build with that birthday goodie?"

He started skillfully winding tape around the batteries.

"Lots of them."

"How many?" the batteries were done. Now, for the motor.

"Okay. Just three or four. But only real advanced stuff. Then I got bored. No challenge."

"Bullshit," Nebraska said. "Never met a kid in my life who got past much more'n a dinky kinda car. Come on. Tell me true. How long 'fore you lost half the parts?"

"First weekend," Jeff confessed. "But I couldn't tell my folks that. Hell, I was on them most of the year for that thing."

"Same here," Nebraska said. "Saw a big damned erector set Ferris wheel in the toy store window in town."

"Same here twice," Jeff said. "I figured with one of those kits I could build anything. A submarine. Rocket to the moon. Jeff Katz. Master Engineer."

"Stick to doctorin'," Nebraska said. "Anyway, that sucker hit me about the same way. Hell, I laid siege to my ma and pa. Better part of a year. Finally got it for Christmas. Started right in on that Ferris wheel. And you know what?"

"Couldn't finish it, right?"

"Man, I couldn't get the motor platform down. Took me 'til Easter to figure out no kid *ever* built anything like they put in a toy shop window. I figure the Erector Set company has guys with PhDs in engineering runnin' all over the country. Knockin' shit like that together to mess with our heads and steal our folks' money."

"You got it," Jeff said. "Big damned ripoff. Like Clover Brand Salve. %Kids! Make big money! Win big prizes! Be the first on your block with a nifty Red Rider Bee Bee gun!' What a racket."

Nebraska tied a wire to one pole. Taped it. Touched another wire to the opposite pole. The little motor whirred into life.

They stared at it, intent.

"Doesn't sound like much to me," Jeff finally had to admit.

"Ah. But you ain't gonna be the guy listen', my friend," Nebraska said. "That old boy will have stethoscope ears and brown shorts, brother. Believe you me!"

Alexis had Tripster up against the wall. "You sorry assed excuse for a human fucking being," she was shouting. "We are here to calm people down, remember? We are supposed to be professionals. Musicians don't scream fire in a crowded theater, stupid. They keep playin' until the shit has quit hittin' the fan. What kind of a head trip are you on? You tryin' to start a goddamned riot?"

"Pigs started it," Tripster mumbled.

"Of course they started it. Pigs always start it! What's that got to do with anything?"

"I'm just doin' what I think is right," Tripster snarled.

"Well, quit it! Now, let's get up there and cool these people out. Okay?"

Tripster glared at her. He wasn't budging.

"I *said*: Okay?"

The struggle of wills continued.

"THIS IS THE FIRE MARSHALL SPEAKING," a loudspeaker voice boomed from outside. "I REPEAT: THIS IS THE FIRE MARSHALL. WE HAVE BEEN ILLEGALLY DENIED ENTRY TO THIS BUILDING."

"Oh, shit," Alexis said.

Tripster sneered. "I guess they wanna play."

Before Alexis could nuke him, Nebraska blasted by, trailing Sunshine in his wake.

"Keep a lid on it, honey," he yelled at Alexis. "Me'n Sunshine'll handle it."

Tripster started to say something pissy, but Alexis spotted something. A scary something. She was gone in mid jawflap.

"You the owner?" the beefy man in the fire marshall's uniform wanted to know.

"Not exactly, sir," Nebraska said. "I'm sorta watchin' out after the place, 'till they get back."

"Too bad. But I got a complaint about serious overcrowding. They're way over the fire code limit in there." The man seemed honestly sorry. "I have to close it down. No choice."

Sunshine piped up. "Say, you remember me, don't you Captain Cherney?"

"Sure I do, Sunshine. How could I forget?"

"Everybody's real uptight tonight," Sunshine said. "We're worried something bad might happen. People might get hurt."

"I worried about the same thing when I got the call," Captain Cherney said.

"From the police, right?"

The captain didn't answer. He didn't have to.

"Pow. Pow. Pow," the kid meth freakin' was going. Pointing the pistol

Allan Cole & Chris Bunch

around. "Pow. Pow. Pow."

"Whatcha got there, baby?" Alexis purred.

The meth freak whirled on her. A cartridge box burst" in his hand and bullets spilled all over the floor. He saw Alexis. Gave a wild laugh. Aimed the gun at her.

"Pow. Pow. Pow," he said.

"That's a real pretty toy you got there, honey." Alexis crooned. "Wanna let momma see?"

The boy cracked the hammer back. Took a steady bead through the pistol sights. His finger whitened on the trigger.

"Pow," he said.

"Come on, baby. Let momma play."

The boy started crying. "Pow," he sobbed. "Pow. Pow."

Alexis reached out as gentle as you please and slipped the pistol out of his hand.

"Come on, sweet thing," she said. She led him quietly away.

"We were sorta hopin' to ease 'em out soon," Nebraska said. "If you go in there now... I don't know. Say my prayers if I were you."

"Just give us an hour, huh?" Sunshine said.

"I have to report this," Captain Cherney said. "It's my job. Besides... I'm not sure... you have that long."

"All we're asking is a chance," Sunshine said.

"I don't know... I'll probably be real sorry, if I do."

"Yessir, you might," Nebraska said. "But maybe not as sorry if things get outta hand."

Captain Cherney looked Nebraska and Sunshine up and down. Hard.

"No bullshit?" he said to Sunshine.

"I promise," Sunshine said. "On my Karma."

Amazingly, the captain took her at her word. They got the reprieve. However brief.

"Woof! There's actual blow in that blow," Angel Dick said, pinching in one nostril and snurfing in mightily.

"Yes, indeedy. But now you lack balance, my Angel friend," Supersplib said, touching up the other line.

Angel Dick honked it down and returned the straw to

Supersplib.

"Fuck me, you were right," he said, wiping at his nose. He looked at the madness around him. "Whaddaya think the odds are we go to fist city? Pigs oughta be here any time now."

"I would feel myself disloyal if I contemplated such a wager," Supersplib said. "Our optimistic friends, you understand." He waved into vagueness. But Angel Dick knew who he was talking about.

"They're okay," he said. "Nebraska is, leastwise. Still... Sure is lookin' to be one helluva night. I swear, man. Pigs fuck with us. I'm fuckin' back."

Supersplib was surprised. "It was my.,. uh... understanding the Angels were out of this."

"Officially, fuck yes, we're out of it. Unofficially... Shit, I wouldn't mind thumpin' cop heads."

He glanced at the little white jar on the table.

"Lay out a couple more, Supersplib," he said. "The kid is feelin' good!"

"Yes... Certainly... Although, might I recommend some delicious hashish? Very smooth. Very mellow."

"Fuck a buncha mellow, man! Let's get *fucked* up."

Supersplib laid out the lines.

Up at the Park Street cop shop, uniforms were gathering by the scores in the parking lot. Riot helmets were passed around. The tear gas teams were passing through the crowd, their leaky canisters leaving a trail of weepy eyes. Batons were being twirled. Holsters nervously snapped and unsnapped. Hideout guns went into socks. Contraband narcotics and other jail- sentence- boosting items were being tucked away to plant on suspects.

A lieutenant shouted an order and cops came to straggly-assed attention.

"Men... We have reports of an in progress riot..."

"Kill a hippie for Christ," one wag shouted. All his cop buddies laughed.

"Knock it off, Betts," the lieutenant snarled. "Now... You are to proceed by the numbers. You know the drill. Wait until your squad is called. Not before. Not later. Okay, girls. Let's move it!"

And the count off began.

"Who you lookin' at, asshole?"

The little man in the San Francisco Giants' baseball cap jumped a mile. He'd been admiring his own reflection in the mirror at the Pall Mall bar. Tugging at his hat and dreaming of double play glory.

Apparently his gaze had inadvertently strayed. And had given offense. He turned to the man sitting next to him.

"I'm very sorry, sir," Giants' Cap said. "Entirely my fault. Let me buy you a drink."

Grancell put an obstinate hand over his glass. His eyes were bleeding. His forehead bulging. His senses aflame with brandy and ginger ale.

"Buy my own damn drinks," Grancell snarled.

"I won't insist then," Giants' Cap mumbled. He turned as far away as he could in his stool. Trying to make himself smaller than he already was.

"Hey, I'm talkin' to ya, buddy!" Grancell wasn't gonna let it go.

"Really, sir," Giants' Cap said. "I've apologized. I've offered recompense. What more—Gurk!"

The gurk was the result of a tie gripped in a beefy paw.

Grancell pulled Giants' Cap close, until the man's face purpled. Breathed nasty fumes into the man's face.

"It was those fuckin' draft dodgin' hippies," he snarled. "Got me suspended. Almost cost me my job."

"I agree, sir! Absolutely!"

"What're ya agreein' about? Fuckin' with me, huh?"

"No, sir. I would never do that. Uh... Bartender... Could we have two more drinkies down here? Please?"

Grancell let go of the tie as the bartender lumbered over.

"Quit fuckin' with the customers, Grancell. The guy said he was sorry."

Grancell was livid. Betrayed.

"Hey, Sam. I'm a reg'lar customer in here. Can't treat me that way... This guy'sa... sa... botherin' me, that's what."

"Sure, Grancell. And I'm Henry Cabot Fuckin' Lodge. Now, why'n'tcha go on home. Sleep it off."

Grancell slammed to his feet. Came to his full, considerable height.

"You are speakin'... speaking to a... an officer of tha law. You realize this. Don'cha?"

"Okay, okay. Settle down, pal. One for the road. I'm buyin'."

The bartender grabbed a clean glass and started filling it with ice to build a make amends drink.

But Grancell wasn't having any.

"I'll show you," he bellowed, startling the little man and sending the bartender scrabbling for the sawed off bat he kept under the bar. "I'll show allayouse. Fuckin' hippies will be sorry they messed with Old Grancell."

"I'll learn 'em!" And he stormed out of the bar.

"Say, he's a little out of control, isn't he?" Giants Cap said. Suddenly brave now that Grancell was gone.

"Not my problem," the bartender said.

"Maybe we ought to call the police," Giants Cap ventured.

"Jesus Christ, jack," the bartender said. "Didn't you hear him? He is the police."

"I feel weird digging a hole I'm not supposed to climb into," Tyrell whispered.

"Ssshhh" was Jeff's reply.

"Don't shush me," Tyrell complained, leaning against the shovel. His voice still a whisper. "If that sucker can't hear us diggin', he's not gonna hear me whispering."

"Let me spell you, son," Nebraska said.

"Typical REMF," Tyrell said. "Fox hole's almost done and all of a sudden he's a big help!" But he gave him the shovel just the same.

Nebraska let the dirt fly. In a few minutes, the deed was done.

"Help me spread out this dirt," Jeff said, scooping up big handfuls and hurling it around in every direction.

"You got it all wrong, man," Tyrell said. "That's not the way it oughta look."

"Oh, for crying out loud. Who's going to look that close? Who'll know."

"I'll know," Tyrell said, his artistic sensibilities offended. "Who used to BDA Arclights? Stand back and let a master show you how it's done."

Rattle scrape hurl and dirt and debris flew from the hole. Tyrell's artful pattern involved jagged peaks in a semicircle. A clatter of rocks bounced on the pavement.

"Sssshh," Jeff said again. Automatic.

"Sound like a busted tire," Tyrell said. "Get over here, you two. 'Fore the square wakes up!"

Jeff took a step forward, lost his footing in the dark, and went sky ground into the hole. With a nice loud THUMP.

"Ssshh" Tyrell said.

"Fuck you."

"Never go back to white mice, you do."

Nebraska stuck out a hand and hauled Jeff out. By the time Katz had dusted off his britches and dug dirt out of his ear, the job had been completed to Tyrell's exacting specifications.

They lugged the big gray cylinder over and propped it up in the hole. Crammed dirt down in and to hold it in place. Nebraska opened the top of the cylinder. Fumbled inside and a soft, constant, whirring sound began.

"Now for the fun part," Nebraska said.

He toted a trash can over from the curb. Picked up a bat he'd hauled along for just this purpose. He spread out his legs, hefted the bat, and took a Babe Ruth Stance.

"Incoming!" Nebraska screamed. WHAM! The bat smashed against the can. It took off like a rocket. SLAMMED against the front porch.

Nebraska ran like the wind. He got about twenty steps before he realized no one was following. Tyrell and Jeff were still standing in front of the house. There was not a sign of life inside.

Nebraska wearily retraced his steps. "What's the guy, deaf, or something."

"A little more subtlety required here," Jeff said."

"We're back to that subtle business again?" Nebraska said.

"Let the good doctor show you how it's done," Jeff said.

In one motion he scooped up a hefty rock and pegged it through the front window.

A CRASH and six or seven tinkles later, and Jeff was a half block away and still gaining on himself.

Nebraska and Tyrell, however, were frozen in place. Gaping at what Jeff had done.

Shouts.

Lights.

Heavy, pissed off footsteps.

"Let's git!" Nebraska shouted.

They got.

Just in time, as the front door slammed open. Standing there, blearing out into the night, was the square Supersplib had promised.

The name on the mailbox said Reynolds. First name, Tom. Middle

Allan Cole & Chris Bunch

name, who cares? The freaks called him R.J. Or aluminum head. Or Fuck Face. Depending on the strength of the available drugs and Mister Reynolds' temper.

He was forty or so, going on a hundred and eighty two. Mister Reynolds was said to have had a wife... once. Word was, after many years of suffering, she split when her hubby demanded she withdraw from the Ladies Auxiliary of the Veterans of Foreign Wars. Mr. Reynolds had absolute proof the commies had taken over.

Mr. Reynolds lived on the blessings of important relatives, who never visited or called. A permanent disability check from the DMV, where he'd clerked until he'd thrown his back out while tormenting a young applicant for a driver's license. And the sale of old copies of "None Dare Call It Treason" and Senator Goldwater's "Conscience of a Conservative."

Some stoners swore they were a helluva read on Owsley's best.

He was also the most notorious complainer on the Haight. His small house was just down the street from The FBI Girl. Mr. Reynolds waged constant battle for All That Is Good And Decent In America. Meaning, sneeze within vague earshot of his home, and the cops were called to roust the offender.

"But don't they get tired of the grouch?" Samantha had asked. "Seems to me, even pigs have better things to do."

"They do. Yes indeed they do," Supersplib said. "But this is no ordinary grouch. We are contemplating supreme grouchiness, here. A grouch with connections!"

Mr. Reynolds' beady eyes swept the darkness. Looking for the source of the offending noise.

He gasped with fear.

Mr. Reynolds had found it.

It was a bomb!

The mother of all bombs.

Poking out of the crater it had formed when it had plummeted from the skies.

The bomb was a tasteful, battleship gray. Although Mr. Reynolds was not appreciating its beauty just now. He was gaping at the markings on the side:

USN
MK. XII/LC
INCENDIARY
250 LB

And sideways, down between the rear fins:

**WARNING: Do not attempt to defuse
MARK 27 Anti-Handling Device Installed**

Mr. Reynolds heard the ultimate voice of doom: Whirr. Whirr. Whirr. On and on. Whirrwhirrwhirr...

"My God! It's alive!" Mr. Reynolds screamed. He thundered back into to his house. "Help! Police! Help!

"The Commies are attacking!"

"No, I am not drunk," the police sergeant yelled into the mike. "I ain't had a drink in six years. Although if you don't get me some help in about six seconds, the AA can kiss my ass goodbye!"

"Whaddya mean, how do I know it's a bomb? Jesus Christ, I'm lookin' at the sucker!"

He was. From the nonsafety of his squad car. Red bubble gum light flashing weird across the scene. Illuminating the deadly, finned presence. Mr. Reynolds' frightened face was looking through the hole where his window used to be.

"Whose bomb? Jesus, who—. Okay. Says USN on the side. Gotta be Navy, right? Some goddamned swabbie pilot musta fucked up and lost the sonofabitch right over my beat!"

The dispatcher's next query brought even a louder howl.

"Fuck you, it's a dud! I can hear it, I tell you! Listen!"

He shoved the mike out the window for the whirrwhirrwhirr. Pulled it back in.

"See? Oh screw you! How do you know a bomb goes ticktick? Not whirr whirr. You get your ass out here and see for your fuckin' self! Better yet, call the bomb squad.

"And I am warning you... get those assholes out here lickity split before the whole thing blows. Wipe out the damned neighborhood. Along with your fuckin' pension!

"Hear me?"

The dispatcher heard.

The sergeant keyed off, slammed the mike home, and tore open the

Allan Cole & Chris Bunch

glove compartment.

Hoping like hell some poor cop slob from the last shift had left a half-pint behind.

"... Cool out, people," Alexis said into stage mike. "We have an emergency announcement to make."

The crowd noise level dropped as she got everyone's attention.

"There's some kind of sewer main or gas main problem... just down the street," Alexis continued. "Now, nobody thinks anything real bad is gonna happen, but we don't want to take any chances, okay?

"So. We want all of you to leave. Now."

There were groans from some stoners who didn't much care if they went kabang. Long as it was served up with music.

"Don't give me any shit," Alexis said. "We can all . get together tomorrow night. Over in the Park. Or maybe Bill will let us, have the Fillmore. Mulberry Street will play, I promise. And maybe we can rope in the Dead... And the Jefferson Airplane. Really get down!"

Some light weighted cheering. It was working.

"Now, we want to do this orderly, people. No reason for anybody to get hurt. So... Line up quiet... Like you were back in school for the A Bomb drills. We have volunteers at the exits to guide you. Do what they say, alright?"

It must have been, because the crowd started pushing for position to leave. But it was mostly quiet. And oddly enough, orderly.

Samantha had been opposed to the A-bomb reference. It might panic people.

"No way," Alexis said. "Listen. This is one generation that *knows* bomb drills. Shit, we were hidin' under our desks and wrapping ourselves in old newspapers from kindergarten on."

Alexis was right. The evacuation of The FBI Girl began without a hitch.

"Sunshine. Hey, Sunshine."

"What's the haps, Robbie?"

"Trouble haps, that's what!"

"Oh, no!" She had visions of riot police swarming all over the place. Robbie had been posted to keep watch on their activities. "I thought we

293

had more time! Why didn't you warn us?"

"Don't sweat the riot pigs, Sunshine. Not yet. They're five... six blocks away, yet."

"I don't get it. What's the problem?"

"It's Grancell, man!"

Grancell's red-rimmed eyes took in the hippies streaming out of The FBI Girl. Shit! They were leaving. He was too late. What the hell happened? Couldn't be much past ten.

It wasn't too big of a stream yet, but even drunk he could see the place was quickly emptying. Nobody was hanging around under the big marquee like they usually did. He bleared this way and that up toward Haight. Not a sign of the riot police. Fumblefingered fuckers. He wobbled back into position - missing the red gum ball revolving down by Mr. Reynolds' house.

Considered his problem. Not that he was worried. Grancell had come prepared. He took an experimental swing with the old cavalry saber. The sheath was belted around his waist. There were pins hanging from the sheath that used to fix the beast to his living room wall - beneath the portrait of Jefferson Davis and the Confederate flag. It was the closest Grancell had ever come to Dixie, except in his lurid cop dreams.

Another swing of the saber. It hissed through the crisp night air. Fuck with Grancell, will they? He'd show them he had an ace or six up his sleeve. Awright! He lumbered to his battered Ford pickup. Tossed the saber through the window onto the seat, beside his baton and rummaged through the debris in the bed of his truck. It was a quarter ton pickup with maybe two tons of old hamburger wrappers, cardboard coffee and cola cups, oily rags and so on in the bed.

It also contained his secret weapon. Weapons to be more precise. There were many many multi-colored rocket flares. Equally multi-colored Smoke bombs he'd scored from Sanders. And a big, fuckin' tear gas grenade. He grabbed it, ooozed into the truck and cranked the starter. The engine stuttered into life.

He was off. Swigging from a Christian Brothers Brandy bottle in one hand. Steering with the other. The tear gas grenade in his lap.

The pickup oopsied over a curb and the bottle went flying. Grancell sawed at the wheel. Straightened the sucker out. Got the pickup in the sortof center of the street and put the pedal to the metal.

He hefted the tear gas grenade from his lap. His plan was to steam up to The FBI Girl. Toss the grenade under the marquee. Then withdraw out of range of the fumes and wait for the hippy kids to bolt his way.

Grancell chuckled at the vision of all the heads he was gonna break. Belched up sour brandy fumes from an even sourer stomach. He was getting close, now. Real close. He took his other hand off the wheel, eased the pin out of the grenade's pin, and edged the grenade out the window, bracing for the throw.

Holy shit! Who put the fuckin' fire hydrant in the middle of the street?

SLAM. As the pickup said hello to the hydrant. The tear gas grenade whipped from Grancell's hand. Tumbled into the back of the truck.

The truck came to rest over the geyser where the hydrant used to be. Grancell muttered cocksuckermotherfucker, kicked open the passenger's door, grabbed his saber and baton and slid out.

He stood there in the street. Wet. Drunk. Pissed. Murder in his heart. Kids were looking his way, now. Wondering what the fuck was goin' on. Fuck *em. They'd see.

Meanwhile, the tear gas grenade had made a pass at a hamburger wrapper. It was love at first sight.

"I told you he had a fuckin' sword," Robbie said.

Tyrell and Sunshine were gaping at the madness down the street. Along with the emerging crowd. There was water geysering from hell to three stories worth of heaven. A crunched up pickup. And this bizarre figure shouting and waving a big mother—

"It is a sword," Sunshine said.

"What the hell's he gonna-"

There came roar of engines. Crowd shouts. Crowd screams. Tyrell whirled to see four olive drab 2 1/2 ton trucks skew across the street. A flash of fancy uniforms as MPs came boiling out of those deuce and a halfs.

Leading the charge was Nebraska's old buddy.

Lt. Sanders kicked the legs out from under a fleeing hippie. MPs swooped on the young man. Punching, kicking, screaming shit about draft dodgin' commie creeps.

Paradise bloomed all around him in the form of many possible draft

Allan Cole & Chris Bunch

dodgers and AWOL GIs. Another hippie went down to a flying tackle and was hauled off in cuffs and purpling bruises.

This was going to be a great night. And it'd barely started.

Sanders started looking around for Nebraska.

The crowd reeled back from Sanders' attack. Scrambling in the other direction to get away.

The first flare kabooshed into the night sky. Red flame ate at the darkness. Then another. Gold. Another. Green. The back of the pickup exploded into fiery life. Purple smoke. Then red. Sparks and flames and all kinds of colors bursting up and up and up. Smoke bombs boiled inky midnight.

Grancell howled in laughter. Danced in the street with his saber and club like old Ben Gunn over Long John's Treasure.

"Come and get it, you hippie motherfuckers!"

The challenge came ten seconds after Angel Dick had thrown a chair through a window and had clambered out of The FBI Girl. He saw Sanders kicking ass on one side. Flames puking into the sky on the other. And the madman Grancell.

More Angels came pouring out the window. Richard and Road Captain Dirty Dog led the charge.

At that moment, Grancell got reinforcements. It was in the form of about one zillion - possibly two zillion - riot- ready cops. They stormed through the water, past the fire and fumes and the railing Grancell.

The riot cop lieutenant shouted them into line just past Grancell's truck.

Hell's Angel Dick and his forces hesitated. Momentarily stalled by the sudden show of force.

There was a surge behind them, caused, domino-principle. by another charge led by Sanders. The crowd was still relatively small. There were still people inside the FBI Girl. And many more were escaping in the confusion.

But the pressure was growing.

There was only one direction for the valve to blow.

The line of cops braced as the Angels stalked down the street.

"What're we gonna do?" Jeff shouted.

Allan Cole & Chris Bunch

"Jesus, I don't know," Nebraska yelled back.

The two of them were jammed up against a wall by the weight of the crowd. There was no way they could move. Jeff could make out Samantha and Sunshine taking refuge behind the towering figure of Supersplib. He had his long arms outstretched and was shoving and pushing people away to keep a space.

This was not turning out the way they'd planned.

T

he bomb squad captain could not believe his eyes. He'd set off with his team and his truck expecting the usual nail-biting and possible maiming his line of work included.

Instead, they'd driven into a budding riot.

Which was no big deal to the captain, except his goal lay beyond the insanity that had stranded his truck.

A goal that might go bang. Any second. Which would end any possibility of a riot. Mainly on account of because there would be a large, smoking hole in the ground where the riot used to be.

This would not do.

Captain Kowalski unhitched the mike. Turned the loudspeaker volume up to full twist.

Sanders didn't find Nebraska. So, he took second best. It came to him on a platter.

Tripster and three largish types burst out of the pack and stormed straight for him. They were zonked to the tits with piss off and semi dangerous drugs.

Sanders blasted on his whistle. Before the shrill note had died, MPs came out of nowhere to club Tripster's forces down.

Now Sanders had Tripster slammed up against a deuce and a half.

"Where's that bitch, Alexis?" he screamed at Tripster.

"Don't hit me. Don't hit me." Tripster pleaded.

Ho, ho, ho. Sanders gloated. A chickenshit. Okay. What's he got to be chickenshit about? Besides just gettin' thumped?

"Let's see your draft card, asshole," he shouted at Tripster.

"Please don't hit me," Tripster babbled on. "Don't hit me." Scared out of his skull.

"Will you shut the fuck up about hitting! Do what I said!"

"Oh, pleasepleaseplease," Tripster babbled on.

What could Sanders do?

What the hell. He hit him. It felt good. So, he hit him again.

"THIS IS CAPTAIN KOWALSKI OF THE SAN FRANCISCO BOMB SQUAD!"

The loudspeaker voice cracked over the chaos.

"Say fuckin' what?" Was Angel Dick's reaction.

"Holy shit!" Was the riot police lieutenant's.

"Yea!" Was Jeff's.

"*Bout fuckin' time." This, from Nebraska.

"Thank you, Jesus!" As Tyrell rediscovered religion.

"THERE IS A REPORT OF A BOMB IN THIS VICINITY," the voice continued. "PLEASE, CLEAR THE AREA. I REPEAT. CLEAR THE AREA. DO NOT PANIC. WALK SLOWLY. DO NOT RUN... I REPEAT... THIS IS CAPTAIN KOWALSKI OF THE SAN FRANCISCO BOMB-"

"

I have my orders, Captain," the riot cop lieutenant blustered. "There are law breakers here. I have to take them in. It's my duty! Besides, you have no jurisdiction or authority over me."

"There's my jurisdiction, asshole," Kowalski roared, pointing off in the direction of Mr. Reynolds' house. "And my authority. It's called a bomb. B.O.M.B. Bomb. A 250 pound kinda bomb, according to a certain sergeant of yours.

"Now, move. Before the bomb does the moving for you! "

"How do you know it's not a fake?"

Kowalski sighed. He was 35. Felt more like 75.

"I don't. Only one way to find out for sure. Wanna go look see?"

"Uh..." the lieutenant uhhed.

"Sure. You're a big man. Come on."

"Yeah... right... uh... How close we gotta get?"

"Belly close," Kowalski snarled. "Me, anyway. You get to stand across the street and see me shake hands with the devil. Or the Holy Mother, if it blows the other way."

"Nebraska. Hey, Nebraska."

"Yeah, Robbie."

"Sanders busted Tripster."

"Sumbitch. Best news I heard all night."

"Thought you'd say that, man."

"Wait up," Nebraska said. "This could get even better."

He strolled over to where Kowalski was getting remotivated to deal with Bomb.

"Excuse me, sir," he said, snapping a salute as if the guy were a by god Army officer and he was still a lowly noncom. "But we got this little problem... Might get outta hand. If it does... Well, it sorta might get stuck to your shoes."

Kowalski looked Nebraska up and down. For a hippy type, he seemed pretty okay to Kowalski. He guessed Nebraska was just out of the Army. Polite, too. Probably had some kinda rank. And/or hot rod responsibilities.

"Make it quick, son," Kowalski said.

Nebraska was quick. He told him about Sanders and Tripster. And Tripster's old man. The big wig general type old man.

"I see what you mean about stickin' to ray shoes," Kowalski said. "Thanks. I'll take care of it. Later."

Then he set off to regather his team and brace the bomb.

Angel Dick watched him go.

"A bomb, huh?" He said to nobody in particular. "This I gotta see."

He started after Kowalski. "Yeah, me too," Robbie said.

In no time at all, a small crowd was trailing after Kowalski. On the way to Mr. Reynolds' house.

"We did it, Ty-Rell. We did it." Sunshine said, giggling and hugging him and covering him with kisses.

"Yeah, I guess we did," Tyrell said.

They came unstuck. Tyrell. leaned back against the big plate glass window that was the front of the old Laundromat. The crowd around The FBI Girl complex was thinning out into nothingness.

"I think there's something to this karma business after all, Sunshine," he said. "We thought good thoughts. Well, sorta good thoughts... depending on your point of view. And it all worked out"

"I told you, my Ty-Rell man. Karma rules!"

She leaned over to kiss him again. Instead, she screamed.

Tyrell was doing a holy shit what's happening and then he saw what she was screaming about.

Grancell!

Sword high. Charging him like he was leading the Light Brigade. Tyrell, unfortunately, had no cannon.

Grancell lowered the sword in mid rush. Fully intending to spear Tyrell.

Several thoughts occurred to Tyrell. All involved the various skills the Army had drummed into him. Killing skills.

"You dirty hippie motherfuck—"

Tyrell went on automatic.

Just before Grancell struck he stepped to one side.

In theory, when Grancell went past... carried by his own drunken weight... Tyrell would spin and break his piggie cop neck with a single blow. If not, the follow up kick should complete the task.

It was a damned good theory. One that Tyrell dismissed the moment it came to mind.

Let Karma do what Karma has to do, was his brand new theory. Not courtesy of the U.S. Army.

Grancell hit the plate glass window at full force.

He spilled into the room in a hail of glass, and collided head first with the opposite wall.

Miraculously, there was no blood. As for Grancell... He groaned once. Twice. Three times. Then he began to snore.

"He's gonna have a helluva hangover," Tyrell said. "Too bad that's all he'll have. Short of an unemployment check."

Kowalski finally got a looksee at his bomb. "I've never seen anything like it," he confessed to one of his assistants. "What the hell's a Mark 27 Anti-Handling device?"

Across the street, he was being watched by the lieutenant, five or six of his men, and growing crowd of young people. Curious about the bomb.

"Maybe somethin' new the Navy came up with," his nervous assistant said. "We could call."

"Get that thing out of here," Mr. Reynolds screamed from his front porch. "Cowards!"

Kowalski craned an ear at the whirwhirwhir coming from inside the bomb.

"Never heard nothin' like that, either," he said. "Scares hell outta me. Screw the Navy. By the time they even 'fess up it's their goddamned bomb

- which they dropped on our fair city, I might add - we will no longer have a hefty portion of Haight Street.

"Plus this Anti-Handling. Which I guess is some kind of bullshit jargon meaning the bastard's boobytrapped!"

"Let's be safe. Haul it off to the beach and blow the sumbitch!"

Many agonizing minutes later, the mother of all bombs was aboard the truck and Kowalski was slowly, carefully driving down the street in the direction of the beach.

Robbie watched it go. Disappointed. The excitement was over. It'd been a heck of a night, though. Music and dope and cops and near riots. Good thing that bomb dropped out of nowhere. Lot a folks mighta got fuuckked up! It was. a weird kinda gift from heaven.

Shit! That it was it. The bomb was a gift, man. A holy, spiritual thing. An object with a soul, like the Indians said. And when the captain blew it up... why, he'd be setting that soul free. To join the Great Spirit. Or, something. Yeah. Free.

He imagined all that power released and soaring to the skies.

"Free the bomb!" Robbie shouted. "Free the bomb!"

He marched after the truck, intent on seeing this thing to the end.

Others took up the chant: "Free the bomb. Free the bomb."

Scores of hippies fell into place behind Robbie. Parading after Kowalski and his truck. Other young people heard the chant and came pouring out of their crash pads.

Flashlights and candles came out of nowhere. In no time at all, Robbie was leading a torchlight procession.

"Free the bomb!" The crowd chanted. "Free the Bomb. Free It. Free It!"

Jeff watched them parade out of sight. He turned back to his five friends. They were about the only people left on the street.

"Pretty good job, boys and girls," he said. "We've prevented a riot, screwed over Sanders and Tripster... Wow, can you imagine what's going to happen to Sanders? He'll be pulling duty on DMZ by the time Tripster's dad is through with him."

"Don't forget Grancell," Sunshine said.

"Never, Sunshine. I will never forget that dear man. So, here we are. The world saved from evil and it's not even midnight yet."

"I oughta be tired," Nebraska said, "but, shucks. I'm just gettin' my second wind."

"Shame to waste a great night like this," Tyrell agreed.

"We could go swimming," Samantha said, indicating th rapidly widening and deepening gush from the fire hydrant, a gush that'd somehow gotten ignored because of Bigger Things.

"Naaah," Nebraska said. "Not deep enough for skinny-dippin'."

"Well, we've also got a whole club to ourselves," Samantha said, indicating The FBI Girl.

"Gee, I don't know," Jeff said. "It's dead empty. What kind of a party can we have with nobody around?"

"Come with me, my pretty," Samantha said. "But be warned: I have every intention of teaching you the answer to that question."

She took a hand from her pocket, and held it out, palm up. There were six deformed-looking vitamin-looking capsules.

"These, according to our always trustworthy dealer man Supersplib, are 1965-vintage Bear Manufacturing Augustus Stanley Owsley III LSD25. Think Mouton Rothschild. Think Kobe Beef. Think Beluga caviar. Think Blown Mind. Think Terminally Fucked Up!"

Now, how could Jeff turn down an offer like that?

Allan Cole & Chris Bunch

CHAPTER TWENTY-TWO

Oh nobly born
One pill makes you larger
The time hath now .come For thee to seek the Path
And one pill makes you small
Tell 'em a hookah-smoking caterpillar
hath set thee face to face
With The Clear Light
And now
Thou art about to experience it
In its reality
When men on the chessboard
In the Bardo state
Get UP and tell you where to go
And the naked Spotless intellect
Have fallen sloppy dead
The time to seek The time to seek The time to seek
Feed your head Feed your head
Feed your head The Path
Breathe ... DEATH

GETTING LOADED DIDN'T didn't work out to be that simple. Jeff, having had an outstanding Thursday night ripped to the gunwales on acid, with no problems other than the Snake Lady and the Stilt Giant, wanted to drop the Owsley right then and there.

Alexis started to caution him, but then caught herself. If this was, indeed, real Owsley - and there was no question to doubt Samantha - it would almost certainly be a Big Trip. A lot more psychedelic - and she wished that somebody would come up with another word because that one was already showing its age - than whatever Jeff would've sucked down out of the punchbowl.

She didn't say anything because one of her first acid trips had been Formal. With a Guide. In a Clean Quiet Room. And the Guide said cheerily if Alexis happened to see a giant spider with a woman's face, it could just be her mother if she was having any problems with her home life, and she wasn't, was she?

And so Alexis saw a giant spider.

A huge goddamned spider.

It took her ten minutes of deep breathing before she could walk up to that spider, and see it shrink down to a teeny little daddy longlegs on the wall that bounced away on her before she could set it free out a window.

Build Your Own Bummer should not be part of the agenda.

Besides, Sunshine took over.

She led them through the almost completely-deserted maze of The FBI Girl to a large and flowered chamber.

This, she explained, had been Bill and Teddy's own apartment. They'd invited her up once.

"But all they wanted was for me to watch," Sunshine said, a bit primly. "So I left."

The FBI Girl might have been a community effort, Alexis thought, looking around. But its legal owners had done themselves proud.

One of them must've seen some old engravings of a Turkish pasha's chambers. Or harem. There was a monster bed with flowered sheets and blankets, closed off by curtains. There were poufs large enough for ancillary orgies. The carpeting was plush, colorful and thick.

Against one wall was a super-Macintosh stereo that dwarfed even Alexis' houseboat blaster. Every record ever released, it seemed, was haphazardly stacked in cabinets around the stereo.

There was a bathroom. In it was a cabinet, filled with... well, devices.

There were two refrigerators filled with munchies and drinks.

But who was she to object, Alexis thought, remembering her own Porsche. Billy and Teddy had worked hard enough for some Creature Comforts.

"You said these guys cut out for India," Nebraska marveled. "Leavin' all this?"

"I guess," Jeff said, "they really believed that he who travels lightest travel fastest."

"Wonder what'll happen to their stuff," Samantha said.

"Take it with you when we leave, if you want," Sunshine said.

"I couldn't do that. I'm not a thief."

"Neither am I,." Sunshine agreed. "But somebody'll come along who doesn't think like we do... and it'll be gone. And if they're wrong in what they believe... it'll be their karma."

Allan Cole & Chris Bunch

She searched through the refrigerators until she found a large bottle of apple juice. She filled glasses, and started handing them around.

Not a bad Guide, Alexis thought, amused.

...and a little child shall lead them...

Jeff wanted a beer, if there was any.

"Taking drugs and drinking alcohol," Sunshine said, "is like peeing into the wind."

Jeff took the apple juice. Nebraska wanted - and got - a sixpack of Coors.

"First... my Ty-rell," Sunshine said.

Tyrell's lips were dry.

"Uh..." he started to say.

"Go ahead, baby. Or don't, if you don't want to. But.. I'm here. With you, my Ty-rell man."

...take me on a trip/upon your magic swirling ship...

Tyrell hesitated. As did Sunshine.

Then he grinned.

"Airborne/Airborne/All the way..." and swallowed the tablet, chasing it with the apple juice. Sunshine smiled.

"I knew there would be a right time," she said.

Alexis figured out the stereo system, found a copy of Sergeant Pepper, and they sat down.

Six friends.

Waiting.

After awhile, after the record had been turned over, Tyrell giggled.

...We were talking—about the space between us...

In his own mind he'd never *really* thought this music everybody was going on about was that special. What he'd grown up on was gospel. Memphis/New Orleans jazz "Dixieland," although that was mostly for the white tourists. Sometimes some old blues - although that was pretty raw, trashy and old-fashioned. As for rock and roll -hell, most of that'd been ripped off from race records or R&B.

Tyrell's main men were people like James Brown. Major Lance. Martha and the Vandellas. Aretha. For older guys, Clarence Frogman Henry. Ray Charles forever, Smokey even more forever.

But now...

...And the time will come when you see/we're all one/and life flows on within you and without you...

Allan Cole & Chris Bunch

Yeah. Time will come, he thought.

And hoped he'd be around to see it.

But the hell with that. He was suddenly happy, very happy. He hugged Sunshine. Gave her the long, long kiss she deserved for helping him.

She kissed him back.

"Later," she whispered, and her tongue traced the inside of his ear, "we can let our bodies... just flow."

Then Nebraska started laughing.

Loudly and long.

Everyone chuckled along, and waited to see if there was an explanation forthcoming.

"I was... just thinking," he said. "You know. Like this place we're in... I kept thinking that we'd see ol' Douglas Fairbanks in a turban and one of those big mother swords they call a Sukimitar or something come out... or maybe Sinbad... and here came Daffy Duck. And his turban kept unraveling. But the funniest..."

But at this point, Nebraska started laughing again. The loud guffaws of a happy, happy man. His chortles died away, into occasional giggles.

Alexis leaned back against him.

Yes, she was thinking. I was right this morning, wondering why I haven't taken acid for awhile. Gives you a chance to step back. Not like you're somebody else like the scare stories say. But...

But stoned on acid, you're sort of...

Detached?

Yeah.

Probably it'd be a good idea to get the band together, before they saddled up for LA, and get everybody righteously stoned.

Tripster, too?

Mmm, she nonthought and decided she'd deal with that problem tomorrow.

A thought floated through her brain:

We don't need all this electricity, do we?

"Jeff... do you have a lighter?"

Very slow-motion, walking underwater, Jeff squirmed to one side, and dug into his pocket.

"Don't want to get up," he explained. "Because of the steps."

Steps?

Allan Cole & Chris Bunch

The lighter spun, spun, spun through the air toward her, and her hand flashed out. Had it.

She started lighting the candles around the room.

Then turned the lights out. She took the lighter back to Jeff, whose attention took a bit of time to attract, since he was occupied running his hand up and down Samantha's bare and long leg.

She was smiling at him. Content.

Alexis went back to Nebraska and sat down.

"Much nicer now, isn't it?"

"Mmmm."

A phrase floated through Alexis' mind:

Oh nobly-born. the time hath now come for thee to seek the path...

From... from what was that book?

Oh yeah. The Tibetan Book of the Dead. Yeah. That weird book that the monks were supposed to read aloud to somebody who was about to Cross Over The Great Divide. Right.

Alexis decided this really <u>was</u> Owsley pure quill,

and sighed, waiting for the rush.

AFTER DEATH - THE CLEAR LIGHT

Oh Nobly-born, listen.

Now thou art experiencing the Radiance

When logic and proportion

Have fallen sloppy dead...

Music was still playing, Jeff realized.

But now, it wasn't The Beatles. Or, anyway, he didn't *think* it was them.

His eyes opened. No they didn't. They'd already been open.

He looked around the room. His friends sat, transfixed. Each alone. This, he thought in a moment of "sanity," probably due to his brain having less capacity for spinning because of Thursday's tripping out, would make a good Scare Picture.

Drug Addicts. In Their Solitary Hell, would be the caption.

This was the infamous Rush.

But everyone seemed quite happy.

Nebraska was crying quietly - but with a smile on his face.

What time was it?

Jeff lifted an arm, and his wrist felt heavy, heavy, suddenly heavy. A goddamned anvil around it. Fumbling fingers undipped the band. He

307

looked at the watch. Omega. His high school graduation present. From his folks.

He'd never realized the reason Swiss watches lasted so long was because they were built out of lead. But that seemed dumb for the Swiss to do something like that. No wonder everybody didn't wear one of them. You could get a wrist hernia. He threw the watch away. Heard it land somewhere.

His arm floated free. His body lifted. And the wave caught him again, and he was away and gone.

...my senses have been stripped/my hands can't feel to grip...

Samantha had been about to draw Jeff's attention to a poster on the wall. FLY JEFFERSON AIRPLANE its scrambled lettering read, but the picture under it that she saw was a beach somewhere in the south seas.

In the Marquesas, her mind told her. You saw it when you were twelve, no thirteen. In a copy of National Geographic. On a right hand page.

But instead of a deserted beach, she and Jeff were in the picture. Walking hand in hand toward her.

They were naked.

Samantha wanted to tell herself that she'd better get some suntan lotion on herself quickly. She wasn't an experienced nudist. But she decided to just watch, from behind the shelter of her eyelids.

Tyrell was suddenly struck by the smoothness of his skin. Its browness. He'd never really realized this was the color people's skin was *supposed* to be.

White was... no, he corrected himself before the thought finished, sliding his hand under Sunshine's blouse, and admiring the contrast... no, they went well together, didn't they.

He wondered why everybody didn't realize that. But they didn't. Not Mister Kelly. Not even his mother. Bummer was the word. He was going to ask Sunshine why this was so, when she giggled suddenly.

"Tickles," she said. And opened her mouth for a kiss, her tongue sliding slowly around the inside of Tyrell's mouth, and his fingers were moving over her suddenly-erect nipple.

She put both arms around him.

"What would happen," she said softly, breaking from the kiss, "if we

Allan Cole & Chris Bunch

put acid in everybody's drink at my parents' barbecue?"

Tyrell thought. Then shook his head.

"I don't think they'd like it."

"Mmm. Maybe not," Sunshine said. "A turned on square is a square that's turned on.

"But wouldn't it be groovy if everybody could, like, be on acid? But without taking any?"

Tyrell started to agree.

Then thought what it'd be like, say, be.ing like this and hearing the jumpmaster's final shouts: Stand in the door... Ready... Go...

And the greenlight and the slipstream tear-..

No. He didn't think so.

Or at least he didn't think he thought so.

He went back to admiring his black, black skin and feeling Sunshine's fingers moving against his chest.

"Why were you crying," Alexis wondered.

"'Cause... 'cause it felt good," Nebraska said.

"You aren't unhappy about anything, are you?"

"Uh-uh. Couldn't be happier. I could lay here on this floor for years.

"Or anyway till breakfast."

"Jesus Christ," Alexis said. "So much for take acid and lose control."

"Hey, I <u>have</u> lost control," Nebraska said, injured. "I could be thinking about how good a fried egg sandwich and some hashbrowns would go, right about now."

"Food? Ech!"

"Okay. Okay, if you feel like that. I'll just shut up and try to figure out how they got the whole damned wall mounted on hinges."

There was silence again in the room... except for the music.

AFTER DEATH - THE LOSS OF REASON

The spirit strives to be liberated From the cycle of Reincarnation.

The strivings become weaker And

Black clouds

Surge around him, blind him, and slowly engulf him

In darkness In darkness In darkness

Go ask Alice

When she's ten feet tall...

...we came UP *with a new plan. One we know you're*

Allan Cole & Chris Bunch

going to like...

No, you didn't, Dad. And no, I don't like this one any better than the others. Jeff blinked. Had his father's words really echoed through the room? And had he made an utter ass of himself answering them?

Maybe. Maybe not. Nobody seemed to notice, except Samantha, who looked at him seriously.

...I have plans for you, Jeffrey Katz...
In a half-dream, he sees his relatives His friends His house He rushes forward crying out and Dashes himself against an invisible wall.

Later, all of them said they'd heard some kind of voice. Jeff's voice: *....Hell. We were kids. Anyway.. Five of us. But... only three guys caught the Bird...*

A pause.
Like I heard somebody in a movie say once... departed friends...

Jeff thought of the lagoon at Guam where some long-since-decimated unit headed for Vietnam must've had one helluva beerbust, because the lagoon was still one solid float of shiny empties.

Tyrell remembered Atherton. When Tyrell'd passed out, puking, Atherton had right-shouldered the paratrooper and carried him all the way back to the airfield. Catch anybody in Memphis doing that, ever, he thought.

Nebraska smiled to himself, remembering a poker game. He'd heard about cardsharks and marked decks, but he'd never seen either one, until Mills sucked those Air Force guys into the poker game. Later Mills had said they were called bicycle readers.

Hell, he mourned. The world needs a few more rakehells. He wondered where his mind found that word. Not straights like me.

But was he that straight. Now?

He decided to ask Alexis.

But she'd gotten up and walked over to a large map, hanging on the wall. He joined her.

Odd. It was easy to walk, even though in some ways the floors and walls were like on a boat. But they weren't, really.

310

The map was interesting. He put an arm around Alexis. She put her head on his shoulder.

"Mexican guy drew it," she explained. "I think somebody called Covarrubias or something."

Yeah. It was an artist's conception of the United States. Here there was a cowboy. Here somebody working steel, about where Detroit should be. Way down there, a tourist enjoying the Florida sun. Here, down below the border, was an Eagle with a Serpent in its beak.

An Indian. Further up, there was a small harvester, a tiny man at the wheel. Nebraska grinned at the farmer, and the tiny man waved back.

"Over here," Alexis said. "Here's home."

Yeah, Nebraska thought. Right there, halfway up the coast. Just above the movie cameras. Home? For Alexis, maybe. But for him?

No. He went back to looking at the harvester, which wasn't quite in Nebraska, he thought. That was home, wasn't it?

He wasn't sure, very suddenly and very dizzyingly. He thought it was time to sit down.

And think.

This acid, he realized, was different. It wasn't a sixpack or a case or a fifth or a joint. It was *not* something you sort of took just because it was Saturday night.

At least, not at the moment.

"You would've liked my dad," Tyrell was telling Sunshine. "Big guy. Hands that'd fit all the way around a bollard, I swear."

"What's a bollard?"

"Those things that they tie ships up with."

"Oh. My daddy took me sailing once. Do you think our folks would have gotten along?"

Tyrell had this great image of his father, mildest of men but someone he'd once seen pitch a drunk off the Embankment, twenty feet out into the Mississippi without taking a deep breath or losing his smile. And the only books he'd read were the River Pilots, Mark Twain, Pilgrim's Progress and the Bible. Talking to that college professor?

And his mother and Sunshine's? What would they talk about - which course to bring out for the white guests, next?

He started to answer. Then rethought.

Maybe they would have - at one time. After all, that professor and the stiffsmiled woman <u>had</u> produced Sunshine.

He just shrugged, as a wave of mourning slammed down over him.

Dead. His father was dead. Tyrell had a vision, of sorts. There was a long line of people coming toward him. Some smiling, some not. Far, far down the line was his father. Then...oh yeah. That was the kid in school – Timmy Hayes. His folks were Christian Scientist. He'd gotten the flu or something. His folks wouldn't call the doctor.

Died, senior year. About two months before graduation.

He knew them. Knew them all. Some by name, some by face. The poor guy who'd had the only cigarette roll back in jump school and who hadn't gotten his reserve out in time. Then there was Lieutenant... oh yeah... Gaines, over there. Tyrell was suddenly real glad he was seeing these people like they'd been. Not like they'd become. Gaines been shouting orders to get Guns Up when the B40 disappeared everything below his crotch.

There were others.

Tyrell knew just how bad it'd been in his platoon. How many people'd gone home in bodybags or in pieces. But you didn't sit there and run percents. Not if you wanted to stay sane.

Dead, all dead, he thought.

The line came right up to him. Stopped.

He was afraid to turn. Afraid to look in the other direction. Would this drug let him "see" what was coming next? Next in... it could be next in two or three months for him.

He noticed Sunshine was crying. He told the line to go away. Told his mind to stop moving.

"What's the problem, baby?"

"I was wondering... when we'll be together next."

"We're... together right now."

"I know. I know. And we'll *always* be together. But I mean... being able to... touch each other. Like... like this," she said.

"But we can't, can we? I'm sorry, my Ty-rell man. I'm not trying to be a bringdown. But I'm still learning about things. And sometimes... what's today is something I want to be there tomorrow.

"And that's being a little baby, isn't it?"

Tyrell found the sobriety to hold her close. He was thinking that if that makes you a baby, then we're all babies, aren't we?

...and we've all got to change our heads so we can change the world. Right?

Allan Cole & Chris Bunch

And the words were coming in too fast on Jeff. Words from his folks, words from Rachel:

..I remember what it was like when I was mustered out....I really think, under the circumstances...you're confused...it would be wrong for us to continue seeing each other... get your thoughts straightened out....much less, get married.

He had his hands pressed over his ears, but they were still there.

...So I urge you, son, that if you are having any doubts about.... find it in your heart to at least forgive me... to set your goals in your own mind...

Samantha's voice from yesterday:

... I know a good soap opera when I see one...

And the voices and what they were saying faded, faded, still talking, still pleading, still manipulating, but there was seasound over them, and Jeff was on the boat, pulling out of straightcitizen/Army Oakland, toward San Francisco and there was no Bridge between the two cities and he and Samantha had only one thing ahead of them. He'd heard it called Baghdad by the Bay. Maybe pretentious... but not now. Not now at all.

"Hey, Babe," he said. "Wanna take a walk?"

Samantha's eyes changed from infinity focus to middle distance to being somewhere in The FBI Girl.

"Sure," she said. "Here we are, in a nice safe room, with good music, our friends, plenty to eat, stuff to drink, a bed over there if somebody gets romantic, and you want to go walk down Haight Street after midnight.

"Sounds great!"

She pulled Jeff to his feet. Goodbyes or explanations did not seem necessary to any of them.

...take me disappearing through the smoke rings of my mind...

A few minutes later, Sunshine and Tyrell decided they, too, needed to go out and listen to their night.

"...that's San Francisco for you. Guaranteed to
blow your mind, one way or another...
The wind of karma carries him away

313

And drives him on toward sheer precipices
Violent flashes cause him to lose
His reason...
PEACEFUL DEITIES
However, along the wayside
The gods of light and wisdom Smile on him and
Await his coming"

Jeff was standing on a street corner... somewhere.

Somewhere, his quite sober mind asked, in San Francisco?

Uh... yes. Certainly not Los Angeles. He could see a hill.

Maybe Reno? No. Reno wasn't this built up.

And he had been standing here for... fifteen, almost twenty minutes, his mind went on.

Now, how did he know that? He'd stupidly taken off his watch and left it back at The FBI Girl.

He was holding Samantha's hand.

"Do you realize what we've been doing?"

Samantha nodded. "We've been standing on this stupid corner," she said, "where any cop who comes by will bust us, thinking that sign is the most profound thing we've ever seen."

"I never thought that."

"Yes you did. You said so, not five minutes ago."

"Oh."

The sign read, in red neon: BRUNO'S CORVETTE REPAIRS.

Jeff looked at it.

"Yeah," he said slowly. "It is trickshit, isn't it?"

"Hey," Sunshine said, as they drifted, drifted, summer flowerpetals through the Haight... and boy would anybody back in the company bust a gut if they heard I thought something like that ran through Tyrell's mind... "was I right?"

"Uh... you're always right. 'Bout what?"

"About soldiers needing love, too?"

"Yeah. Oh yeah."

A traffic light changed. They waited for it, even though the streets were deserted.

"Sunshine?"

"Ty-rell?"

"I love you."

"I know. I love you, too."

"No. I mean I *love* you."

"And I fell in love with you all over again when I saw you walk out of that store with your new friends."

Again?

Three shadows came out of a darkened storefront.

"Hey, people. What's happenin'."

Deliberately casual. Too deliberately casual.

Tyrell came back to earth. Wishing he had an Ml6, his Kabar or even his bootblousing irons. He was as unarmed as a baby. Now, what I'll do, he thought, a little unclearly, is put my back up against the wall, and—

"Hey! It's Sunshine! Wha's haps, chile?"

"Crasher! You big meanie! You scared me."

"Oh... I'm sorry."

"You mean we can't," one of other shadows complained.

"We sure as hell can't. This your new friend?"

"Isn't he pretty," Sunshine said. "His name's Tyrell."

"Hey, man."

"Hey."

"Boy, Sunshine, you sure sound messed up. You got any to spare?"

"No. This was a present," Sunshine said, sounding regretful. "But tomorrow... or the next day, I'll see if there's anything around."

"That'd be cool."

"Goodnight," Sunshine said. "You have a good one, too. Oh yeah. Here." And the larger shadow handed Sunshine a lit stick of incense... and a joint.

Alexis, once the roar had slowed, had suggested to Nebraska that a good game of Monopoly would be fun.

Nebraska gaped at her.

"You mean?"

"Yeah. Sure. It's great... you get into being a stone capitalist. You know. J.P. Morgan... Carnegie... toss them widows an' orphans out into the street. Repossess the family homestead.

"Like that. Real decadent stuff."

Then Alexis looked around.

Allan Cole & Chris Bunch

"Oh. But we need more people, don't we? Oh well.
She pulled Nebraska up.
"Come on. Let's go find some trouble to get into."
...down the foggy ruins of time...
Downstairs, in the main room they found the lights still gleaming, and heard a dull thump-thump-thump. Then the snarl of a snare drum.
Somebody, in the mass exodus out of The FBI Girl, had forgotten their instruments - onstage were drums, guitars and a big old standup bass.
Behind the drums and the bass were two boys. They looked to be about ten years old.
"What're you kids doing out," Nebraska wanted to know.
One kid looked defiant, the other thrummed the bass. "Aw, Mikey was stayin' over at my house," he said. "An' we was readin' Tom Sawyer, an' all about drainpipes an' all.
"An' my folks went to sleep, an' me an' Mikey looked an' we got a drainpipe.
"So...
"You know, Mister, I'm gonna grow up an' play rock 'n roll."
Thrumm.
Nebraska started to say something. To roust them. Tell them get their little butts back home. Then he chose not to.
Instead, he got up onstage, and picked up a guitar.
Started picking at it.
And very suddenly there was music there. Not the awkward, stiff-fingered twanging Righteous Brothers back at Gramps' house, but free, easy flowing, the music coming all around him.

There was a drum. And a bass.
But of course not played by two children.
Strings.
And a voice.
That was Alexis:
"But of all these friends and lovers/There is no one compared with you/And these memories lose their meaning/When I think of love/As something new...."
She broke off, and watched Nebraska's fingers moving with a sureness that was purely tactile and had nothing to do with knowledge, ability or memory.

"You could cut it," she said. "There's been worse people play guitar for a living..."

Nebraska's fingers CLAAAANGED, but Alexis picked up the song once more:

"Though I know I'll never lose affection/ For people and things that went before/ I know I'll often stop and think about them/ In my life, I'll love you more..."

WRATHFUL DEITIES
Even the awful
Goddesses of wrath Conceal
Behind their terrifying cries
A call to ultimate liberation.

...far past the frozen leaves/The haunted frightened trees...

Tyrell came back to himself, and knew where he was. Out somewhere.

Beyond the wire.

The trees of Golden Gate Park lifted around him, twisted and became triple-tier rain forest.

Tyrell started to check his '16. Magazine seated... round in the chamber... finger touching the safety...

There was no rifle, he realized. No grenades. Behind him, no flankers, no pig gunner, no radioman.

Just Sunshine.

"Where..." she said, suddenly sounding afraid, "are we?"

"West of Kon Turn. I think."

"Oh. Where's that?"

"Where... where I was."

Part of him knew where he was... and would not let him use the name to Sunshine.

"But we're not in any danger," Sunshine went on.

The jungle reached out fingers to him. In the trees were snipers. Overhead boobytraps. Just in front of him... a tripwire. Over there, in that brush, a cleverly camouflaged RPD.

Oh, sweet Jesus, Tyrell thought.

"Go out there," Sunshine said. "With your mind. Be a Viet Cong. Would you hurt us?"

"I'm an American... a grunt."

"No you're not. You're my Ty-rell." Tyrell was in the darkness. He was an NVA Regular, looking through the notch-sights of the Soviet machinegun... at a tall, thin, strangely-dressed black American. Standing in a glade with his arms around a beautiful girl. A girl barely a child.

"No," Tyrell said. "I wouldn't hurt us."

The rainforest wavered. But returned.

Tyrell slumped down. Put his head in his hands.

"Thanks, Sunshine. But... I'm going back. Back to that jungle.

"He'll still be out there."

"Maybe," Sunshine said.

"Do you know what I'm talking about? What I went and did today?"

"I know," she said. "But it doesn't matter."

"Shit," Tyrell mourned. "I just wish... wish there was 'some way we could just be together, without all this black and white shit."

"There is. There was. There will be."

"This isn't fair," he said. "I just meet you... and we're in love, and... tomorrow I go away again."

"That is the karma," Sunshine said. "But we'll be together again."

"You know, they could send me back to Viet Nam. And... and something could happen."

"We will still be together," she said. "We were one once before, in another life.

"The wheel turns," she said. "The wheel turns, my Ty-rell man."

And generations/generations of white baptistbullshit broke around him, if only for this one stoned moment, and Tyrell, too, could see, once more, a line.

A line that stretched back, back through Roman costumes, Greek costumes, African warrior costumes. Ahead, space suits like they wore in Forbidden Planet. The costumes changed, but the faces did not.

Always it was Tyrell and Sunshine.

Sometimes he was white, sometimes she was black. Sometimes they were both the same race and wore the same costume.

Damnfoolish acid drug stuff, his backbrain found the energy to whine. That isn't *real*.

But still, always, it was Sunshine and Tyrell.

Tyrell got up, and took Sunshine by the hand.

He walked forward... into the overhanging trees. He smelt vicks

Allan Cole & Chris Bunch

vaporub and touched rough eucalyptus.

"Next time," he said slowly, "we will be trees... and you can be people."

Sunshine, too, touched the tree.

She smiled...

Nebraska found himself back in the bedroom, staring intently at that now-animated map,

He turned around. He was the only one in the room. Then he looked back at the map.

The voices, who'd been singing, talking, almost inaudibly, suddenly changed. They became harsh.

Unfriendly.

Strangers. Nebraska shuddered. It was if he was sitting in one of those big cranes he'd seen in pictures of Hollywood directors. He was looking down at himself, standing there in this strange room.

In this strange city.

All around him were people who did not know him, who did not care to know him. Each day started, different from any other day, and peoples' tasks changed. Changed but did not change, and the men and women grew older and grayer and then they died.

But the great city went on.

It had not known they lived, and would not know their bodies were under the sod. Nor did its people. And, if they had known, would they have cared beyond the moment of the tear.

It was gray, gray and black, and Nebraska could see the people in this city, marching. Like that film his history teacher had shown, of one of the Nazi rallies, with people marching, marching, shouting with one voice.

Coining in, coming at him, coming in, marching, marching...

He heard the beep of a horn.

A tiny horn.

It was the little harvester.

It was getting dark on the plains now. The harvester had its headlight on, and was turning for him. He thought he could see a welcoming smile on the driver's face.

Ahead of <u>him</u> would be the farmhouse, yellow light gleaming as summer's heat cooled down. There would be laughter from children, and a hug from his wife.

319

She would have a frosty pitcher of iced tea. The driver would wash, eat, talk to his family and then to bed.

The next day, his task would recommence. The same task, but different. Different as the seasons changed, one into the next, in a slow spiral like the earth's movement around the sun.

Death came here, too. But death as the end of life, just as winter followed autumn, but to be succeeded by the brightness of spring.

Nebraska felt a wash of longing...

...and Alexis' head, pillowed on his shoulder.

She, too, was looking at the map. She reached out. Touched a dancing Indian.

"So much," she said. "There's so much to see.

"And be."

Nebraska turned away from the map and put his arms around her.

...out to the windy beach/far from the twisted reach of crazy sorrow...

Jeff and Samantha were somewhere in Golden Gate Park, when the voices came back at him. He heard, loud and shrill, real jealousy in the shriek from his father's shade:

...You've made promises to that girl... if you are having any... most honorable... doubts put them aside... you won't regret it... we came up with a new plan. One we know you're going to like...The bullet to be bitten immediately is your future... enough time has been wasted...

All this has been our fault
All this has been our fault
But you know that better than I
But you know that better than I..."

And Jeff's mouth was O-ing for the scream and he heard Samantha's voice:

Is that the only medical school in the world?

Doctor Daniel, from the Free Clinic:

...There are lots of doctors, and some of them didn't go to the University of Southern California...

Samantha once more:

You loved every minute of it. Jeffrey Katz..

Yes. Yes he did.

Allan Cole & Chris Bunch

And it was Samantha, and he turned to where she lay beside him on the grass, and saw, shine-illuminated by-headlights out on Kennedy Drive, a tear. Samantha was looking straight up, at something, not infinity.

Jeffrey Katz, ready to slaughter whomever or whatever being in the heavens who'd made his Samantha cry, snarled up.

At, far, far above, an airliner's blinking lights.

Samantha spoke, nearly in a whisper.

"Good, sometimes to be alone," she said. "Not so good, others. Sometimes...

"Looking up at that plane," she went on. "I saw me. Ten years from now. Still going up and down the aisle. Coffee... tea...well then, how about a mar-<u>tooni!</u> Just a flying waitress."

Jeff saw things very clearly, very suddenly.

It was not unlike somebody had just stepped up behind him, and swung a huge, padded sledgehammer at the base of his skull. And in that moment of explosion, he realized:

Here he'd been, wandering around with his head up his ass. Just like he was still back in high school, feeling sorry as all hell for himself, nobody loved him, nobody cared, and meantime feeling quite free to say and do anything he wanted no matter who it hurt. And never stopping to see that maybe his problems were... maybe not pissant.

But he sure as hell didn't have cancer.

Or... and he didn't want to consider it... a black skin in a white world. A white world that was driving Tyrell back... back to...

Same thing with Samantha. He tried to think if, once, just once, he'd actually talked to her about what she wanted, or what she thought in particular?

Not very much. Nope. It'd been nothing but Jeff Katz, from when he'd crawled up the steps to her apartment.

<u>Goddamit!,</u> his mind cried, there you fucking go again! Now you're starting to feel sorry for yourself because you spent all the time talking about yourself.

More I, I, I, ego horseshit.

Then, like a film shown in reverse, glass-shattered pieces collecting, he had the moment:

"Wrong vision," he said calmly.

"The stew just looks like you. You're sitting up forward, in first class.

Allan Cole & Chris Bunch

"You work for the United Nations now. As a translator. You just got promoted and you're heading for Tokyo. Oh yeah, and you're drinking a martini, not a martooni."

Samantha's eyes came back from the airplane.

"Oh brother," she said. And chuckled.

"That was the *worst* calm center rap I've ever heard."

"Worked, didn't it?"

Samantha sat up.

"Interesting thought," she said. "You know, I never thought of going international. I mean, there's a lot of the world out there besides Braniff... or the Peace Corps, either."

She poked Jeff.

"Hey, Doctor. *You* don't need to practice in LA, either. "

"Or San Francisco. Think Global."

Jeff was not thinking globally, however.

Other things came up.

His fingers touched the silk cascade of her throat, crept down, buttons unbuttoning as he went, and Samantha was slipping out of her blouse, heel coming back and then her leg falling to the side. The miniskirt was hiked above her thighs.

Samantha was not wearing panties...

THE COUPLING
The spirit is condemned to be Reborn
Male and female beings Surround him
An irresistible force
Draws him. Draws him. Draws him.

Jeff's tongue twisted through curly hair, then down, across Samantha's inner thigh, then, pointed, up the parting cleft of her lips. Gently around her clitoris, back, and in, warmth meeting warmth, wetness meeting wetness, then back out, back up, as one, then a second finger moved into her, softly curling, curling.

Jeff's right hand was under her buttocks, lifting, and holding as his head moved.

Samantha hissed breath out, then began turning slowly. Jeff muttered protest, but she kept moving.

Her hands found his belt buckle. Zipper. Slid his pants down. And

322

then her mouth found his as they turned onto their sides, and for Jeff the universe narrowed, nothing more than his tongue, endlessly circling/her tongue, moving around and back and down and he shouted ecstasy into the park silence...

....to dance beneath the diamond sky/With one hand waving free...

Tyrell wondered, without much curiosity, what had happened to their clothes.

But not very much. It was very right to be here, naked under the dying stars as morning came toward them.

Here, in the Children's Playground, as Sunshine's blonde hair caressed his chest, spidersilk moving, and then her milky body lowered itself down on him, his cock sliding, gentle resistance into her, and her knees on the ground beside him as her hips lifted, fell, lifted and he moved deeper and deeper into her, her fingers moving on his chest, her breath rasping, her head back and her moaning:

"...My man... my beau-ti-ful Ty...Rell. man.. ..

...Alexis' buttocks were hard against Nebraska's thighs, her hands digging at the bed, pillow under her stomach, and then once again, they were turning, bodies shifting like a kaleidoscope, like they had been making love for days, bodies familiar maps, yet still fresh, still new, still unknown, now on their sides, her knee coming up and Nebraska sliding onto it, once again going into her easy warmth and her hands grasping/unclasping on his shoulders, stomach sweat sliding, her breasts against him, oiled bodies moving, moving, in a night that would never end...

....let me forget about today until tomorrow...

Male and female come together. The doors close.

BREATH 2 - REBIRTH

The ear once again perceives the sharp wind Of reality.

Breath takes possession again Of flesh and blood The memory vanishes.

Jeff and Samantha dressed each other.

"I'm still buzzing a little," she said. "Correction. A lot."

"Yeah."

Samantha buttoned her blouse, then waved at a rather shocked old man in black, taking his dawn walk.

"How do I look?"

"Uh.-"

"Like I've taken acid and been fucking all night?"

"Well... maybe if you changed... you know. Into a miniskirt that didn't have grass stains on the back."

"Yeah," she said. "You just worry about Jeff Katz. Doctor, heal thyself, and all that."

Jeff looked down. Grass stains on his knees. Other stains on the front - they'd used his pants as an occasional mattress.

"What are they going to think at San Francisco International?"

Jeff's smile vanished. He forced it back.

"Uh... like I've taken acid and been fucking the most beautiful woman in the world all night?"

Samantha attempted laughter. And failed.

Sunshine was crying.

"Come on," Tyrell tried to soothe. "Hey. It's like you said. We'll be together... some other time."

She cried, even harder. Then found control, hugging Tyrell.

"Yes," she said, her voice gradually finding control. "And... and it'll be in *this* life.

"Won't it?"

Her teary face, suddenly the face of a sixteen year old girl, looked up at Tyrell.'

"It will," Tyrell promised. Without the power, without the hope.

But still, he promised...

.....Stone Free/To do what I please...

Alexis came out of the bathroom, brushing her hair. "What would happen, Nebraska, if you suddenly decided to stay? If you called SFO and told them to take that ticket and give it to charity?"

"Stay here... in San Francisco? For good, you mean."

"For the moment, anyway," Alexis said.

Nebraska thought, choosing his words through the still-swirl of LSD.

"I've been wondering that myself. Probably not much. My folks'd understand.

Allan Cole & Chris Bunch

"I don't have any other strings. At least... not ones that've been talked about.

"My brother could handle the farm. Hell, he's twice the worker I am, anyway."

"Say you did."

"Say I did," Nebraska wondered.

And they both looked at the wall, where a calendar hung. And their minds together ran through three absolutely perfect days, days that could never, should never be duplicated...

SHANTIH SHANTIH SHANTIH
....In my end is my beginning...

Allan Cole & Chris Bunch

SUNDAY: THE LAST DAY

"...And it really doesn't matter if I'm wrong/I'm right/Where I
belong I'm right/Where I belong..."
—Lennon/McCartney

"...There are places I'll remember/All my life though some have
changed./Some forever not for better/Some have gone and
some remain..."
—Lennon/McCartney

"...Who is the Underground? Think—look around— maybe
in a mirror maybe inside..."
—Boston Avatar

And we're at:
San Francisco International Airport

CHAPTER TWENTY-THREE

"…GET UP AND TELL you where to go./And you've just had some kind of mushroom/And your mind is moving low./Go ask Alice/I think she'll know…

Or you can ask Young Doctor Katz, Jeff thought. He might know, too.

The public address system quit mournfully paging a Mister Frank Harris to please call his office... crackled with a new message:

"This is the last boarding call for American Flight 763 for Omaha. Would all military standbys please report to Gate Twenty Six at this time."

"That's me," Nebraska said. He drained the glass of brandy and shuddered. "Whoo. They pour strong here."

"Got to," Tyrell said. "Whyinhell would anybody even get in an airplane unless he was drunk?"

Jeff dropped money on the bar, and the three of them walked out of the airport bar and down the long, echoing halls of the terminal.

"I don't want to hear nothin' about airplanes from you," Nebraska said. "You're the jerk who jumps out of them!"

"Just what I was talking about," Tyrell agreed. "I know enough to get away from those bastards before Gravity Strikes."

All three of them laughed, slightly.

"How do you feel," Jeff asked.

"A little fizzy," Nebraska admitted. "I think there was some acid in that acid."

"You got that right," Tyrell agreed. "If I go and relax and stare at the wall longer'n a few seconds, it starts tryin' to do the twist on me."

"That's the price of being a dope fiend," Jeff said,

They were at the Gate.

All three of them looked at each other. Nebraska shifted his cheapjack carryon from hand to hand. Uncomfortable.

"Well..."

Again, no one said anything.

"It was one *hell* of a party," Nebraska offered.

"It was that."

"Guess I better get my seat," he said.

"Yeah. Get your drink order in before takeoff. I mean you don't want to show up the conquering hero sober, do you?"

"I have no intention of doing that."

Again, The Silence.

"You guys... thanks a lot," Nebraska said.

"Hey," Tyrell said. "I think we owe you."

"That's the truth," Jeff agreed.

"Darned if I know why we're standing around like we're at some kind of funeral," Nebraska said. "I'll be back out here... Someday."

He would not.

"Sure," Jeff said. "And you've got my folks' address. They'll know where to reach me."

"And Mrs. Andrew Harris is in the Memphis phone book," Tyrell said.

"Yeah. I'll give you a call sometime. Both of you. "

He would not.

"Sir? We're on final boarding."

"Oh. Sorry. Hey. You guys take care." And with a final wave, Nebraska disappeared onto the airplane.

"You know," Tyrell said/ "for a peckerneck farmer, ol' Nebraska wasn't too bad a guy."

"No, he wasn't."

Neither of them realized they'd automatically fallen into talking about Nebraska, in the past tense - just as they'd done in Vietnam... after a casualty had been dusted off.

"Come on," Jeff said. "I'll buy you another drink."

"Better not," Tyrell said. "I come off that plane one wing low, and Momma'll have me for lunch. She's probably gonna have the preacher there with her anyway. An' the church choir."

"Ugh."

"Don't knock it, man," Tyrell said. "Some *serious* foxes sing gospel where I come from.

"But you better get your butt on a plane," he went on.

"Yeah. I ought to."

Jeff didn't know how to ask - and so he blurted: "How much leave did they give you?"

Tyrell froze. Then his gape of surprise vanished.

"How'd you know?"

"When I picked up the bomb. Down on Market. I saw you coming

Allan Cole & Chris Bunch

out of the recruiting station and I knew right then you'd reenlisted."

"Whyn't you say anything before?"

A long silence. Then: "I didn't exactly know *what* to say. Hey, man, I'm having enough trouble trying to figure out what to do with my own life."

"They gave me forty five days," Tyrell said.

Jeff hesitated over the next question Then: "How long did you reenlist for?"

"I took three more," Tyrell said. Real casual. "They were after me to reup for six years - but I said I wasn't that sure."

"Where'd they assign you to?"

"Fort Bragg. They'll gimme my sergeant's stripes as part of the deal."

"Bragg? That's the 82nd. What's the chances of..." and Jeff stopped. Shit! But Tyrell knew what he was going to say.

"Of goin' back to Nam? Real, real fuckin' good, I guess. But that doesn't mean it's gonna happen, does it? I mean, Grancell and Sanders couldn't nail my fly young ass - and I've already ducked the Cong for fourteen months.

"Somehow... someway... I'll get out from under. Hell, Smokebomb Hill's right up the road. I can always go Green Beanie and tell 'em I'm an Indig Specialist. Black Russian type. Don't you have any worries about me."

Jeff didn't say anything for a very long while.

"But speaking of worries," Tyrell said, breaking the uncomfortable gloom settling in. "What are *you* gonna do?"

"Shit, I dunno," Jeff said.

"Only advice I got - don't be leaping first time somebody says frog."

"Good downhome southern wisdom, huh?"

"Yeah. From a damn' redneck bluecap at Benning, back at jump school who said I was gonna do just that for him."

Jeff grinned. Tyrell clapped him on the shoulder.

"Go ahead on," he said. "And... stay loose."

Jeff's eyes were a little foggy around the edges as he turned away. It was just a reminder, of course, of the acid still percolating out of his system. Riiight!

They were calling the PSA flight to Los Angeles. Every hour on the half hour.

329

Jeff already had his ticket in his pocket - although he could've bought it on the plane. He started back through the terminal, toward the loading gate.

He went past the PSA desk. There was a line of people waiting to buy their tickets. Most of them wore suits and harried business-type expressions.

One man stood out. He was a stocky Mexican-American buck sergeant. On his brand new greens he wore the Combat Infantryman's Badge, three rows of ribbons and, on his right shoulder the horseblanket combat patch of the First Cavalry Division.

Jeff looked at him for a long time. The Latino saw the stare, and stared back.

"Hey," the man said. "You got a problem, hippy?"

Jeff laughed - it was the first time he'd found anything really funny since they'd gotten to San Francisco International. And he suddenly knew what he was going to do.

"No, Sergeant," he said. "And thanks. You going to LA?"

"Yeah. Goin' home."

"Here." Jeff handed the man his own ticket. The sergeant looked at it - suspicious.

"It's good. It's real," Jeff reassured him.

"How much you want for it?"

"Merry Christmas."

The soldier looked very puzzled.

"Man, I heard there were weird cats here in Frisco... Why're you givin' your ticket to me? Don't you need it?"

"No," Jeff said. "I don't. Not for a good long time, anyway. I got too much business here in San Francisco."

Jeff started toward the terminal exit and the cab rank. The Mexican was sort of coming out of his surprise, and about to say thanks. Jeff turned back.

"Oh yeah. Peace, brother..."

And he was gone.

...I'd love to turn you on...

THE END

Allan Cole & Chris Bunch